PENGUIN BOOKS

ME IN YOUR MELODY

Deborah Wong is a Rhysling Award and Pushcart Prize nominated Malaysian poet. She holds a LLB (Hons) from the University of London and the Associateship of the Malaysian Insurance Institute (AMII). A devoted fan fiction writer, she finally answered the call to be a storyteller by attending the summer intensive creative writing programme at the University of British Columbia, Canada. Her writing can be found in *Ricepaper Magazine*, *Thought Catalog*, *Blood Bath Literary Zine*, *Strange Horizons*, *Dark Matter Magazine Halloween Edition*, and many other local as well as international online literary journals and anthologies. Recently, she self-published *Autopsy of Sentiments*, a personal and intimate confessional poetry chapbook about grief, unrequited love, and kinship. Deborah writes full-time and lives with her dancing-queen mom, melodrama-enthusiast mama, and a feminist calico cat. *Me In Your Melody* is her debut novel.

Me in Your Melody

Deborah Wong

PENGUIN BOOKS

An imprint of Penguin Random House

PENGUIN BOOKS

Penguin Books is an imprint of the Penguin Random House group of
companies whose addresses can be found at
global.penguinrandomhouse.com

Published by Penguin Random House SEA Pte Ltd
40 Penjuru Lane, #03-12, Block 2
Singapore 609216

First published in Penguin Books by Penguin Random House SEA 2024

ISBN 9789815202021

Typeset in Garamond by MAP Systems, Bengaluru, India

www.penguin.sg

This book is for Mom and Mama,

and

for 슈퍼주니어,

thank you for the music!

♪ Playlist

♪	**Unsteady**	X Ambassadors
♪	**Only One**	Yellow Card
♪	**Set Fire to the Rain**	Adele
♪	**Summertime Sadness**	Killin' Baudelaire
♪	**Have You Ever Needed Someone So Bad**	Def Leppard
♪	**Once Again**	Mad Clown and Kim Na-young
♪	**A World to Believe in**	Céline Dion
♪	**The Center of My Heart**	Michael Bolton
♪	**I Almost Do**	Taylor Swift
♪	**The Second You Sleep**	Saybia
♪	**Almost Here**	Delta Goodrem and Brian McFadden
♪	**From the Bottom of My Broken Heart**	Britney Spears
♪	**No One Else Comes Close**	Backstreet Boys
♪	**Somewhere Only We Know**	Lilly Allen
♪	**Exile**	Taylor Swift (feat. Bon Iver)
♪	**Hate You**	Jungkook
♪	**Without You**	Samantha Cole

♫   **Come As You Are**   Wild Orchid
♫   **2 Become 1**   Emma Bunton (feat.
                                         Robbie Williams)
♫   **One More Chance**   Super Junior
     (비처럼 가지 마요)
♫   **This Is My Now**   Jordin Sparks
♫   **Catch Me I'm Falling**   Toni Gonzaga
♫   **Lost (지독하게)**   Super Junior-D&E
♫   **I Will Show You (보여줄게)**   Ailee
♫   **Come to Your Senses**   Alexendra
                                         Shipp and
                                         Vanessa Hudgens

Part I

One

'I drag you to hell, bastard!' The bus driver raised his middle finger, honking at the sedan that could've caused them to skid.

I breathed a sigh of relief, peering out the tinted window.

Particle-laden beams of sunlight were separating the shadows. I stroked my temples to ease the mild headache I was having, put on the wireless bluetooth Hello Kitty headset—Edward's gift to me—and scrolled through the Spotify-recommended playlist.

Then, Mom's best wishes text appeared on my phone.

I swiped from my lock screen—*to reply later*.

This cable-stayed bridge connecting the mainland to Penang Island resembled the Brooklyn Bridge—Edward's favourite walkabout.

He was to spend the whole of December in New York; a reward by his management company in recognition of his success with chart-topping hits and sold-out gigs—achieving all this while also working on his next album. He would talk of being inspired by everything—enjoying a hot brewed americano, visiting the public market, the coffee shops, art museums, and galleries as well as admiring the Hudson River while chatting with strangers whenever their fates would align. And Edward had promised to take me to the Big Apple. *One day.* But that promise had surpassed 365 days.

The bus reached the Nibong Tebal terminal station.

One by one, the passengers stood up from their seats. Some were complaining of their bladder bursting—getting ready to leave, although there was no worm to catch for any early birds.

I would rather immerse myself in lip-syncing to the crescendo of Beyoncé's 'If I Were a Boy' than be trapped in the scramble to exit.

The bus driver helped me unload my hand-carrier and suitcase from the automobile trunk, reminding me to beware of pickpockets.

'Are you not a local?' the bus driver asked.

'I'm from Kuala Lumpur,' I said.

'Enjoy your stay, miss.' He had a smoky odour, must be a chain-smoker.

Approaching the waiting hall, the hawkers at the food stalls haggled with the foreign and local backpackers to market their home-cooked *nasi lemak*—the aromatic infused coconut rice stirred my appetite for a second helping, which I hadn't had for a while. And then, I spotted *kuih lapis* among the varieties of traditional sweet cakes in the plastic trays.

I remembered Mama would make them like a Tesco bulk purchase, to satisfy my sweet tooth, patiently ladling the batter in red and white, layer after layer, despite using only rice flour, sugar, and coconut milk. Childhood moments had always been the most innocent.

'Biu-jie . . .'

I turned and smiled when I saw the familiar face of my cousin, Daniel Lau, jogging along the sidewalk, gesturing a stop sign while crossing the traffic-congested intersection. I playfully ruffled his bleached blonde hair as he reached me.

'You still look the same,' he said.

'That was taken six months ago.' I peeped at his phone.

He pulled me in with open arms.

Sheltered by his slender embrace and towering height, neither of us wanted to be parted from this belated embrace. This cousin had grown up to be a man.

'I've no problem identifying people, even if they turned to ashes.'

I smacked Daniel's shoulder and winced because it hurt—he must've been religiously working-out at the gym. 'I will tear your lips off—'

'Don't get angry on your vacation, a'ight.' Daniel winked.

'Thanks for the reminder.' I then ordered two pieces of sweet and savoury *apam balik*.

'Think you were twenty-one when I last saw you,' Daniel said as I inhaled the earthy and popcorn-like sugary nuances, too exhausted to hold a conversation. He then asked cautiously. 'Let me have that duffle bag.'

'It's okay.' I paid the stall owner.

'What's in there?' Daniel whispered. 'A golden goose?'

'For you to guess, for me to know,' I said, munching on a mouthful of pancake.

'Have you not been getting any food throughout the journey?' Daniel asked, wrapping his arm around my shoulder, my body covered with a pang of intense comfort.

'Need to put on some weight.' I swallowed before answering.

'Count your blessings. You know lots of women would murder each other to be in your place. Anyway, Old Bean has prepared a hotpot banquet for you tonight.'

I snorted. What a crude way to address his father—typical Daniel.

It was a quarter to seven.

The open-space parking opposite the crosswalk was a full house. A man with a ponytail, dressed in a suit-and-tie, was ogling us, seemingly observing my asymmetrical bob hairstyle, dark-under-eyes, and my oleaginous complexion—the tropical heat was getting to me. I played the staring-game until he reached the pedestrian overcrossing—I lost against time.

Thereafter, I pulled my hoodie over my head.

'Whoa,' Daniel said the moment I rolled up the sleeves to my elbows. 'Check out your three-dimensional black rose tattoos.'

I felt a little sheepish. 'Two months to complete both arms,' I told him, feeling proud of the work adorning my arms.

'Calling grief and death—' Daniel gestured in the Mudra ritual style.

'Black roses symbolize rebellion and strength,' I clarified. 'These babies are a steadfast reminder of when everyone thought I wouldn't have passed that threshold.'

'Strength of armour compelled by dark elegance,' Daniel said. 'Forget those who wronged or misunderstood you. Your intellectual skill always seems to be a step ahead of everyone. Anyway, meet my girlfriend!' Daniel said, gesturing to his car.

Way to go cuzz! I ran my fingers over the glossy surface of 'his girlfriend', which was a Volkswagen campervan—the icon of a hippie counterculture—with sprayed-on graffiti in assorted colours on its exterior. The only thing missing from making it a stereotype was the lack of a gigantic 'PEACE' sign scrawled in a happy colour.

Daniel closed the storage boot, listening to me comment on the lack of a peace sign as he fiddled with the latch to ensure that it was firmly shut. 'Don't give me that look! The peace sign is so overrated.'

'Does it have . . . a name?' I asked, admiring the rainbow-design interior. 'How'd you even get her?' I briefly entertained a lame thought, thinking that my cousin had stolen the van from an ice-cream seller.

'Beatrice,' Daniel said, 'and I saved up enough money for this makeover. I am striving hard to be different from my peers.'

I buckled the seatbelt, scoffing at his haughty tone. I changed the subject. 'Supposedly *it* is preoccupied at the soup kitchen now.'

'Yeah, Old Bean is able to handle it with the maid's assistance,' Daniel said.

'Shouldn't you have some respect for your stepmother?'

'But she did not give birth to me,' Daniel said, turning the engine on.

Everyone had a backstory buried six feet under their brain.

Lacking parental love was our curse, our backstory grave.

Daniel's mother had passed away when he was five, while I'd suffered childhood with an emotionally abusive father. The Lau descendants appeared to cope with abandonment issues quite well.

'Hey, let me help you.'

Edward's voice claimed my memory.

Out of nowhere.

That evening when Edward had snuck into the Saujana Residence aparthotel's employees-only room. Time halted when he appeared with the reindeer headband over his head alongside the bittersweet boundary that I should've drawn with a renowned international figure. My heart was beating for Edward's alluring and delicate gaze, as I counted the food packets for the homeless.

'You should stay in your suite,' I had said to Edward.

'I wanna see you. Anyway, I've latched the door.' He had slung the acoustic guitar over his shoulder, smiling at me. 'This year's Christmas is so meaningful. All because of you, Emily.'

'I'm sorry Biu-jie,' I heard Daniel muttering.

Along the road, the traffic lights had just turned green.

Edward's memory in me mellowed, for now.

'Old Bean should be volunteering at the soup kitchen,' Daniel said.

'That's your biological father. Have some respect for him,' I said, softly exhaling while glancing ahead at the road.

'Old Bean is an intimate term from a son for his father. And the word "bean" is the politest metaphor for "sperm" from a paternal viewpoint.'

'All right, save the remaining info,' I said.

Daniel then turned up the stereo. 'My favourite song,' he gushed, clapping.

A K-pop ballad was playing on his curated playlist.

As Daniel was crooning the lyrics, my memory shifted to the glimmering Ferris wheel that Edward and I had planned to visit; a quick date night at the amusement park but we weren't able to because of Edward's manager—Mr Han's—radar system. Mr Han was a business-carnivore who gnawed at the artist's cells, platelets, and bone marrow. His prying eyes on Edward's privacy allowed Mr Han to determine—and eliminate—any potential dating partners.

'Is my hairdo swoon-worthy?' Daniel asked, trying to break the silence.

'Yeah, I'm mesmerized.' I laughed. The roots of my cousin's hair had grown to push out his original roots in black; identical to the skunk of twinning colours.

'I'd prefer to be baked under the sun at the food drive than squabble in the temper-rising, mundane kitchen. Sorry to bother you with the kitchen's hierarchy but trust me you really have to join in on the fun one day as a volunteer . . .'

Along the ride that was filled with Daniel's babbling, I spotted the rolled up shutter of every shop that had started its day. Day shift staff should be clocking in at the twenty-four-hour convenience stores. Wandering, my mind drifted to that breezeless Christmas. My first and last with Edward.

* * *

'Your company has always been feeding the poor?' Edward asked.

It was approaching late evening in Kuala Lumpur. The aparthotel's colleagues and I had been distributing food packets and bottled waters at the homeless centre.

'Usually, we do it on a weekly basis but because December is the month of giving we do it every day.' I said, as Edward placed the Santa hat on my head.

My heart skipped a beat at the sweet interruption.

'Was Kuala Lumpur your first choice?' I asked.

'Ubud was my first.' Edward's eyes shut to enjoy the night.

His quiet and magnetic demeanour, strong as a gust of wind, swept me off my feet.

'I chatted with a few homeless people over there,' Edward said.

'For creative inspiration?' I smiled.

He shook his head ruefully. 'They were rich and wealthy, then they became bankrupt overnight. Some are old and indisposed. You see that man over there? He was a breadwinner, and now he's a penniless liability, all because of one big loss in an investment. At times, I wonder how to help them.'

'Are there a lot of homeless people in Seoul?' I asked.

He nodded. 'I miss going out alone since moving there as a trainee. There's a café situated one block from where I lived. After I debuted as an idol, I tried going out wearing a hoodie, a face mask, and shades just so I could grab a coffee in peace. But a woman started following me, and then, before you knew it, there was a locomotive-like line of fans waiting by the time I reached the café.'

'Yeah, not to mention the airport chase.' I chuckled.

'Sorry about that.' Edward looked at me.

'A priceless experience for me, though.'

Later, the Christmas carol medley hollered towards the celestial befallen night in Korean and English. Except there won't be winter rashes, only tropical warmth.

* * *

The automatic gate slid to reveal the Serendipity Sanctuary signage that was scribbled in a big, cursive font on the stone retaining wall. How sacredly the place had been named—in hopes of providing a safe haven.

It was a non-profit community food centre, overseen by the St Paul's Church, where Uncle Raymond served as a committee member.

Daniel parked the campervan in the garage.

Murmurs trailed from the soup kitchen, where a long queue had formed.

I stood before the gated door that separated the food centre and the Edwardian, Anglo-Malay bungalow that was to be my stay for the subsequent days.

The first time I'd come here was with Mom to attend my cousin brother's full-moon celebration. I saw the same white Champaka tree at close quarters that had been majestically standing there ever since I could remember. I remember playing hide-and-seek alone under the horizontal striations of its vigilant bark. Its petals would bloom with a hauntingly beautiful scent, especially during the night.

'The wall is sound-proof, separating the kitchens and the bungalow, so no one can hear the clung-cling Chinese New Year medley,' Daniel said.

'Emily-baby!' A woman squashed into me.

I didn't even have a moment to react to Aunt Bridget's greeting.

'Let me take a closer look at my big niece.' This woman, who smelled like a lavender-scented love potion, grabbed my shoulder, inspecting for any possible defects and parts that needed to be fixed. 'Too old to be a screen siren, wait, have you been taking care of your skin?'

'Your accent is *so* weird, Aunt Bridget.'

'This is cockney-accented Cantonese.' Adjusting her Audrey Hepburn's *Breakfast at Tiffany* hairdo, she radiated a holier-than-thou aura. 'I was the one and only Chinese-Malaysian living on Kensington Street.'

Daniel made a circling motion around the ear, signifying that she had a few screws loose. He then whispered to me, 'This is a post-occupational habit of a retired actress.'

Aunt Bridget logged into her phone, asking for my number. While reciting it to her, she glared at me, indicating that I should slow down. The annoying bubbling sound set off as she was typing from the keypad. 'You're in our group chat now.'

'Lau-d & Praud—' I read from my phone.

'This is the only gateway to our *kaypoh* sessions, just the three of us.' Gossiping, she meant; pointing to herself, Daniel, and then me.

'Isn't the spelling L-O-U-D,' I asked, to clarify.

My aunt cleared her throat. 'It's U-N-I-Q-U-E. If the Americans were able to dissolve the "u" from the word "colour" then I should've the right to change the "o" to an "a".'

'So, what's this B-F-F stand for?' I asked.

'Bombastic-Fabulous-Fantastic, and not best-friends-forever,' Aunt Bridget said.

'Emily!' There stood a grave-looking man at the stoop.

I threw my arms around Uncle Raymond like I had just returned from the real Mortal Kombat. It was his suggestion to Mom that I should get away from the capital city for a better lifestyle and health improvement. A person of few words, birds would start speaking if Uncle Raymond ever smiled three times a day, which put off a great number of those that didn't know him.

I choked slightly. 'Thank you so much, Uncle Raymond.'

'Remember, you're part of the Laus,' my uncle said, patting my back. 'I won't allow anyone to hurt you or any of my family members.'

* * *

In the bedroom, I ran my fingers over the photo garland on display, captivated by the 3D, glittering, gold and metallic stars and heart-shaped paper banners that were clipped with mini wooden pegs along the multicoloured strings. A whimsical homecoming. Forget the high-density apartment facing the panoramic Petronas Twin Towers that I'd formerly lived in.

'Hope you like them,' said Daniel.

'They're so pretty. Thank you.' I smiled at my cousin.

'See, I told you Biu-jie would appreciate my effort,' Daniel said to his father.

'Being pampered by the Laus is a real blessing,' I replied cheekily.

My uncle would keep quiet as and when compliments were showered upon his only son. There is a superstitious Chinese phraseology that says a son is his father's enemy from past life. My uncle would remain reticent even if Daniel reached the moon for him.

'On the other hand, there's a no refund and no exchange policy if you think it's too feminine for your romping attitude,' Daniel said.

Folding my sleeves, I grabbed the extra pillow and threw it in Daniel's direction, a warning for having an unfiltered mouth. Uncle Raymond was gazing at my black rose tattoos and then at me, probably readying himself to judge while Daniel nonchalantly pursed his lips. 'Breakfast should be ready.' Uncle Raymond eventually cleared his throat, tapping on Daniel's shoulder. 'Help me set the table.'

Despite him being *po*-faced, I assumed my uncle just needed some time to adjust to the new Emily. 'How come I didn't see Mama?'

'She is resting in her room.'

That was weird. Mama had always been a morning person.

'Take your time, Rome wasn't built in one day—but I also don't think you'll need two-hundred years to do so,' Uncle Raymond said as he chuckled.

I smiled briefly at his encouraging words. My eyes shut, listening to the sound of the lawn being mowed outside. Then, the whiff of the apple-white wall paint teleported me to *that* night.

Refusing to be home alone, I had decided to hit the bar. A few rounds of vodka and a few beers later, I drove aimlessly around the capital, then passed by the Titiwangsa Lake, watching the water shimmer. The lake overlooked the Ferris wheel at a nearby amusement park. The gradual rotational movement of the wheel set me adrift. I infiltrated the world that was reserved exclusively for Edward and me—imagining bliss; locking lips and making up for lost time in one of the cabins.

If only I had turned off the engine.

It was a stupid mistake that almost cost me my life.

Two

Mama didn't join us for breakfast.

Instead, she preferred to eat in her room these days.

It felt shady.

Yesterday, she had fired the maidservant—Gordon Ramsey style—for walking, and not tiptoeing, into her room—violation #1 of her bedchamber policy. The sulking brought on by Mama's early-onset dementia was more deliberate and calculated than the tantrum of a child sulking about her missing candy.

It was, however, my fraternal duty as a granddaughter to be here.

'Remember, whatever Mama says, just nod,' Daniel said after knocking.

'Are you serious?'

Daniel just looked at me, too high-strung to repeat himself.

'So, no jumping from the window?' I asked attempting to lighten the mood.

'Come in,' Mama's sparkling voice sang.

Mama gathered her permed soft grey hair, clipping it back with a butterfly-shaped jade hairpin. Daniel and I walked in—making sure to tiptoe—feeling like small-time robbers. Clad in a loose bat-sleeve dress, Mama turned around in awe the moment she saw our reflections in the vintage vanity table.

'Cheryl, is that you?' Mama asked me.

Gobsmacked at being mistaken for my mother, I mouthed to my cousin for clarification, 'What's wrong with—?'

'Do what I said. Just nod,' Daniel murmured.

My hands, which were holding onto the serving tray, started to shake uncontrollably.

Mama's condition would've fluctuated since we last spoke. When had that been? Ah, yes, I'd called her on her birthday. Uncle Raymond hadn't informed me of her decline, as he probably didn't want to slap me with bad news the minute I arrived in Penang. Such an incident could impact me negatively, as Dr Erica had advised me 'to be thankful for every living day and to stay positive'.

I began to perspire; guilty—should've visited her more often.

Mama's smile hadn't lessened a bit as I ambled to her bedside.

Suddenly, Mama hit Daniel's forearm with her walking cane. 'How dare you let your sister hold the tray, Raymond?' Gosh, my cousin had transformed into his father.

'It is not heavy at all,' I cut in, emulating my mother. 'You should be hungry by now,' I said, placing the tray on the sleek bedside table. 'Today's breakfast is plain congee with spring onions and other condiments. Eat it while it's still hot,' I mixed the congee with the tiny chunks of salted egg yolk and sprinkled in some deep-fried shallots and canned, pickled lettuce.

'I can eat by myself.' Mama tried to grab the bowl. I patiently pulled it back to me. With that trademark Boss-Baby-Tim frown, Mama tried stealing the bowl again, acting like a preschooler refusing to share her Mars bar with the boy next to her. She turned to me, 'That Mrs Phang will ask you to stand outside if you're late for Maths class.'

'Don't worry about it,' I said, holding a spoonful of congee near Mama's mouth after blowing on it to cool it a bit. 'She wouldn't dare to lay her hands on me.'

She finally relented, allowing me to feed her. 'I want more pickles in my congee,' Mama spoke around a mouthful of food.

'I'll go get some for you.' Daniel escaped in a millisecond.

An intense quiet permeated the room as the door closed softly.

Mama's hand reached for my cheek, caressing it. Her emotional touch had me withholding tears.

I steeled myself and scooped the last portion of the congee, bringing it to her mouth. I then reached for the paper napkin. A chill settled over me at the sight of the congee dripping from Mama's lower lip. I carefully dabbed at it, trying not to cause a stir and disturb her aloof smile. I should've taken leave to visit Mama more often.

'Oh, why are you crying?' asked Mama.

'You can't recognize me, Mama?'

Mama blinked, smiling slowly.

'I'm Emily, your granddaughter.' I tried controlling my tears. 'You've taken care of me ever since I was a baby.' Gripping her hands, I listened to Mama chew and swallow. I felt as though I was being spiritually devoured.

'You . . . Emily . . .' Mama's hand slowly cupped my cheek.

'You remember me now?' I grabbed her hand quickly. 'So sorry I couldn't come back for your eightieth birthday. I was—'

'Emily should be a baby. You are Cheryl,' Mama interrupted, relinquishing my grip on her hand to stroke my head. 'I will bring you to "hit the villain" at the temple tomorrow.'

'You don't have to hit anyone, Mama,' I exhaled.

'I will hit anyone who hurts you . . . or Emily,' she hollered.

I remember the one time I'd gone with Mama to the temple to 'hit the villain'. The villain was a neighbour who Mama suspected had stolen her wooden clogs. Despite several ensuing arguments and the neighbour's vehement denial, Mama remained unconvinced of his innocence. So, we had headed to the temple. If memory served me right, Mama clamorously thwacked a human-form made out of paper with her sandal—the paper a personification of the 'neighbour', his name written in

Mandarin-Chinese characters—while chanting offensive words to invoke his inauspicious fortune. She stopped when the paper became crumpled; ruined beyond repair.

I remember watching the spectacle, overcome. I, too, wanted such catharsis. 'I've been chasing the wrong people, people that don't give a shit about me.' I had chuckled painfully. 'Learned a painful lesson, I know I've got to start somewhere, but . . . it's hard, Mama . . . '

Mama had wiped my tears. 'Before this, we could not see or hold each other because you were living very far away. I'm always there for you and with you. Just close your eyes and listen to your heart. Always remember this is your home.'

* * *

'Watch where your hands are touching Smelly-Egg,' Aunt Bridget snapped at Daniel, struggling to get into the campervan.

'What a nickname! I feel like a badass,' sneered Daniel.

'I wanted to name you Stanley. But your father wanted Daniel. Just because Dan, as pronounced in Chinese, is like an egg,' said Aunt Bridget, clad in a skintight red embroidered *qipao*.

Daniel air-punched his fist and bounced on the leather seat. 'Yay! Dan-Has-Balls . . . '

'Where are we going?' I placed the batik tiffin carrier on my aunt's lap after climbing onto the passenger seat. I turned to her, noticing the lacquer rouge gloss that outlined her cupid's bow lips.

'Don't ask. Just follow.' Her Bette Davis eyes peered at me.

'Why Stanley? Did the name remind you of a sexy director you once dated?'

'Daniel! Your mouth is worse than sewage,' Aunt Bridget rebuked him, exasperated.

Their comical squabbling infused with the mellifluous alto saxophone melody on the radio. They were playing an hour-long tribute for Kenny G, and sadly, we'd missed the first half.

Growing up, I had been partly influenced by the saxophonist's *Breathless* album.

Loitering at Tower Records, unable to afford the imported CDs, I would listen to the selected music at the stand, checking out the officially licensed band t-shirts, *just for fun*, while avoiding the store manager's eagle eye.

I had then became a seasoned downloader of Napster in college. From Metallica to Nirvana, Oasis, The Cranberries, Hole, The Smashing Pumpkins, Eminem, Tupac Shakur, Joan Jett, and then Alanis Morissette—I had their songs in my computer's yellow folder icon and transferred part of the folders on my Sony MP3 as well as burned the music on a blank CD.

Daniel slowed down the campervan due to the slippery road.

Aunt Bridget was counting the heavy raindrops on the windshield. I'd been awake due to the heavy downpour from two to five last night and had then slept through the petrichor, inhaling the earthy scent produced when the rain condensed from the dry soil permeating the air, singing its lullaby, reminding me of the bittersweet life I'd been living.

I looked at Aunt Bridget's manicured finger pointed at the five-star hotel she had stayed at with the *Anna and the King* film crew—a crew that included Chow Yuen-Fatt and Jodie Foster.

The movie had paved a breakthrough in my aunt's career in Hollywood, despite not having many lines of dialogue, let alone a kissing scene with the King.

She was well known for a scene where she endured the long-haul slapping—and then being pushed into the makeshift reflecting pool—by the actress who had played the King's wife. The whole scene took three days to film, only to be edited into a nine-minute scene.

'My skin's grown thicker after years in this gruelling industry.' Aunt Bridget's gaze looked staid. This was the first time I'd heard my aunt talk about her post-acting life.

Edward's celebrity aura suddenly resurfaced in Aunt Bridget.

Daniel shook his head. 'You've said that the whole time.'

My aunt continued, 'The Hong Kong film industry has been so competitive. My name wasn't mentioned at the end of the movie credit as a stand-in. My diet was boiled potatoes and steamed broccoli, and I shared an apartment with five artists from the same talent agency. I'd sneak in *char siu* rice with extra spicy XO sauce when I felt like indulging myself.'

'Did you ever get caught by your manager?' I asked.

Aunt Bridget tapped her temple, gesturing to her wit.

The rain splashed with the intense screeching swipe of the windshield wiper along the road towards Armenian Street. 'I spoke to mom last night. She sends her regards to all,' I said.

'What time was it?' my aunt asked.

'It was a fifteen-minute call,' I said.

'You should've let me talk to her,' she added.

'Ah, it was just to inform her I arrived safely,' I said, looking at the rows of Peranakan-inspired shophouses, the Penang Islamic Museum, and the Sun Yat-sen Museum. I turned to my aunt. 'So, what's it like working with superstars?'

'Tony Leung is just . . . chef's-kiss.' My aunt's expression turned austere. 'Natural-born actor, a philanthropist, and a faithful husband. His charisma has literally widowed me.'

Daniel and I glanced at each other and turned to look straight ahead, trying not to laugh at her figure of speech.

'So that's the reason you remained single?' I said, my thoughts turning to Edward.

'It's hard to explain unless you've experienced it yourself,' Aunt Bridget replied.

A sense of forlorn triumph emerged within—I had experienced it with Edward.

Daniel stopped before the hawker centre. 'Dearest aunt, your fish ball noodle soup stall will be closing soon.'

'Let me get off, quick.'

I watched her get off, lurching to avoid her five-inch bejewelled Manolo Blahnik stilettos—sharp enough to puncture my toes. Postured up, Aunt Bridget fixed her chignon and her qipao's collar, and then, holding the tiffin, she headed towards a narrow alleyway.

She suddenly stopped. I watched in shock as she whispered something into a hole in a graffitied wall. I side-eyed Daniel. 'So, retirement blues have set in heavily here.' It felt like the movie reboot of *In the Mood for Love*.

Daniel nodded. 'Apparently, she's working on a movie script.'

'Are you serious?'

He shrugged. 'Heard straight from her horse's mouth.'

Three

I returned to my room—another hotpot for dinner, the second after yesterday.

The dim LED lighting clipped onto each photo on the wall, vehemently streamed into an everlasting afterglow. I stretched to reach for the pink teddy plushie, squashing it to my chest, so homely and secure. My kindred had spoiled me with a teddy bear collection in rainbow colours, glamping as one happy family inside a canvas tepee.

I heard someone knocking on the door while unpacking my suitcase. Auntie Noon—Uncle Raymond's wife—walked in holding a tray of Thai mango sticky rice.

'Hmm, smells nice...' I inhaled, smiling. 'Should be delicious...'

'The coconut milk is freshly squeezed, and I place it to simmer on low heat,' she whispered. 'My husband will kill me if I ever use the store-bought ones.'

I chuckled. 'You could've just yelled, Auntie, I would've come down to pick it up.'

'Ma-in-law is asleep and sis-in-law doesn't like anyone shouting, as it chases away her creativity,' Auntie Noon said as she placed the tray on the writing desk, passing me the bowl.

Taking a scoop of the mango chunks, I mixed it with a spoonful of glutinous rice. Auntie Noon observed me with her Colgate advert smile. I smiled and said, 'The stickiness is way too sweet for my heart and soul. How're you able to maintain that hourglass figure?'

'Hey, I eat a lot too, but all my energy is used up in working the family kitchen and volunteering at the soup and gourmet kitchen.'

'That's interesting,' I said. 'This place . . . has expanded a lot. So, how many kitchens are there in Serendipity Sanctuary?'

'The soup kitchen serves mostly walk-ins. But some will pack the food for their children and ailing elders back home after their meals. The gourmet kitchen is where the ingredients are prepared and then cooked. And the pastry kitchen is where the kuih and breads are freshly made daily. Volunteers bring back the leftovers if there are any. The church's stakeholders planned to have a food bank that opens from nine to five. As for the food drive—'

'There you are. I've been looking through the whole house for my pretty chef-wifey,' Uncle Raymond interrupted, pecking Auntie Noon on her cheek. 'May I have a second helping?'

I continued to eat from the bowl, catching a glimpse of Auntie Noon's shyness.

Uncle Raymond gazed around. 'Bridget's been treating you like a little girl. I stopped her from painting the bedroom pink.'

I smiled affectionately at the lovebirds.

'Eat more, Emily. Mango sticky rice is my chef wife's specialty,' my uncle continued to praise her then suddenly let out a sigh. 'If only that rascal could appreciate it.'

'Daniel had a disproportionate amount of meat slices of hotpot just now,' I said.

'Emily-*ah*, I know my son. Don't have to help him say good things.'

I finally learned to shut my mouth—for good.

'Let me get some more for you both.' Auntie Noon retrieved the bowl from my grip and walked out of the door.

I pursed my lips. 'Daniel still needs some time, perhaps.'

'It's been twenty years. This boy's neck is hard like steel.'

'Intractable' was the word that described the Laus' razor-sharp tongue and harsh attitude best—that difficult to control the hatred we might embrace for certain people, stuck in a noxious emotional loop, ingesting the poison of our own. Perhaps, the Laus had once been a family of alchemists who sought the elixir of immortality for Emperor Shi Huang Di and, in their endeavour to procure it, were forced to consume any failed potion. Perhaps our predecessors continued to bear the curse, seeking the impossible and swallowing every failure, feeling it rip up our insides.

Ever since he was young, Daniel had labelled Auntie Noon with distasteful names from 'second-class-mamie', to 'slutty-home-wrecker', and then 'Old Bean's whore'—the most unpleasant one, which I'd reprimanded him for, but he did not change until Uncle Raymond and Mama threatened to erase his name from the family's genealogy register.

I remembered meeting Auntie Noon for the first time, a year after Daniel's mamie passed away. Both Mom and Mama had brought Auntie Noon for textile shopping at the capital. I was put in charge of babysitting Daniel in the country club's playroom while Uncle Raymond and my father were having a drink in the beer hall. Later, at the Chinese restaurant, Daniel was behaving restlessly during dinner and throwing tantrums. Uncle Raymond lost it when my cousin started hurling food from his bowl onto the floor. Auntie Noon managed to stop my uncle from hitting his son. Instead, Daniel tossed a plate of soy sauce onto her Chut Thai. Such was the curse, the inability to accept defeat. Daniel hated Auntie Noon because her presence was a reminder of his mother's permanent absence.

The breeze outside the window evoked a sense of subtle bitterness in me, lingering on my lips and my palate, engulfing that imaginative lump in my throat. My fingers were tracing the patterns on the quilt cover; my mind transported to that sundown

when the aparthotel's kitchen called it a day, the eve of the
Mid-Autumn Festival—with Edward.

* * *

I winced the moment my head bumped into Edward's chest.

'Didn't I tell you not to stay so close behind?' I murmured.

He gave my forehead a brisk rub. 'I'll take the blame if we
get caught.'

'Then you won't see me again.' I switched on the hanging lights.

'*Wae-yo*,' mouthed Edward, inspecting the free-standing cooker.

'I'll be fired by Mr Krishna.' I frowned, exasperated and
in disbelief.

'Your senior manager? Well, good. Then you can come to
Seoul with me,' Edward said.

'What am I going to do there? Get windswept by the foliage?'

'We can have a picnic and then ride our bikes at Hangang
Park, listening to street poets and musicians who perform in the
late evening. At night, there's a water and lights show at the Banpo
Bridge. And Han River is Korea's greatest pride.'

'My manager has permitted a two-hour utilization of this
place and we've literally wasted ten minutes,' I said.

'What's with the hush-hush?' questioned Edward, his
tone snappy.

'The day shift employees are still working,' I replied, gritting
my teeth.

'Let's get going.' Edward clapped.

I shushed him.

He leaned closer then. 'Thanks. I get to spend another
worthwhile day with you.'

My heart fluttered. Clearing my throat I said, 'It was
kind of last minute. The rice flour at the Korean mart is all

sold out. I never knew Chuseok falls on the same day as the Mid-Autumn Festival.' I turned to Edward. 'Do you get any holiday for the celebration?'

He gazed at me deeply. 'Chuseok doesn't have a set time frame. It depends on the lunar year. At one time we had an entire week off. For this year, I guess it should be five days consecutively including the weekend.'

I grabbed a glass bowl from the wall cabinet, pretending to avoid him. 'We don't get a day off because it's nothing more than eating mooncakes and children playing with lanterns. I used to do that with the neighbourhood kids and had no curfew just for that day, especially if it was all through the weekend,' I reminisced.

'Are we making mooncakes today?'

'We're making *onde-onde*, a sweet treat almost similar to *songpyeon*.'

His eyes beamed. 'You know about songpyeon.'

'Hey, I'm not a total idiot, I know some Korean culture.' My voice echoed, loudly.

Edward shushed me then covered my mouth with his hands.

Noticing my narrowed eyes staring at his hands and then at him, he pulled away.

'Well, it isn't songpyeon without pine nuts,' Edward pretended to digress, still glancing at me. 'That incomparable aroma mixing with the beauty of pine needles . . . and those with the sesame-seed filling are affordable and easily accessible. Besides the plain one, my all-time favourite is the mugwort-flavoured pastry.'

Trying not to sneer at his nostalgic reminiscing of home, I opened the cabinet. 'Despite its different taste, the pandan green could replace mugwort for its colour.' I retrieved pandan leaves with stalks, a packet of glutinous rice flour, two blocks of palm sugar, and some leftover grated coconut, placing them on the table.

'Are these the ingredients?' Edward asked.

'Yes.'

Impishly, he smiled as I mixed the hot and room temperature water from the water dispenser into a separable glass measuring cup.

At the stainless-steel, commercialized table, Edward arranged the ingredients in a meticulous line as if preparing for an intercultural explosive cookout. I picked up the micro-cutter blender from another cupboard. Edward cut the pandan leaves with a pair of shears into smaller squares.

'These green coloured leaves are as soft as . . . clay,' Edward said.

'This Malaysian vanilla is mandatory for almost every dish, from curries to desserts. Now, be my watchdog for a bit.' I ambled away to turn off the lights and to extract the juice using the blender.

Edward shielded the lighting from a dimmed bulb that shone into the kitchen from the corridor. I pressed the button on the blender once and then twice, restraining from doing it for the third time, trying not to blend it entirely. I wished I could use the mortar and pestle, the traditional way to pound and extract the concentrate. The blade could be high-speed and straightforward, but the pestle determined the estimated texture through pounding by the sense of touch. Edward stood beside me, forced proximity by choice. I knew he had been experimenting with the new cotton flower cologne from his endorsement.

'Done, please switch on the lights,' I said.

'Tada!' Edward exclaimed childishly, showing a Calypso mango.

'So, that's the purpose of putting on that windbreaker.'

'That's how I hid banana milk, honey butter chips, and shrimp crackers as a K-pop trainee.'

I tried hard not to laugh at his forwardness, pleased at the solid, emerald-green pandan concentrate dripping from the strainer, diffusing an earthy scent.

Suddenly, I heard footsteps getting closer and caught glimpses of torchlight piercing into the kitchen. I pulled Edward by his collar to hide under the table.

The female employees from housekeeping to the front desk, and the food and beverage departments had set their attention on Edward ahead of his arrival, and I had been apprised to not engage in any skinship with their *oppa*. Heck, if they had listened to me, I would have told them this 'sweets-making' mission had been organized by Madam Ong—to bring a sense of hospitableness to Edward.

'What's the mango doing here?' I asked.

'Of course, we're going to eat it with that green Oh-de,' said Edward.

'Say it properly—onde-onde.' I rolled my eyes.

Once we were certain the danger had passed, we abandoned our hiding spot and resumed work. I measured half a cup of glutinous rice flour into the bowl, then sprinkled in some hot water, doing so by intuition and the touch of hands, as taught by Mama.

As the clumps began to consolidate with the pandan green concentrate, I sprinkled in more hot water for that extra chewiness.

'I look forward to eating the Oh-de-Oh-de,' Edward said, pinching in some salt to mix well with the grated coconut. My ticklish bones couldn't stop laughing at his mispronunciation. 'I've been drinking coconut water my whole life, but this is my first time seeing a freshly grated coconut.'

'Coconut water has cooling properties and helps with dehydration, but its consumption is not recommended if you're taking traditional Chinese medicine.' Feeling pleased to have the dough resting in the bowl, I smiled at him. 'Wanna knead it one last time?'

'At last . . .' Edward folded his sleeves and revealed his forearms. Then, I felt an abrupt pull on my blouse. 'Let's do it together, Em.'

'I have to work on the bowl of *gula melaka*.'

He gazed at me softly. 'Can we use mango as its filling?'

'Told you, the combination is not right—'

Edward's arms intertwined with mine. Rude, without permission. Physically, I tried to shrug him away, but my heart wasn't into it.

'Love your well-cropped nails, Em.' His breath warmed my neck.

My body froze. I bit my lips, and my face grew hot hearing the word 'love'. The similar lip-service he would give to his fans, to acknowledge their existence on the concert stage or during the radio interviews. But I couldn't help enjoying that cloud-nine moment, as the heels of our palms flattened and folded outward, till there were no micro bubbles to press out of the dough. My heart fought to stay unaffected. Our eyes met after some time—I felt a little disoriented, feeling his arms wrapped around me. A magnet. *Intimately compelled.* And this was not playing interactive fun games at the fan meetings.

I pulled away as our lips were about to touch.

'I'm sorry.' My lips trembled and I swallowed hard. I'd almost gone off the deep end.

'What's wrong, Emily?' he asked, searching my face for any expression.

I looked at him. 'We don't have much time.'

'Are you . . . are you seeing someone?' Edward asked.

'Let's finish this quickly.'

Four

The hotel-style breakfast bar overlooked the tropical gardens.

The morning gleamed over the carved, jade-stone bonsai tree that stood in the middle of the ceramic tea table. The Peranakan-style teakwood crafted mirror window was hanging above the Victorian rosewood chair. St Paul's Church had purchased this colonial bungalow from the former British colonialists below market value.

'Mama and Aunt Bridget aren't joining us?' I asked, curiously.

'Bridget is like a nocturnal animal. Sometimes she sleeps throughout the day, and mistakes dinner for breakfast.' My uncle flipped over the business edition. 'Ma's been staying up all night, experiencing irregular sleep patterns, which could affect her circadian rhythms.'

Auntie Noon walked in with a pot of plain congee.

Uncle Raymond stood up, pivoting from one side to the other corner along the breakfast aisle, filling up his plate with food, then grabbing a glass of milk, before pulling Auntie Noon to the chair. 'How many times have I told you not to work on an empty stomach?'

Blushing, Auntie Noon picked up the fork and started eating.

'What a lucky wife to have such a husband,' I said to her.

'Gone are those days when women were being married, only to cook, do laundry, and bear offspring. Be very careful if you ever make a woman cry. God counts her tears, especially a wife's. And you—!' My uncle pointed at Daniel.

I laughed as Daniel froze—hands up.

'You're late for work, young man!'

Auntie Noon wiped her mouth with a cloth napkin once she finished eating. 'I need to return to work, a lot of food to be packed.'

Uncle Raymond then eyed Daniel in his own sweet groove, picking and choosing the food. 'Hurry up, there's an added food drive location at Kapitan Keling Mosque today.'

Daniel's loud groan echoed. Planet Pluto would've heard it too. 'Rushing here and there all the time, even a death row prisoner needs to breathe before hanging.' I agreed, there has to be a break in-between no matter how busy that person is.

'Let me help you at the food drive today,' I said to Daniel as he emptied the glass of OJ, chomping down on the baked beans, hash browns, and cocktail sausages.

'We need to talk about your internship, Emily,' Uncle Raymond said.

I turned to Daniel, who seemed bemused by his father.

This was out of the blue.

'What internship?' I asked, narrowing my eyes.

Silence prevailed for a few moments.

'What are you talking about?' I asked once again.

The sound of the grandfather clock ticking had me growing impatient.

Uncle Raymond put down the newspaper, smearing one of the pages with marmalade and toppling the salt and pepper shakers and the cup of unfinished coffee. Known as the no-nonsense Lau, his cold, ballistic harshness stung me as he looked at me with that killing-me-softly stare. He was the most feared, as told by Daniel, as if being caught in the headlights as a deer. 'It was a last-minute arrangement. I spoke to your mom yesterday and she agreed.'

That was . . . indeed *beautiful*—thanks for keeping me in the dark.

It's part of the Chinese elders' typical character traits to blindly treat their younger generations like they can never ever grow up. I turned to my cousin. *Damn.* Daniel left behind a paper serviette with a single word scribbled on it.

F.E.A.R

I quickly slipped it inside my jeans pocket.

I felt mystified, like I was walking into a trap. Was this Mom's plan? Her attempt to sign me up for holistic Catholic retreats had failed several times. Sweat emitted from my every pore. Too late to map out a prison break.

Uncle Raymond stood up. 'I'll be in my office. Come over once you're done.'

I stalled, trying to buy time, helping Auntie Noon to clean the dining area, then vacuuming the hall. The staff at the laundromat were congenial and helped me learn how to operate the industrial washing machine and the dryer. It felt like I was back at work in the aparthotel. The spinning sound and soft thunderous roar of the washing machine was indeed therapeutic. However, the ill-at-ease Auntie Noon grabbed the linen cloth from my hands as I readied to toss it over the dining table.

She pulled me behind the pillar. 'I seldom question my husband's decisions, but he has his way of settling things. I'm sure he'll listen to what's been troubling you,' said Auntie Noon.

So, it was confirmed—I shouldn't expect a bed of roses from this staycation.

Unaffected by such an array, I stopped at the veranda, breathed in, enjoying the sound of the irrigation sprinklers. A rabbit came to mind—Edward's favourite animal—galloping to chase after its mates on the lawn. Stung by a pricking needle straight into my heart, the memory of Edward's voice, scent, and touch once again uprooted my impervious demeanour, making me want to repeat that stance.

I shook my head to wave the thought away.

It was of no use. In a matter of minutes, I found myself gasping outside the door, flabbergasted the moment the door swung open.

'Your footsteps are like a tsunami alert,' said Uncle Raymond, handing me a few sheets of facial tissue. 'Are you being chased by a phantom?'

They're my own demons, I thought. I didn't answer him as I reached for the tissues.

Uncle Raymond closed the door, sat on the director's mahogany chair, then shoved a paper at me and said, 'Take a look at this.'

'Letter of Internship,' I read. 'No monthly salary. Allowance in cash is to be paid on a weekly basis. The job scope is to assist mainly in the pastry kitchen and sometimes in the soup kitchens as well as the food drive,' I inhaled and then continued, 'to assist in collecting fresh produce from the distributors from either the wholesale marketplace or directly from the local growers, whichever is applicable.' I stopped reading.

'Is there a problem?'

'Probation period ends in . . .' I looked at my uncle.

'C'mon finish it.'

'Probation period ends in three months,' I read out loud.

'What do you think?'

'Definitely a surprise.'

He knew I was fuming from my expression. 'Looks like I've spoiled your vacation, huh, by telling you to volunteer in these bustling kitchens.'

I exhaled, choking on my words, then pursing my lips to curb the part of me that was eager to retaliate. 'That's ninety days of work. Why not make it one hundred days then?'

'Oh, the senior pastry chef will be overjoyed at your recommendation.' Uncle Raymond stood up, placing his hands on the desk in slow-mo.

That was the most respectfully sarcastic I was capable of being to a father-figure. I pushed the letter back towards my uncle. 'Thank you for the offer. I used to love baking more than reading law books.'

'Any plans after returning home? Or getting a job? Everyone has got to start somewhere, Emily.' He ambled over to me. 'You're here for a productive vacation.'

The weight on my shoulder had blown-up. My eyes closed. I breathed, fingers scraping the upholstery that should have blanketed me in solace. The internship seemed to be no escapade. Hands buried in the strands of my hair and toes tapping like a metronome—to be in one's right mind. Work could perhaps substitute this emptiness.

'He's not coming back, Emily.' Uncle Raymond brought it up. It'd been a year since Edward left.

'He promised to return,' I said, half-heartedly.

'It is not easy to accept it, I know.' My uncle's voice became unprecedentedly emotional. 'Life is an unexpected journey. Not everyone will be by our side along the way. We chance upon people who teach us, who we learn from, sometimes even fall in love with. Beautiful memories are the times spent in happiness or sadness, from arguments to long embraces.'

I forced a smile and wiped tears from my eyes—*he's right.*

* * *

Most of the photos in the garland were discoloured with foxing stains.

I remembered Mom would develop two extra copies of every birthday photo of mine; one for Mama and the other to send to Aunt Bridget's private address in Hong Kong. Edward and I shared a common interest in old, black-and-white, vintage photographs.

'These photos were taken from Mama's albums at 3 a.m.,' said Daniel. 'Her snoring was the loudest, so loud even a burglar on the roof would shit his pants.'

'Thank you for fixing the lighting on the garland,' I said, adjusting the photo of one-month-old Daniel and adolescent me with a new wooden peg. It was a photo I'd been carrying ever since I'd moved to live by myself.

Daniel made a disgusted face at the photo. 'I look like a Chinese red egg to be eaten to attain good fortune.'

I pinched his bleached hair. 'Anyway, this egg has grown up so much.'

'Of course, I can now eat three to four bowls of rice per serving,' Daniel boasted.

I smirked and spotted a photo from my fourth birthday.

I remembered waking up early that morning. Mom had been busy in the kitchen. My father had gone to the bakery to pick up the chocolate cake he'd pre-ordered. That small celebration was to my contentment, and I was not expecting gifts—improvident or not—but Mom and Uncle Raymond had an additional surprise treat planned, just because Mama missed her granddaughter. Later, Aunt Bridget showed up in a bathrobe-like sapphire-blue wrap dress, with a tall, lanky, handlebar-moustached man. But they had to return to Hong Kong after the cake cutting. And that was the first time I'd gotten to hold a life-size Elmo plushie.

'I should've been born in your era, Biu-jie,' Daniel exhaled.

'Why?'

'In order to join in the fun and be the hairstyle police,' Daniel said. 'The man next to Aunt Bridget had a screwed-up Paul McCartney college boy hairdo.'

'Didn't you want to be a hairstylist at one time?' I picked up the duly signed Letter of Internship from the table, browsing the terms and conditions.

'I want to be a cinematographer now,' he said. 'A long shot, but there's no glass ceiling in Daniel Lau's dictionary. Those are for the lackadaisical and the indolent. A man should have unlimited dreams,' he recited with elegance. 'I believe I am, therefore I am. The world is not a forlorn stage, and God loves stubborn people.'

That's why I'm still alive.

'Hey, this isn't Juliet's balcony.' I shooed him off.

Daniel shot me his notorious impish grin and jumped off my bed.

My room had literally become an art space. The garland twinkled in an exuberant glow, coruscating through the surroundings. Still early for Christmas, the least it'd do was broaden the horizon, filling the desolation with subtle positivity and nourish my inner peace. 'Whose idea was it to install a mosquito net canopy?' I asked.

'Aunt Bridget.'

'Really? Cool . . .' I raised my eyebrows.

'Old Bean was shocked when she first suggested that you would love it and then insisted on the pink netting while I suggested a white one, though Old Bean had told me you love blue. If you don't like it, I don't mind removing it for you.'

'I love it, really,' I said. In fact, the mosquito net reminded me of a bridal veil as I looked up at the constellated sky. 'I'm lucky to have the Lau-d & Praud with me.'

'I see you've acted on the note I gave you this morning,' said Daniel, eyeing my internship letter.

'It is impossible to Fuck-Everything-And-Run,' I said. 'Be sure to look out, as I shall Fight-Everything-And-Rise.'

'Bravo! Old Bean must've given you a lecture about his life adventure, like "I've eaten more salt than you've eaten rice", and "what kind of wind and rain haven't I seen",' Daniel impersonated his father. Uncle Raymond had gone through a great deal in life.

I laughed at Daniel's antics but stopped when I noticed a silhouette standing by the door.

'I am Bei-er, at your service tonight. Do you want some wine?' said Aunt Bridget, alternating between an English and a Shanghainese pitch.

'We will leave soon, thank you,' Daniel said.

I mouthed, 'What did she just call herself?'

'Told you she's writing a movie script,' Daniel whispered.

'Rui-er, what are you doing here?' Aunt Bridget dragged me away.

My cousin stood up but was told to mind his own beeswax.

'You shouldn't be seen with a man in this decadent lounge.'

Who is Rui-er? What the F is wrong with my aunt?

'I—I was . . . ' I stammered, pointing at myself.

Just how *great* it was to be held hostage by the dark, immodest, smokey-eyeshadowed Aunt Bridget. Confusing thoughts and sarcasm aside, I had to immerse myself in her actress mindset. I channelled my instinct to counter-and-combat, ready to pounce with confidence.

'I'm a secret agent,' I said proudly.

Aunt Bridget spookily beamed. 'Serial number?'

'A secret agent can't reveal her serial number.'

'Have you forgotten your pledge for the exploited women?' Aunt Bridget recited. 'The Moonlight-God is going to punish you for not upholding the role as the member of Women's Knighthood.' Then, I shrieked when Aunt Bridget held me at knifepoint. 'Say your serial number and I shall let you go.'

'Double nine eight four eight six,' I said in a quivering tone.

'Now go. Don't look back, Rui-er!'

I ran off without looking back. Gosh, my cousin was right about my aunt. If only he could have foreseen the possibility of her waving a knife at me. Luckily, my bad improvisations had set me free.

Five

Next morning at the dining table, Uncle Raymond and Daniel were exchanging glances—the first time my uncle could see eye to eye with his firstborn. I was too busy feeling relieved upon being informed that the knife was an acting prop to pay the father—son duo much attention. Aunt Bridget had stolen it from the filming set in Zhejiang, supposedly to appease her compulsiveness and to keep as a memento to commemorate her last movie.

'Just who are *these* . . . Rui-er and Bei-er?' I asked, perplexed.

'Aunt Bridget's latest characters in her script,' Daniel said.

'It's difficult for her to imagine living in this mansion without spotlights and accolades,' said Uncle Raymond. 'Zero flamboyant clothing and no media to report your private life.'

'There're three kitchens to pick from and volunteer at but Aunt Bridget refuses,' said Daniel. 'Maybe try matchmaking her with a man, so at least she has a life-partner.'

'That will be done for you, soon,' Uncle Raymond said to Daniel. 'I'll be delighted to slaughter a chicken for the purpose of worshipping the deities for three-days-and-three-nights if you ever stop behaving like a kid and bring a girlfriend home.'

'I love babies but I don't want one.' Daniel impersonated an infant's cry.

As I laughed, I held my belly, almost choking on the scrambled egg in my mouth.

'I'll throw you out if you ever bleach your hair again,' my uncle said, changing topics.

'I want to try pink next time,' said Daniel.

'I'll dye my hair ash-purple if Dan-Dan is going pink,' I said.

My cousin gave me an instant high-five.

'The Lau daughters are consecrated to their profession,' said Uncle Raymond, 'as well as doing church work—like your mother, Emily.'

'I'm not as pious as her,' I said.

'Cheryl called last night. She's happy that you're giving this internship a try,' Uncle Raymond said, 'especially since she's known Sean since her teens.'

'Step by Step and Rise'—Emily's mixtape of the day.

'Who says your mom isn't concerned about you?' Daniel nudged my elbow. 'Don't worry, Uncle Sean is very, *very* pleasant to work with.'

* * *

I bowed with arms behind me, a sign of respect for this man who stood—approximately six feet high—before me with polished, tanned skin. I peeped at Daniel, stomping on his foot, humming in soft cadences, eyes moving in every direction.

'Shaking legs will dispel good luck and prosperity,' said the man in a low, nasal pitch.

Daniel stopped immediately. 'Sorry, Uncle Sean.'

'You must be Emily.'

'Yes, Uncle Sean.'

'Can I call you Little Niece from now on?'

I tried not to stir. 'I normally go by Em—'

Daniel pinched me, signalling I shouldn't have rebutted. I wasn't prepared for such instant-family-recognition. I would give this grave-digger expression man with a greasy face the benefit of the doubt to dip my head inside this pan of hot oil.

'I'll never force anyone to obey me.' Uncle Sean couldn't stop staring at my tattoos. His features were softer than my uncle's.

Those grave, deep eyes flared like a beeping lie-detector. 'Very bold to ink floral pieces on your skin.'

I bowed. 'Thank you, but I prefer to lay low instead of bragging.'

The silence was replaced by the sound of the cooking pot stewing.

'I honoured you as Little Niece because we're on the same path.'

Stripping off his shirt, Uncle Sean revealed a fire-spitting dragon tattoo on the left side of his torso encircling a Celtic crucifix. He turned around, exhibiting the statue of the infamous military warlord Lord Guan Yu of the late Eastern Han dynasty on his laboriously chiselled back. The tattoo emphasized the blood dripping from the Green Dragon Crescent Blade wielded by the deified figure. Legend has it that the enemy's blood would coat the blade in a layer of frost when battling in the snow.

Daniel blinked.

'Every tattoo has its backstory,' said Uncle Sean.

Man, was he right. 'But I don't intend to join any . . . badass gang,' I murmured.

Uncle Sean shushed me. 'Doesn't matter. There's a price to pay. It is worthwhile for the one we honour and truly love.'

I quietly swallowed.

'Little Niece, your face is becoming tomato-red. Why?'

'The kitchen is . . . humid,' I muttered.

'Wear lighter coloured clothing to avoid the heat from the hot, pressurized ovens,' Uncle Sean started. 'No tight-fitting jeans and . . .' I looked at him staring at my fashionably torn denims. 'You look like a beggar. And don't complain if you have muscle cramps, which you will feel if you continue wearing such impractical clothing while working in the kitchen.'

Fussy Uncle Sean was worse than Mom. 'So, what's my first task?'

'Cut up the mozzarella cheese with the knife.'

'Don't we have an industrial grater?' Daniel asked.

'Today is Little Niece's first day of work. I'm here to test her resilience, just like any master would.' Uncle Sean put his shirt back on. 'I want these done in two hours.'

* * *

Daniel sighed in exhaustion the moment Uncle Sean left the pastry kitchen for Uncle Raymond's office. I guarded the door as Daniel filled the jar from the dispenser with water, then gulped it down like a disconsolate fish, dabbing at the remaining drops on his neck. 'You want some?' My cousin handed the jar to me dramatically.

'What's that for?'

He shrugged. 'To show others that you've worked impressively hard . . .'

'I don't look sexy when I sweat. You said that, remember?'

'Take it easy. Uncle Sean has no interest in women.'

I laughed. 'We better hurry up, else we'll have to put up as all-rounders here.'

'The pastry side is a gruelling rush. Makes you feel worse than an overworked grinding-machine.'

'But it's still better than working in a restaurant. Haven't you heard there's no life if you work in the culinary industry? No proper meal time and distressing peak seasons. I've done a stint on the pastry side and despite the gruelling conditions it was. . . fun.' I ran my fingers over the heavy-duty, KitchenAid stand mixer, giving in to a feeling of nostalgia. I remember Edward had a sore throat after finishing an angel cake straight out the oven—it had been my first attempt at baking for someone . . . special.

Daniel scooped up the finely cut cheese into the container. 'This place has ridden the British colonialism wave and the nationalist movements. Japanese soldiers have probably executed and decapitated their enemies and war victims where we're standing. I also heard about a torture chamber where prisoners of war were held captive. The church informed the interfaith council of this when they invited groups of different religions to minister prayers before the demolitions and dismantling.'

'Serendipity Sanctuary should become a thrilling tourist attraction,' I said.

Daniel grinned. 'What an aptitude for business.'

'What about the lush garden with the land and waterscape?' I asked.

'That used to be a mass grave. The church decided not to build anything on it as a mark of respect to the countless innocent souls buried there.'

'I don't remember catching sight of this pastry kitchen when I last came here,' I said, passing a stainless-steel tray to Daniel after wiping it with a chequered kitchen cloth.

'The pastry kitchen was built in 2010. Initially, it looked like a cottage with second-hand ovens stacked like corpses. It was then fully renovated two years ago, with all these brand new baking appliances and utensils.'

'Was it fun working at the food drive?' I asked, pulling the last carton of carrots towards me after moving the julienned ones into plastic containers.

'Better than working in the three kitchens. You might think what a mundane life it is—setting up tents, arranging food packets, calling out for people to queue up. Some insist on having additional packets for their elderly parents or children.' Daniel stopped. 'Does your internship include working for the food drive?'

'I think so,' I said. 'But I'll be working on the pastry side this week.'

'Hey, you wanna hear an exclusive tattle?' Daniel whispered, 'Old Bean and Uncle Sean are like brotherhood . . . in love.'

I took the knife he was waving around, lacking faith in Daniel's culinary abilities, then cut the block of mozzarella. 'Isn't that a bromance, like sisterhood on the runway train?'

'Mama said so. She's the family's storyteller, only when her brain is *tuned* accurately. I'll run the hook when she talks about the Japanese Invasion during World War Two,' Daniel illustrated. 'Listen, they'd once painted their names along Acheen Street, the infamous hangout spot for youngsters and the dropouts, especially for the gangster-wannabes. Who knows, these could be Old Bean and Uncle Sean's deplorable stories, ones they'd like to take straight to the grave.'

'I think you need to stop dramatizing everything.'

Daniel pretended as if I were a fool. 'There's something amiss between those two. I'll continue to dig deep, just mark my words. Uncle Sean's tattoos have a killer vibe, like he'll tie you down and torture you for hours. My balls will curse me in pain.'

It had been a *long* time since I'd laughed this hard.

* * *

Daniel and I were cutting the second batch of cheddar cheese when Mama barged into the pastry kitchen, accompanied by Aunt Bridget.

Uncle Sean had to agree with the Empress Dowager Mama, permitting my cousin and I to attend the relative visiting session at the Chew Jetty. Throughout the journey, I was stunned by Mama's phenomenal lucidity, however, Aunt Bridget stated that it could be a sign death is near as awareness fluctuates then. I chose to look at the brighter, more positive side.

I was baffled by Mama's next-of-kin who lived by the jetty. I knew none of them, no thanks to how fluent I was in Hokkien. I excused myself to enjoy the view from the Chinese floating temple when Mama was offering her prayers at the ancestral shrine. Once upon a time, I had wished to show Edward the wonderful clan jetty and floating villages.

A rugged man was scraping anti-fouling paint off the boat beside me.

Aunt Bridget was blotting away the matte foundation along the creases of her cheekbones and lips. 'No one in their right mind should put you to work under that Sean-the-Monk in his Shaolin Pastry Kitchen.'

'Uncle Sean was formerly a monk—?' I asked, confused.

'Have you seen a tree-climbing pregnant sow? No, impossible. I called him a monk because he doesn't eat meat.' Aunt Bridget laughed, tugging at her lace collar, flustered by the sweltering heat. 'He is Tan Sanzang, the main character in *Journey to the West*. The longevity monk doesn't kill to source meat—protein—but he abstains from coming into close contact with real meat, like this one . . .' My aunt showed off her creamy skin tone.

'I think you should advertise for Nivea body lotion,' I claimed. Aunt Bridget's glare made it clear that she didn't appreciate my sarcasm. 'Okay, okay, I get you.'

'He's also called me Baigujing in reciprocity,' she added.

'Isn't that a demoness shapeshifter?' I turned to my aunt. 'But the real question is: Are you going to devour his flesh to gain immortality, like the character does?'

'Hell no!' Aunt Bridget's pitch reflected a middle-aged dolphin's sonic sound wave.

I remained quiet for a while. 'How long have you known Uncle Sean?'

'Hmm . . . since before you were born,' Aunt Bridget said.

'What do you think of his tattoos?' I asked curiously.

She turned in slow motion. 'How have you seen his body ink?'

'Well, it was the first day of my internship. And Daniel was there too,' I said. 'I think Uncle Sean is a hero, enduring excruciating pain as thousands of needles gnawed at him. The process must have dragged on for weeks or months, with the possibility of inflammation that can only to be treated with antibiotics and painkillers.'

'Confirms he's got a tattoo fixation,' said Aunt Bridget. 'Everyone has that lust-for-life history. I'm not talking about poultry or pastrami. Someone like Sean would rather be demoralized by needles than get laid. He truly is a rare breed from Middle-earth.'

I pivoted to leave the dock due to the scorching heat and high tide, and also partly because Aunt Bridget's Sensual Meat Sermon wasn't my cup of tea.

The rickety walkway had me bouncing and heaving with every step. I quickened my pace as an eerie screech-to-break sound prevailed. The smell of someone refurbishing the hull with the shellac primer lingered, melding with gusts of sea breeze, making me feel nauseous.

'Don't be influenced by the Monk, working to death in the kitchen.' Her voice still reached me. 'At least treat yourself to some meat.'

I flipped my hair back and turned around. 'Of course, I've had some . . . *meat* before,' I said.

Aunt Bridget walked until she was right in front of me and leaned closer, slapping my arm so hard that I almost stumbled over. 'Let me guess, handsome white man?'

I played along, a dismayed lover. 'Separated by miles, and oceans apart, I still remember his scent like it was yesterday; overshadowed by his presence, imagining him in a bookstore aisle or shuffling his albums at the record store. I see him everywhere—while waiting at the bus stop or disembarking the MRT. Like you, I . . . won't be kissing another man in this lifetime.'

Aunt Bridget's fingertips dabbed my cheek. 'You really did cry.'

I peered at the teardrops, surprised; thinking of Edward. I thought I'd been kidding, but my heart clearly wasn't on the same page as me. 'Life has to go on without him.'

'I managed to harvest the acting chromosome in you.' Aunt Bridget patted my back.

'There you are!'

We turned towards Daniel's voice.

Aunt Bridget wiped the lingering tears under my eyes with a facial tissue. 'I'll tell no one you've slept with a white man.'

Slap me hard, Lord Zeus. 'I didn't . . .'

'You two look like you've stolen some gold from a treasure chest,' said Daniel.

'We're having a girls chat, not for men to nosedive in,' Aunt Bridget jeered.

* * *

We then stopped by a Mamak stall restaurant for afternoon tea.

A man in a long kurta and baggy pants from the cash counter escorted us to an empty table. The menu list and its pricing were printed unambiguously on the wall. The man repeated our orders then left. Meanwhile, an honest mistake had ingrained in my aunt's head that I'd slept with a white man.

Ten minutes later, the man sauntered to our table. 'Masala tea,' he said.

'*Sini, terima kasih,*' I asked him to bring it over, thanking him. The milk foam diffused its dairy fragrance as I sipped from the glass.

Daniel was savouring the *roti canai banjir*, an Indian flatbread, with *dhal* and chicken curry gravy. Aunt Bridget refused to order, citing that this wasn't the kind of place she eats at. The aromatic spices were apparently digging up her unforgettable memories of her time in Marrakech. The eatery was inundated with sizzling, overpowering pungent spices. The kitchen staff brought out trays of food—spicy-red-chilli squid, spinach cooked in spicy turmeric sauce—arranged side by side on the stainless-steel stall with wheels. The queue extended to the next few shops.

My cousin let out a hoarse burp.

Aunt Bridget slapped the back of his head in agitation. 'Where're your manners?'

I almost spat out my drink, looking at the drama queen.

'The way you hit on my head,' Daniel said, savouring the thick gravy, 'would have turned me into a handicap if you were my mother.'

'What's taking Ma so long? I'm bubbling with sweat,' said Aunt Bridget.

'After the prayers at the ancestral shrine by the in-house Taoist priest,' Daniel said, 'they should be crying each other a river, hugging and digging reservoirs in their tear-ducts, talking about how mercilessly their sworn siblings and families were killed in World War Two.'

Aunt Bridget smirked. 'She'd call me an ungrateful daughter whenever I told her not to think about the past, just because the war was over when I slipped out of her womb.'

'I wonder how people could live permanently in a village built on stilts. It's so dangerous, walking on rickety connected planks, though it was interesting to see a post box attached outside every household.' I said, eating the fried Maggi noodles.

'The villagers have the superpower to walk on the water,' Aunt Bridget said.

'I wonder what Mama and the elders are discussing,' I said.

'As long as they aren't matchmaking me with some girls,' Daniel said.

'You never know.'

Six

Edward adjusted the air-con to his desired temperature, divulging the KL city skyline. It was after torrential rain that the sunset gradually embraced the overspreading of blue and silvery grey. I pulled over the linen curtains, missing out on the whispering dusk.

I nosedived into the ocean of music drafts, face down onto Edward's unkempt bed. 'Don't go.' His fingers ran over my work badge.

Such an act was deemed intruding, as there'd been great comfort in just lying beside him. 'I'm on duty Mr Edward Ahn,' I said, covering part of my face with his leather journal.

'Guess who's been on my mind as the wind was bending and breaking the tree into half out there?' Tapping on the guitar's neck for an inspiring rhythm, he focused on the lyric draft. 'I thought the building would collapse any time.'

My gaze couldn't leave his. 'You're over-exaggerating.'

'I still feel the icy chill, it was like living in an igloo.' Edward pressed my hand to his cheek, and I could feel his heartbeat on my palm, aligning mine. 'Creative people aren't only hungry for passion and love. They're also hypersensitive.'

Slowly, I moved away, stealing a glimpse at the music draft—'Sajin'.

'It means photograph,' Edward said.

I listened attentively.

'I love conjuring up new ideas and usually won't be out of them for a week. I've beaten many music producers and singers–songwriters, at composing and penning lyrics for a dozen tracks, including a few K-drama theme songs.' Edward's reflection was observing mine in the window. 'I think the fearless ones should compete to race against the monstrous monsoon.'

'Don't most Koreans love the warm, fuzzy summer?'

Edward was strumming the guitar, sampling the chorus. 'Along with the beaming sun, we've been whipped often by the cold breeze, the parks are filled with children and adults in short-sleeves and cotton pants, or dresses.' He caught me looking at him. 'Seoraksan National Park located in the northeast region is best to experience the first autumn foliage in mid-September. I'm sure you'll enjoy the spectacular canopy of colourful leaves.'

I opened Edward's bento box and put down a pair of disposable chopsticks. The purple rice was sprinkled with sesame seeds. 'Come, it's dinner time,' I said, sneezing and coughing at the whiff of the burning spices travelling down to my throat.

'My favourite—*jjimdak*.' Edward gestured with a surprised smile.

'Aren't you the one who placed the order?' I asked, blowing my nose.

'Should be my manager,' he said.

I grabbed Edward, stopping him. 'You sure it is from Mr Han? Maybe some . . . fans?'

Edward drew me to the seat and then pulled out two stainless-steel chopsticks from a pouch, stirring the pointers in the gravy. He smiled as he lifted the chopsticks. 'No blue-black means no poison. *Gwisin* is in no hurry to take me.'

I rummaged through the plastic bag for a receipt. 'Mr Han ordered this from Ampang.'

'Oh, can we go there by foot?' Edward asked.

'Ampang is on the east side. There's a Korean grocery store, souvenir shops, and shops selling Soju. You'll definitely feel at home. I went to an authentic Korean restaurant with a visiting Korean poet after an open mic. I still remember that extra spicy *tteokbokki*.'

'I look forward to going there with you,' said Edward.

'Will you be able to sneak out from here?' I asked.

'I'll think about it, *gwaenchanhayo*.' Edward's arm was trying to get closer.

'Enjoy your food.' I reluctantly let him go as he pouted playfully. But I couldn't stop sneezing. 'You . . . *achoo* . . . just killed me with the capsaicin,' I said, blowing my nose with facial tissue. This food was a silent killer despite being served without the usual red pepper flakes and red pepper paste.

Edward went to the mini fridge and poured an isotonic drink into a glass, prodding me to finish it. I gave it a try. 'Where'd you learn this from? It does help ease the allergy a bit,' I admitted, finishing the rest.

'A *sunbae* taught me back in my idol trainee days. A mild rhinitis got the best of me and increased my sensitivity to chilli peppers. This helped to alleviate the trigger. But hey, this has proven its authenticity. This is the kind of wonderful dish I could see myself enjoying with my family at the marketplace.' Edward slurped the cellophane noodles, letting out a noise of satisfaction. 'Whenever my mother made this dish back home, there wouldn't be a morsel left in the pot.'

'What's the main killer ingredient in jjimdak?' I asked, passing him the *banchan* set of fermented kimchi, fried anchovies, spicy braised potatoes, and stir-fried oyster mushrooms with French beans.

'The secret ingredient is . . . *cheongyang gochu*.' He was waving a piece of a scallion-like vegetable with the chopsticks. 'Green chilli pepper, grown only in South Korea's soil. Like the warlord Thanos and his mad titan characteristics, it is even stronger than the red chilli pepper. Either eat it fresh or make a dipping sauce with diced onions to go with *pajeon*.'

'I love the Korean pancake as it is.' I stood up to leave. 'And my favourite is the seafood with the balance of iodine taste with the rest of the ingredients.'

Using a clean spoon, Edward picked sliced carrots, diced potatoes, vegetables, and chicken strips from his bowl and put it into an empty bowl. 'Here, try it.'

'Your manager is coming back soon. He told me so.'

'Please don't talk about him.' Edward rolled his eyes, leaning closer. 'Should I bring this bowl into the closet, so we can eat together?'

'You almost got me in trouble the other day,' I said, as I felt him tug me towards the closet. He gazed at me in the dim lighting.

'Your company is ridiculous. Mr Han wasn't around when I had a throbbing spasm in my shoulder. You're the only one I could ask for a massage. Why is that a problem?'

'But you're muddling things up,' I said.

His stare turned grave. 'I don't understand, Emily.'

'It's better if we draw a very clear line between us from now on.'

Tears had begun to emerge; as if a layer of glass barricaded his beautiful eyes. I looked away—wouldn't have precipitated that aching if I had a second choice. Like a black, tangled heart, I had hurt him, yet I felt the same as well.

Edward slowly put the bowl aside. 'Your colleague Sabrina told me you are not seeing anyone. Then, why are we not—?'

His words stung me. Impossible to reveal that I'd signed the non-disclosure agreement supplemented by his record label, prior to his reservation. His management had the right to seek compensation from the aparthotel if I were caught or suspected of being involved in an illicit affair with Edward. With the possibility of losing my job, my bad reputation would be an uncalled for.

Then, I bluffed my confidence. 'I don't date superstars.'

Clenching his teeth, Edward let out a sigh.

* * *

Daniel was howling.

I rubbed my eyes, tried *erasing* my past memory with Edward.

'Look at what you've done!' Uncle Sean was pulling Daniel's ear. 'Did I not tell you to go slow and steady with the curry powder?'

I dabbed at the sweat beading my forehead using the towel around my neck.

Uncle Sean wailed, eyes bloodshot. 'Little Niece, we're making the curry puff potato filling, not mashed potatoes. Now, how am I to rate your performance today to Ray-Ray?'

'The way you address my uncle is so . . .' I shivered, looking at the pot.

'I think we should hire one or two helping hands,' said Daniel. 'I've found my passion on the pastry side of things. I should stop volunteering at the food drive now.'

'Waste of breath, nobody wants to do unpaid work,' said Uncle Sean.

'I'm putting up the notice tomorrow. I don't care,' Daniel said.

'Okay, good luck,' Uncle Sean replied sarcastically.

I gave Daniel a high-five and said, 'The traditional curry puff filling must be cooked in Malaysian curry powder with chopped onions and curry leaves. Its simplicity counts. And don't substitute potatoes with sweet potatoes to minimize the cost.'

'No way, we're operating on a tight budget,' Uncle Sean said.

'Let's switch-up the puff's filling using *gochugaru*,' Daniel said.

That night, Daniel and I had to finish the pot of a failed potato-filling experiment.

* * *

'Red pepper powder, here we come.' Daniel found parking in a designated yellow box. I would've guessed the state government must've paid the topiarist a decent amount.

At the seafront promenade, the signage—'Welcome to Karpal Singh Drive'—was installed within the gated landscape of the well-kept botanical garden with shrubs meticulously trimmed into decorative terrestrial and floral shapes.

The unique, sulphury seawater smell was considerably pleasant as we headed towards the two high rise office blocks in the commercial complex. Food trucks selling fusion fast food were parked under a row of tall palm trees, and an incandescent sculpture stood at the shoreline corner—sculpted by a reputed visiting artist from Tokyo, the best futurist forefront after dark.

Daniel stopped in front of the commercial podium, right beside an auspiciously shaped pond with striking, neon red and blue water features. 'Here we are,' he pointed, seemingly proud to be in front of K-Licious-Delish, a high-concept Korean convenience store chain.

'*Annyeonghaseyo*,' two women attired in navy green uniform stood at the entrance acknowledged in unison, handing out a shopping basket to us.

'Aren't we here for the gochugaru only?' I asked Daniel, receiving the basket.

'The red pepper powder can wait. This store is full of surprises every day.'

I trailed along as Daniel headed to the first level, avoiding the rushing customers descending the stairs. Embarrassingly, my face almost slammed into a cardboard standee. Armed with a swoon-worthy, killer smile, the store's ambassador, with a dulcet Korean full name, gestured two thumbs up. Then, a schoolgirl implied that I'd blocked her view for a selfie with the standee, professing a flying kiss at her cardboard-lover.

'So obsessed, bet she's forgotten what her surname is,' I murmured.

Daniel cackled at my sarcastic comment.

'Why are we leaving downstairs out?' I asked.

'The ground level is mostly ready-to-eat snacks, our last destination to strut-and-strike. Now, we have to divide and conquer.'

I felt as if I was in the midst of an ongoing subtle looting. Customers rummaged, fumbled, and swept across a variety of confectionery and beauty items, dropping them into their shopping basket with the power of their hands. Some were conjointly carrying two to three baskets, one on their arm, while kicking the other, moving along from one aisle to the next; this scene could be almost be compared to *Shop'til You Drop*—my favourite game show. The mess somehow resembled *Hell's Kitchen*. I had once watched an amateur local chef with condiments, sauces, readily chopped fresh produces—julienned and grated, drenching the gigantic wok with blistering oil and then ladling in the ingredients.

'Why are you standing there? Come and help me,' said Daniel.

'People actually buy things without looking at the expiry date?' I shook my head.

'I forgot to mention,' Daniel said. 'Those who purchase items worth of MYR 100 with a single receipt stand a chance to win a meet and greet with the ambassador. And the promotion is for today only.'

'What—you mean that cardboard-lover?' I asked, pointing my thumb behind me. 'This is far worse off than the BSB-N'Sync obsession of the late-nineties.'

I winced as the woman's shoulder hit mine.

What on earth! Her facial skin was egg white and translucent. This resurrected one joined the crowd as they were picking and dropping the facial sheet masks—ranging from collagen essence to volcanic mud, to hyaluronic acid and tangerine pore-tightening—into their baskets. In seconds, these wizard-like shoppers had cleared the items from the K-Beauty and Skincare aisle.

'So long as he's a tall, fair, and handsome Korean-oppa,' Daniel was fantasizing. 'You're the one in a million who isn't riveted by the Korean Wave. But I'm sure within your internship period, I'll manage to turn you. I don't mind giving you some K-pop music lessons.'

'Thanks, I don't think I can buy more than MYR 20.' I hastily looked around, wondering if I could escape as my heart started to palpitate and pins-and-needles started taking over my body. 'I'll get that gochugaru, just tell me where it is.'

'Are you sure?' My cousin was paying full attention to my condition.

'You can have this,' I said, pushing my basket to him.

Daniel pointed at the last corner. 'Right over there. You can do it!'

As advised by Dr Erica, I invited positive energy into my space, navigating myself away from this misery. These customers and I coexisted, and they won't inflict any harm to me. Instead, I should learn to share my space with them. I slipped past two stocky women at the confectionery aisle and happened to discover Pepero—chocolate-covered pretzel sticks of assorted flavours. I don't know why it felt like I was seeing it for the first time. And, among the extensive selection, I spotted the flavour 'Nude'—Edward's favourite, with chocolate in the centre and a biscuit coating on the outside.

But I made it out of there! *Alive!*

The soft background music continued to veil the sound and the voices of the customers. Along the cooking ingredients aisle, I was overwhelmed by the types of gochugaru displayed on the shelves and picked the one which was of a lesser quantity. Some had 'Extra 100% Spicy' stickers on them. I was impressed with their meticulous and resealable packaging.

While I was wondering whether I should get a packet of Pepero or not, a slow track entered the AirPlay. It commenced with an upscale piano melody and was then accompanied by soft drums; to fit the hand brushing along the reeds growing on estuary, perhaps as it does in the wetlands. The melody depicted silhouettes of coupledom finally allowed to meet and channel their burning desire. They swayed to the dance, in togetherness, giggling at their bad steps, falling slowly into each other. The melody arrangement felt somewhat familiar.

'Are we done here?' Daniel asked.

I blinked at his shopping baskets. 'That should be more than MYR 200.'

'You're always my brilliant Biu-jie. Hold this.'

I took it from him, dropping in the red pepper powder packet. 'I picked this one with only 250 grams as the first starter. We can buy the larger packet later.'

'No problem,' Daniel said. 'We're going to pay separately for two receipts, so we'll stand double chances to win the contest.'

'Not us. Only you.'

'The winner is allowed to bring a friend.'

In the checkout lane, Daniel pointed effortlessly at the menu billboard, ordering two portions of *kimchi bokkeumbap*, three cheese corn dog skewers, and two *bingsu*—one with strawberry topping and the other with adzuki beans.

'I'm wowed by your cow's stomach.'

'The spicy rice cake is yours and the shaved ice too,' said Daniel.

'You still remember my favourite,' I said.

'Of course, we are cousins of unsound like-mindedness.'

'Bribing me in advance to accompany you to the meet and greet,' I said.

'Can you stop being so sharp-witted?' Daniel rolled his eyes.

There was a short jingle before the announcement.

'Annyeonghaseyo, dear shoppers, this is your store manager Elisa Park taking over the AirPlay for the next hours, wishing you a pleasant shopping experience at K-Licious-Delish. The song you just heard is the brand-new single "Sajin", which translates to "Photograph", from the most anticipated comeback of the former K-pop-idol-turned-soloist Ahn Myeongjun . . .'

The world fell apart as I began to see fragmented butterflies in discotheque flashes.

Seven

I wasn't able to describe the exact place where the throbbing pain that refused to dissipate resided in my temples. Anything could happen. Like a nightmare in retrogress, I waited for something to run me over.

Thereafter, the daylight surmounted through every window, casting a rosy hue—

—with elegance and solitude.

A silhouette in a black suit was serenading the crowd sitting behind a transparent, acrylic grand piano. The silhouette was revealed to be Edward, who was gazing at my every meandering step while playing the melody of 'Sajin'. I bit my lips, in tears— beset by emotion that saturated all my inner thoughts. Every note was orchestrated with great finesse. The mellifluous, sharp, and augmented flat keys were congruent to a meteoroid at its highest speed, ready to burn up every unhealed wound. Edward took my hand, tugging me to sit beside him. I gasped as his lips met mine, a kiss long overdue, yet abstruse.

Finally, the barrier between us had fallen apart.

'Don't leave,' I whispered.

Edward's voice was trembling—wordless.

'You left the writer's retreat all of a sudden,' I choked out.

Edward didn't reply.

'Is that . . . how you want me to remember you?' I shivered.

Edward then pressed his lips against mine, a way to shut me up.

The piano started to crack and then sunk into a progressive split. The keyboard was stuck in a distorted autoplay like the symphony of an eerie music box. Clutching my fist, I whimpered. Tears fell like a flurry of snow. The room slipped into darkness, and Edward was disappearing. The surrounding energy resembled a smouldering fire.

* * *

'Emily-baby, can you hear me?'

'Haiyoh, move aside, lah. Bridget, I can't see my granddaughter's face. This is Mama, you hear me?' Her grip shook my brittle shoulder. 'Raymond, call the *bomoh*.'

'There's no need for a witch doctor, Ma.'

'Should we bring her to the emergency room?' asked Aunt Bridget.

Please don't.

I tried opening my mouth, but no voice came out—paralysed by unseen demons sitting on my belly. Blanketed by terror, as if trapped in an amorphous rumble with debris and wreckage in a collapsed building, I fought deliberately to shuffle.

Suddenly, I felt a slap across my cheek, then another one, nastier than the previous.

'How can you be so, so selfish, my Emily-baby, to see a white-head person sending off a black-head person?' Mama was crying, refusing to bury her granddaughter before her.

'Hmm . . . no . . . don't.' I could hear myself. My eyes blurred.

'Emily, can you hear me?'

'You're breaking her eardrum, Bridget,' Uncle Raymond said.

'Where am I?' Finally, my voice had gotten clearer.

'In your bedroom. Take rest. Everything is okay now,' Mama said. 'Noon, I leave my granddaughter with you. Raymond, where's my lion-mouthed grandson?'

'He should be back by now.' Uncle Raymond's voice trailed further.

Rubbing my eyes and still in a daze, I asked Auntie Noon to draw the curtain from the window to let in a piercing sunbeam. I put the compact mirror away, realizing how ghostly-pale my complexion was. I'd lost my ability to taste despite finishing a glass of ginger tea with lemon juice. All I could ascertain was that the concoction had tasted slightly off-balance. The ingredients had been washed, peeled, and then pounded by Auntie Noon.

This was the first time I'd dreamed of Edward. Those hovering nuances of his, stimulated a feast for my perception and apprehension. I could still feel his lingering touch as my arm stretched to retrieve the plain congee sprinkled with chopped torch ginger flower and spring onions right next to a Suvarnabhumi-patterned lampshade.

I took a small spoonful in my mouth, chewed to digest it with Edward's lingering kiss. 'What are those for?' I asked, pulling the comforter to my chest.

'To appease the spirits,' said Auntie Noon, looking at the three stalks of crushed lemongrass bound with a bright red, woven string in the corner.

I thought of the unfortunate historical events of Serendipity Sanctuary that Daniel had told me about. 'You mean . . . someone died here, in this room?'

'Shhh . . . don't talk about it.'

I narrowed my eyes. 'So, all of you thought I was being possessed?'

Again, Auntie Noon didn't respond.

I placed the empty bowl on the night table. How on earth could they be that superstitious? And my no-nonsense Uncle Raymond couldn't beat them, so he couldn't help but join in.

Counting to three, I tried balancing on my feet then with aeroplane-spreading-arms. I felt like an anchor struggling to secure myself in the ocean of emotions under rough terrain.

'Careful,' Auntie Noon grabbed my hands. 'Can you walk?'

'I still feel a little woozy like someone drained my blood—'

She covered my mouth. 'This bungalow is two hundred years old. Souls that are listening could be searching for substitutes. One night, I saw sister-in-law running up and down the stairs, dressed like a French maid, and mumbling in a weird Chinese dialect.'

I laughed. 'Aunt Bridget's working on her movie script.'

Auntie Noon then expressed with doubt, 'Spirits of the dead never stop looking for victims, especially the vengeful ones. In my village, we always use essential oils to chase away the bad ones, even though black magic has been utilized widely and is performed using corpse oil, which is harvested from a dead pregnant woman.'

'Are you serious?' I asked.

'Karma will catch up to both parties in unfortunate ways.'

'You mean "ketchup-sauce".'

She cleared her throat. 'Catch . . . up . . . I am serious.'

'Thanks for the delicious congee, Auntie Noon, I feel much better now.'

'Not me. It was ma-in-law.'

Mama's unique culinary creativity was to add chopped torch ginger flower in her cooking. This was then passed on to mom, who drizzled these fiery bright pink petals into my soup. Damn the bland hospital food. Its citrusy-forward flavour would rid my mouth of the metallic taste that was a side-effect of the short-term antidepressant pills. Stroking my sore cheek, I felt how Mama's slapping and her paradoxical lucidity had spelled consistency, in flow.

* * *

'I see the Wi-Fi speed is much better here,' I said, looking at Daniel.

'Old Bean's wife has changed your bedding to a fresh bedspread.' Relaxing his posture on the bed, Daniel's thumbs pressed the keypad, playing an online game. 'You're sweat drenched like a monsoon spell of love. Take a look at the newly erected essential oil shrine right beside the desk. It's turned this place into a cabaret-style massage and spa.'

'I don't mind sharing the collection with you.'

'I don't want to smell like a walking love potion,' Daniel said.

'My room looks more like *Exorcist* meets *Moulin Rouge*.' I sighed and rolled my eyes. 'Did Aunt Bridget know about the removal of the mosquito canopy net?'

'Old Bean was like a hostage, sandwiched between the witches of Serendipity Sanctuary, as in Mama, Aunt Bridget, and Auntie Noon,' Daniel said, shifting left and right, pressing the keypad. 'Their argument sent the roof flying to the Straits of Malacca. Our prima donna aunt lost the verbal war. Mama and Auntie Noon have combined forces to remove the mosquito canopy because its netting is a spirit trapper—you know, the cause of your blackout.'

'No. My blackout was due to—' I stopped myself from explaining further.

First, I was misunderstood by Uncle Sean when he thought my tattoos were gang-related, then there was Aunt Bridget's meat-philosophy, and now this whole thing about being possessed. The last thing I needed was for Edward's true identity to be exposed to my *beloved* and tensed-up, conflicting, and *sort of* misbehaving family members.

'How're you feeling?' Daniel put his phone aside. 'You really scared me.'

'The dizziness is slowly subsiding.' I tried to banish the cause by massaging my head.

'You . . . really don't remember a thing?'

'What did I do?' I asked, distraught. Daniel shook. I exhaled, panicking, thinking unreasonably, and striking out the non-viable. 'I took off my clothes?'

Daniel looked at me and said gravely, 'You vomited on me.'

* * *

My index finger and thumb were pressing on my left wrist, then above my upper lip—an acupressure self-healing technique to calm the mind and emotion. Today marked the last talk therapy session with my therapist. 'Good day to you, Dr Erica.' I smiled as the video call began, feeling disgustingly bad that I had thrown up on my cousin.

'A blessed day to you too Emily, it's been a long time since I've heard from you.'

'Yeah, sorry I've taken quite a while to call you back with all the settling down and hotpot reunion with my family members. How have you been?'

'I've been doing great, just the usual business with clients' assessment files.' She dragged the chair closer to the screen. 'You still have your make-up on.'

'I was out the whole day with my cousin.'

'That's awesome. Where did you go?' Dr Erica picked up a pen, preparing to chronicle my confession on the patient's consultation sheet.

'I went to K-Licious-Delish, a Korean convenience store,' I began to summarize the incident, from customers cluttering along the item aisles, to those fan-girling selfie shots with the cardboard standee being their lover–husband, the endless broadcasting of K-pop idols' provocative dance moves on the LED flat screen TV, and then the delectable selection of popular Korean street foods; all to avoid mentioning the blackouts.

Dr Erica looked me straight in the eye. 'Did you buy something nice?'

'Daniel bought twenty boxes of assorted Korean ramen noodles,' I said.

'I want to know what you bought,' Dr Erica said.

I began reminiscing about that gigantic Pepero and my indecision about purchasing it.

I'd failed when trying to overcome Edward's presence in my head, becoming disoriented after hearing only the song title and his name. And what's worse, my behaviour must've been caught by the store's CCTV. My mind then shifted to Pepero Day, one of South Korea's biggest day-marketing events. It's an occasion marked by gifting or exchanging the choco-stick snacks with the intention of conveying love and friendship. I remember Edward had waited at my employee's locker with eleven boxes of assorted-flavoured Pepero wrapped in a bouquet at 11.11 p.m. on 11 November. My heartbeat went haywire the moment Edward kissed my hand.

I felt as if my seven chakras were blocked, stopping me from confessing further.

After sniffling several times, I felt dizzy. No, I shouldn't lose it again, not in front of Dr Erica. Time for a breathing tactic. Grateful to feel my feet against the floorboard, breathing in sharply at three-second intervals, I reached for the chamomile essential oil, applying it on my belly.

'I read your email,' Dr Erica smiled, switching the subject. 'Good to know you're focusing on an internship, try embracing a new hobby if possible.'

'I'm taking things one step at a time,' I said. 'Thanks for your patience and for trusting this headstrong patient of yours.'

'I'm an advocate for talk therapy supplemented with prescriptions. In the end, it is still your effort and that driving force within you that matters.' Dr Erica smiled. 'Try making some new friends in this new environment you're in, keep yourself busy, remember to take a break in-between work, surround yourself with positive, vibrant energy. Your mother and your uncle have been your supportive pillars, remember that.'

'Love heals, and it could be poisonous at the same time,' I murmured. 'Guess I'm fated to be *widowed* by this love,' like Aunt Bridget's celeb-crush with Tony Leung.

It hit me then. Suddenly, unexpectedly.

'Stay with me.' Dr Erica's voice was like a reverberation. 'Can you hear me, Emily—' The palpitations vanished after thrashing my drifting flow. 'I want you to close your eyes and follow the flickering flame. Don't be afraid.'

Dr Erica had previously recommended ECT to improve my rapid depression. Brain damage could be a side effect, and I might forget pieces of Edward.

'I heard "Photograph" today at the store,' I started.

'I'm all ears if you need to talk,' Dr Erica said.

'I wrote the lyrics in English with him, in his arms at the writer's retreat that night.' I then wondered, 'It shouldn't be sung in Korean. That's odd.'

* * *

Late into the night, the sounds of cymbals clashing aroused me from my deep sleep. I walked to the bathroom to cleanse the excessive facial sebum that had accumulated on my face and then bumped into Aunt Bridget, who was yelling, 'Somebody tell Ma not to do this anymore.'

Doors flung open one after another; first the yawning Uncle Raymond, then Auntie Noon, scratching her ears. My cousin's eyes were partially shut as he emerged with an electrocuted bird-nest hairdo and drool.

'Ma, it is bedtime,' Uncle Raymond pleaded.

'You can't stop me from doing my job!' Mama said, clutching onto the cymbals.

'It's past midnight, Ma.' Slices of lemon were atop Aunt Bridget's face. She'd probably put them on after applying a moisturizing cream as the rejuvenating base. My sleepy-zombie aunt ambled to her mother. 'Ma, you took my acting prop without telling me, again!'

'You stole this from a film set,' Mama said.

I blinked as my aunt was revealed to be a kleptomaniac.

'Ma,' Aunt Bridget covered Mama's mouth and Mama struggled to escape her hold. 'Stop embarrassing me in front of my niece and nephew!'

'Didn't I teach you? Stealing is a sin!'

'The production house deducted my pay. I was teaching them a lesson.'

'That's enough. You both.' Uncle Raymond was massaging his head.

Aunt Bridget pushed Uncle Raymond aside and folded her arms as she faced Mama. 'First of all, you removed that mosquito canopy from Emily's room and now you've stolen my cymbals. Are you going to kick me out of the house next?'

'My Chew family hailed from a generation of ghost-chasers in Fujian,' Mama said. 'It is for Emily's good. Cymbals are the most ideal instrument, other than fireworks.'

'That's news to me,' I murmured to Daniel.

'Whatever. This is what we've got to suffer after midnight,' said Daniel.

'Mama.' I held her arm. 'Actually, my blackout was—'

Suddenly, Mama clashed the cymbals, *hella* loud this time.

We plugged our ears with our fingers, shaking off the intense vibration.

It felt like a reverberating slap on the face, I blinked and cringed, and couldn't hear myself properly. Playful-Daniel was rolling his eyes, as if conjuring the spirits. Aunt Bridget's curses were shrouded by splitting echoes, as she yelled at Uncle Raymond—something about the local council slapping us with a letter of summons for being a nuisance and disrupting the peace of others.

'This will cast out the evil spirits and pervert demons in you, Emily!' Mama roared.

I raised my hands—giving up.

Eight

Over breakfast, Uncle Raymond announced a new batch of volunteers assigned by St Paul's Church to Serendipity Sanctuary (Shaolin-Three-Kitchens as politely mocked by Aunt Bridget). On the flip side, I was exempted from working this weekend due to my sudden unforeseeable blackout.

Daniel wound down the campervan's window in the driver's seat. 'You smell all floral and earthy, Biu-jie.'

Ignoring him, I gazed at two squirrels crossing the road then disappearing into a bush, one after the other. 'I feel relaxed and comfortable this way, also it helps me avoid puking on you again.'

'It is much better than smelling the stinking *petai* beans and durian, at one go.' Daniel never failed to trigger my ulnar nerve.

'I thought your nemesis has always been the fishy, rancid *belacan* paste.'

'That'll make me puke the whole day.' Pointing a warning finger at me, Daniel took a turn towards the junction. 'The week before a volunteer had belacan paste fried rice for lunch. Boy, it's like the second coming, havoc all the way.'

I couldn't stop laughing. 'I miss eating durian from the freezer, like ice-cream.'

'The Laus love the king of fruits, not me.' Daniel looked to his left before taking a turn. 'Guess I must've gotten it from my Mamie.'

There'd always been emotional _thundershowers in my cousin's voice, that sting of pain and the reluctance to call out this endearing term. I remembered Auntie Candice fondly for her cool and reserved demeanour, Farrah Fawcett-esque mane-like, antigravity hairstyle, and her natural-born, Michael Douglas-esque prominent chin dimple. However, her demise happened too suddenly. I remember getting back from school to Mom packing her dark-coloured outfits in a suitcase, off to attend Auntie Candice's funeral in Penang. Later that night, Daniel had called me from the funeral parlour phone booth, crying for failing to wake his mamie up from sleep.

Daniel turned to me. 'Remember your version of *Sleeping Beauty*? Honestly, I can't wait to grow up to become a prince and then revive Mamie back to life with my kiss.'

'You were too young to understand death.' I wiped my eyes. 'If that could stop you from crying and start eating . . .' I shrugged. 'Have you ever thought of paying respect to her?'

When stopping at the traffic lights, Daniel switched the gear to neutral and turned to look at me. 'I really wanted to. If only Old Bean would be willing to reveal mamie's plot number.'

I looked straight ahead, steadily breathing, and then tapped on his hand.

'Maybe he can't even face her,' Daniel murmured, bitterly.

I zipped-up the conversation. 'I don't remember this being the route to K-Licious-Delish.'

'We're going to St Paul's Church,' said Daniel.

'Someone's becoming religious.' I nodded.

'Over my deadly-handsome body.' Daniel took a sharp U-turn.

I let out my ticklish-bone laughter.

Making a right turn, Daniel said, 'I believe there are spirits keeping us company in the kitchens and also the bungalow. Hopefully, I didn't scare you.'

'Sometimes, ghosts are more straightforward than humans.'

'Right,' Daniel said. 'At times, the back of my hair would stand on end to sing the unexplained goosebumps' anthem.'

'Try asking for four digits, who knows you might win the lottery.' I unbuckled the seatbelt.

'I wished for a third eye to see Mamie,' Daniel said. 'I don't care if she looks like a zombie from *Train to Busan*,' he continued, parking the campervan, walking beside me into St Paul's Church.

A youth leader in my former church ministry had affirmed that a place of worship is for sinners—from coveting spouses to indulging titanically in food fellowships—who are then taunted into fervent praying. The edgy, cuckoo spiritually sick ones utilized 'hell' as eternal punishment, cloaked in wolf's skin but beneath the disguise is the flesh of a meek lamb. I was too naive to comprehend what he meant back then. 'Hello, it's great to see you again Dan!' A man in a long sleeve turtleneck walked to my cousin, giving him a hug.

'Hello, Uncle Clement. This is my cousin, Emily.'

This stranger gazed at me with his thick bushy brows and observant eyes.

'Emily, nice to meet you,' he said as I extended my hand.

He shook, it with the friendliest smile ever. 'Finally, we get to meet.'

* * *

At the marketplace, the fishmonger was feeding the Arowana and Butterfly koi flakes and floating pellets in aquariums decorated with small stones and ornaments. They believed to have the capability to produce positive energy, attracting prosperity and absorbing negative *chi*.

A woman who looked to be in her fifties was instructing a staff member to extricate two live groupers from the running water tank. 'Give me fat-fat ones, more meat to eat.' She then paid the man. The grouper pair wiggled to escape from the clear, extra large plastic bag filled with fresh water the moment she gripped onto the handle.

Daniel and I averted our eyes from the glaring gaze of the woman's resplendent glossy jade bangle reflecting a beam of light.

The fishmonger layered the crushed ice on the seafood produce, covering the lid. Daniel and I stacked the Styrofoam packing boxes on the heavy-duty hand truck above the fruits in the cartons. Later, at the vegetable stall, we saw the same woman from the seafood stall, bragging about her recipe to the seller. She claimed, 'I marinate them with Shaoxing wine.'

'At least the pair isn't sober when they die.' I lowered my voice.

'What if they're enemies?' asked Daniel, pouting.

'Hopefully, they won't meet again in the next life as fish or humans.'

We thanked the vegetable seller, collecting the last two packaging cartons.

They were the Serendipity Sanctuary's sponsors, at least that's how Daniel referred to them. They had signed an agreement with St Paul's Church's committee members on an annual basis, supplying daily produce based on a coordinated pick-up time, that was set to be three hours before closing time, to avoid any last-minute rush. Then, there was the scrupulous job at the gourmet kitchen, it was an enormous task for Auntie Noon and the volunteers to separate the rotten seafood from the good, and the wilted, decolourized vegetables from the fresh, tender ones. These had to be done with no delay, once the greens began to spoil, they would become stale and 'ripe'—slimy with foul odours.

I halted the trolley at the bumper pavement, with a shrouded disposition of goodwill that came straight from the heart. No monetary reward, just pay it forward.

'The church had to subsidize part of the cost during monsoon season due to the soaring prices. There are times not even a slice of fish fillet, only salmon, mussels, tiger prawns, and lobsters are available. Serendipity Sanctuary isn't a five-star pescetarian restaurant.' Daniel wiped beads of sweat with his folded sleeve. 'Here comes Santa Claus Uncle Clement digging out his one-month pension scheme for the fresh *tenggiri* and *kembung* fish, red snapper and squids.'

'Let me guess, red snapper curry and fried calamari—?'
I clicked my tongue.

'Also, fried kembung and tenggiri fish cakes curry.'

'Uncle Clement seems to be kind-hearted,' I muttered. My
sixth sense felt he behaved in an over-friendly way. 'Pension
scheme. He previously worked as a civil servant.'

Daniel started, 'At the stall where we collected the seafood,
the boxes were formerly ready for pick-up only. My campervan
smelled rancid as fuck. The battalion of volunteers at the gourmet
kitchen must've fainted when they opened the boot. I had to send
my poor Beatrice to an auto spa. Those arseholes gave us goods
where three-quarters of the seafood was rotten. I immediately
lodged a complaint to Uncle Clement.'

'My cousin's initiative in his work,' I said, hands clapping
in slow-mo.

Straightening his posture with pride, Daniel continued, 'Don't
ask me how or what Uncle Clement did to those dishonest folks.
His way of dealing with things was successful. There have been
no more hiccups since then, it's been smooth as silken tofu and
we get to witness the staff pack the produce before us.'

'You're all prepped to take over the sanctuary.' I sipped from
the water bottle.

'I started working in the sanctuary ever since I finished upper
secondary,' Daniel recalled. 'It's been eight years. I'm satisfied with
my method of working thus far. Don't really mind earning big
in the corporate world and receiving an allowance as a token of
appreciation. Still, I'll never ever give up being a cinematographer.'

'Indeed, one may distinguish oneself in any trade.' I patted
his shoulder.

After unloading the cartons into the campervan, Daniel and
I arrived at the fruit stall to pick up some imported fruits at his
expense. Daniel introduced me to Fruit Tan, the owner.

'It is easier to identify.' Fruit Tan smiled, revealing a set of
polished front teeth that could be dentures. 'There are so many

Mr Tan's in this marketplace, just simply cast a stone and they'll stand up in hundreds. The one over at the further end is Chicken Tan,' he pointed. 'The handsomest poultry seller and the one at the farthest corner, everyone calls him Asparagus Tan of scallion hairdo, always no time to upkeep nicely, and sells mostly imported vegetables.'

'Hmm, should we call you Cherry Tan instead?' said Daniel. I covered my mouth and laughed. 'Your complexion is soft and supple.'

'Better stop teasing Uncle Tan, look at him all flush-up,' I said.

'Girl-ah, my sons are married or else I will introduce you to them,' he said. 'Take your pick: accountant, criminal lawyer, and cardiologist. I've known Raymond since when you both were just a speck of dust. Daniel is like my reputed godchild.'

Daniel bought two packs of strawberries and handed one to me. I insisted on paying him back. He refused, saying that he hoped its antioxidants would help treat the cause of my blackout. Such an involuntary reaction would have stemmed from a bad lifestyle, a change of environment, and the inevitable work anxiety from Uncle Sean's Shaolin-Pastry-Kitchen—

—and Edward's constant intrusions in my mind.

En route the church, Daniel discussed the inclusion of two volunteers in the pastry kitchen. No volunteer from the gourmet side wanted to switch rosters with us. They preferred to work under the kind and benevolent Auntie Noon than the temperamental Monk. We continued the discussion with Uncle Clement when we reached. I soon realized Uncle Clement had his eyes on me throughout the discussion. One of which was to seek my approval in certain matters with regards to the sanctuary's administrative department, handled by Uncle Raymond. However, I refused to gain admission because it would go against my role as an intern. Then, the topic of the fundraising food drive project—Daniel's brainchild—was raised suddenly. Uncle Clement suggested that I should partake in it.

'How close are Uncle Raymond and Uncle Clement?' I asked Daniel later.

'Think they've been friends for more than a decade.'

I nodded, unwelcome thoughts crowding my brain.

Nine

Daniel had almost lost his marbles when I passed out and had forgotten to collect our official receipts at K-Licious-Delish after checking out. So, I promised to accompany my cousin to the convenience store after our day shift.

It was in my cousin's bucket list to meet and greet this cardboard standee in this larger-than-lifetime opportunity. On the way, he even chided me for being ruthless like the Empress Wu Zetian when I told him to forget the proof of the transaction. The probability of winning it was zero. Though I wasn't a K-culture enthusiast, I was partly to blame for Daniel's shattered hopes. Who knows if he could have won if not for that unforeseen blackout.

We ambled to the checkout lane after entering the store.

Keeping my head pointed straight at the menu billboard as Daniel was ironing out the matter with the store manager, I blinked. My fingers couldn't stop drumming the counter. I felt as if I was being hypnotized by the name tag—Elisa Park. I remembered she'd gracefully introduced Edward and his latest single at the music station to the shoppers the other day.

'They need to check with the finance and billing department,' said Daniel to me.

'Hopefully she won't recognize me,' I murmured as the store manager left.

'Stay cool Biu-jie,' Daniel said. Fishcakes on skewers dipped in the clear, hot broth filled with chopped spicy green peppers had been tempting our appetite. 'Let's order some *odeng*.'

'Honestly, I only want this to be over quick,' I murmured.

I remembered my father's frown-to-throttle expression the moment I had dropped my Coke. My new dress soaked with the artificially sweetened carbonated drink, while Mom cleaned the stains on my lap. How I wished I could dig a hole and hide my head as the restaurant crowd ogled the six-year-old mini-Emily. Since that incident, my father would taunt me periodically in front of his relatives at any family gatherings and after that to his office colleagues, who at the Christmas party called me 'butterfingers', a worthless daughter who couldn't even hold a cup.

'Sorry for keeping both of you waiting,' the store manager said. 'Thank you for your patience. I've validated all the purchased items according to the date and the estimated time you've provided. I'd checked the in-store CCTV and the one—'

'Wait a minute,' I cut in. 'How many people have seen the footage?'

'Two from the finance department and myself,' the store manager said.

'What did the three of you . . . see?' I tried to stay calm.

The store manager glanced at Daniel then at me. 'Please come with me.'

Outside the room, she unlocked the door, leading us into the control centre and then switched on the lights. Daniel and I waited as she scrolled into the surveillance files after logging in with her ID and typing out the password. Daniel and I looked at me in the crystal-clear CCTV footage, behaving in an unsettling manner at the checkout lane. I was patting my chest, to calm myself down, perhaps. Daniel rushed to my aid when I staggered out. Next, I vomited on him outside the store before collapsing.

'I need some air,' I murmured as I left.

I vowed that this'd be the last time I'd set foot in the place.

* * *

Back from the convenience store, on the rooftop terrace, I lounged on the turquoise-coloured sofa. Then, I attentively inspected the pergola-design gazebo. I decided that this living space should've won Southeast Asia's 'Best Architectural Design' award.

'The total amount from our purchases has been split in two for an additional chance to win the meet and greet.' Daniel uncapped the carbonated drink bottle and handed it to me.

I took a sip from it.

'Old Bean said no alcohol for you. Sorry . . .' Daniel sat beside me.

'I've been sober for quite a while now.' Wishful thinking had set in. 'I love the tranquil, mysterious ambience here. Is there a reason I can't see this place from the entrance?'

'Mama's geriatrician recommended her to go for a morning or an evening stroll.' Daniel sipped from his beer. 'None of us have the time, although Mama adamantly stated that she could do so by herself. Old Bean hired a contractor to build this reflexology garden path.'

'I'm surprised the church allowed this so easily,' I remarked, relaxing my feet on the portable footrest cushion. 'It's . . . quite a dubious claim that Uncle Clement made, about knowing me.'

'I guess Old Bean must've told him,' said Daniel, applying a sheet mask over his face.

'How many complimentary sheet masks did the store manager give you?' I asked.

'About ten of them, I think,' Daniel said, while dabbing and massaging his face. 'Don't tell Aunt Bridget or the supply will only last for two days.'

'Why is that?'

'She'll apply them seven times a day instead of as instructed.' Daniel cringed.

'Confirmed! Aunt Bridget is obsessed with looking good,' I said.

Daniel nodded. 'The store manager gave me some tea samples too—honey citron and aloe pomegranate, both with antioxidants. Miss Park also informed me that jujube tea would help with blood circulation.'

'That's five-stars in customer satisfaction feedback and experience.'

'Even a stranger cares for you, Biu-jie,' Daniel added, nudging my arm.

'I never thought I'd be a part of another embarrassing *stunt*, even in Penang.'

Daniel raised his bottle in agreement, proposing for a toast. 'Whether it is a shameful act or what, you're still the champion among trillions of ejaculated sperms.'

I almost spat out the boiled chickpeas. 'That's . . . so profound.'

Daniel took a gulp from a third bottle, seemingly just because.

'Studying law is hard, in terms of stress and the workload, the committed long hours, similar to resistance training.' My gaze was lost in the dark, constellated sky. 'Owing to my only child syndrome and characteristics, I'm quite the believer of Nietzsche's infamous motivation—the determination to not lose heart. If I must die, I'll go down with dignity.'

'Old Bean has been calling me futile soil, saying he'd have preferred to give birth to a *char siu*—at least he could eat it with Hoisin sauce,' Daniel said. 'Now, the fundraising food drive has to be a success so I can rub it in Old Bean's face. But first, we need more vo-lun-teeeersss—'

Lifting the bottle from Daniel's grip, I looked on as his head dropped to my shoulder, groaning away. I hummed the chorus of 'Sajin' as if Edward was beside me. The breeze kissed my face as his aquatic scented cologne settled in this state of mind.

I finished my cousin's bottle.

The cola and the beer amalgamated on my tongue as my mind trailed off . . .

* * *

Fiona Chin snatched the guitar from me. 'I see you have a new hobby.'

'A friend lent it to me,' I said. 'Hey, give it back.'

'Why so anxious . . .' Fiona hid the instrument behind her, analysing my expression like an expert. 'From a male friend perhaps,' examining the headstock and then the body. 'It's a Gibson Hummingbird! What a wealthy friend you have there.'

I gently took the guitar back, thinking that I should've returned it to Edward earlier. Fiona walked towards me with an apprehensive expression as I was checking for possible scratches.

'Guess how much my dress cost,' Fiona pivoted, asking suddenly.

'Must've cost you a fortune,' I said, gathering the tutorial notes on the floor.

'Well, someone paid for it.' Fiona said, glancing at me. 'Envy my paid-to-travel job? Meeting rich bachelors . . . I was in Bel Air for a massive house party last week.'

'Good for you.' My fingers, which were practising the G major chord, stopped. 'Currently, I love working in the aparthotel, especially the late-night shift,' I said as I briefly thought of Edward.

'You don't live in a destitute state.' Fiona poured herself a glass of bourbon.

I changed into my loungewear, pouring Smirnoff vodka into the glass, squeezing in some lemon juice, and shaking the glass, as the liquid started to quench my thirst. 'I've fulfilled my father's dream by completing the Bachelor of Laws with a second-class upper, getting my Certificate of Legal practice, and working in prestigious firms to gain experience and corporate exposure. The price to pay as a good daughter. And I'm done with the legal industry.'

'I'm so lucky that my parents never force me to do the things I don't want.' Fiona wiped her eyes. Her crocodile tears. Those I'd shunned ever since the first day in secondary school, as I'd watched her flaunt her leather strap Guess watch to our classmates. 'By the way, is there a person named Ahn Myeongjun lodging in your workplace now?' she asked, out of the blue.

I slightly choked on my drink. Random and direct.

'Are you okay?' Fiona was quick to check in.

I nodded, pretending to grab a bottle of water from the fridge.

'Well, my coworker is a huge fan of ParadiZo. A source told her that their lead rapper and visual is in town for several months for his solo project,' Fiona held onto the fridge door, held onto my gaze. 'And, he is lodging in Saujana Residence, your workplace.'

'Not that I know of.' I kept a straight face.

'I'll ask Sabrina when she's home.' Fiona crossed her arms.

'Maybe your co-worker got it wrong.' I took my unfinished glass in one hand and the guitar in the other. 'Time for some beauty sleep. Good night.'

Fiona looked on as I walked into my room.

Ten

At the rooftop terrace, the psychedelic rock'n' roll of birds chirping felt a distance apart. To bless my barely opened eyes, echoes of chitter-chatter with the clanging sounds of utensils from the soup and the gourmet kitchens resounded. Delicate beams glazed across the room.

I stretched, cautious of any possible sudden muscle spasms from sleeping through the night on this sofa. Wrapped in a duvet, Daniel was sucking his thumb, still asleep, like a newborn delivered by the mythical stork to the terrace.

'Enjoyed your sibling's gathering last night?'

I jumped up immediately, hearing my uncle's voice. 'We happened to fall asleep while engrossed in talking.' I whacked Daniel's shoulder. 'Hey, wake up. The sun's out.'

Uncle Raymond's keen eyes were surveying last night's evidence of empty beer and carbonated drink bottles, scattered and rolling off the floorboards. Some were untouched. 'Oi, get up!' He patted Daniel's cheek. When Daniel didn't wake up, he did it again harder. I sighed as my cousin cursed in his sleep.

Uncle Raymond threw a bucket of ice water on Daniel. I leaped two steps behind. My calf was drenched by splashes of this cold baptism. My cousin jumped up. The whole thing reminded me of the single jolt that's used to incapacitate an electric eel. Drenched from head to toe, Daniel took a while to finally come to his senses. I quickly grabbed a towel to wipe his body.

Daniel shook off the water like a wet hound. 'Tryin' to murder your own sperm?'

Uncle Raymond came to sniff me, then Daniel. 'Didn't I tell you not to give Emily beer?' He narrowed his eyes in a killer-stare. 'Are you not happy with your life, Daniel Lau?'

'That's because I dislike being your son.' The words hastily slipped from Daniel's tongue.

'What—!'

Blocking my cousin from receiving another blow, I said to my uncle, 'I just wanted a few sips.' I patted my cousin's cheek. 'Look, I've eight fingers and two thumbs. Not drunk.'

'Yeah, so long as I'm here, Biu-jie won't do stupid things.' Daniel picked up an ice cube from the floor and rubbed against his forehead.

'Didn't I tell you to vacate the rooftop by midnight?' Uncle Raymond asked.

I peered at Daniel. Two adults were being held captive at night by a curfew, even under the same roof, without a war or an emergency ordinance. This was something strikingly new to me. Daniel was scratching his head, again, disguising his brain-gone-elsewhere forgetfulness.

'Of course, I know about the *Cinderella Rules*.' I quickly nudged at Daniel's arm.

My cousin was nodding cordially.

Uncle Raymond narrowed his eyes even more.

'I honestly had a great time with Daniel, apart from being fascinated by such a breathtaking rooftop terrace that was co-founded by you, dear Uncle Raymond.' I then patted Daniel's shoulder with sarcasm. 'We shall continue our sibling's chat one day sometime soon, right cousin? Think we're late for work. Better go now.'

My uncle exhaled. 'Both of you should sleep early after working in the kitchen for long hours, especially you,' he pointed at me, empathetically. 'You're still recovering from a traumatic emotional blackout.'

The remorseful silence was punctuated by a strong gust of wind.

'Be downstairs in half an hour. Put on an outfit of a pleasant colour, Emily. No black for today.' Uncle Raymond left with the bucket as the water continued dripping from Daniel.

'Where are we going again this time?' I whispered to Daniel.

Daniel yawned. 'The bed knows best,' he said, pretending to snore on his duvet.

* * *

Auntie Noon unlocked the door to the Laus' ancestral hall.

Aunt Bridget stood between Daniel and me, clad in a velvet jumpsuit of Lana Del Rey's summertime theme and a LV-monogrammed, limited-edition saddlebag. I often wondered who bought her these extravagant souvenirs. Maybe that Hong Kong-based Goldman Sachs banker she was previously linked to? When asked about her script's status, Aunt Bridget told me to steel myself to prepare for something unforgettably explosive.

Mama walked towards us with a walking cane.

I hugged Mama tightly after she pecked my cheek. Her vintage pressed powder and fruity Avon lipstick took me back to childhood. Uncle Raymond shushed Daniel and I, as we were giggling at Mama's lipstick mark that was now smeared on our cheeks.

Mama sat on the eastern rosewood chair, smiling. 'Today's tea ceremony is to confirm Emily as part of the Laus' lineage. As a matriarch, I started this bloodline for equality, to cherish and appreciate the women, and cherish and appreciate we will, even if your surname is Chung.'

Auntie Noon poured from the pot of Chinese tea into a *gaiwan*, a traditional Chinese lidded bowl. 'Emily, you have to present the tea to ma-in-law.'

I rested my bent knees on the golden-phoenix-embroidered kneeler, received the antique gaiwan from Auntie Noon, and recited words of respect with gratitude in Cantonese. 'Mama, I ask God to bless your health, granting you the age of longevity likewise to the mountain and the roaring sea, in wisdom, with abundance of joy and always protected by the merciful Guanyin.'

Mama nodded with that stretched-dough smile, wide and pleased.

She drank from the saucer, gently swiping it with the cover before sipping, then passing it back to Auntie Noon. She took my hand. 'No matter the hardships, we do not leave any Lau daughters behind, they are our blood and soul.'

'I shall remember your essential wisdom, Mama.' I bowed.

Auntie Noon discarded the unfinished tea, rinsed the utensil, replenished its contents, and then passed it to me. 'This is to be represented by Emily, on behalf of her mother.'

Daniel inhaled, emotionally.

I looked into Mama's wrinkled eyes as she received the tea with lips stretching wider, happier in a sense, taking one sip after another. I exhaled as Mama finished the tea, feeling a peculiar sense of emptiness. I wished mom could be with us, instead of volunteering full-time at the church. Then, Mama stroked my arms. 'These tattoos are beautifully inked. Must be hurting a lot? I feel sad to see you going through such pain. You're to be cared for and guarded by the Laus from now on.'

My heart swelled. The return of a prodigal granddaughter.

Life had been a process of riding the wave, always riddled with unpredictability and in need of experimentation. A self-absorbed attitude shouldn't exist in my head. The Laus, with their supportive spirits, had been compassionate towards my ugly, inglorious past. Weirdly, the hardest pill to swallow had been Mama calling me by Mom's name. Time had rung its final wake-up call. Edward already had a major comeback in his career, dominating the music charts. His future endeavours should be as bright as the moon, as I'd prayed.

'Watch me as I rise from the ashes,' I said, steadfastly bowing.

* * *

'This floating temple isn't as crowded as the one at Kek Lok Si or Khoo Kongsi, even the prayer incense had to surrender to the smell of BO,' said Daniel.

I shook my head as my cousin burped like a horse after overindulging in the seaweed *siu-mai*, with gluten, minced mushrooms and MSG-flavourings.

'Indeed. Such a beautiful sight when dusk approaches with its twinkling lights reflecting on the north channel,' I remarked.

'Never ever underestimate this historical shrine,' Aunt Bridget cut in. 'It was built on stilts and fortified to last against the daily high tides even before Ma was born.'

Mama stomped around with her walking cane after getting out from my uncle's black sedan. Daniel and I accompanied her to the temple's main entrance. Aside from a wide-open area, this two-storey building had lively dragon columns and red lanterns decorated along the arch-like ceilings. Water lily bowls were constructed at the pavilion, to bring forth peace and harmony.

Upon entering the temple's main hall, Mama and Aunt Bridget received three burning joss sticks from the temple's caretaker. I waved a 'no' when it was my turn to receive the joss stick. Thereafter, the caretaker apologized for his ignorance when Mama referred to her eligible-to-marry beloved granddaughter as a 'religion-eater', or, simply put, a Christian.

I took shelter from the heat under a canopy. Aunt Bridget and Mama were in a trance, mumbling prayers. 'Guess what their prayers are?' I whispered to Daniel.

Daniel pouted, pretending to foretell. 'Our prima donna aunt must be praying for a filthy rich husband while Mama is asking god to bring you a new husband.'

I shook my head. 'Mama's praying for more wifey candidates for you.'

'Her prayer won't come true. Mark my words.'

'Have you got someone in mind?' I asked.

'Your interrogative tongue could easily scare men away.'

'Then stop bringing up the "H" word,' I said, my arms folded. He whispered, 'What era is this? "H" can be a woman too.'

A grin slid across my face. 'Since when did you become so witty—'

'"H" is for homies,' interrupted Daniel. 'Someone you're comfortable with; whom you love to share the same space and breathing air with—that includes the bathroom and bed.'

'You two noisy mosquitoes follow me,' Mama's voice synchronized with the tapping of the walking stick. Aunt Bridget looked over her shoulder and mouthed, 'Faster.'

I remained in solitude, confronting the elevated Goddess Guanyin's gold statue. Besides the wafting incense, the light, floral scent of burning sticks in the prayer hall was pleasant, casting a veil of calm. I missed the smell of sage and the frankincense that were there during Eucharistic celebrations. However, being a Catholic, entering a temple was a forbidden issue.

The monks were chanting with the wooden fish. Eyes closed and manifesting the high-minded beacon of love, I felt Mama's grip on my right hand.

Led by the hypnotic percussion beats, I began to visualize last night's dream—the lotus by the lake, attached with a jewel. I tried reaching it, was disappointed when it slipped away, and vanished on my second attempt. A dream trapped in a wetland, alone, somewhat ascertaining that Edward's presence could be within reach. In a deep trance, my body stumbled into the lake.

Waddling and struggling at the same time, I couldn't breathe. Then, all eyes were on me as I was devoured by reality, waking from the hallucination. The monks and Mama helped me up as I fell from the prayer cushion. I gulped, mortified by my actions, and bowed in apology.

'I apologize on behalf of my granddaughter Emily for being weak like a soft-shell crab today,' Mama prayed. 'Please take the negative energy from her and replace it with a happy, vibrant one. As for my grandson Daniel, bless him with a good wife, one that will provide him with enough children to fill the hall. For my daughter Bridget, may she find a man to take care of her, preferably a chef because she cannot cook. My other daughter Cheryl, bless her for the church volunteering activities but maybe slow her down a bit so she can come back to visit me. Lastly, my eldest son Raymond,' here Mama stopped for a bit. 'I hope to be a grandma one more time, before I come to you.'

Everyone looked over their shoulder at the non-expressive Uncle Raymond.

Mama grabbed a set of crescent-shaped wooden moon blocks from the altar.

Known as a *jiaobei* divination, the devotee had to seek divine guidance in this *godly* Q&A praying session. Each block was carved to look rounder on one side and flatter on the other, to balance the yin and the yang on both sides.

'Emily, you go first.'

'Mama, I'm a Catholic,' I whispered.

'So—'

'It's a conflict of interest—' I spoke clearly.

'*Cornflake* of what—'

'Ma—' Uncle Raymond started. 'Don't force Emily if she doesn't want to.'

'Everyone has three chances to throw unless you get a *shengbei*,' Mama said.

Daniel rolled his eyes.

Biting the bullet, I clasped the moon blocks several times, threw them higher, believing them to be motivated by gravity, doing so just to make Mama happy.

Mama held her breath till both the blocks lay flat. 'The symbol of laughter means the gods are confused. Throw the blocks and ask the question as clearly as possible.'

I repeated the process; throwing higher, much harder. I don't believe in this crap, but I still respect all deities. Both the blocks fell even harder and louder on the ground, trailing echoes as they dropped consecutively.

Aunt Bridget and Daniel were scratching their heads.

'How come it's the same, again?' Mama exhaled with disappointment. 'My goodie-good granddaughter, ask Goddess Guanyin sincerely. You shall receive the blessing dearly.'

Picturing the authentic meditation of falling into the deep current, the mind was perfectly at peace. One of the blocks bounced backward, then stood diagonally as it hit the ground, once and then twice, while the other lay flat.

Everyone's expressions stagnated.

'The gods cannot understand your question still,' said Mama. 'Let's try again. This time I hold your hands. Make sure no more stupid mistakes.'

* * *

Mama approached the plus-size woman seated at a pop-up stall under the tenebrous tree. The Phra Phrom statue, the Four-Faced Buddha, decorated with a necklace made of orchid petals and its feet sprinkled with jasmine flowers. The spirit cloth in royal yellow in Sanskrit was hung against the wall fencing. It included the woman's lifetime achievements and prominent skills written and framed in traditional Chinese. She'd even had a photo taken with the Dalai Lama.

'My blessing to all, it is God's destiny that has brought us together. I'm one of the last sidewalk fortune tellers in Penang.' The woman looked to be in her sixties. She scanned Daniel and me from top to bottom then turned her gaze to Mama. 'Is there anything you're seeking to clarify?'

'How much do you charge?' Mama asked.

'MYR 30.'

'Whoa! Very expensive . . .' Mama covered her mouth.

'I won't take one cent if you think my prediction is inaccurate.'

Daniel and I rolled our eyes at the woman's high-pitched, nasal accent.

'Good. My granddaughter's turn first, and then my grandson's.'

'Madam, you're so lucky. Your grandchildren are like golden-boy and girl-of-purity.' She had a gold chain talisman amulet around her neck and a gold ring on her left middle finger. She gestured to me. 'Come, let me read your fortune from your face.'

The woman must've felt my uninvited polar-opposite aura as I reached my hands out, trying to balance on the white plastic stool that felt like it could break at any time. A smile deliberately formed on her face as she studied every line and facial pore while rubbing the lines on my palm. She seemed to be in a trance, chanting the reserve of abracadabra, which sounded like an Indo-Chinese dialect.

'The condition of your health and wealth shall be abundant if you choose to look on the brighter side,' the woman said. 'Happiness is not only making big money. It is what makes you able to sleep well at night, have no worries, and be happy.'

'How will her marriage fate be?' Mama asked.

I pulled Mama's sleeve, glowering at her.

The woman smiled. 'We meet many people on all accounts. But there's always one that will be in every reincarnated lifetime. The one who has left shall return either in this life or the next. If both are meant to be, no fire and storm is greater than the gift of true love.'

Eleven

The melodious 'ding' from the multi deck oven overlapped with Mama's clashing cymbals. Not only was Mama carrying on her ancestor's profession—the ghost-chaser—but the clanging had also triggered a vibration so loud that Daniel and I temporarily lost our hearing. We were still able to read Mama's lips, saying, 'Spirits, spirits, go in peace.'

The awkward silence broke. Edward sprung to mind when the clock hit 11.11 p.m. Be it the sign of his return, as the sidewalk fortune teller had prophesied.

'It's rehab night.' Daniel's hands waved. 'The prison warden is away.'

'Poor Uncle Sean,' I laughed, retrieving the piping hot pineapple buns from the oven. 'Even Aunt Bridget calls him a monk.'

'So underrated,' Daniel laughed. 'He resembled the Diyu Grim Reaper. Ya'know the rumour about him having a fling with our aunt.'

'Really—that's news to me.' I yawned.

'From Mama's horse's mouth,' said Daniel. 'They've been on a movie date.'

'Impossible, Aunt Bridget's manager has been on the lookout for her.'

'Their rendezvous happened in Penang,' Daniel cleared his throat, picking the buns with a pair of tongs. 'Aunt Bridget sneaked back to celebrate Uncle Sean's birthday, watching *Ghost* at the Majestic Theatre and had curry noodles for supper. After that night, they don't talk to each other anymore. Weird . . .'

'More like lovers to sworn enemies situation,' I shrugged.

'Our aunt definitely enjoys sprinkling some BFF drama into her love story,' Daniel said. 'Ticking to-sleep-with boxes on each producer's name, director, stylist, and actor.'

'Well, I'm blindsided,' I said, glazing the fluffy buns with less-sweetened strawberry jam. 'There's the one Aunt Bridget had given her heart and soul to.' Emotionally, I'd think of skin-to-skin intimacy—whenever Edward put his hands on me—replacing clay with dough, like Demi Moore and Patrick Swayze's characters living rent-free in my head.

'Aunt Bridget and her curated United-fucking-Nation camp.'

I threw a wet towel at my cousin.

Daniel leaned closer. 'Have you done it with a celebrity before?'

Rolling my eyes, I retrieved a tray of vanilla cupcakes from the cooling deck. 'Anyway, Uncle Raymond is excellent at solving domestic problems, getting Mama the new cymbals.'

'Sometimes Old Bean really has got a way.' Daniel poured hot water into the Korean ramen cup noodles, then covered both with the lids. 'I learned to keep the unnecessary bickering down from him, to manifest good positive energy within.'

Noise started to escalate from the gourmet kitchen. The volunteers from the previous shift had left. Lady Di (named Diana Sim) walked in. She was a retired secondary school teacher volunteering at this indistinguishable non-profit food centre. Lady Di talked about her thirty years of teaching experience in rural Malaysia and I, in turn, shared my experience of my final year at the University of Sheffield. Lady Di laughed when I told her of how London's high-end restaurants replaced the coconut milk in Malaysian curry with fresh milk.

'I smelled pineapple buns,' Lady Di said to us.

'You're welcome to take one,' Daniel said. 'Uncle Sean's on leave.'

'I know or else we can hear his thunderbolt voice from here,' Lady Di smiled.

Daniel and I laughed.

'Hey, nice try on the buttercream swirl,' Lady Di said to me.

'Thanks, I still need a lot of practise though,' I said thinking of how I needed to get better at controlling the piping bag with my hand movement on the cupcakes.

'My Biu-jie is the Jackie-of-all-trade,' said Daniel.

'Oh, bribery of sweet words,' I said. 'Thanks, much appreciated.'

Daniel smiled. 'Aren't you supposedly on day shift, Lady Di?'

'I decided to switch my roster with Uncle Cabby. His wife is working a late shift, and he should be hands-on with his four lil-buzzing-kids and that mischievous toddler at home.'

'The cupcakes should be ready by now,' I said. 'Why not take some home for Uncle Cabby and his family? It is my new project for the soup kitchen. Hopefully soon.'

Lady Di beamed. 'Sean has seemingly been softened by you.'

Daniel gazed at her then made eye-contact.

Lady Di was quick-witted. 'Raymond and Clement should be back from the wholesale by now. I'm heading back to the gourmet side.'

I turned to my cousin thereafter for some kind of clarification.

'We're short of volunteers already,' Daniel said, eluding my question.

'Is there something I don't know about between Lady Di and you?'

Daniel did not play along. 'Luckily, that prison warden has peeled, sliced, and then cooked the pineapple filling. Otherwise, our hands would've been eaten up by its enzyme and citric acid.'

Daniel's garrulousness was to disguise what had been going around the kitchens lately. This loud mouth had been keeping *something* from me. The night's fall breeze enunciated the echoes of Mama's clashing cymbals. It must've been difficult for my cousin to zip his mouth for ten seconds. 'All right, I quit.' I threw down my plastic gloves and gestured a farewell.

'Uncle Sean is planning for a sworn relationship with you.'

Daniel is predictable. 'Are you serious?'

'I swear that this is not a drill,' Daniel affirmed.

'Let me guess, the Monk has fixed a date with the temple's head of authority to conduct a blood oath before the Lord Guan Yu's towering statue, witnessed by the Laus as we recite the uncle-and-niece-kinship vows,' I snapped, looking hard-nosed.

'Maybe that's a little dramatic, but nothing's been confirmed yet.'

'This isn't wartime. Count me out.' I piped out the remaining strawberry jam into a container then kept it inside the fridge. 'Maybe my tattoos gave him the wrong impression?'

'Right.' Daniel nodded.

'Does Uncle Raymond know about this sworn-in arrangement?'

Daniel shook his head.

I heaved a sigh of relief.

'Otherwise, Aunt Bridget would be restlessly bugging you and Mama would be parading her ceremony costume.' Daniel rolled out the dough then cut it into wedges. 'Does your head still hurt from the nasty temple cushion fall?'

'Nah, I feel a lot better.'

'I was bewildered when you asked the fortune teller for dream interpretation.'

'The dream was indeed intriguing and engaging,' I said, shaping the cut out dough into a crescent.

'Women are like men too, trapped in relationships and finances; distraught.' Daniel smirked. 'So, what's your dream about?'

'I dreamed of the lotus flower.' Measuring each ball of dough on the digital weighing machine, I pinched off the excess amount to form another one.

Daniel wiped his hands, then typed something on his phone. 'There's an article here that says a lotus flower dream symbolizes purity, self-regeneration, enlightenment, love, and rebirth. Despite its roots that slither into muddy beds, the flower itself is beautiful. In your case, a new beau might be on his way.'

I pretended to not listen.

'Take it as an affirmation,' Daniel said, arm over my shoulder. 'A positive sign to find a goal in the life you deserve to have. Be selfish for your own sake, time to press the restart button.'

I pre-heated the oven for the next baking. I had always been a swashbuckler, moved out from a cozy home and got a job at the aparthotel, tackling housekeeping chores, and handling frivolous and thorny guests. None of this was enough to make me whine and complain about earning a lot less than when I was working in the preeminent legal chambers. Mom was proud of my promotion to assistant public relations officer. However, nothing compared to Edward, an uninvited guest who *reorganized* my life.

Daniel uncovered the lid, scooping the pineapple filling from the bucket into the dough and then rolled it on his palms. 'You have the balls of the Laus.'

'Oh, don't put me in such a plinth of grace,' I said.

'Perhaps, a new man is walking into your life . . .'

'Based on the lotus dream and that . . . foretelling?' I shook my head, disbelieving.

'You never know,' Daniel said. 'Keep your options open.'

'I'm aiming for a new career opportunity after the internship,' I said, packing the bun inside each transparent pastry bag then sealing them for hygiene purposes.

'You've the guts of the slain-feminist poet Qiu Jin.'

'Whoa, you know about her too?'

'She inspired Aunt Bridget to write her latest script,' Daniel said.

'Cool. I love her poetry and essays. Been hunting for the English translated version.'

'Once you're a poet then you'll always be.' Aunt Bridget's voice was heard, suddenly.

'Speaking of the hidden green ghost,' Daniel said.

'You really scared us, dearest aunt,' I glazed the buns with melted butter. 'It is a quarter past three. You're up early to write.'

'I couldn't sleep. Thanks to Ma's cymbals,' my aunt yawned. 'Your father is responsible for this bloody antique instrument.'

'Go talk to him. I don't answer for a third party,' Daniel said.

'I had an argument with Ma at the temple just because I couldn't get a shengbei,' said Aunt Bridget. 'Screwed-up the second round of jiaobei, received angry answers from the gods. I had to redo the throwing process until my tough luck kicked in.'

I patted my aunt's back, fetching a cup of water for her.

She thanked me. 'I need an alternative valerian to knock me off.'

* * *

'Bridget is in the Emergency Room . . .'

It'd been an eerie morning to begin with. After which, we pulled an all-nighter.

Appalled by the phone conversation with Uncle Raymond earlier, I dropped flat on my cousin's spreading futon, rubbing my face. Like a noose twisting his voice, Daniel politely told me to do what I should while he took some time to digest the misfortune.

In Aunt Bridget's bedroom, the so-called wall of cinema was furnished with posters of Charlie Chaplin, Buster Keaton, Greta Garbo, and Janet Gaynor. Then, the Category III movie posters of Johnnie To, Herman Yau, and Tsui Hark's films with explicit content.

I opened the wardrobe and was greeted by Nancy Kwan and Audrey Hepburn posters while searching for a bag to pack her essential items.

There were manuscript papers scattered on the writing desk, some on the floor, spilling out from the trash bin. Other than English, I never knew Aunt Bridget could write effortlessly in simplified Mandarin-Chinese. I unfolded the creasing paper. My hands continued to shiver, questioning her sudden overdose. The *alternative* to valerian, as she'd briefed us last night.

'Act 1, Scene 1: The night is warm and floccose. Bei-er is in bed, waiting for Kenji Yamashino. Her back is facing the door. He doesn't want to be seen kissing her; from shoulder to her unclothed spine. A blindfold to hinder her sight as their lips cement the forbidden promise. After tonight, they have to go their separate ways.'

I tightened my grip on the script.

A small padlock was left dangling at the door. Uncle Raymond had to break in, when he realized his sister's non-responsiveness. I turned off the stand fan that had been spinning eerily. Emotional density took over as I was reading the script's final line—

Farewell, my celebrated life. Bei-er rests her pen.

Aunt Bridget might've taken method acting a little too seriously.

My aunt had lived her dream, sacrificing her seething youth, walking with the rise and fall of the film industry. And her personal life had always been sensationalized by the HK tabloids. An incident that sent the roof flying was when my father's colleague saw my aunt entering the elevator with a tall handlebar-moustached man at The Peninsula Hotel—the man she'd brought to my fourth birthday party. Arguments got heated when my father accused my mom's baby-sister of being a promiscuous and materialistic siren-queen who had lots of affairs.

I should've supported my aunt, understanding the strength of these inherent temptations. Then again, I hadn't grilled Edward

about his private life. In an industry of negative influences—
fuckboys and humping-girls—what were the chances of a former
K-pop-idol-turned-soloist to get down on one knee and propose
to his non-celebrity girlfriend? *Absolutely not.* Inevitably, in the
K-entertainment industry, the celebrities would have to face
the music and would probably lose fan support; one of their
revenue streams. The *sasaeng* fans would stalk their idols and their
non-celebrity partners. It wasn't like the West where the late Kurt
Cobain still enjoyed mainstream success despite being married
and having a child.

Fandom with a hefty price. I shook away my thoughts.

'Biu-jie, have you packed Aunt Bridget's stuff?' Daniel asked.

I blinked, snapping back to reality. 'No suitcase here. Think
I should lend her my duffle bag instead. What do you think?'

Daniel nodded, massaging between his brows. 'By the way,
Uncle Clement wants us to be in the conference room for a short
meeting. Do you need my help?'

'It's okay. Uncle Raymond's told me what to pack.'

Back in my room, I tossed out the contents of my duffle
bag, spreading the sea of indispensable junk on my bed. There
were crinkled, loose papers—some were my poetry drafts that
I'd been working on without reservation, a worn-out stationery
bag, three winter beanies in turquoise, indigo, and pantone pink
though I don't remember having the latter one hardback A5 size
journal, a bunch of scarves, a half unconsumed preserved sour
plum candy, and a strip of the antidepressant Fluoxetine.

I chucked away the bitter pills and then locked the drawer.

In the veranda, I heard drowning voices coming from inside
the conference room.

I knocked on the door. Uncle Clement opened it with a
brief smile.

I greeted him and then passed the duffle bag to
Uncle Raymond.

'How's Aunt Bridget?'

'She fell down the stairs. Quite bad,' my uncle said, sounding concerned.

Could it be the inauspicious shengbei effect? *Oh, my irrational brain.*

'Let me introduce you to our new volunteer,' Uncle Clement said to me.

The stranger slung his backpack, ruffling his undercut to the back, and then extended his right hand. 'Annyeonghaseyo, Michael Kim, nice to meet you.'

I firmly shook his hand as his deep-seated eyes looked on.

Part II

Twelve

'Welcome to Kuala Lumpur,' I greeted.

'Nice to meet you, Miss . . .' Edward looked at my nametag, 'Emily.'

An airline announced its flight landing in Malay and English.

Captivated by his energy, though hidden beneath a pair of sunglasses and a cerulean blue bucket hat, I cleared my throat. 'Just Emily. So, where are your suitcases?'

'Only my backpack for now.' Edward was looking elsewhere, surveying.

I gingerly looked over my shoulder, spotting about three to four women disperse from a crowd that seemed more like an army or troop. They moved as though strategizing a plan and were soon joined by others. Two of them had aimed their phones at Edward, taking photos in periodic pop-up flashes. Trying to get different angles. It was as the security admin had warned us. The arrival hall was inhabited by Edward's fans, putting up with the long night along the corridor, just to get up close and slightly personal with their favourite pop idol.

'I swear the Saujana Residence management didn't leak the . . .'

'Calm down, Emily.' Edward chuckled.

'Shouldn't your manager be here with you?' I tried to loosen the tense situation.

'Yeah, being pushed towards the mad crowd like a flap of pancake.' Edward adjusted the backpack's buckling strap around his chest.

I snickered uncontrollably.

Edward's gaze caught mine. 'He's scheduled to arrive later with my guitars.'

'These fans have ample time to chase their idols. Don't they have life?'

Edward shot me a look.

I didn't reply—*supposedly* a blatantly honest opinion.

'Anyway, do you have any backup plans?' he asked.

'Of course.' I pressed the bluetooth headset, paging the necessary personnel to stand-by.

Count to three. Edward and I trudged along the moving walkway, passing the travellers checking the departure board. The panic had started to rattle me, exacerbated by the jittering voices and plodding footsteps. Edward grabbed my hand. We hastened off as one of them tried to pull me back, then another hand grazed me, preparing to grab and grope Edward. Oh hell, what a perilous melange.

The fans turned hysterical when Edward threw his bucket hat in the crowd—thankfully able to divert their attention. I looked over my shoulder, out of curiosity, at the rampage. The shouting matches and altercations had slowed down our fleeing. The airport security had safeguarded the priority lane. I waved my one-time access pass—courtesy my workplace—at the officer, permission to enter for Edward and me, hearing the fans attempting to climb over the barricade panels.

Exhausted, I let Edward go as we got into the elevator. Initially, I had thought Sabrina was overestimating the power of the fans. Thankfully, Madam Ong always planned ahead. As the doors closed leading us to the basement parking, I dabbed off my sweat, breathing hard with my knees bent.

He gazed down at me, panting. 'Welcome to my world . . .'

* * *

'Little Niece, hello . . .' Uncle Sean's fingers snapped at me.

I blinked at the meandering crowds and the bustling sound of the marketplace.

'Didn't you hear Fruit Tan's recommendation?' Uncle Sean's tone had hit the impatience zone. 'Today's blueberry is all the way from Peru.'

Michael was chatting with the talkative fruit seller. The trolley was filled with green and red apples in boxes. Edward's memory had repossessed me, a fate oftentimes unavoidable.

'You're knowledgeable,' Michael said to Fruit Tan.

'I was a professional tour guide, leading interpretive tours locally and abroad until the 1997–98 Asian financial crisis.' Fruit Tan's lips pursed, reminiscing.

I hadn't fully been resuscitated from the recollection, worse still, I'd forgotten how many packets Daniel had asked me to purchase for the mixed berry pie experiment—as approved by Uncle Clement and seconded by Uncle Raymond. Michael was sharing his knowledge behind the Korean strawberries' success, listening to Fruit Tan on the demographic differences of the strawberries' soil type in Australia, New Zealand, Egypt, and USA, as well as in Cameron Highlands, where the local growers resided.

'I always appreciate the farmers' sweat,' said Michael. 'The large-scale containers are filled with water to prevent the fruits from losing water through evaporation, allowing them to breathe and grow, and preserving the freshness for three to four days.'

One Korean man's gone, another's visited.

Uncle Clement had asked for Michael's opinion to improve the desserts for the community food centre. Uncle Raymond had an appointment to meet up with Aunt Bridget's physiotherapist in the hospital. At times, it didn't sit well whenever Uncle Sean was around.

'Please pack twenty packs of blueberries and strawberries, thanks,' I said to Fruit Tan, cutting into Michael's strawberry harvesting conversation.

Uncle Sean turned to me. 'That's a lot of Vitamin C, you'll get diarrhoea, Little Niece. Also, these are imported fruits, of course not cheap.'

'Some are for my aunt,' I said. 'The rest are for the mixed berry tart making.'

'She . . . she's . . . a . . . awake?' Uncle Sean stammered.

'Yes,' I said, in an annoyingly loud voice.

'Is that true she hurt her backside?' Uncle Sean murmured to me.

'Go ask her yourself.'

Uncle Sean cleared his throat and shot me a look. 'Who approved of the tart making?'

'Uncle Raymond and Uncle Clement,' I replied quickly, hoping to switch topics.

Michael cut-in, 'I suggested it too, so I don't mind paying.'

'I'm not going to pay for your failed experiment,' Uncle Sean said.

'I am positive that this is definitely going to be a success,' Michael said.

Uncle Sean gripped his waist, obliquely gawking at Michael like he thought the young man was bouncing off the walls. 'Today is your first day volunteering, yet so snobbish. But I forgive you. You've had it rough after all,' he gestured a V-sign at Michael.

I snickered, even though I sympathized with Michael—being mugged and staying at the church for a week, as we'd learned from Uncle Clement at the meeting earlier.

Michael glared at Uncle Sean but didn't say a word.

'I have enough money,' I said, then, to Michael, 'keep your allowance.'

Fruit Tan said to me, 'You can always pay on your next trip. I've debited all items into two separate invoices addressed to—' he showed the tallied amount without a digital calculator.

Each item looked to have been billed unambiguously.

'Here is the exact MYR 300 in crisp new bills,' Michael said. 'Have a good day. May your family and you be happy and healthy.'

'Nice doing business with you.' Fruit Tan gave me a thumbs up behind Michael's back.

* * *

'Being busy is a blessing, isn't it?' I said to Daniel, on the way to visit Aunt Bridget.

My poor cousin loosened his tie, tossing the suit to the back of the campervan. 'For you, maybe. How was your first bonding session with our handsome oppa?' He meant Michael.

'Five minutes seemed like forever,' I said.

'That bad, huh?' Daniel chortled.

On the way back from the marketplace, I'd caught myself staring at Michael's side profile. He resembled a proportionally carved Roman art sculpture, a pore-less one at that—could be the deliberate recompense from the comprehensive hell-bent skincare routine. The folded long-sleeve shirt exhibited his muscular arms and his unchapped lips were similar to Edward's. He was metrosexually attractive.

'Why has Aunt Bridget been transferred to Gleneagles? Has she been keeping up with her former celebrity hiatus, being unresponsive on the group chat, not even replying to a private message. And now, I'm doing Uncle Sean a favour by bringing this over.' I yawned, holding onto the thermos flask.

'The prison warden and his no-gravity balls,' said Daniel, yawning aloud.

'And he didn't even bother paying you a transportation fee,' I said.

'Good luck milking anything from that miser,' Daniel smirked.

'Will Aunt Bridget's medical insurance be able to cover the hospitalization cost?' I asked. 'We're talking about a private medical centre here.'

'Unfortunately, everything is being dug from her pocket,' Daniel said.

'But she hasn't been working for the past five years,' I said, curious.

'Old Bean is Aunt Bridget's conservator. Her legal guardian,' said Daniel.

'Are you serious?'

'Take it from me, Biu-jie. Live a stress-free life and concentrate on your internship. Just slide . . .' Daniel yawned again, distorting his following words.

* * *

'We're visiting someone in the presidential suite,' Daniel said, after making an inquiry at the nurses' counter.

We had fifteen minutes before the hospital's visiting hours ended.

The lighting along the left-wing corridor looked dim, harmonizing with the intense tension crowding the space. However, observing the artificial bouquet at the mahogany table somewhat minimized the tension of the admission episode. A man attired in a black suit greeted us, holding a luxury stainless steel meal tray. There was a steak placed artfully on the tray.

'Butler service,' I said, eyes widened. 'Is she staying in a hotel or what?'

'Only the filthy rich can afford this.' Daniel pressed the room bell.

'Indeed, a vacation before embarking on the stairway to heaven,' I added.

'Come in,' our aunt sang.

Daniel and I gasped.

Holy moley! Splendour, opulence, and grandeur—a trail of fast-moving cars sped along the skyline. Overlooking the sea, the sporadic brightness was cascading along the Penang Bridge. A lighthouse situated in an islet, known as Pulau Jerejak. Formerly an asylum for patients with leprosy, it was rumoured to have been inhabited by disturbed spirits for the past century. The islet had attracted teams of paranormal researchers from around the world to track-down any ghost sightings for reality TV-shows.

'Help me finish all these.' Clad in a kimono silk nightie, Aunt Bridget was munching on toast. She smiled, as I complimented her good appetite. Not only had my aunt hurt her bum, she'd also complained of numbness afflicting her whole leg.

Daniel jumped onto Aunt Bridget's bed, enveloping her in a tight embrace. 'I thought we might never see you again.' He started to cry. Aunt Bridget patted his head, enjoying rare display of familial love.

'Careful with her back,' I said to my cousin.

'Speaking of that . . . I thought you'd split into two.'

'Hey, easy on my humping-asset.' Aunt Bridget smacked his shoulder.

Daniel covered his mouth, guffawing.

'Oi, quit your rubbish Smelly-Dan,' I said, then looked at my aunt, letting out a relieved sigh. 'We were so worried about you when Uncle Raymond told us. At least you're eating well and still able to joke.'

My aunt blinked, arms wide open, then mouthed, 'Come here'.

I placed the thermos flask on the table, then threw my arms around her. Her palms rubbed my back, comforting my worries. My eyes turned glossy with a sheen of tears.

'Did you get your bum bandaged?' Daniel tried peeping behind her.

Aunt Bridget pinched her nephew's lips. 'I'll throw you out if you don't shut up.'

I waved my hands at her. 'Right, Aunt Bridget, what really happened?'

She exhaled. 'I . . . missed the steps and slipped. And blessed be, I was able to reach for the handle rail or else I really would've broken into two.'

'Wearing your contact lens at that time?' Daniel asked Aunt Bridget.

'Yeah.'

I looked to Daniel and mouthed, 'Bad shengbei effect'.

He nodded supportively.

Aunt Bridget snapped her fingers. 'Stop whispering. What are you two going on about?'

'Nothing,' we said in unison.

'Spill the beans. Now.' Our aunt pointed a threatening finger at us.

'We thought the jiaobei gods had snatched your life.' My cousin rolled his eyes. 'Also, Biu-jie had to lie to Mama and tell her that you're shooting a movie in Hollywood.'

Aunt Bridget patted the back of my head. 'My lawyer niece is excellent at white lies.' She pulled us closer to her and turned contemplative. 'Who knows this might be a second chance for my movie script to shine in Hollywood. Good luck comes with the Hell God's reversed plan.'

Daniel shook his head at our aunt's artistic, optimistic narrative.

'But Uncle Raymond said you were unconscious in your room.'

'Heard of dead asleep?'

Daniel and I blinked, then exchanged glances.

Aunt Bridget looked on, making the annoying, tsak-tsak, sound of a house lizard at us. 'This is what unmoving, peaceful sleep means. Mind you, my creative juices are spilling over, I can't wait to write.'

'Pray hard there's no fire in the house?' Daniel shook his head.

'Think Ma sprinkled ice water on my face when I was late for school once . . .' Aunt Bridget grimaced. 'Don't believe me? Ask your mom, Emily. She knew me too well.'

I turned to Daniel and snickered—it really runs in the Lau family.

Daniel side-eyed me, then cleared his throat.

For now, I should take Aunt Bridget's word for it.

'Do me a favour, Emily. Tomorrow, bring my Chanel and Anna Sui perfumes and a few sets of nightwear—the silk ones. Also get the scripts and the stack of blank papers on my table.'

'Get some rest, Aunt Bridget.' Daniel said as he yawned.

'The script should be done in three days, and it needs a villain.'

'Whatever.' Daniel added, 'There's a volunteer at the sanctuary; a teapot.' A Hokkien labelling of a male's penis, pointing out its resemblance to the spout, from where liquid could be poured.

That's it. I picked up a neck pillow from the armchair and tossed it at Daniel for being disrespectful. A warning to curb his risqué humour. His snickering laughter resembled Muttley, the Hanna-Barbera cartoon fictional dog, eyeing me. 'That Korean volunteer is compatible with Biu-jie. Not you, dearest aunt.'

'Assessment before confirmation,' Aunt Bridget said. 'Send him in tomorrow.'

'Come on, he's just another person, not some alien.' I closed my eyes on the couch.

'Did you tell the Monk about my situation?' My aunt changed the topic.

'No,' Daniel said.

Aunt Bridget looked at us. 'Good, or else I'll kill you both.'

'But we brought you supper.' I sniffed from the thermos flask, opening the lid. 'This soup tonic is made with lots of love, simmered with immense passion.' I ladled it into a bowl, then passed it to my aunt. 'Finish this and take your painkiller. Bedtime soon.'

Aunt Bridget hastily gulped the soup down. 'In exchange for my co-operation, bring that Korean bloke over.'

Daniel and I rolled our eyes.

* * *

Uncle Sean's pupils dilated with hope. 'What'd your aunt say?'

'Look inside the flask. That's the proof.' I walked into the pastry kitchen.

Uncle Sean clasped his hands, on the verge of tears. 'She finished the soup.'

Daniel and I shared a look at how romantically infatuated the Monk was.

'What's her comment on the soup? When will she be discharged?' Uncle Sean asked.

'Ask her yourself,' Daniel said.

'Why can't you tell me?'

'I had a gruelling meeting today with Uncle Clement and the rest of St Paul's committee members, brainstorming about the fundraising for the food drive project, including budget expenses and volunteers' recruitment,' Daniel said. 'If not for doing you a favour . . .'

'Young people doing more work won't die,' Uncle Sean said ridiculously.

'A man is in his most feeble state of mind when he's asleep. A woman is at her weakest when not feeling well,' Daniel added breathlessly.

'Also, time to reignite that old flame with Aunt Bridget,' I said.

Uncle Sean avoided us while heading out with the flask.

Thirteen

Daniel hadn't taken his eyes off Michael since this morning.

It started on the terrace when my cousin caught a glimpse of Michael clad only in sweatpants, doing yoga half-naked on the piercing-soles reflexology path. That being said, Daniel should've been Aunt Bridget's scriptwriting assistant and should have been doing more writing and less ogling. I'm not entirely sure how his illustrations of Michael's abdominal muscles and protruding hip bones was helping with the script.

I shunned Michael as he climbed in the car on the seat, looking at me. 'Emily-ssi, why aren't you sitting closer? There's a wide space between us.'

'No thanks and scrap that honorific,' I said.

'Formal greetings are a sign of respect.'

My cousin whistled, trying not to laugh.

Immediately, I nudged Daniel's arm. 'Aunt Bridget is waiting.'

The gear squeaked with a loose, deafening sound when shifting. Daniel spoke to me in Cantonese, 'Even Beatrice is excited to have Mister Kimchi on board.'

'By the way, why does Miss Bridget want to meet me?'

I turned to Michael. 'All volunteers are like family members to one another.'

Even a fool could sense the awkwardness throughout the journey.

Daniel's sudden and temporary personality reversal seemed impractical. His boisterousness had been swept under the rug, and he'd bid farewell to his limitless energy and endurance. And I missed his bright outlook. It'd seemed weird when he rushed through breakfast then rocked up in that despicable suit and tie to meet with the St Paul's godfathers for Episode #2 of the fundraising food drive discussion without his usual jovial demeanour. The only Daniel-esque comment he made was when he told me that none of the committee members resembled Marlon Brando or Al Pacino. Instead, Uncle Clement could easily have achieved the role of a benign and compassionate godfather.

'Let me talk to Uncle Clement,' I said to Daniel.

'What for?' Daniel asked.

'I don't want him to overwork my cousin.'

'I'm blessed to have a kind-hearted Biu-jie,' he said, playfully leaning his head on my shoulder. He quickly adjusted his posture to concentrate on the road. 'My manifestation is working. Now that we have the resources and manpower, it is my time to shine, for I'm not a piece of char siu.'

I patted my cousin's head.

'Count me in then.' Michael smiled. Those dimples should be enthroned with Swarovski diamonds. 'Certainly Mr Clement Ho would be happy with two more participants, right? To come up with more ideas?'

Daniel elbowed me, whispering. 'He is definitely the lotus flower from your dream.'

* * *

Two nurses were giggling and covering their mouths in the elevator, sort-of drooling over Michael, behaving sheepishly and then waving at him on the way out. My cousin let out a fake cry, claiming that Michael had indirectly been sent by the universe to promote the phenomenal growth of K-culture, and eventually the whole nation would be Koreanized in no time.

Hello to Hallyu-ism. Bye-bye to whitewashing.

I accidentally spilled essential oil on Michael's wrist while rubbing it on my temples, quickly apologized, and then wiped the ointment on him with a facial handkerchief.

'How're you feeling, Miss Emily?' Michael asked.

Before I could answer, the doctor held onto the gate, hurrying us to clear the elevator space. On the gurney, a patient recoiled in horror, pressing his hands to his chest as he was wheeled into the elevator assisted by two nurses—one of them was carrying a portable intravenous drip.

I released myself from Michael's grip, then courteously thanked him for saving me from a probable meltdown. Luckily, I didn't vomit or collapse on him. Crashing into the patient or being stuck in an elevator with someone in such acute pain would have probably triggered me.

'That was close.' Daniel, appalled as the medical team left, was looking at me then at Michael. 'You all right, Biu-jie? Look like you've seen a ghost.'

'I'm fine.'

After binge-watching TED Talks on YouTube, I'd trained myself to design emotional talks to invigorate my lucid mind. *Go with the flow.* I could perceive immeasurable difference between Edward's intimate sense of touch and the more utilitarian one of Michael. There was no immediate high level of dopamine, only Michael's friendly rapport—based on the feelings in one's bones.

'It is a man's responsibility to protect women and children,' Michael vowed.

I kept my gaze on the elevator panel, moving upward.

We reached Aunt Bridget's heavenly staycation suite, and she gave my cousin and me the warmest hug as we walked in. She stopped, fluttering her permanently laminated eyelashes at Michael. 'Well, well, well, is this the Korean wowser?' she asked, scanning Michael up and down.

Michael greeted my aunt with hands on his belly.

'Anyeonghaseyo, Bridget *ibnida*, can I call you Michael K?'

'Michael or Mike only,' he said, no skin contact still.

'Michael K sounds like a model. You're qualified for that,' said my aunt.

'Again, please call me Michael or Mike.'

'I'm calling you Mikey from now on,' my aunt said, annoyingly.

Daniel clasped Aunt Bridget's right hand. 'Your highness, please don't scare our new volunteer away or else you'll be working on the pastry side with . . .'

'Having to work alongside Uncle Sean is a great honour,' Michael said.

I broke out in laughter when I realized Michael had aggravated Aunt Bridget's peskiness. The first rule when talking to Aunt Bridget is you do not talk about Uncle Sean. However, Michael should really be forgiven, despite Daniel's eye contact with me, confirming that Michael was probably in deep shit.

Aunt Bridget raised her finely trimmed eyebrows to observe our silent movements, then moved her gaze to Michael.

'Uncle Sean is a talented pastry chef,' Michael started his *advertisement*.

'I won't be discharged if you continue talking about him.' Aunt Bridget waved her hand to cut him off.

'Hey, take that glimmering accessory away from me,' said Daniel. 'I'm going blind soon, for the sake of Saint Adonis.'

Aunt Bridget showed off. 'I found it inside Emily's duffle bag.'

I ambled over and then took her hand, examining her index finger.

'It was in the side pocket,' Aunt Bridget added.

A blazing streak that had echoed to scrape like a deer running towards the headlight, the persistent thrust of memory was lashing forward. There was a saturated blue box with a pair of prominent hands delving into it before me, familiar and devoted.

I pursed my lips.

Oh, Emily, what if Edward were to know this promise ring had been worn by someone else, instead of guarded by you. How could I have forgotten to check the duffle bag thoroughly? Had I been this absent-minded my entire life? Whether it was a precursor to an engagement ring, this fidelity and commitment band had a sense of confidentiality I should have protected.

'May I see it?' Michael's tone was calm, yet unconvincing.

'What are you trying to do?' I hissed, almost bending my aunt's finger.

'Emily, honey-dear, you're gonna pull my finger out,' my aunt pleaded.

I let go of her, and instead, confronted Michael.

'Biu-jie, your tone is frightening. Stay cool.' Daniel smiled cautiously.

'The craftsmanship is so distinctive, undeniably elegant with the most brilliant cut,' Aunt Bridget analysed like a gemologist. 'Who gave this ring to you, Emily?'

I chimed in. 'The promise ring has the engraved initials of EAMJ.'

Aunt Bridget's mouth was agape. 'So, you were engaged to that white—?'

'No,' I revealed, affirmatively. 'He's my . . . former lover.'

Daniel's jaw dropped. Aunt Bridget pressed the back of his head, asking for some clarification, sheepishly and evidently not believing me.

Michael, though, his eyes were rooted to mine.

* * *

Daniel was sprawled on the deck of the rooftop terrace, grabbing a handful of tacos from me. 'Uncle Sean will crush our muscles, and drain every drop of your being and mine by churning our inner labourer when you've spilled his secrets to our aunt.'

'Stop being a coward. Some secrets aren't meant to be kept forever.'

'Don't change the topic. Well, you're my Biu-jie. I've no right to be angry at you but look here, you're getting me into hot oil. It's been two weeks of spending daytime at the church and peeling root veggies in the pastry kitchen at night. I'm so fucking exhausted.' I cleaned off the crumbs from his Rolling Stones graphic black tee.

'Think about it,' I said. 'We helped Uncle Sean deliver the soup-tonic to Aunt Bridget. He should give us some grace.'

'Very conniving.' Daniel glared at me.

'Hey, look here,' I pulled my sleeves up, revealing the black rose tattoos. 'I'm Uncle Sean's Little Niece. We've done a favour for him. Staying out of their romantic fling is the best way. Three relationships you shouldn't mess with—a husband-and-wife, a mother-and-daughter, and lovebirds madly in L-O-V-E.'

Daniel exhaled. 'You should consider giving classes on love philosophy.'

I bluntly tapped on his shoulder back, relaxing against the turquoise-coloured upholstery foam cushion. Daniel pretended to cough to check my subtle harshness. 'Next time, don't start the blame game before listening to the whole explanation,' I said.

Daniel furrowed his brows. 'Are there any men that could keep up with you?'

I leaned closer to him. 'Don't you think tonight's a fair bit quiet?'

Daniel popped the *xiaolongbao* into his mouth and then spat it out instantly.

I laughed. 'Oh, where art thou handsomest Michael Kim? Daniel has burned his tongue.'

'Keep your voice down,' Daniel gritted out, his hands covering my mouth.

I dodged him immediately, rubbing an ice cube around Daniel's mouth, taken from the beer-galvanized bucket. 'You've been ogling him since he first arrived.'

'He is not my type. I repeat. He is not my type.' Daniel raised his voice, took the melting ice cube then dumped it in his mouth. 'It's the fault of the steaming hot xiaolongbao soup,' he said, peering at it cautiously. 'I won't be fooled by your resting-bitch-face. Please tell me how your raging hormones aren't compelling you to eat him up?'

I munched on the popcorn. 'Honestly speaking, I don't feel a thing.'

'I don't believe it. Don't let me catch you both kissing one day.'

I threw a popcorn kernel at Daniel, and it landed safely inside his mouth.

'I don't get why he was so interested in the ring?' I murmured.

'I know the reason you aren't interested in Kimchi-Mike!' Daniel jumped up so suddenly, it shocked me. 'Must be that EAMJ engraved on the ring! You better spill now.' Snacking from the dried fruits and nuts bowl, Daniel scrunched his face.

'It's a quarter to midnight. Uncle Raymond will throw another bucket over your head.'

'Well, it is never too late for one more love story,' he winked.

* * *

I retrieved the clothes from the washer, including my aunt's kimono sleepwear that she'd handed over. The fabric reminded me of the first time my fingers had run across Edward's strong breastbone. An ecstasy that could spellbind, stoked to caress.

'Is everything all right?' Michael asked. 'I heard some noises upstairs.'

'Everything is fine,' I tilted my head up to match his height. Well, except for a Daniel vs Uncle Raymond combat show that was going to go down soon.

The Virgo-son had accused his Aries-Old Bean for imposing the cinderella rule. Instead of a bucket of ice water, Uncle Raymond was chasing after his son with a slingshot. Daniel then regimented my romantic tale to save his arse, encouraged by Uncle Raymond's appeased grinning. I couldn't stop blushing. Back then, in order for Aunt Bridget to return the promise ring to me, I'd lied that EAMJ was Edward An, a Chinese surname, instead of 'Ahn'.

Reason—stopping others from inquiring Emily's Love File.

'Don't take your bath so late. You may catch a cold,' Michael said to me.

'Thanks for your concern.' I shut the bathroom door.

The water from the shower poured softly, tickling my senses. The pitter-patter of drops amalgamated with my body heat— hydrotherapy. The promise ring was a mechanism to maintain my rationality when the intention to abuse myself with alcohol, when the mood swing tsunami had summoned me to swallow a whole bottle of Fluoxetine.

* * *

'I don't deserve such an expensive acoustic guitar.'

I remembered returning it to Edward.

'Oh, I can get you another if you don't like this.'

'I cannot accept this expensive gift,' I said.

'You played very well,' Edward said, hand on my waist. I stirred a little. 'The guests were cheering in the lounge bar. You deserve the standing ovation.'

'Thanks for the short tutorial.' I lowered my stare. 'Sabrina, Madam Ong, and the team are happy with my performance too, though I was very nervous back then.'

'All you need is to practise more. Have some confidence,' Edward added.

'It's really late. I should get going.' I said hurriedly.

Edward took me to his bed, instructing me to hold onto the electric guitar by its fret while adjusting the chord from the amp. 'Strum the E chord for me, will you.'

Reluctantly, I sat down, picked up the plectrum and did as he'd instructed, but the roaring sound amplified to an eerie screech. Apologizing softly, I counted to three, strumming the first chord ranging from the highest to the lowest.

'Let me show you.' Edward tugged my hair behind. His fingers were stroking mine.

I gulped when I felt him stroke my back. Slowly, I repeated the pentatonic scale positions, feeling amused, and yet my concentration had to match the height of the Empire State Building. As the scent of the reed diffuser began to permeate, his fingers intertwined with mine to experiment with the range of rhythmic positions on the fretboard to create a melodic riff.

'Try to relax,' he whispered.

Eros could be within reach, shrouded in hotness, like sanguineness brewed to last. Each prolonged gaze bore affection. I tried avoiding eye contact. Edward murmured a 4/4 time signature as the principal guide. I felt pleased when I realized I'd begun to meet his pacing.

'You're doing well.'

His words tickled my neck as his arms encircled my waist.

Synchronicity transpired that lick of sweetness and the melting passion of an ice-cream; my neck flushed with mild headiness. Our hearts thumped to supplement the sound of the pedalling drum. I envisioned the soft ocean waves by the beach. Edward leaned in slowly and then kissed me. Then, his touch swirled over me with intensity. I kissed him arduously, with the intention to unbutton his shirt. Edward smiled, cupping my cheek, as our lips locked.

My fingers wrapped around the nape of his neck as our lips met with intense desperation. We pulled away. His lips pressed against my forehead, hands sliding along my back. Edward softly pinched my chin, surveying my face, as the candlelight flickered. Stupefied and breathless, I blinked, responding to his gleaming smile. *Do not wake me from this dream*, I thought as I began to remove the notably-tested cautionary tape. I knew he was that missing puzzle piece I'd been searching for—the one I'd always wanted to come home to.

Yet, there was *fear*.

After another quick kiss on my lips, Edward moved to the drawer.

'What is this?' I asked, looking at the velvet sky blue box.

He beamed, carefully picking up the ornamental silver jewellery. 'It's been five months since we've known each other. And, this ring is my commitment, my promise, to be faithful to each other, and to begin this relationship with love.'

The taste of melancholy stayed in my windpipe.

He added, 'It may not be something expensive, but it represents my sincerity.'

'You've made progress and have achieved this milestone. But this relationship will be subject to public scrutiny, leading to a negative impact on your career.'

His watery eyes were fixed on mine, 'Your actions have proven *this* doesn't matter.'

'This isn't a blessed love, Edward,' I said. 'We'd be burned.'

Fourteen

On Friday afternoon, Daniel was as engrossed as an irregular bubble laser buzzing in the St Paul's Church conference room, competing in the Candy Crush Saga challenge—against me. Michael was flipping the official documents, which were in Hangul with English translation below the questionnaire bracket, from one page to the next.

The door opened, letting a breeze in.

'Sorry for being late,' said Uncle Clement. 'I had a prayer session via a video call with a parishioner.' He then turned to look at me. 'Emily, you look different today.'

'My cousin sister's been foolishly smiling since this morning,' Daniel said.

Stroking the promise ring over the platinum chain around my neck, I smiled to myself. 'Thank you. There's nothing better than to wake up feeling blessed.'

In fact, I'd been pulling an all-nighter, hustling in the pastry kitchen with my cousin—the reason being Uncle Sean had taken a half-day leave of absence to make offerings at the Guan Gong Temple at a stipulated, auspicious time, three times a week on alternate days, as it'd effectively benefit my aunt's rapid recovery. Additionally, I'd even started a one-week internship at the gourmet side. The promise ring had been my source of emotional perseverance.

'Praise the Lord Almighty,' Uncle Clement said, lifting his hands in a quick prayer. He dragged the executive chair. 'Michael, have you compiled the supplementary documents to be sent to the Korean Embassy?'

'Yes, I have. It should be complete in two days.'

'Let me know if you need a lift to Kuala Lumpur.'

Hands on his chest, Michael expressed his gratitude. 'Luckily, only my wallet has been stolen. I didn't sustain any major injuries except minor abrasions on my arms. Thank you for providing me with shelter, Mr Clement Ho.'

'You may call me Uncle Clement.'

'All right,' Michael agreed easily. 'In fact, I called the consulate officer yesterday morning. They should inform me if there're any important undertakings. Meanwhile, they need Uncle Clement's full name, contact number, and occupation in case of any emergency.'

'That's not a problem. I should be able to provide those.'

Michael murmured a word of quick gratitude, shifting between English and Korean.

Uncle Clement clasped his hands on the table. 'This is a pickpocket syndicate that allegedly targets tourists then uses their credit cards to make purchases. It is not safe to travel alone even in broad daylight nowadays, unlike thirty years ago.'

'I'm curious about your past occupation, Uncle Clement,' Daniel said. 'Were you a private investigator specializing in— catching cheating spouses?'

'I worked for an "authoritative organization",' said Uncle Clement, ever-so-calm. 'So, how has your stay and your work at Serendipity Sanctuary been so far, Michael?'

Michael's lips stretched wider. 'I've just started assisting at the soup kitchen after a week of volunteering at the pastry side. Daniel's father and the volunteers are very supportive. And Emily was not only helpful but also invented stuffed mango compote filling.'

Uncle Clement nodded, beaming like he'd just won the lottery.

'If only . . . ' Michael glowered. His expression looked like a duck's bill. 'If only Emily would wear gloves when handling the fresh chicken and fish fillets.'

'Well, I prefer to do so by touch, as Mama taught me.'

'I think it's important to improve the food and kitchen hygiene of the food centre,' Michael said. 'The basic sanitation requirements are a key element of quality control. In Korea, a QC programme was introduced to modify the—'

'I'm here to discuss the fruit of Daniel's labour, the fundraising food drive.'

'And my cousin sis will kick your Kimchi-butt out if you behave like a Mister-know-it-all,' Daniel said to Michael. 'Don't say I didn't warn ya.'

Uncle Clement became the referee to this bickering game.

Goalkeeper-Daniel had kicked the ball to Michael.

My cousin's rubbish tongue was testing Michael's resilience towards Shakespeare's retelling of how to handle Emily-the-shrew. My lips pressed together, trying not to laugh at Michael's long face. He exercised his right to remain silent though.

'That's awesome,' Uncle Clement broke the silence, beaming. 'I'm overjoyed to know that you're lending a helping hand. Raymond will be so proud of you.'

'My cousin's turning into a zombie,' I said. 'Pity him for not having good sleep. I was hoping to add this meaningful event to my resume for future reference. In the past, I've helped organize and have even participated in volunteer programmes for the underprivileged locals and the refugees, especially during Christmas and Malaysian festive seasons.'

Michael raised his hand. 'I want to be part of this fundraising food drive too, in addition to undertaking all tasks at Serendipity Sanctuary.'

Michael had been trying hard to convince us to include him—like an intelligentsia's last chance to market his knack. Now, the ball had been kicked into Uncle Clement's court. Kimchi-Mike was seemingly a godsend. It should've occurred to Uncle Sean that a genuine, authentic volunteer did exist.

'We're lacking volunteers,' Michael added. 'Let me inform my trustworthy manservant to send my university's reference letter by email to confirm my contribution to the volunteer programmes.'

'What's your opinion, Emily?' Uncle Clement asked.

Damn, Clement the sly fox was a crafty hunter but I wasn't a dumb bunny either. 'Would the Korean Embassy hold Serendipity Sanctuary and St Paul's Church accountable for approving their citizens over-volunteering under a tourist pass?'

'Yeah, we don't want to be sued for mistreatment.' Daniel supported me.

'My suggestion is,' Uncle Clement said, 'that Michael should be given a week to read this fundraising proposal.' He passed Michael the blue folder. 'Let me know if you need any clarification or you're always welcome to check with Daniel.'

'It should take me a day to finish,' Michael said.

'Better quit if you can't handle it,' said Daniel. 'It took me ten months to drill my brain to come up with this project.'

'I love challenges,' Michael said, looking at me.

I showed him a victorious fist—I wasn't going to back down.

* * *

Later that evening, Daniel and I accompanied Michael to shop for extra comfortable T-shirt to work in the kitchens. While waiting, Aunt Bridget asked us, on our group chat, to purchase facial sheet masks for her extended stay in Gleneagles.

'I'll drop you two off and then send these to Aunt Bridget.' Swinging two separate black and white logo paper bags, Daniel let out a regretful utterance, reading from another chat message. 'Look now, she wants a lip scrub.'

'What time did you tell Michael to wait for us?' I asked.

'That Kimchi should be here by now. I told him to hurry up. He was supposed to shop at H&M only. His family must be growing money on a banyan fig tree.'

'You stay here and wait for him,' I said. 'I'll go get the lip scrub.'

I walked into Sephora, thinking of how half of my former bathroom counter used to be filled with my personal skincare and beauty products—I never went without my non-comedogenic concealer and my full-coverage powder foundation, matching my lipstick colour with my skin tone; tweezers to pluck-and-shape my brows, sculpting powder for nose contouring. I was influenced by the *America's Next Top Model*. Those happy days should arrive again before long.

> Kimchi is missing

Sent by Unicorn-Egg.

Daniel's username on the chat app.

I sauntered to the men's clothing section at H&M, searching for Michael in every hidden corner. A retail salesperson looked up, squatting and retrieving a pair of jeans while inspecting the other denims under the merchandise rack. Black, acid-washed, and cobalt blue. I wished for Edward to be there. It had been the first and last time I stepped into the men's section—with him. The supervisor's perfunctory bashfulness betrayed her expression. I cleared my throat and asked if she'd seen Michael— roughly six feet tall, Korean, with a slender build, wearing faded blue jeans, and a black regular-fit polo shirt. 'Oh, and dimples on both cheeks,' I added as an afterthought. Wait . . . how did I even know this?

'He left about fifteen minutes ago,' the woman said.

On the other hand, Michael's phone seemed unreachable.

'Is that Kimchi with you now?' I spoke to Daniel over the phone.

'No,' Daniel replied. 'Probably kidnapped by K-crazed maniacs?'

Then, a familiar tone of voice from Uniqlo perked me up.

I couldn't believe my luck. 'I found him,' I replied to my cousin then hung up.

Michael turned to me as I yelled his name.

'You arrived just in time, Emily. Hold this bundle. The sales assistant is getting a collared shirt in my size now.' Michael said.

'How long are you planning to stay here?' I asked, looking at his elaborate shopping.

He shrugged. 'Pay it forward should be an unlimited timeline, shouldn't it?'

'The maximum authorized stay is ninety days for all foreigners. Extension is, of course, allowed for an additional two months subject to immigration's confirmation,' I said.

The cashier smiled from ear to ear receiving the Amex gold card from him, then started folding the apparels in assorted colours—hooded slip-ons, flannel long sleeves, loose cotton pants, and a pair of faded, baggy ripped denim jeans.

'Why did Uncle Clement want to see you after the meeting?'

Michael kept the receipt and the card inside a brown leather wallet. 'He told me to strive for my very best.'

'Is that all?' I shot him a suspicious look.

He exhaled without looking at me. 'Yes, that is all.'

* * *

In the pastry kitchen, I was folding the beaten egg whites into the custard batter. The air-ventilating blade echoed the sound of destructive, rattling shackles due to the greasiness and trapped dust that hadn't been cleaned.

'Are you free this Wednesday?' Uncle Sean asked in Cantonese. 'Thought of visiting your aunt.' Uncle Sean poured the tapioca flour onto the weighing scale. 'But you follow me to the hospital, just in case—'

Michael interrupted before I answered. 'I don't think Miss Bridget will chase you away if you're going to visit her with sincerity.'

Uncle Sean looked at him. 'You—understand Cantonese.'

'I worked in Hong Kong for a brief stint.' Michael said. 'It is awesome that Chinese-Malaysians speak Cantonese as well.'

'Great-grandpa was from Guangzhou, settled in the Perak state, worked in the tin-mining, and met a beautiful Samsui woman. They travelled to Penang by foot, got married, and had my grandpa in the Guandi Temple,' Uncle Sean drizzled the canola oil, brushing it on the tray before pouring in the corn batter.

'Your clan must've been blessed by the deities,' I said.

'Great-grandma's water broke when she was praying to Lord Guan Yu. It's a blessing from the God of War that she survived. Many women died of childbirth due to lack of medical breakthrough, trusting only traditional medicines.'

'Samsui woman, that sounds interesting,' Michael said.

I backed away when Michael noticed me. 'These women are Guangdong immigrants and work as manual labourers in Malaya and Singapore. Their heads are wrapped in red cloth to keep their hair clean from dust and debris.'

'But why can't they use white, black, or blue?' Michael asked.

'Oi, don't waste time,' Uncle Sean said. 'If you want to know more, go to the public library. Here, we talk about baking and kuih-making only.'

'What has been the most difficult kuih to make so far?'

Uncle Sean turned to Michael, 'Are you trying to steal our kuih recipe?'

'No, no, no, I don't mean that—' Michael's eyes grew quickly to the size of ping-pong balls, anxiously pleading innocence.

'I'm surprised you can pronounce "kuih" like a native speaker,' I said.

'Your grandma taught me,' Michael explained.

'She seldom talked to strangers,' Uncle Sean spoke to me in Mandarin.

'Really, I'm honoured to have learned something from her,' Michael said.

'You can understand Mandarin too?' Uncle Sean felt his stomach drop.

'I took Mandarin lessons in my teens. It was difficult but also pleasantly challenging. Hangul is the world's most scientific alphabet. Japanese is the easiest.' Michael turned to me. 'Every language is distinctive, the pride and joy of each diverse culture and identity; furthermore a language creates a special bond between people, like we're able to converse in English.'

'Hanzi writing should begin at a young age to develop the linguistic reflexes,' I said, hoping Michael wouldn't have picked up Hokkien or Malay in a short time.

'Little Niece, your hands and mouth are so productive,' Uncle Sean was being sarcastic, after inspecting the finished custard mixture in the stainless-steel bowl.

'I don't mind helping Michael finish the rest,' I said as I washed my hands.

'Very considerate and so cooperative, you see that Kimchi?' Uncle Sean peered at Michael—hard at work stirring and then removing the custard from the stove—seeming agitated by that nickname. Uncle Sean continued, 'The sky has turned upside down, and snow will fall soon.' He did not believe in my team spirit. 'My Little Niece has been very patient lately.'

Suddenly, as if these tools were his enemies, Uncle Sean dropped the garnishing brush, throwing in his apron as he realized how late it was. To the garage he sped off like a ball of chaotic fury, to wait for my cousin, who was supposed to have returned from the gym.

I stretched my arms the moment I heard Uncle Sean's footsteps fade.

'Time for some exercise,' I said.

Lifting the head in a circling motion clockwise and then anti-clockwise, I relaxed, eyes closed. I formed my hands into fists then gently released them. Repeating this motion several times and practising the breathing technique, I pushed forward and stretched my hamstring slowly, protruding my back to emancipate the muscle tension. Michael's arms circled, slightly imitating mine, stretching out to the right then to the left, rolling his shoulders with bending arms towards the bottom, then moving up with his hands on his hips. The hem of his shirt was displaying part of his abs and those pelvic bones. Sweat lines had dampened his torso, outlining the brawny muscles under the white shirt, emphasizing the length of his personal workout duration.

Edward had been the first man I'd seen half-naked.

I shook off the thought and then set the three pans of corn pudding in a separate ice water bath to cool them.

'Folks coming to the soup kitchen love the corn pudding because it's made from fresh ingredients.' Michael poured in the sweetened kernels into the wok, stirring evenly.

'It's Mama's recipe, passed down from her mother.'

'You guys can open a kuih shop in the future,' Michael said.

Not just interested in my promise ring then. Michael seemed to try his involvement in our traditional kuih venture too. I grinned. 'So, have you tried corn pudding before?'

'I did, but it was too sweet for me.' He glanced at me.

'I thought Koreans love sweet desserts, like red bean paste.'

'My mother is a health enthusiast. She'll send the food back to the kitchen if it's not to her taste. She did that many times, in the restaurant or to our private chef.'

'Hey, maybe we can sneak in a piece or two.'

'Are you sure, I don't want to get myself into any mess,' Michael joked.

'It's been ages since I've had it. There's more than enough for the soup kitchen.'

'Careful with the blade,' he said suddenly. 'It's really sharp.'

I took a deep breath. The audible cutting had relinquished the echoes as the blade hit the chopping board. *I could do it steadily—I have to be good at this.* The blade had sliced through the cob, and then stuck, deep. Fear seeped into my bones, but I tried to control the movement as the blade ascended to some degree with a deliberate wiggling motion. I relaxed my grip then angled to pull the blade out, counting to three. On failing, I repeated the process. But the blade refused to act jointly with me.

'Come, let me do the rest,' Michael said.

Then, the blade poked right into my index finger.

My blood, initially just dots, then started to trickle.

Michael grabbed my hand and led me to the tap, quickly turning it on. The gushing of my blood provoked the disturbance within. I felt Michael's hands rubbing mine, pressing the side of my finger to drain the blood. I grabbed the promise ring, tugging the platinum chain around my neck. The water had turned cold. Or was my body feeling the chills? The smell of chlorine made me vomit. I emptied my guts in the kitchen sink.

At least I didn't vomit on a human this time.

'Let me carry you to your room,' Michael's tone was soft.

'You . . . go back to the kitchen—' I was almost collapsing.

I felt Michael's arm around my back. Before I knew it, I was being lifted off the ground.

The chandelier swung like a pendulum in the hall. The sound of a pushed open door, the vision came in flashes as I braced myself for the next meteor crashing episode. Edward had finally returned and was lying beside me with that familiar scent. I cried out his name. I wanted him to see the promise ring, kept in immaculate condition. He should be proud of me.

Very proud.

Fifteen

Mr Han suddenly barged into Edward's suite.

I was arranging the bottled water in the pantry as the soloist started the domestic war of locution with his shitty-faced manager in their native language. Angrily, Edward removed the clear tapes from his papillary ridges, throwing them aside after long-hours of guitar practise.

Mr Han then ambled over to me. 'It is all because of you!'

Panicked, I gazed into his predatory eyes.

'You . . . finish already!' He pointed, then stormed out.

Edward rolled his eyes at the door. 'I'm sorry if he scares you.'

I shook my head, despite my heart accelerating. 'What's wrong?'

'Don't bother.'

'Did he . . . find out about us?'

Edward was stroking my arms to soothe me. Then, I felt his lips locking with mine. I couldn't deny that the intimacy felt good and banished my fear.

'He's always a pain in the butt.' Edward whispered on my lips.

Surprisingly, he could still joke.

'I've to return to work,' I said, biting my lips.

'I saw a cut on your hand.'

'Just a papercut,' I said to him.

Edward quickly pulled me into the bathroom, retrieving an elastic medicated plaster from his toiletries pouch then applied a Band-Aid on my open wound. 'The peppermint extract will soothe the pain. You'll feel the cooling effect.'

The soft touch of Edward's callused thumb had aggravated my emotional pain, doing so with a slow-burn kiss on my wounded skin. I stayed silent, looking at the adorable cartoon animals on the bandage. Such healing magic, the urge to kiss Edward was overpowering, it felt like my desire had turned its blade on me and was stabbing me, over and again. I didn't have the heart to push him away. He took my hands while my feet compelled me to run from him. A flickering spark of tension emerged. I avoided Edward's gaze—Edward who that had composed millions of lyrics, just to make me stay.

'Thank you for the cute Band-Aid,' I said.

Edward's arms circled around me, stopping me from leaving. He then whispered. 'The day will come when I put that promise ring on you.'

* * *

I stirred as Mama's finger was trailing along my black rose tattoos, claiming them as a broken China art piece. I'd considered adding red dots to denote cherry blossoms, shading the unfolding petals with a vibrant rose colour, an ode to my love for Edward, the soulful, enigmatic artist.

As I drifted awake, I realized two things.

Edward hadn't been in my room last night.

Michael Kim had.

'Why not go over to join him?' Mama said, pointing at Michael, as she half-walked half-limped on the reflexology path, dewy with sweat.

'I prefer to spend more time with you and your radiant smile,' I said to Mama as the morning sun kissed my skin.

'Your mouth is like honey. But very slow in pursuing a man.' Mama pinched my cheek. 'Should let down your toughness and behave daintily. The way to a man's heart is through his appetite, so learn to cook. Let me teach you to make sweet kuih to melt his . . . everything.'

'That poor guy is gonna get diabetes.' I chuckled lightly.

'Then, heal him with your sweet, magic words,' Mama whispered.

I blushed. 'Thanks, Mama, but I'm not interested in having a new relationship.'

'Is that why you've been touching and smiling at that ring around your neck?' Mama asked. 'It must be from someone you loved. Bring him here, I want to meet him.'

'There have been some complications in this relationship, so I can't bring him to you for the time being.' I bit my lips feeling like my heart was being sliced again.

'Like the sidewalk fortune teller's prediction, your destined love encounter is auspicious this year, but you've to act fast and quick. No delay,' Mama said.

I changed the topic. 'Who bandaged my index finger by the way?'

'Me—' Pain-proof Michael grimaced, furrowing his trimmed, bushy brow.

'TQVM,' I waved. 'Hope you'll enjoy therapy-ing your soles on the concrete substrate. The painful congestion and the tightness are just hurdles on your path to immortality.'

'Come and join me,' Michael said, panting and clad in one of the Uniqlo t-shirt he'd just bought. 'I don't want to be the one stepping on these stones alone.'

'Leave Emily out of this,' Mama said. 'I saw you carried Emily back to her room last night. It breaks my heart to see her not moving, laying like a dead fish. At least I didn't have to slap her face and she got up by herself this time.'

'Just overworked in the kitchen. No big deal.' I was massaging my forehead. That was part of it.

Furthermore, Aunt Bridget's post-fall second-chance-to-live episode had served as a wake-up call. Whether or not her movie script would be chosen by Hollywood, she was driven by a passion to create. I got goosebumps thinking of her perseverance.

It resembled Edward's. My cousin had thought of not keeping Mama in the dark whenever she asked about her daughter. It hurt me to my core to lie. But I was sure Uncle Raymond would have the matter in hand. The niece and nephew's duty was to fulfil their filial obligation wisely.

The painful recollection of Edward and my time together had also been doing me in.

'I told Raymond to give you a three-day medical leave,' Mama said.

'Thanks Mama but one day is enough.' I gratuitously pecked her cheek.

'It includes weekends, Emily,' Michael chimed in, drinking from his water bottle. 'Lest you need a tetanus injection. Luckily, the blade wasn't rusted.'

'Thank you for your help yesterday,' I said to him.

'Oh, Emily is blushing,' Mama said, clapping like a child.

'Everyone should bloom beautifully on this beautiful morning,' I said.

'Tell me, are you interested in my granddaughter?' Mama asked Michael.

Michael quickly looked elsewhere, then at me as I pursed my lips.

'Did I say something wrong? I'm just asking. Curious,' Mama said.

'I see your condition has improved a lot.' I placed my arm over Mama's shoulder. 'The recent medical report shows you're back on your feet,' I leaned in and whispered, 'also planning for your kuih-making as comeback.'

Mama kept playing dumb, avoiding my interrogating gaze.

Thanks to Aunt Bridget of exposing her mother in our Lau-d & Praud chat group.

'Emily is like a friend to me,' Michael said, not one to be tongue-tied. 'I have a lot of respect for her. Not only that, she's . . . beautiful inside out.'

The last line, you idiot! Over exaggeration was not it.

'Oh, so you've seen Emily's *inside*?' Mama cackled, then said to him, 'The Lau daughters are hard to pursue. But I can give you some tips and tricks.'

'Mama, he meant by my heart, right Michael?' I made eye contact with him.

'Of course it's her heart,' Michael clarified, deadpan. 'What else?'

Mama looked at us, back and forth. 'All right, I'll let it go, only for this time.'

* * *

Aunt Bridget's eyes were closed as she enjoyed her Balinese massage, courtesy the hospital's by-appointment service. 'Runway-Mikey has taken your job. That's why you're here.'

'Please not his name for at least five minutes,' I said.

'Be grateful, would you?' Aunt Bridget said.

'What—?'

'For saving Emily-damsel from last night's kitchen distress.'

'How'd you know?' I raised my voice, *loving* my comedically slapstick family.

'Bridget's receptive antenna is better tuned than CNN, BBC, and Al-Jazeera.' She exhaled in relief as the masseur massaged her neck.

It must've been Uncle Sean who told her, his story no doubt corroborated by Mama. Resting my folded arms on the couch, I smirked. 'I guess the pastry-side-someone finally worked up that courage to drop by.'

My aunt kept quiet. I would've bought it if her facial muscles hadn't been twitching in an attempt to display that hidden bliss within. My dear Aunt was in sweet, sweet denial. 'I . . . don't know what you mean.'

'Far on the horizon but close at hand,' I drew a love shape with an arrow struck across on the sheet. The blush on her cheeks betrayed her stoic silence.

Aunt Bridget rubbed the memory of the heart I'd drawn off the sheets and took my hands. 'That short stint-romance with the ex-lover has become part of your memory. Runway-Mike has the height, the face, and the—'

'Michael is yours if you're interested.'

'If only he was twenty years older,' my aunt said as the masseuse placed two slices of lemons on her eyes, applying an avocado-paste mask on her face.

'Don't try to matchmake me with him,' I said.

The citrusy slices immediately dropped on Aunt Bridget's lap the moment she sat up. 'You're not young anymore. Need I remind you of your date of birth?'

I flipped through a *Cosmopolitan* magazine, humming the twelve major scales.

'Wake up, Niece! That EAMJ is in the past, a memory that you can swim and dive in but do nothing else about. A good man is difficult to find. You'll be missing another boat.'

'Think I want a yacht this time.' I smirked, took a bite from a red apple, the healthiest and the most cursed fruit of knowledge, a ripened ovary.

'Stew this kimchi, my niece.'

I couldn't sit there with Aunt Bridget resuming her Meat Sermon.

I owed no one an explanation about my private life.

* * *

A scrawny looking man dressed in a poncho-like robe of the Tao religion was offering prayers, hands begging the bluest clouds. Then, a man in a bright red shirt and black pants, holding a feng shui compass, pivoted to the opposite direction, moving his index finger to emulate the magnetic flow of the needle. 'What's going on here?' I asked.

'This is for your good fortune, Little Niece,' Uncle Sean said softly.

A new kitchen god had just been installed, facing the pastry kitchen entrance. Traditionally, the altar had to be located right above the stove. The deity could watch over our conduct from where the incense and the offerings were to be made on a daily basis. It was a sudden decision, with no prior memo or notification from Uncle Raymond.

'The pastry side is closed for today only for the newly installed kitchen god to adjust to the kitchen's surroundings,' Uncle Sean said.

I wondered how Uncle Clement would think of this ridicule.

The Taoist priest greeted and then spoke to Uncle Raymond in Taishanese, a dialect so close to extinction that I couldn't possibly understand its linguistic syntax.

'This is to improve your weak Ba-Zi, Emily,' Mama said. Ba-Zi referred to the Four Pillars of Destiny, the Chinese astrological concept to understand and strengthen one's fate.

* * *

After dinner at the food truck, my cousin said he had a place to take me to.

We crossed the intersection from the seafront promenade towards the alley, bypassing the lit Whiteaways Arcade, the commercial avenue with a historical charm. Then, a sign written in chalk pointed upward from the stairs turning to the left—'The Hyde Park Skinhead'.

Just, what a name!

Daniel was squeezing past a line of people descending the stairs.

Following closely, I heard a trail of laughter and cheering with live music and glasses clinking inside, a neon green haired woman was guarding the entrance.

Daniel pointed at me and then himself.

A woman with buzz cut tilted her head, smiling at me.

Two men walked out the room, looking tipsy. Daniel then pulled me to the side while the woman spoke through a handheld intercom.

'How come there's no signboard outside?' I whispered.

Daniel covered his mouth while replying. 'Not many know of this place.'

'I would've dressed differently if I knew we're going clubbing,' I said.

Daniel batted my concern away and smiled. 'Trust me, you'll love this place.'

'How much is the cover charge?' I asked.

The woman called us over, pressing the self-inked rubber stamp on the back of our hands. 'It's a peace sign,' I marvelled, shoving the luminescent marking in Daniel's face.

'I told them many times to change it.'

How many times has Daniel been here?

My cousin opened the door to the noise within.

Although I was concealing my amazement, I was in awe of the interior of the cocktail lounge, which was painted in fluorescent amber using what seemed like the multicoloured palette knife scraping technique. A collection of vinyl records was displayed near the entrance, varying from international and local indie artistes to the legends and the living. I spotted a crowd gathered in a corner, flipping through poetry pamphlets and chapbooks.

A woman with fluttering long hair was conducting a sound-check on the keyboard. Next to her was a guitarist and a bassist while another man was setting up a drum kit.

The hanging chandelier was below the mic stand, reminding me of the open mic, where the amateur and the professional performers supposedly stood. Next to the bar, customers were queueing up to surrender their coupons at the paying counter to collect their free drink.

'What do you think of this place?' asked Daniel.

'That's the pride flag,' I said. It hung against the wall, flying parallel with the AC vent mist. 'It reminds me of this open mic I attended at a bar back in Kuala Lumpur.'

'The washroom is right behind you just in case there's any emergency. But it is shared by everyone. They don't have different ones for men and women. Just thought I'd inform you, so you won't be shocked.'

'Dan-Dan-*Sambal*—' A smooth voice hollered from the Americana-retro diner table. A man stood up and then hugged my cousin tightly, pecking his cheek.

'Ken-Ken-Belacan—' said my cousin, patting the man's back.

'Belacan' means spicy shrimp paste chilli, a condiment—Gen-Z's love language.

'You've brought a new guest over.' The man smiled from ear to ear.

'Meet my cousin from the capital city,' Daniel introduced.

I extended my hand. 'Nice to meet you, I'm Emily.'

'Kenneth Woo,' he said as he shook my hand . . . daintily.

I shot Daniel a surprised look.

'Finally, I get to meet my Sambal-boyfriend's relative,' Kenneth said.

I felt a little faint and slowly extricated myself from his excited grip.

Kenneth giggled then showed me the rustic menu scribbled across the display, made up of baked goods, sandwiches, sparkling juices, mocktails, and alcoholic drinks. 'I must arrange for you both to meet my family. Let me know when you're free, Emily.'

I knew why Michael was out of my cousin's league. I looked at my cousin and smiled, murmuring 'Congratulations' under my breath.

'What . . .' Daniel blushed. 'Ken and I are just . . . friends.'

'Order whatever you want, Emily. I'm the owner of this place,' Kenneth said, raising his right hand with poise. 'We still have some dough in the fridge, right? Let's bake a pizza or two, maybe toss in a plate of spaghetti marinara. Let's hold a feast. Go big or go home!'

'By the way, the stage looks dead-quiet tonight,' Daniel started.

'We have one more slot for a spoken word up for grabs,' Kenneth said.

'Your therapist wants you to concentrate on your hobby. There's already a spot here where you can perform.' Daniel winked at me. 'Whenever you're ready.'

'Thanks.' I eyed the front stage. 'Hopefully soon.'

Knowing that I'd been a seasonal spoken word poet, Kenneth invited me to the first-class seat on the sofa. The crowd had taken their respective places as the chandelier dimmed, conveying a sense of fellowship. I clapped as the performer recited her line, reminiscing about a particular moment with Edward.

* * *

I bowed to the crowd on the stage of the open mic night.

'Love your beautiful poetry, Em.' Edward was screaming from the crowd.

I pulled him out of the bar and headed upstairs, being vigilant about his safety. 'How'd you find me and this place?'

'Thanks to Sabrina,' Edward said. 'She called an e-hailing cab for me.'

I gazed deeply into his eyes.

'I gave my manager a long list of things to buy,' he confessed. 'He's going to be damn pissed.'

Edward chuckled. 'I can only stay for an hour.'

I held his arm, trying to comfort him and tell him to stay cool as the chattering from downstairs got louder. An interracial couple was standing halfway from the stair railing. I exchanged a polite nod then raised my glass at them.

'I hope this surprise didn't scare you,' Edward whispered.

I shook, taking his hands. 'Thanks for coming.'

His pupils dilated, like they did whenever he felt like he was being appreciated.

We hadn't had any physical contact since the paper cut incident. It was all I could do to stop myself from helping him escape his manager and drag him into the wild. A place where no one would know him, the start of our very own dangerous adventure.

'Back there, the female cashier mistook me for a Korean actor,' he said innocently, ignorant of what was going on in my mind.

I chuckled.

Edward pulled me to the next floor. Our footsteps were quiet and my shoulder almost bumped into a stack of empty bottles that were camouflaged in partial darkness. Dim lighting shone from the headroom below. I whispered, 'Stay here. Don't leave me.'

He glanced at me as my grip tightened on his wrist.

Edward stroked my cheek and then took my hands in his. 'Even ghouls will have to ask for my permission before taking you away.'

I leaned against his broad chest, feeling safe.

'Sabrina told me you took a day off.'

'I'm one of the opening acts for two international poets and an indie musician, it's best to steer clear of any unnecessary mixed energy before the show.' I gazed up at him.

Edward pursed his lips. 'If you don't mind, may I have the last two lines of your poem? Don't get me wrong, I'm not stealing them.'

'It is still a work-in-progress.' I copied the lines from my phone onto his. 'I'm lucky to have a famous singer-songwriter-soloist praising my work.'

'For each love it holds so dearly, for each breath it becomes you,' Edward recited from the Notes app. 'What inspires you to write these beautiful verses?'

'Well, my muse is everywhere.' I had to lie.

'I agree,' he said. 'I do get inspired even in the washroom.'

I laughed. 'That's pretty awkward, but that will do as well.'

Faint echoes from downstairs were a reminder of rationality. Hindering our laboured breaths, our eyes were caught on one another.

'Has anybody ever complimented your beauty?'

I bashfully shook my head, watching my reflection trapped inside his eyes. 'You're the first.' *That matters.* I didn't say that part out loud.

He grinned. 'What's your impression of me then?'

I felt his breath along my neck. 'Hmm . . . you're a compassionate and free-spirited human, despite several endorsement deals, and millions of followers on social media.'

'Are those threatening to you?' He frowned.

'I don't give a damn, frankly.'

He cupped my face. 'I really want you to be my—' His words were cut short as he stumbled, a little off-balance.

My arms encircled Edward's waist in an effort to steady him as his body leaned against mine. 'How many glasses have you had?' I carefully sank to the floor, taking him with me.

He let out a little laugh. As I was about to open my mouth, his thumb gently brushed over my lips. His passionate gaze suddenly turned teary-eyed. I vowed to be strong in the face of whatever was to come as the agonizing pin-drop silence persisted. I heard Edward inhale shakily. 'Mr Han's forcing me to return to Seoul,' he choked out.

The nightmare that had haunted me had just come true.

Sixteen

'Meet and greet here I come!' Daniel waved the passes.

Uncle Raymond looked on, stopping me from getting up to help as my cousin lost balance while imitating Michael Jackson's antigravity lean. However, he picked himself back up, ending the slipshod breakdance with an awkward, rotational arm movement that ended with a crotch grab and a high pitched 'Aww'.

My cousin had always been a devout jester.

'That's so great, I'm happy for you!' I clapped in encouragement. 'I know there will be a K-Army Stew party tonight.' *Now, let's get back to the documents in-hand.*

'There's just one thing stopping me,' Daniel said. 'I need a leave application form. The event is in KL next Saturday. I care not whether you'll be angry or not. Biu-jie is coming with me to this once-in-a-lifetime meeting with the Korean ambassador.'

'Well, both of you are booked for next week,' Uncle Raymond handed the duty sheet to Daniel. 'And the week after.'

Daniel tossed the paper aside. 'Since when has Uncle Clement taken over your position as the HR manager?'

Uncle Raymond looked at Daniel. 'This was a unanimous decision taken by the committee during the organization's internal meeting session.'

'The godfathers should've stayed at home, doing yoga and meddling with their own family affairs instead of dipping their hands in ours,' Daniel said.

'Have you lost your mind?' Uncle Raymond raised his voice.

'I guess even the toughest nail gets rustier as time goes by,' Daniel said.

'I'm not being demoted, it's just a minor shift in authorization.' Uncle Raymond rolled his eyes. 'Look, this whole place and this bungalow sheltering your potato-head would not exist without the help of St Paul's Church. Be grateful, my son.'

'Can we speak to Uncle Clement to rearrange with the two other volunteers? I'm sure Daniel and I won't mind replacing their—' I began, hoping that would cease the brewing civil war.

Uncle Raymond cut in. 'Daniel Lau, both your wings have become steel it seems. You know we are lacking volunteers at the food drive during the weekends especially. All you think of is having fun. You're so irresponsible.'

'Fine.' Daniel stormed out of the office.

My uncle stopped me as I was about to go after Daniel.

* * *

Outside the pastry kitchen, Uncle Raymond passed me a lingfu amulet to be worn around my neck. The yellow paper with the Taoist symbol, painted with the talismanic incantation, had been folded into a triangular shape and tied with a red string.

The feng shui master and the Taoist priest had predicted that my blackout at K-Licious-Delish and the pastry kitchen meltdown could've possibly stemmed from clashes with my *Ba-Zi*. They'd prophesied my astrological birth chart based on the month, the day and the hour of the birth year provided by Mama through the Qi-Men forecasting under the *Book of Wealth and Life Pursuits*. Honestly, if these pseudo-science masters could identify everyone's Four Pillars of Destiny by taking control of their fate, the world would've been the playing ground of humanity, not crying for apocalypse in the unending war.

'The *lingfu* is to protect you from the unseen spirits.' Mama said. 'You were born in the Year of the Rat, under the Wood element. You need a Tiger to protect you.'

I didn't pay much heed to her and was inspecting her *kuih bingka* recipe. I noticed she added the tapioca starch into the grated cassava, sprinkling an equal amount of sugar and a pinch of salt, and then mixing it.

Edward was born in the Year of the Tiger.

Luckily, Mama knew nuts about my 'failed' suicide admission.

'I want to compile your recipes in a journal,' I said.

'Don't change the topic.' Mama smiled, pouring the mixture into a tray.

I took the tray and kept it to cool inside the fridge.

She patted my head. 'Remember, you've to leave by midnight.'

I gave this fairy godmother a long hug, feeling her peck my cheek as she let go. I vowed to never forget to add that pinch of salt as an additional ingredient. I bit my lip and frowned when I noticed Mama's slouching figure, reaching to hold Auntie Noon's hand for comfort. Auntie Noon winked at me when Michael wasn't looking. Aunt Bridget's next script should be titled, *Everybody Loves Michael Kim*.

'Are you feeling all right?' Michael said softly.

'Let's start baking,' I said after Mama left with Auntie Noon.

Michael retrieved the tart crust from the fridge, which I'd told him to prepare in the evening. 'We're going to have a tranquil and peaceful night starting now.'

I poured in the strawberries and blueberries from the packets into a steel colander, rinsing them with water from the filter tap. 'That's something new to me.'

Michael sprinkled some flour on the table and then dropped the cold dough on it. 'Mama has stopped clashing the cymbals. I told her those aren't needed to scare evil spirits when you're protected by the lingfu amulet.'

'What a brilliant idea,' I murmured. 'And none of us thought of that.'

'It is just a reasonable thought,' Michael said. 'By the way, how's Miss Bridget?'

'She's doing fine and should be discharged soon after completing her script.' I turned on the stove, adjusted it to low heat.

'How's it like to have a retired actress aunt?' Michael asked.

'I'm proud,' I said, trying to disregard her unusually strange behaviour.

'I would agree with that.' Michael narrowed his eyes, staring at the promise ring on my neck. 'The accessory looks like it complements the lingfu.'

The powerful forces of the universe might've forced some sense into this proper stranger. He should be credited for empathizing with my private emotion—doing so with a dash of humour. Aunt Bridget would probably have praised him if she had been here and strongly coaxed me to reconsider him. I even had to her from comparing Edward with Michael. The lingfu was meant to protect, and the other accessory—the promise ring—was a living memory of Edward that I carried with me. The latter was irreplaceable. Meanwhile, be ready for civil war between Mama and my pious mom, if she ever stumbled upon this Taoist amulet.

'Do you have any idea what the ink on the amulet was made of during ancient times?' Michael rolled up his sleeves, changing the topic.

'It's made from a rooster's blood.' I shot him a purposefully eerie stare.

Michael raised his eyebrows. 'That's gruesome.'

The mixed berries simmered inside the saucepan, forming bubbles. I scooped up a bit to taste the sweetly sourish compote and then turned off the stove so as not to overcook it.

Michael gave me a thumb's up after tasting it, struck speechless by how good it was.

'Don't finish it,' I warned.

'Why not—?' Michael licked the last traces of the compote from the wooden spoon. 'Didn't we buy enough of the straw-and blue-berries?'

Michael's phrasal inventions weren't as impressive as the illusionist David Copperfield's attempts to make the Statue of Liberty disappear. 'Mama just reminded me not to stay here after midnight. It's bad for my Ba-Zi.'

'And you really believe in the feng shui master?'

'I'm accommodating for Mama's favour,' I muttered.

Our gazes suddenly met.

I looked away. 'Any Korean superstitions you wouldn't mind sharing with me?'

Michael pursed his lips. 'I grew up in a non-religious household and was sent to a boarding school in the US when I was twelve. I used to stay in a relative's house, so I adopted Korean-American culture, eating mostly fast food, pizzas, and spaghetti and playing basketball and baseball. And when summer came, I'd have a backyard barbeque with my cousins. To me, Seoul is somewhat in-between a familiar stranger and a long-lost lover, too far to grasp.'

I looked up at the ventilator fan against the wall. 'You've cleaned that too?'

'Daniel did that,' Michael said.

'My cousin is acrophobic despite his towering height,' I said.

'He's also cleaned the fridge, washed the kitchen sinks, the cookware and the utensils, and mopped the whole floor,' Michael continued, slicing the extra pastry crusts from the side and then grouping the dough strips to set them aside. Poor Cousin Dan must be distressed at not being granted the chance to meet and his one-and-only Korean oppa.

I let out a chuckle looking at Michael's face.

'Why? Is there anything there?' he asked, rubbing his cheek.

I handed him a clean white cloth. 'Wipe that flour off.'

He thanked me and took the white cloth, wiping slowly, like his face was made of glass. Fragile and thin-skinned. He clumsily missed the spot. Instead, he smeared the stain all the way down to his chin. I took it from him. 'Stay still. Don't move,' I said as I wiped it off. Once and then twice. Doing him a favour— repaying his kindness for being there during my blackout.

His eyes fixed on mine. I avoided his gaze, despite, or perhaps because of, the tenderness there.

'Thank you, Emily.'

I smiled. 'You're welcome.'

As informed by the geomancer, Daniel had to be absent from tonight's mixed berry pie experiment because his Ba-Zi was clashing with the Grand Duke Jupiter, a legendary god who supervised people's fortune from heaven. My cousin was also born in the Year of the Rat (of the fire element)—twelve years my junior.

Michael preheated the oven after pricking holes in the rolled-out pie dough. 'I heard the feng shui master had chosen someone born in the Year of Tiger to take care of the pastry kitchen and its administrative tasks.'

'Yes,' I said then turned to him. 'Wait a minute, were you born in the year of—'

I was interrupted by Michael's playful roar. He laughed. 'You're two years older than me, Emily-*noona*.'

'Emily,' I pointed a spatula at him. 'You get that through your head.'

* * *

Daniel messaged the Lau-d & Praud group chat, informing us that he won't be joining us for breakfast; a daredevil defying traditions upheld by Uncle Raymond. Meanwhile, Aunt Bridget uploaded her Sunday roast breakfast photos. Mama looked pleased when she noticed that Michael had taken the seat beside me.

A plate of Javanese-style *mee rebus* were before Mama. 'Thank you Noon for fulfilling my request,' she said, devouring the thick yellow gravy.

'I asked a volunteer from the gourmet kitchen to get the recipe from the chef at the Rasa Sayang hotel. I heard he hails from Java, Indonesia,' Uncle Raymond said.

'A recipe is dead without the chef's magical hands and sensitive touch,' Mama said, grabbing Auntie Noon's hand. 'You've worked very hard in the family and gourmet kitchen. We're short of volunteers, I know.'

'I can handle it, ma-in-law.'

'I think, from next week onwards, ask Emily and Michael to assist you on the gourmet side for one week,' Mama said.

'I'll be interning at the food drive with Daniel next week,' I said.

Mama tapped the table. 'Girls cannot stay under the sun for so long, later their skin becomes burned like coal. Men will run away.' Mama pursed her lips.

I tried hard not to laugh at Mama's concern, finding it frivolous. I gave Uncle Raymond a meaningful glance, indicating that the underlying contradiction in my roster had to be discussed later. I finished my soup and moved to the meal section, filling my bowl with pressed rice and ladling in the coconut milk soup with assorted vegetables and deep-fried tempeh—an Indonesian-inspired dish made from fermented soybean—then combined it with peanut sauce.

'Emily's problem has been solved! If you happen to faint again,' Mama said to me. 'Michael will be there to catch you.'

My face flamed with embarrassment. I did my best to reply nonchalantly. 'No need to be scared when I'm wearing the world-class amulet.'

Patience was the best virtue to combat any stress aggressor. Thank god I hadn't dropped the pair of tongs. 'It provides confidence aside from warding off evil.'

Michael chewed on the sourdough toast and gave Mama a wide grin. The garlic smeared on the toast spread on his teeth, reminding me of Edward shoving his face at me, I would ignore his impish greetings, nonetheless enlivening at heart, especially the morning shift.

'Daniel will be there to catch me if I were to fall again,' I said, apropos of nothing.

'Oh, I think Dan-Dan should be in the soup kitchen more often,' Mama said.

Wiping his mouth, my uncle said, 'Ma, let me talk to Clement about this.'

'Why does it have to be him?' Mama said.

'Three authorized persons rather than one to be responsible.' Uncle Raymond sipped his Kopi-O, a highly caffeinated 'Penang Espresso', then poured some into Mama's cup. The robust and aromatic hand-roasted coffee was nostalgic for me. 'I still remember Ma used to make it in a big teapot, drinking it like water from morning to night.'

'Very good, past memories still stick nicely in your brain,' Mama said.

'I'm going back to work now,' I said.

'All of you remain seated,' Mama tapped her walking cane.

'No one is supposed to leave, not until I get all things right and straight.'

Everyone froze at Mama's command.

I remembered my father being asked to leave when there had been a dispute among the Laus to be discussed. I was too young to be involved in adult matters, and so he'd take me with him. Auntie Noon finished her *curry laksa*, eyeing her husband, then glancing at me. However, even the most obtuse person would've been able to ascertain that Mama had somehow accepted Michael as part of . . . our family.

'I want to volunteer at the gourmet and the pastry kitchen,' said Mama.

'Ma, I do not agree with this,' Uncle Raymond said.

Mama narrowed her eyes. This was where the emperor began to mellow as his mother, the Empress Dowager, spoke. 'I want to assist in the soup kitchen too.'

'Those kitchens aren't a safe place for you, Ma,' Uncle Raymond said.

'Someone planted a C-4 under the stove?'

'Ma, I'm concerned for your safety and health. I'd be a bad son if I let anything happen to you.'

'I've been rolling in and out of the kitchen, cooking meals for the cadets and their superiors while taking care of you and your two sisters' kiddie buttholes. An inactive lifestyle will speed-up my dementia according to my geriatrician,' Mama said. 'Unless you've booked a coffin for me—'

'Please, don't say that.' We said in one voice, including Michael's.

My uncle furrowed his bushy brows, inundated with nonsensical-nuisance and his beloved mother's ominous choice of words. 'Sean told me you've been working hard in the pastry kitchen lately.'

'I want to help my Dan-Dan's fundraising food drive project, and secondly,' Mama looked at Michael and me for an alarming amount of time. 'I want to showcase my kuih-making skill, testing my brain and the muscles in my hand to avoid any rusting. When you're working with a looming deadline, you learn to grab any chance to do what you have to.'

'I'm sure you'll live a long life, Mama,' Michael said.

'Michael is such a good boy. Your mother really raised you well.'

Blushing slightly, Michael took a bite from his buttered toast.

'How come my grandson isn't here for breakfast?' Mama asked.

'Daniel's at the Rifle Range Flats for the food drive,' I said.

Mama started wiping her tears with a handkerchief. 'A mass grave had been discovered over there in the sixties when the construction of the flats was underway. All remains found were of the victims who perished during the Japanese occupation.'

'Ma, what are you trying to say here?' Uncle Raymond said coolly.

Oscar nominee Mama weaved the story of her intergenerational trauma as I slowly chewed the pandan steamed cake. She had merely been three when the WWII air-raid siren threatened her village, barely giving her time to digest the extensive chaos and bombing by the Japanese soldiers invading Malaya. 'The war was as painful as a family argument between a parent and a child. You could be angry at Daniel, but your heart will always hurt for him.'

Uncle Raymond flipped to the finance section. 'Daniel is old enough to get married and shouldn't be fanboying over celebrities. He's lucky that I didn't throw him out for spending the entire night on the rooftop terrace, dirtying the floor with ramen noodle bits.'

Michael stood up, bowed. 'I'm so sorry, Uncle Raymond. I should've cleaned it for him. Daniel is like my *dongsaeng*. I should take care of him.'

Tenderly, I tugged at Michael's t-shirt hem. 'Take it easy, sit down.' Having a stranger volunteer for breakfast had loosened Uncle Raymond's tense shoulders a bit.

Mama turned to Michael and me. 'The making of the mixed berry tart last night was great, huh? Be sure to let me have a slice. Don't finish it all by yourself.'

'It was a success, Mama,' I said with a straight face.

'Do you not feel well after wearing the lingfu?' Mama said to me.

'No, I feel exceptionally well.'

Mama nodded. 'You are all dismissed. I need to talk to Raymond only.'

My uncle suggested that they continue the discussion in his office.

Seventeen

I stood beside my buffoon cousin at the KLIA arrival hall.

After clearing the immigration lane, we looked on as an inscrutable looking officer interrogated Michael at the international check-out line before slapping the rubber stamp on his passport.

Three days ago, Daniel had entered my room in a blustery mood, grabbed my hand for a beat-deaf dance move, squeezed the meet and greet VIP passes into my grip, hollering—'Dan and Em Take Kuala Lumpur'. Uncle Raymond had 'surrendered' and had arranged for volunteers to replace us. Mama must've orchestrated this with her crown-prince during breakfast.

Mama had one condition: Michael had to tag along.

My Ba-Zi wasn't fit for travelling this year, at least that's what the geomancer had told Mama, warning her that I would meet an undiscovered fatal disaster if I did.

Hence, Michael-the-Fire-Tiger had to be the Wood-Rat's chaperone. Just to accompany dear-Daniel, I was to allow such collateral.

'The immigration officer must've thought we're drug mules teaming up with a handsome gangster to sling the bling-bling,' Daniel said, slinging his backpack over his shoulder.

'How disappointing, I've been missing Fashionista-Smelly-Dan for a while.' I glared at the mundanely-styled Daniel, from top to toe.

'I'd advise you to embrace open-mindedness, and brace yourself for what you're about to see'—Daniel put on his shades, dragging his suitcase—'at the convention centre.'

We hopped into a high-speed train and had quick lunch at KL Sentral—only because I'd been craving Hainanese chicken chop rice and cold brew coffee.

Michael ordered the same as me.

The digital display of arrival time showed it was 10.15 a.m. as we disembarked from the light rail transit, reaching the KLCC rapid transit station right at 11.11.

My cousin gestured to be quiet, closing his eyes and praying.

There was a busker entertaining the crowd with retro music, playing the best slow rock ballads. The lead performer initiated the applause while serenading the crowd with an upbeat mash-up, to liven up the sequestered atmosphere along the indoor underpass tunnel, which connected to the most iconic shopping mall and the convention centre where the meet and greet was held.

'Welcome to Suria KLCC!' Tour-Guide-Daniel said, sipping from the venti-sized boba tea with extra tapioca pearls.

There were pop-up retail stores at the concourse level selling modern and traditional clothes in addition to handmade cookies of assorted flavours, hand-woven straw clutches, colourful headscarves, and bejewelled accessories. Some items were tagged with lower prices to clear stock from the previous festive celebrations. Five men-in-black mall security personnel were on duty, speaking through their earpieces as two were guarding the centre stage. The digital pixel bulletin was showcasing the attractive tourists' packages and destinations with the 'Visit Malaysia' logo.

'This must be your first time here, Mike?' Daniel asked.

'I've been here for a luxury-brand watch's roadshow.'

'Have you been modelling part-time for the timepiece company?' Daniel asked.

Michael seemed to be allergic to such compliments. 'I had a two-day stopover before heading to Thailand and Laos. I stayed in a traveller's inn. The capital city is truly beautiful.'

'That's what all tourists say.' Daniel shot me a look.

'Suggestion,' I raised my hand. 'Let's check into our rooms.'

'Should we go get some cake and a cup of coffee?' Michael asked energetically.

'I'll see you guys at the convention centre.' I walked ahead of them.

* * *

Moments later, I marched confidently into my favourite bookstore.

For now, I'd kept myself away from Michael Kim, enjoying my short stint of freedom. The Fire-Tiger must've thought I was taking a nap in my hotel room.

Uncle Sean had some concerns about Michael's undiscussed identity and his interest in Mama's traditional kuih-making craft. Daniel's surveillance had also confirmed that Michael had been ogling my chest non-stop. Honestly speaking, his attention always seemed to be at the area around my neck, at the promise ring. While packing my suitcase last night, I'd expressed clearly to Mama that Michael and I were just teammates. Mama, however, would not give up on her matchmaking endeavours without trying harder.

Suddenly, a figure stood beside me. 'What a dense text you have there.'

The voice sounded familiar.

I turned and was startled. 'How—how'd you find me?'

'Daniel has been a very great friend lately . . .' Michael winked.

'You're stalking me, dammit!'

Immediately, a couple in the thriller/mystery aisle turned in our direction.

Michael shushed me and then surveyed the premise. 'Nice bookstore.'

I didn't reply.

He continued. 'I've been to their main store in Shinjuku. I'm happy to recommend the mega-size Kyobo Book Centre in Gwanghwamun Plaza to you. With selections of international and local books, including music CDs and DVDs, a huge stationery section, and officeware and decorative items.'

I moved to the Asian literature section.

'The place is accessible from the Gwanghwamun Station on the Seoul Subway Line.'

I looked up, and his gaze stuck to mine.

Kinokuniya at Suria KLCC had been a literary, magical escapade for me ever since college years—a timeless peacekeeper, a solace of contentment for bibliophiles. Their homophonic background music was good for relaxation, I'd brought Edward here for a quick browse-around. He'd joked that the footsteps of the children running from the mezzanine to the main level could've been ours. We realized we were running late and rushed from there. Things got worse when we spotted Mr Han at the aparthotel's front entrance. I had to loiter around for fifteen minutes before returning to work. Madam Ong gave me a verbal warning. However, I felt like it had been a risk worth taking.

I typed unfeigned lines in my Notes app, ignoring Michael.

'The wind caresses the cobalt sea/beneath the unfurling words,' Michael read out loud from my app. 'I prefer non-fiction over poetry, but this is—' He took a snapshot with his phone.

'That's an invasion of privacy.' I put my phone away.

'Pardon me for being in love with these captivating, awe-inspiring verses.' He trailed after me. 'By the way, what's the title of the poem?'

'Untitled.' I turned to face him. 'Trying to plagiarize it? What a *great* idea.'

'I know what copyright infringement is,' Michael said.

'And stop following me,' I muttered.

'I need to make sure you're safe and sound throughout this trip.' He ascended the spiral staircase leading to the open-plan café.

'How can I possibly *hate* you,' I turned. 'I've trained my brain to manifest self-love and self-care through the practice of positive energy,' I said, moving towards the counter. 'FYI, I've been a patron at this mall as well as this bookstore before. I won't get lost.'

Ignoring me, Michael imprinted his palms on the pastries and cakes display.

I ordered an iced vanilla latte and a slice of American chocolate cake at the counter. 'Anyway, it is the weekend, happy thoughts only, please.'

'I've promised Mama to keep an eye on you. We, the young ones, shouldn't have to let our elders have any worries about us. It can cause health disturbances.' Michael finally placed his order. 'One americano, chilled.'

'Iced americano, you mean?' The barista looked perplexed.

'Fairly similar but remove the ice cubes,' Michael said.

'Be specific if you don't mind,' the barista said.

'This is how to make it chilled,' Michael gestured. 'Shake the coffee with the ice cubes but don't include them in the drink. Easy, isn't it?'

A chill ran down my spine upon hearing his preference; it was identical to Edward's.

'I prefer hot coffee, but the scorching weather won't permit it,' Michael added.

I paid for my order as well as his and grimaced when Michael took my credit card away. 'Hey, give it back!'

'Ma'am, please take mine,' he said to the cashier.

I sighed and handed cash to the cashier, as the front of the line wasn't the place to have a debate. The cashier smiled at me, returning the cash to me and taking Michael's card.

Once the payment was made and we walked away from the counter, Michael extended my card to me, which I promptly snatched from his hand. I spotted an empty table with a plastic cup of unfinished Americano on it. Michael moved towards it. He placed our tray on the table, picked up the half-finished cup and handed it to the barista at the collection counter. We waited for the table to be cleaned before taking a seat. Michael looked on as I sliced the chocolate cake into half.

'Here, you have some.' I said, passing the cake to Michael.

'That is meticulously separated.' Michael smiled.

'You paid for my cake and for my drink . . .'

'You can always have a share of my Americano.'

'I'm fine.' I kept my gaze on my Notes app, preferring not to be disturbed.

There's breakfast shared by two, drinking from the same chilled Americano mug. I'll hold you as you fall asleep while you work on your poetry drafts, consumed by the quiet Han River view. Don't mind me soaking you with my kisses to unblock your creativity.' Edward's voice echoed through my head.

'How long have you been writing poetry?' Michael suddenly asked.

I swallowed, dislodging my attention from the unresolved intrusion. 'Ever since I was studying A-Levels in college, and I only started to hone my craft three years ago.'

'I bet you've been complimented for your talent and beauty.'

I smiled at him, finished my cake then took a sip from my drink. The weirdest diluted Marmite taste lingered on my tongue. I grimaced forcing myself to swallow. Turns out, it was Michael's drink. *Argh! Goddamnit.* I quickly pushed it back to him. He didn't seem bothered, nonchalantly humming throughout.

'I'm so sorry. I really didn't mean to,' I said, embarrassed.

'Perhaps, it's time for a change,' he muttered.

I briefly grinned. 'Interesting, you talk like you know my destiny.'

Michael's gaze remained steady as he silently looked at me.

I got up from my seat, grabbing my tote. 'Daniel must be waiting,' I said, hurrying out of the café, brushing off whatever his implication might be.

* * *

All attendees—from adolescents to middle-aged people—simply couldn't take their eyes off Daniel, who was queuing for registration outside Hall A at the convention centre. Weird was not enough to describe Daniel's open-mindedness. A madcap in such an anticipated moment. The pageant—if there was any—should've crowned my cousin the next fashionista.

'You two are really a pair,' Daniel teased Michael and me.

For once, Michael couldn't restrain himself, joining me as I covered my mouth laughing. I shook with laughter and disbelief. 'My cousin bro is pretty as fuck.'

'May I see your proof of winning,' the event staff said to Daniel.

Daniel adjusted his blonde wig and handed over the pass.

'May I take a look at your identification card?'

'Is there a problem?' Daniel asked.

The woman couldn't take her eyes off my cousin's emblematic white cocktail dress and his seductive, fluttery fake long lashes. 'It is my responsibility to make sure the name on the pass and the name on the identification card is the same person. And verify that the photo on the identification card is of the person holding it.'

'Am I not allowed to cross-dress? Yes?' Daniel crossed his lean, muscular, waxed legs. I had to force myself to press the 'do-not-laugh' button.

Michael was quick to evolve into the see-no-evil monkey emoji. 'No, Miss—I mean Mr Lau.' The woman smiled, embarrassed.

'If there is a problem, my cousin sister shall be my legal advisor and that gentleman over there is our family bodyguard. I'm Marilyn "Daniel" Monroe. Have you watched the movie *Seven Year Itch*? This dress was inspired by that.'

'I'm sorry, but I don't know who that is,' the woman said quietly.

Daniel exhaled. 'You should watch old Hollywood movies in addition to chasing K-pop idols. You know, to broaden your horizons.'

And with that Daniel strutted away.

'So, that's the reason you had an enormous carry-on with you,' I said as I followed.

'Hey, this is a precious-as-fuck kind of dress,' Daniel hissed.

'Question is where'd you get this in such a short time?' I asked.

'One of Aunt Bridget's props—'

I shook my head. 'Then, how come she's never boasted about it?'

'Go ask her if you don't believe it.' Daniel rolled his eyes.

'I've gone through her wardrobe before and found nothing that looks like that.'

'It was right inside that treasure lookalike trunk inside her room, neatly folded and well-stored. She hid it with the same care one would hide an illegitimate child.' Daniel fluttered his eyelashes. As I looked at him, I was overwhelmed with a sudden urge to protect him. His courage for living in *that* moment. My cousin then continued, 'Our prima donna aunt paid her stylist and her PA an undisclosed fee to sneak the dress out after the award show at the TVB broadcast centre in Hong Kong.'

'I think Michael should go into the meet and greet hall with you,' I said.

'Why is that?' Michael voiced his doubt.

'Michael-*ssi* is the family bodyguard, like you claimed.' Eyeing them, I brought these two *objects* closer, arm-to-arm. 'You both look perfectly stunning together.'

'Emily—is that you?'

I turned to the vivacious tone. 'Sabrina Ng!'

Our shrieks of joy echoed along the open corridor as we hugged each other tightly.

'Long time no see!'

'You look really different.' Sabrina said to me. 'Never imagined we'd meet here again, and I wouldn't have even recognized you if not for your voice.'

I ruffled her shoulder-length ash-purple hair. 'You're looking gorgeous yourself. Your old-fashioned boyfriend finally allowed you to change your image?'

She pursed her lips. 'We broke up . . . six months ago.'

'I'm so sorry to hear that,' I quickly brushed my palms across her arms.

'There are many people in life who are going to disapprove of what really makes you a better person,' she explained. 'But you know what, I'm much happier now.'

'Are you here for the meet and greet? I remember you're a Hallyu addict too.'

'I'm working for K-Licious Delish as their PR officer.' Sabrina retrieved her name card from the holder, handed it to Daniel and me, and winked at Michael. 'I'm based in the KL headquarter. They plan to expand from Klang Valley and go nationwide. So, what brings you here, old friend?' Sabrina held my hands.

I squeezed her hands and smiled as I turned to introduce her. 'Sabrina, my ex-colleague from Saujana Residence. Daniel, my cousin and that's Michael.'

'Holy shit.' Sabrina couldn't take her eyes off Daniel. 'He's making the blonde bombshell roll in her grave right now.'

'That's the vibe of the like-minded,' Daniel said. 'I like it.'

'My colleagues kept telling me there's a Marilyn-blondie in the queuing line. Thank goodness, I didn't miss it,' Sabrina said.

'Thank you for checking me out but I'm already taken,' Daniel said.

Sabrina tittered, smiling at Michael. 'I can see that.'

'You don't think I'd have such bad taste . . . in men?' Daniel rolled his eyes at Michael. 'This Kimchi is already taken, although that's yet to be confirmed.'

'Yeah, shoot me like the fireworks display at the Namsan Tower.'

I couldn't stop laughing at Michael's darting metaphors with their impromptu speculative elements. 'The winner is allowed to bring another guest, right?'

'Yes, that should be the rule.' Sabrina tried to take it in stride.

'I'm opting to stay out of this meet and greet,' I said, folding my arms.

'No,' Daniel declared and turned to Sabrina. 'Maybe you can help get the three of us in.'

'Please excuse us for a moment,' I said, then quickly led Sabrina to the side.

'What's going on here?' she whispered.

I exhaled, trying to gather my thoughts. 'Help me put those two inside the hall.'

Sabrina looked over her shoulder, as Marilyn-Daniel-Monroe and Mr Kimchi were peering at us. Then, she started snickering out of nowhere. 'Wait, I thought that's your new—'

'No,' I interrupted.

'Okay, understand.' Sabrina patted my forearm.

I mouthed a thank you.

Sabrina waved at one of her colleagues to bring over the winner's list. After a quick look at the document, she turned to me just as I spotted our names in full. She assured me further. 'Let me check. Give me a minute or two.'

I walked to my cousin and noticed that Michael was browsing on his phone.

'We practise a quid pro quo culture in Malaysia,' Daniel said. 'You scratch my back and I scratch yours to survive in any unpredictable situation.'

'Like the kingdom of the apes,' Michael burst into laughter.

'If Sabrina can help us, my cousin sister has to return the favour.' Adjusting the band around the plunging neckline, Daniel ensured the bust enhancers on both sides of his chest were still firmly adhered. 'Be quiet, here comes Sabrina.'

'Emily, your name can be replaced with another person's.'

An announcement had been made by the organizer informing us that the ambassador was on his way. The queues bustling with banners and fandom lightsticks had walked into the hall, taking their respective seats. Some were clad in customized t-shirts and waving balloons with the ambassador's face printed on them. Triumphantly, Daniel intertwined his arms with Michael's and then mine.

'I need confirmation right now as the event has started.' Sabrina hurried us.

'Put Michael Kim's name in,' I immediately said.

His eyes became round in surprise. 'Wait, no!'

'Yeah, three or nothing.' Daniel furrowed his brow, then side-eyed me.

'Time for the Tiger to chaperone another junior Rat.' My arms folded, proudly.

'I hate you, Emily Chung!' Daniel whirled around and stomped to the convention hall, led by Sabrina's assistant.

When the door opened, I was hit by the shrieks and screams of fans, which were so loud that the noise could probably pierce through the wall. Michael let a fan enter before him. His lips were pursed. Definitely pissed.

But I needed to breathe. Without his presence.

For the next two hours or so.

Eighteen

I took a sip from the paper cup, facing the water fountain.

The chamomile tea was infused with a piquant herbal scent, bringing with it a sense of calm that was interrupted by the extensive clamour brought on by the arrival of the K-ambassador.

I turned, hearing the soft crack of Sabrina's stiff neck. 'Don't you need to go back in?'

'I told 'em there's an urgent call from my boss.' Sabrina smirked. 'The crew can handle the rest without me, unless the stage topples over.'

I chuckled. 'You have Madam Ong's aura in you.'

'Missing those days, huh?' Sabrina said, stealing glances at my black rose tattoos, then at my asymmetrical bob hairstyle. 'This makeover really suits you, like a triad leader heiress, the contender for the Chinese Mafia's sizzling chair.'

'That's a dangerous situation,' I said, a little supercilious of this subculture I adorned. 'Thanks, I'll take that as a compliment. By the way, how're your parents?'

'They're doing fine. We were talking about you two weeks ago.'

'Oh, really—' I turned. 'I've wanted to thank your father for guiding me to the right path in my tertiary studies. My father mistakenly thinks he's known me ever since the day he made me but it was your father's advice that made me give the law degree my bravest shot.' At times, a blessing in disguise could end up with unexpected benefits.

'My dad sees potential in you,' Sabrina smiled. 'He'd always wanted me to become a chemical engineer, but I flunked Physics and Add Maths. How embarrassing,' she said, brushing off the excessive crumbs from her lap. 'Remember my dad's forever motto?'

'Science and art cannot be married,' Sabrina and I said, guffawing.

'I told him numbers and alphabets do sleep together though. Look at Algebra.'

'And give birth to the most controversial . . . Calculus?' I asked, laughing.

'My regret is not choosing Literature,' Sabrina pouted, 'like poetic Em.'

'You still remember that,' I felt pleased and leaned closer. 'Is the guest's name for the meet and greet amendable once confirmed?'

'Terms and conditions apply,' Sabrina said. 'The company has the right to revoke the winner's prize whenever they deem fit. I'm sure you know the usual regulations. There's always a way to get the three of you into the hall,' she assured me, winking.

I smiled at her as my thoughts drifted to how I would inevitably disappoint Mama's anticipation for the budding relationship between Michael and me. Sadly, it was improvident, despite the blessings from my most-loved Mama. There had been many times when I had been tempted to confess to her about my past relationship; scraping off the K-pop idol part, of course. Would anyone believe it, if they hadn't personally seen one with a celebrity.

'How have you been doing for the past few months?' Sabrina asked. 'I was thinking of calling you soon. As you know work has been keeping me busy.'

'I live in Penang Island with the relatives on my mother's side, volunteering at their non-profit food centre. The kitchens are somewhat . . . magisterial.'

'Wow, sounds like the imperial kitchen in an ancient palace.'

'It's been a month since I started my internship,' I said. 'As I'm saying this to you, I still can't forget the smiley face of the person when I handed them a bowl of mushroom or the compliments regarding the delicious kuih or the hot-baked buns, or the flaming wok-*hei* at the gourmet kitchen,' I confessed, peeping at the dreamy-eyed Sabrina. 'You're always welcome to visit me. I live next to the makeshift imperial kitchens.'

'Oh, they even provide a hostel for the volunteers. Not bad.' I snickered. 'So, how did you get a job at K-Licious-Delish?'

'After your admission, an international hotelier bought the aparthotel.' Sabrina exhaled. 'The new management initially intended to combine both workforces. But the retrenchment letter came two weeks later with compensation. And they retained Mr Krishna, must've loved his obsequious behaviour.'

The general rule of thumb about life—everyone is dispensable.

'I worked briefly at Dad's engineering firm. Then, I stumbled upon this job vacancy at a Korean-based artisan café, advertising on behalf of K-Licious Delish.'

'You're always the luckiest, like a four-leaf clover,' I simpered.

'I think it is Fiona's luck. We were having coffee that day.'

'Still keep in touch with her, huh?'

'Yeah, she's been promoted to a cabin manager. And she's back in town, preparing for her engagement. Her future-husband is a senior pilot with Emirates.'

'Oh,' I said, recalling Fiona's chilling words to me during my hospitalization.

'Hey, what's the story with Michael Kim?'

'He's one of the volunteers at the food centre.' I said, absentmindedly rubbing the ring on the chain. 'I'm focusing on my internship, nothing more.'

'Like you've been denying feelings for Ed—' Sabrina paused. I turned as she finished her pepperoni sandwich, patting the crumbs from her lap. 'The platinum chain looks familiar. Is that the one you bought at Lazo Diamond?'

'Yeah, you scolded me for foolishly spending MYR 600 for this.'

'Guess I know the reason now,' Sabrina said, eyeing the promise ring.

'How did you know?' I asked. 'I didn't tell you a thing about this.'

Pursing her lips, Sabrina shot me a grin. 'I knew about Edward's proposal.'

It took me a while to put the pieces together. 'You planned all this for him?' She nodded, with those innocent Bambi doe-eyes. 'Oh geez, so it all started when you wanted to borrow my Forever 21 rhinestone ring for a date, right?'

Sabrina rolled her eyes. 'How else was he supposed to know your finger size?'

I smacked her shoulder, chuckling bitterly. 'You liar . . .'

'Edward sent me a voucher for a Korean restaurant as a token of appreciation for helping him. My advice for him was to love you or else . . .' Sabrina cracked her knuckles.

I exhaled. 'Unfortunately, we met at the wrong place and the wrong time.'

'Edward is a really decent guy and by far the most humble and genuine celebrity I've ever met,' Sabrina said, matter-of-factly. 'A man wouldn't have shown his most vulnerable side if not for the woman he truly loved.'

'You know I still keep his letters to me,' I said, heavy-heartedly.

Sabrina beamed in awe and disbelief. 'All of them?'

I nodded. 'But I stopped reading them. I want him and our memory . . . to stand still at the writer's retreat. Like he left me so abruptly. No closure,' I confessed, biting my lips.

Sabrina instantly pulled me to her. Silent weeping turned to ugly crying in her embrace. I felt her hand patting my back as I curled up and covered myself. Sabrina then stuffed a face tissue in my grip. I could hear her breath. 'Actually, I received a call from Edward . . .'

I gradually lifted my face up at her culpable tone. 'What . . . ?'

'. . . before you were admitted.'

'Then how come you didn't tell me?'

'I was working night shifts that month . . .'

'Can't believe you're doing this to me . . .' I choked out, breathing hard.

She held onto my forearms, shushing me gently. 'I'm sorry . . . I . . .'

A handful of parents with their young kids turned their heads towards us.

My body shivered; new pain reemerged from the kinesics. I closed my eyes to ease my kangaroo-chasing heart. No third fucking blackout. Not in an iconic KLCC park.

'It's my fault for not dragging your sleepy head up.' Sabrina said. 'Maybe I was hard on him, telling him about your forced resignation, the non-stop drinking, and still being . . . so in love with him.'

I massaged my head.

'I asked why he left you,' Sabrina continued. 'Instead, he asked for my address to personally explain everything to you and insisted that the shitty-face manager won't be coming. I told him to check for my availability. In case he bumps into Fiona. Or any fans.' She sighed and looked up at me, remorse clear as day in her expression. 'I'm really sorry I kept this from you, Em.'

Fiona again. My lips pursed. 'I guess we're not destined to be.'

'I still remember that day when your mom called, the police found you in the parking lot . . .' Sabrina bit her lips. 'Thank goodness you survived.'

'Two empty vodka and beer bottles, plus the excessive inhalation of carbon monoxide,' I turned to Sabrina. 'What do you think the police would say? Of course it's a suicide.'

'But I don't believe you'd end your life, Emily.' Sabrina looked at me deeply. 'I tried calling Edward a few days after your admission,' she said, finishing her drink with a sucking sound. 'But the number was out of service.'

I whimpered. Forcing a grin, I was stroking the promise ring, reminiscing and gradually looking at a couple sharing a sundae cone ahead of us. 'I still don't believe Edward had a girlfriend. His manager could have been lying.'

'Whoever that person is, it doesn't matter to me anymore,' I said, feeling sore.

* * *

Next day, we had lunch with Mom at an authentic Korean restaurant.

Browsing the laminated menu, I glanced at Michael, who seemed to know what he wanted to order. Mom's fingers were tapping on the table, while Daniel was sipping on his second glass of Dalgona coffee, his gaze glued to the phone. He hadn't said a word to me since last night when I refused to accompany him for the meet and greet.

Michael stopped me when I decided to order *tteokguk*. 'Mrs Chung, would you mind if I ordered dishes that complement purple rice?'

'It is your call,' Mom said, relaxing against the banquette seating. 'My Emily loves Korean rice cake soup. That is what she orders whenever she visits any Korean restaurant. Once, she ate that for three consecutive dinners.'

'Sometimes I'll add a few slices into my instant noodles, cooked HK-style with mixed frozen veggies and garnished with two slices of crispy fried luncheon meat and a sunny side-up,' I said sipping the iced *sikhye*—a sweet rice drink.

The waitress came to take our order.

Michael whispered, pointing at the menu. 'I'm ordering this, and this—'

Mom smiled after the waitress had repeated the orders. 'I'm looking forward to this sumptuous lunch,' she said, sliding her finger to turn off the phone screen from an incoming call alert. 'Emily, later we'll go shopping for some clothes.'

'I just bought a few with Daniel the other day.'

'I can give you some suggestions if you take me along,' Michael said.

'We shop only for what's necessary,' Daniel said.

'Change your wardrobe, Emily. Always black and blue,' Mom sighed.

'Blue is one of the polite colours in Korean culture,' Daniel protested.

'Also, stains from the kitchen don't look obvious on it like they on white,' I said.

Michael popped a piece of yellow radish in his mouth. 'Mrs Chung, your batik chiffon blazer looks splendid.'

'A friend got it for me as a gift when he travelled to Yogyakarta,' Mom said. 'Malaysians take pride in owning one such piece and truth to be told, no one should doubt Helen's tailoring skill, for who else can turn a bolt of traditional cloth into a blazer, culottes, and a short skirt?'

'You're somehow knowledgeable about fashion too, Mrs Chung, speaking from a fashion stylist point of view,' Michael said.

Mom's eyes widened at the compliment. She looked at me and sighed. 'I'm glad to hear that, Michael, but it pains me to never hear Emily talking about it.'

Who cares about fashion?

I picked a piece of deep fried oyster mushroom, relishing the taste.

Mom added, 'I've known dressmaking since before Emily was born and continued pursuing it till after she turned two years old, but she was a handful, day night in—'

'Mom, your green tea is getting cold,' I cut her off, sparing Michael from having to listen to details about baby-me that he was better off not knowing.

'And our food has arrived!' Daniel kept his phone back into his waist pouch.

'Spicy stir-fried chicken, that's awesome,' Mom said to Michael.

'It is *ddak-galbi*. Emily told me you love *rendang*.'

Mom raised her brows at me. 'Give me anything with rendang in it. That should keep me company, rain or shine. I don't mind eating it for lunch and then reheating the gravy adding in hard-boiled eggs and eating it for dinner. In our home, we call this "recycled egg rendang". Want to know who gave the name? There, that princess.'

'Wow, *japchae*!' Daniel exclaimed, as if on a mukbang live-stream.

'You always wanted to try this dish, especially to know the difference between the two cellophane noodles. This is made from sweet potato starch and the one we usually have at home is made from mung bean flour,' I served the transparent thick treads in Mom's bowl.

Mom gave it a try. 'Nice, despite the fact they're culturally different.'

The statement somehow penetrated within, daggering my heart and bones, even though it was phrased slightly differently than what Edward's manager had said to me.

'I love the ebullient mixture of vegetables,' Mom said. 'Japchae looks fairly similar to *jiu-hoo-char*, stir-fried shredded jicama roots with dried squid, a must-have in every Penangite household on Chinese New Year—a traditional dish that is said to show how skilled the bride-to-be is before marrying into the family.'

'Thanks. Shall I check with Emily on the recipe?' Michael asked.

I pretended to not hear him.

'To whoever is making that dish, I wish that person best of luck, especially the julienning of vegetables that can literally cause the hands to go numb for a day.'

Mom turned to Daniel. 'One day your wife shall make it for you too.'

I chuckled while eating a piece of diagonally cut red capsicum. Daniel rolled his eyes, gesturing at me to check my phone. I read Daniel's message on the group chat.

> My fire is still burning due to your sudden absence, but I tested this Kimchi during the meet and greet. He seemed to be interested in you, so keep your options open.

Then, there came a reply from Aunt Bridget.

> Mom & son-in-law interrogating time. Please remind my sister to roast that Kimchi's butt for more Q&A. Time to hunt for a qipao for the tea ceremony.

After some thought, I replied.

> My matrimony isn't a Snakes & Ladders game. Please keep out! 😒

Aunt Bridget replied almost immediately.

> Betta' wrap your legs over that Kimchi, my niece.

After dinner, I noticed that Mom couldn't tear her eyes off Michael as he paid the bill at the counter. 'Haven't seen a Korean man before?' I grinned at her cheekily.

'I would prefer you to marry a local,' Mom said. 'Seoul is very cold, and I doubt you'll be able to handle the blistering winter, and you're not a fan of spicy food.'

'Aunt Cheryl, you can always Skype or video call,' Daniel said. 'Spicy food isn't the problem. Biu-jie is creative in switching up recipes and can do so unless Michael is a workaholic. Then, she'd have to spend her lonely nights venting at the heater . . . '

Mom covered her mouth and laughed while I kicked my cousin's knee.

'This is just a little revenge,' Daniel said to me, with a silly expression.

'I spoke to *Gor* last night,' Mom meant Uncle Raymond. 'I never thought my Emily baby would return to her sociable personality after being at knife's edge eight months ago. Even my happy crying had shocked my own brother—'

I turned to Mom, dewy-eyed. 'Your daughter is hard-to-die.'

* * *

Sabrina invited us to a famous street food night out in the heart of Kuala Lumpur that evening. My cousin stayed in the hotel room; he was probably still angry at me.

Michael didn't mind trying out the local street food at the roadside vendors. He let out a big burp after eating the fried Hokkien mee, cola-flavoured chicken wings, and fried vermicelli with clams. He said he wouldn't mind eating himself into a food coma, as he would miss these dishes once he was back in Seoul.

Sabrina then took us to a dessert shop that specialized in tang yuan. The menu was written in Mandarin-Chinese. Translation wasn't needed as Michael seemed to understand the script. After ordering at the counter, Michael and I joined Sabrina at the table she had secured, one that was nearer to the entrance.

'Sorry for my lateness.'

That *familiar* voice.

I ceased smiling and rolled my eyes.

Sabrina was smiling.

I turned to Fiona. That same-old sinister grin. That same choking perfume. My eyes met hers, taking me back to the hospital where I had been admitted for alcohol poisoning. I was too depressed to speak to any visitors. I remembered Sabrina sobbing quietly as she touched my face and wished me well. I could only thank her by heart. When she left to go to the washroom, Fiona whispered in my ear, 'You deserved to die with your love.'

That was struck me with immense grief, coming from a long-time friend.

I left for Penang after my hospitalization with plenty on my plate to deal with, which is why I'd missed telling Sabrina about this. . . incident.

Michael glanced at me, seemingly picking-up on my discomfort.

'Didn't I say I'll pass the engagement party invitation to Emily tomorrow?' Fiona said in response to Sabrina's questioning look.

'Ah yes, I'm glad I made it. I have to see the healed Emily Chung with my own eyes,' Fiona said to Sabrina.

'Of course.' I smiled widely. 'Nine lives, baby.'

'The last time I saw you . . . ' Fiona pretended to be in deep thought, 'ah right! It was in the hospital . . .'

Sabrina playfully smacked her arm. 'Show some respect to Emily's friend.'

Fiona's expression did a one-eighty. 'Hi, handsome.'

Michael waved at her.

'This is for you, Emily.' Fiona tossed the peony-pink envelope in my direction. 'You're invited to my engagement party. And you too, Michael-oppa.' Sabrina and Michael looked at the arrogant chick.

'I found mine.' Fiona said, looking pointedly at me. 'While some lost theirs. Forever.'

I stood up, welcoming the endgame. 'I'll be there. Early.'

Nineteen

'Michael was quick to return to his room,' Sabrina said over the phone.

'Uh-huh,' I stepped out from the elevator.

Troubled by Fiona's viciousness, my fingers were drumming against a glass façade in the hotel lobby. Something about Fiona's indescribable resentment didn't sit well with me.

'I wonder what Fiona meant by losing the one,' Sabrina said.

My eyes shut. 'Did you tell Fiona about Edward?'

'Hell no!'

I jumped, surprised by Sabrina's outburst.

'I remember she was exceptionally happy the day when we were heading to visit you at the hospital,' Sabrina said. 'I thought has she won a lottery or what.'

'I was too depressed to even look at her that day,' I told her, dawdling along the corridor, then swiping my key card to enter my room. 'Oh, what the fuck!'

'Are you all right? What happened?' Sabrina squawked from the other end of the line.

'Told you to hang the "Do Not Disturb" sign at the door,' Daniel said.

'I did! Look there! Haiyah, Emily why—' Kenneth yelped.

'I'll call you later, Sabrina.' I hung up. One hand covering my eyes and the other prohibiting Daniel and Kenneth from coming closer. 'Just give me a moment to breathe.' I calmly said. Never in my life had I thought I'd get a sneak peek of gay erotica. Indeed, there was a sign hanging on the door. I was still staring at my cousin—his fault of not informing beforehand.

'Your things are over there.' Daniel pointed at Michael's room.

I scowled. 'I went out for a phone call like fifteen minutes ago!'

Daniel blinked and then shot me a goofy smile.

I groaned at Daniel, then knocked at the adjoining door. 'Open up, Michael Kim! I want my belongings back!' However, there wasn't any sound. It was barely 10 p.m. and he'd fallen asleep. *Oh my god, seriously?* The knocking soon evolved into Lau-d & Feisty banging. My palm was starting to sting. 'I'm counting to three. One, two—'

Kenneth plugged his fingers in his ears, hiding behind Daniel.

Michael opened the door and let out a grimace as my hand whacked his chest. 'I don't think violence is necessary, Miss Emily.'

I shot him a frown, massaging my right hand with my left. 'I want my things back.'

'Then where are you going to put up at night?' Michael asked.

'There're so many budget hotels around.'

'Biu-jie, are you out of your mind? Drug addicts are probably loitering in the dark alleys by now, unless you wanna be mugged,' said Daniel.

'You can have my bed. I can sleep on the chaise lounge.'

'In your dreams, Michael Kim,' I snapped. Gritting my teeth, I turned to a smirking Daniel. 'Tell me this wasn't your . . . mind-fucking idea.'

He bleated. 'Your Honour, I am innocent without the need to be proven guilty!'

Michael couldn't stop laughing at my cousin playing victim.

'Oh Kenneth, did you see my cousin's Best Dressed trophy? And to have a photo session with that K-ambassador while being cross-dressed. Damn . . .'

'What cross-dressing?' Kenneth asked.

My cousin's hand was smothering me, stopping me from continuing.

'Time to explain, Naughty-Dan . . .' Kenneth separated us.

'All right, all right,' Daniel pushed me right into Michael's arms. 'Plus, we shall continue where we left off . . .'

'We're leaving at six tomorrow, Smelly-Dan!' I said.

Daniel quickly whisked Kenneth into the room and locked the adjoining door, shouting from inside. 'Have fun with your lotus flower!'

'Hey!'

'What is he saying?' Michael asked, stepping into the bathroom.

'Ignore him.' I said, massaging my head and my stiff neck, still trying to shake off the unpredictable meeting with Fiona and her bone-chilling narrative.

I leaned against the headboard. I had to be vigilant in this 'only one king size bed' situation. Another sleepless night. Hopefully, I wouldn't blackout.

Again.

* * *

Wrapped in a towel, water dripped down Michael's neck. His abdominal muscles displayed a clear-cut vista with those hip bones. The whiff of aftershave, well-groomed sideburns—I was being terribly influenced by my cousin.

Emily, wake up! 'I need to shower now!'

'Wait for the shower steam to evaporate.' Michael said.

I quickly picked up a perfume mist from my duffle bag, spraying it around the bathroom including the toilet bowl, then the whole room.

Michael sneezed abruptly, then again louder before cursing in Korean. The situation was fairly similar to Edward's typical reaction to this scent. 'The smell is like an acidic ocean,' Michael said.

I ignored him and walked into the bathroom.

I turned on the shower. The water pressure made me feel I was at Niagara Falls. As the droplets poured over me, my breath held at Edward's promise to declare his love by shouting the loudest '*saranghaeyo*' when on the boat tour. If only Michael's bricklayer half-nakedness hadn't skimmed through my mind the moment I closed my eyes. I cringed to shake that away.

I climbed into bed after taking a shower.

Michael gestured, asking me to keep my voice down. I ignored him, taking two pillows from the bed and placing them on the chaise sofa—they were meant for him. Heading to the Nespresso machine, I pretended to enjoy the scenic city skyline, peering at Michael's phone screen.

'Ah, that's your girlfriend!' I was sipping the Nescafé bold and smooth coffee.

'Respect my privacy,' Michael said strictly.

'Calm down,' I said. 'Men are generally the same, flirting with other girls while already taken.'

'That's my mother,' he replied logging off from his iPad.

Relaxing the back of my head on the soft pillow, my arms spread like an angel in a snowbank, in the middle of this dimensional bed, then sprung up suddenly. 'Michael Kim is the opposite of *nappeun namja.*' It meant bad boy.

'That's not a nice word.'

'The less you know about me, the better I feel.'

'Where'd you purchase that acidic ocean scented cologne?' He asked suddenly. But I didn't answer him. 'Why'd you love men's cologne that much?'

'I prefer drenching myself in this particular masculine scent.'

Michael grabbed the ice bucket, cutting off the foil below the bottle with the wine key, twisting the cage counterclockwise as the pressure deliberately pushed the cork. Then, his grip controlled the cork as he separated it from the bottle.

Hearing the hissing sound, I put a pillow over my head.

'When did you order champagne?' I asked.

'Let's play a game,' he said suddenly.

I screamed as the bottle popped.

'Damn, you scared the hell—'

Deep breaths, Emily.

Wiping the bottle of the liquid that had spilled onto his hand with a napkin, Michael licked the remaining drops before washing his hands. 'C'mon, it's gonna be fun.'

'With a MYR 500 champagne?' I checked from the official receipt.

'Daniel is right,' Michael said. 'This is a night that shouldn't be disturbed. You don't mind grabbing a shirt for me, do you? Any colour will do. I need to change.'

'That's your problem for being clumsy.' I lay on the bed and closed my eyes after finishing the coffee in one big gulp. 'Good night and enjoy your champagne.'

I felt a pull and heard something akin to peculiar slithering, and then felt the bed sink. I shuffled away, trying to ignore Michael as my body felt fatigued. The AC was set at a cozy temperature, yet I remained conscious and awake. Why hadn't the magical effect of caffeine kicked in yet? The delicately roasted Arabica could have been a sham. I forced my eyes open, and was startled by the close proximity of a certain someone. I pushed Michael away, smacking him hard with a pillow.

He dodged, smiling as he successfully avoided getting hit and seemed to feel delighted by my agitation. 'Are you not interested in any man?'

You pushed the wrong button, buddy. 'Not ones who love pastel colours,' I said.

'I sympathize with you for discriminating against the metrosexual for their personal taste.' Michael ran into the bathroom with his shirt and closed the door.

Tears welled from deep inside and coursed down my cheeks. Once upon a starlit night, there was an idiot—no, actually, make that two staunch idiots—in Shakespeare-inspired teenage love. Despite being adults with developed brains, the love I had for Edward felt almost unreal, it shaped my life. It was an all-embracing, healthy experience, a bona fide stimulation—steamy and body positive. It'd gotten so physical, which had then transformed into a different kind of intimacy.

Michael opened the door.

I was taken aback, caught by his deep-seated eyes. 'Let's play Truth or Dare.'

'Not sleepy?'

'Too many things in my head.'

He thought for a while. 'I drink the champagne and you drink the coffee.'

I pursed my lips to stop myself from laughing at his serious tone.

'No physical intimacy,' he added.

'As you wish. Truth—when was your first kiss and with who?' I asked.

'Haven't been kissed.'

'What!' I laughed in disbelief.

Michael looked bashful. 'What about you?'

'Liar!'

'That's the truth you asked for,' he said raising his voice. 'Your turn.'

'My first boyfriend,' I said, cautiously. 'I dare you to finish your champagne.'

'What's the rush? His name?'

'Digging in to my personal life?' I was still digesting Michael's never-been-kissed status.

'Like I know your boyfriend personally. Duh.' Michael's tone resembled Daniel's.

'Edward,' I said, handing him the bottle.

He smiled, grabbing it from me, apparently satisfied with my answer.

We exchanged glances at the sound of gulping and the conspicuous up-and-down motion of his throat. The dripping liquid snaked down along his torso down to his navel. He'd returned to the room shirtless. *Shouldn't have said anything about the colour of his t-shirt.*

'It's your turn. I dare you to dress me up.'

'In your dreams.'

'It'll be over this shirt. Don't worry.' Michael passed me another t-shirt.

How cunning. I grabbed the t-shirt from him, not fooled by his poker face.

Our gazes met when I put the shirt through, settling it around Michael's neck then pulling it slightly to adjust the sleeve on his right arm. Made from stretchable, soft material, the shirt had been a loose fit, displaying Michael's sculpted muscles. His lips parted, observing my fingers skim the fabric under his armpits, along his shoulder blade. He gasped as I flattened the wrinkled hems. I was consciously not looking at him, my breathing setting off a catastrophic minuet. I could feel his skin even over the t-shirt.

'Thank you,' he said. 'We did get to know each other.'

'Guess we're done here,' I said, avoiding my reflection in his eyes.

Michael fell asleep beside me.

Lying on the bed with my head on the pillow, I looked up at the ceiling.

The dopamine had kicked in, causing a storm of emotions to brew.

Twenty

'Surprise!' Edward walked into my room at the writer's retreat.

I poked my head out the door to check the corridor, saw that the coast was clear, so I tugged him inside, and then pulled the door closed behind us.

Edward pivoted in circles towards the loggia facing the sylvan tropical forest. 'I can instantly write ten songs to depict this bountiful realm,' he said, shuffling like a free-spirited balletic tap dancer, his arms spread wide. 'I hear the rippling flow of the waterfall from afar.'

'What're you doing here?' I asked.

Edward then pulled me to the bed, which bounced gently under our weight.

Time decelerated as I brushed the straggly fringe that was lying across his face, careful not to probe those lips, feeling his finger outlining the ridge of my nose, and then my chin—an unadulterated sense of condolement had embedded itself in those chocolate brown eyes. There had been an extended period of time where we hadn't been in such close proximity.

He kissed my lips. 'Hello, pretty neighbour.' My heart expanded with ticklish laughter. Then, another kiss on my lips. 'No more interruptions from now.'

'Your manager has finally let you off the hook?' I choked out the question.

Edward hung his denim jacket over the chair and walked to me with a piece of paper he'd retrieved from its pocket. He showed me the letter written in English with a resplendent amber-red logo from Rocking Fire Entertainment. 'Mr Han can't say no to the CEO. This solo English album is to gain more worldwide exposure.'

I looked at him, amazed. 'Is that your reason for this retreat?'

'Well, every company has its ways.' He winked. 'You just gotta be smart.'

'Mr Han is still your manager, what if . . .' I said.

'Honestly, Mr Han's been a pro when it comes to paving my solo career. No one in the management team believed in me and my music, but he did,' Edward said. 'Being a soloist, you take the risk of only having one shot to prove yourself. Nevertheless, he's been managing my idol career for the past decade. He has changed a lot lately.'

I pursed my lips, unsure as to which direction the arrow was aiming.

'It is never about you,' Edward tugged my hair over my ear, gazing at me.

'Sabrina messaged me yesterday, telling me to be ready for today,' I said.

Edward chuckled while helping himself to some water from the mini dispenser. 'So, there's no secret among the sisterhood,' he said, pulling me in for a long kiss.

Rimbun Hijauan was a privately owned artist retreat centre.

Opportunity had struck as the open call for a residency had been announced for unpublished writers and poets in the local community. As expected, Mr Krishna had rejected my two-week leave application. In contrast, Madam Ong wrote a recommendation letter to supplement my appeal letter and then resubmitted it to the HR department.

Meanwhile, Sabrina had become his envoy, passing letters to me during lunch.

'I see you've been working hard on your poetry pieces.'

I grabbed the drafts from him. 'It's not even complete yet.'

Edward narrowed his stare. 'You're indeed the toughest nut to crack. The chef must've overslept while poor Emily was stuck in the open fire.'

'What a lengthy, outrageous lie—' I rolled my eyes.

Edward's arms wrapped around me. 'What's your moaning level? High-pitched? Breathy?'

Lost in his gaze, I bit my bottom lip. 'Depends on how you control the combustion.'

'Think I hear . . . overdue sizzling.' His fingers were outlining my face.

'Where?' My tone was coarse, slowly giving in to his seduction.

I melted, feeling his lips on mine. I would flinch at Edward's infallible features. I had to steal a glimpse, momentarily, eyes partially open to this torrid intimacy.

My lips nibbled along Edward's jaw to his neck. Edward's hands cupped my face. My breath hitched, heart pounding to the resolute beat of his open-mouthed kisses. No Mr Han barging into the room. No screaming fans.

Edward laid me down on the bed.

I wanted him to lead.

His lips returned to seal his claim along my neck, then on my lips. I kissed him harder, a few times, then stopped to catch my breath, smiling at him, memorizing his touch. His kiss. His gaze. On my skin. His jokes. Quizzically playful. A melody that perfectly suited me. It was all as intended.

His fingers caressed my cheek. 'Will you be mine?'

'Always . . . ' I pulled him in for a long, deep kiss.

* * *

'Who is the handsome guy next to you in the photo?' Daniel asked. I snapped back to the present. 'If that's the promise ring-namja, then you have great taste.'

I switched off my phone, thanking the waitress for filling up my glass with Chinese tea. Aunt Bridget was idly turning the lazy Susan on the restaurant's banquet table.

I remembered on the fifth day of the retreat; I came back to an empty room after the poetry writing workshop. Edward was nowhere to be seen. His backpack and his guitar were gone. I searched for him all over the writer's retreat. A sick prank, a slap across my face that made me feel broken. Then, a letter and the promise ring were on my bed.

I will come back for you, Emily, my love.

'Look at that deep-fried *tilapia* with fried garlic oil,' Aunt Bridget said.

'It looks so creepy with the mouth open. I'm not eating that,' I announced, dry humoured despite Aunt Bridget's interruption.

'It's having a screaming orgasm.'

Daniel laughed hysterically at Aunt Bridget's joke, whereas I kept a poker-face.

'Respect the food,' Uncle Raymond snapped. 'Set a good example, Bridget.'

Aunt Bridget crossed her legs primly, sipping from the glass. 'Sorry . . .'

'One important person is missing?' Daniel asked, looking around the table.

'Michael Kim?' Aunt Bridget helped herself to some red wine.

'Oh, I saw him at the soup kitchen today.' I turned to my aunt. 'So, how's your script coming along?'

'Chef's kiss baby. Done and ready for action. Now, don't interrupt me when I'm all prepared to enjoy the food.' Aunt Bridget read from the menu booklet.

'The last time we had an eight-course dinner was to celebrate Mama's eightieth birthday. We couldn't wish Mama loudly just because it'd make the time-keeper deity jealous,' Daniel said.

I remembered that day when I called Mama from the hospital. I had just been transferred to the normal ward. Mom was by my side together with a nurse as I spoke and wished Mama cautiously. A birthday wish for longevity would always bring happiness to any older person.

'Four empty chairs ahead. Who are we waiting for?' Daniel asked.

'Reserved for Uncle Sean and Uncle Clement,' I shrugged.

My aunt pretended to choke. 'Time to reapply my lipstick,' she whispered to me after grabbing her bag. 'Text me when that Monk is here. I'll run from the back door.'

Playing hard-to-get, were we?

'I insisted that I would meet Clement only if Raymond were to allow you two to attend the meet and greet,' Mama said. 'That pee-wee boy was so scared that he agreed. Everyone has weaknesses. Hit on that,' she declared, devouring the fried tilapia with her fork and spoon.

'Let me help you with the fish bones,' I said to my grandma.

'Pity my dear Noon,' Mama murmured. 'Raymond might be in love with Clement.'

Shocked, Daniel spat the food out from his mouth.

I vetoed. Once again, Mama reverted to her babbling.

Uncle Raymond turned towards us at the comedic reaction.

I chortled quietly, hiding under my tote bag.

'The only way is for Noon to be pregnant,' Mama spoke to herself.

'Mama's imagination has scaled new heights,' Daniel whispered.

I wondered if my future mother-in-law would meddle in my pregnancy.

'Anyway, when is your mother coming back to visit me?' Mama asked.

'She's busy at the Communion Ministry,' I said.

'My eldest daughter would rather serve Jesus Christ than her mother.'

Mom's only contentment after my father walked out from their marriage was to serve at the church. The family secret I was supposed to keep, at least for now.

The waitress entered our private room to replenish the braised peanuts. Daniel poured part of it into his bowl. 'Think we're having a match-making dinner.'

'What?' I almost choked. 'For you maybe . . . '

'It's Kimchi and you,' Daniel whispered. 'Maybe, with another man too.'

'Are you serious?' Chills ran down my spine. Perseverant Mama would never back down. 'Then I'll pack up and run back to Kuala Lumpur.'

Suddenly, four guests walked into the private room with Uncle Raymond.

The woman looked to be in her mid-fifties. She was plump and was dressed in all-red with an ear-to-ear smile. It would be fair to call her a firework, as stated by Daniel. She walked up to the table and claimed an empty seat. An elderly couple followed her to the table and took their seats beside Mama. I nodded with a friendly smile as they returned the same. The fourth guest was a young woman, presumably the daughter of the couple. She took a seat beside her parents, behaving shyly.

'My name is Sister Jade,' the firework beamed, and then to Mama. 'I'd forgotten to collect my newly printed business cards today.' She clapped lightheartedly and turned to my cousin. 'We meet again, handsome.'

'Excuse me?' My cousin asked, confused.

'So young but has amnesia,' Sister Jade said. 'At the Chew Jetty temple prayer hall, your grandma introduced Mr Raymond and you to me.'

I turned to my cousin. He mouthed, 'Who the hell cares?' as he rolled his eyes.

Sister Jade was helping herself to the vegetarian noodles, scooping them into her bowl. 'Matchmaking business is so lucrative nowadays and keeps me so busy that I had to skip lunch today.'

It seemed like Mama and Uncle Raymond had met with this Madam Matchmaker at Chew Jetty, the same day as my internship with Uncle Sean started and Aunt Bridget gave me her complimentary sexy-meat lecture. It'd been arranged for Daniel, as the only heir to the Lau name. The baton to continue the nuclear family, to open the branches and spread the leaves, had been passed. A timeworn matrimonial custom my cousin was being compelled to observe in this modern era.

Daniel and I took turns to walk out of the private room.

'What are you gonna do?' I folded my arms.

My cousin exhaled, in deep thought. 'I need your support, Biu-jie.'

'Please don't mess things up,' I said.

Daniel shot me a lopsided smile. 'Just watch me.'

Back in the private room, the young woman was seated next to Daniel.

Mama then instructed me to sit next to the young woman's parents.

Aunt Bridget had just ordered a bottle of white wine to complement the steamed scallops. Daniel's suck-that expression was glazed with the fervour of an impending showdown, ready to explode at the soft touch of a trigger. I overheard the elderly couple discussing, in the mix of rudimentary Mandarin and Hokkien, my black rose tattoos, then Aunt Bridget's flamingo patterned qipao, in the hopes that even those that heard them would not be able to understand what they were talking about.

'What's your name, handsome?' asked Sister Jade, brushing Daniel's arm.

'Daniel,' my cousin murmured, avoiding his father's glower.

'This is Lily,' said Sister Jade.

Daniel briefly nodded at her.

'Look, so perfect, like a match-made in heaven.' Sister Jade clapped.

I pretended to cough while chewing. Daniel shot me a look. Aunt Bridget was typing away on her phone, immersed in a 'do not disturb' zone. Meanwhile, I rotated the Lazy Susan on the table and scooped up a serving from the meat dish for Mama, putting the chunks of meat and slices of braised yam on her plate.

'Eat carefully. Let me know if you want more,' I said to Mama.

'Madam Chew, how old is your granddaughter?' Sister Jade asked.

'She is old enough to be a mother to four children,' Mama said to Sister Jade.

I swallowed, feeling a subtle sense of humiliation.

'Anyway, please call me Betty.'

'Where did that English name come from?' Daniel asked Mama.

'The name was given by a neighbour,' Mama said. 'She thought Elizabeth was sweet, but I can't pronounce the "th" sound well. I chose Betty because of Loh Ti, China's classic beauty.'

'I remember you had an old newspaper cutting with a list of legendary screen-sirens that committed suicide due to mendacious men,' I said to Mama. 'Gone too soon.'

Mama smirked. 'Of course. My head is like a vault with untold secrets.'

'I shall keep an eye out for your granddaughter's potential suitor,' Sister Jade said, fanning off any negative vibes. 'There are tall, rich and handsome, or short, fat and bald to choose from. Some can cook and wash or can go all-night-long.'

Mama and Sister Jade giggled at the last one.

Feelings and emotions come and go. Time will prove love. Love lies in its sustainability. My phone buzzed as a text alert from Daniel lit up my screen.

> The Russian Roulette is in your direction now. You run, I run.

I replied to Daniel's text.

> We need to make a plan 😣

Aunt Bridget replied saying:

> Gamsahamnida, the kung pao chicken is mine

'Singing always brings a couple closer. Can we ask the restaurant manager to help set up karaoke? This should be fun.' Sister Jade said.

'I want to sing "My Heart Will Go On",' Lily said, blushing. 'Daniel will be Jack and I'll be Rose. Let's rehearse one time before singing.'

Daniel laughed. 'Sorry, I can't sacrifice my float for you.'

'The noblest thing is to die for the one you love,' Lily countered.

'I will die . . . but not for you,' Daniel said coldly.

Uncle Raymond glared at Daniel. 'Want me to slap you?'

I made a disapproving face at Daniel when I saw Lily was already in tears.

'Getting married to start a family, owning a small house, having a car and then earning a steady income are the top-five things I wish to achieve in life.' Lily said, her voice quavering slightly.

'Yeah, but that's you. Not me.'

Lily continued, 'My parents brought me up to be an obedient daughter, a docile wife, and a caring mother. They love me so much despite the fact that I'm just a vessel with holes, pouring out water.'

The last line was like a bullet to my heart.

Daughters are like water that is poured out, impossible to retrieve.

Lily was lucky not to experience the most toxic gender crisis in Chinese idioms.

'We just met like what . . . ten minutes ago,' Daniel sneered.

'You may not love me now but who knows in the future,' Lily said. 'We're of marriageable age, and one year is enough to cultivate feelings for each other.'

'I'm not what you think I am.'

Everyone became perplexed except Aunt Bridget, who was savouring the claypot kung pao chicken, happy to have it to herself. Lily's parents stood up after she left the table crying.

Daniel groaned, ran to chase after her, to make sure she was all right. Uncle Raymond told them to calm down and then sent me to check on the situation.

Lily walked back into the restaurant; eyes reddened.

Outside, Daniel stood by the pillar, staring up at the blanketing sky, then at me. 'I told her who—*what*—I really am. Guess my balls are stronger than tiger bile.'

Twenty-One

The pastry kitchen would never be the same again.

Daniel had a slap mark half the size of the Australian map on his cheek.

It happened after returning from the restaurant. Uncle Raymond had finally lost it when Daniel expressed his rejection of Lily. No one was able to stop my uncle. I'd let my cousin down with the ice water bucket incident and then this. Aunt Bridget was quick to flee from the scene. Mama was yelping, pleading her 'fighter-cock-son' to stop, and threatening to leave home if he won't.

Well, the filial son had to bow to his dramatic-mommy.

Since that morning Uncle Sean had been observing Daniel—pulling and trashing the freshly baked butter rolls from the trays onto the rack, then slamming the lid.

A flame was lit.

'Today, I will offer the bread to the Kitchen God,' Uncle Sean said.

'I'll do it,' Daniel volunteered.

'Unless you want to burn the Jade Emperor alive.'

I glared at Uncle Sean, asking him to tone down.

Daniel turned to him. 'You know I've always respected you as my elder, but these fists are ready to talk if you think I don't deserve to be a man.'

Michael swallowed in slow-mo. I was in awe of Uncle Sean's patience in the face of my cousin's volatile demeanour, his sprightly heaving chest, and red cheeks. Both their eyes looked feverish, as if they were about to swallow an erupted, molten rock whole.

'See this mark on my face,' Daniel pointed at Uncle Sean. 'It's the start of retaliation.'

What's running inside your head, Smelly-Dan?

'You'd be long dead if you were just a rookie by the street.'

The smell of kerosene wafted in to fan the flames of a no holds barred conflict.

I quickly turned to Michael. 'So, when are you going to teach us how to make kimchi buns? The soup kitchen needs some Korean-fusion baking here.'

'Oh,' Michael was highly receptive of Lau family tensions by now and swiftly picked up on the need to change topics from my random question. 'Thanks for reminding me, Emily. First, we need to source the best fermented kimchi, which is of course an important ingredient. But we need advice from the finest pastry chef Uncle Sean.'

'Learn from the way your seniors curry favour with me,' Uncle Sean chided Daniel.

Daniel frowned, wiping his sweat off and casting the towel aside.

I picked up the towel, soaking it inside a shallow plastic basin and then rinsing it with tap water. Uncle Sean muttered in dissatisfaction as I hung the towel, for I'd bequeathed my help to pacify my cousin's Peter Pan Syndrome. When my cousin had composed himself, I gave him a pat on the shoulder. He forced a smile. Then, Michael nudged my cousin's arm, taking the edge off tonight's tension.

'You two, go easy on the kneading. Treat the dough with respect,' Uncle Sean said. 'This isn't the pottery scene from *Ghost*.'

Michael looked confused as Daniel and I burst into giggles. Especially at the last line. Not only was the Monk traumatized by Aunt Bridget's unwanted affection, but the movie had also become his Achilles' heel.

'This is my final warning!' Uncle Sean said. 'The two of you really have no respect.'

'Oh, quit shouting,' my witty cousin said. 'The Kitchen God won't be happy despite you having that huge-ass militant tattoo on your bronze greasy back.'

Quiet dogs bite hard—my cousin had been testing the prison warden's equilibrium.

'My aunt is right. You have no-balls.'

Uncle Sean shoved a knife at my cousin. 'I'll cut your tongue out!'

Daniel's fist slammed against the table. 'Be a man. Admit to the rest that you'd gone to visit my aunt in the hospital.'

Uncle Sean gasped.

Daniel struck the Monk with his right fist.

Oh geez! I ran to the corner.

Michael interfered on time, grabbing my cousin.

'Stay out of this, Kimchi . . .' Daniel muttered.

But, Michael needn't have interfered on Uncle Sean's behalf. The man was quick to dodge. 'Let him.' The sound of him cracking his knuckles and neck bones was eerily audible. 'Been a while since I've practised my skill.'

'You're gonna lose and end up licking my arse,' Daniel yelled.

Uncle Sean twisted the towel and flicked it against Daniel's left cheek. I heard the sound of cloth meeting flesh, harsher than it had any right to be. Daniel's left cheek was now blooming red. It had happened in a jiffy. Next, my cousin was knocked off, right onto his knees. I helped him up, checking his *new* wound. Daniel blinked, shivering, rubbing his face, but looking fine—bruised but fine.

'It was just a scare,' Uncle Sean clarified when he caught me glaring daggers at him.

'Thanks,' I replied with all the sarcasm I could muster.

'If I really gave it my all, he'd be in the emergency.'

I gathered my thoughts. 'Honestly, the pastry kitchen is a place for harmony, with blessings from the Kitchen God. We should bake all pastries and breads with unending love.'

Michael gestured a thumb's up at me.

Uncle Sean threw in his towel with a loud thump on the floor, looking at all three of us in a disapproving manner. I'd defied him by being honest. 'Make sure all the dough has been shaped properly, so it rises in soft peaks inside the oven by the time I return,' he said.

'You're my heroine,' Daniel said to me.

'Don't talk while you're working,' I warned Daniel.

'But men don't like Tiger-Women, right Kimchi?' Nitwit-Daniel said.

Michael tried to hold in his laughter. 'I despise the loud and the boisterous, but don't mind the one who mistakenly-takes-my-drink.' His forearm brushed mine.

Airheaded-Daniel was scratching his head while I shot Michael a lethal stare.

I pretended to cough. 'Three of us work as a team. That's the reality.'

'Biu-jie has finally awakened,' Daniel said. 'We should drum-out that full-of-shit feng-shui master. We have to counter this inauspicious *sha-qi* in this kitchen.'

'What're you planning to do?' Michael and I asked in unison.

'I am telling Old Bean the truth,' Daniel said affirmatively.

* * *

'Being gay doesn't mean I'm a terrorist!'

Daniel started the civil war at 4.44 a.m.

An intense rattling—of earthquake potential without a tsunami alert—shook the bungalow's foundation. Footsteps stopped in front of my room. I called out from my bed. The shadow remained immobile outside my room. I called out my cousin's name in full, and then Michael's and there was still no response. If only the dizziness in my head would've subsided. Instead of lying on the bed, I got up and counted to five before walking to the door. Before I could pull it open, a letter was slipped under the door.

I deserve to be who I really am.

I sighed at my cousin's handwriting.

* * *

It'd been a week since Daniel left home.

He'd sneak in and start working in the pastry kitchen in predawn hours and then clock out at 6 p.m. on the dot. His 'I'm fucking alive' text popped up constantly on the Lau-d & Praud group chat. Aunt Bridget had muted him for causing irritation.

'What if I asked for an extended stay?' Michael asked.

'What for?' I passed a bowl of ABC vegetable soup to a homeless man.

'Daniel's been working on the food drive in major cities and then the evening shift at the pastry kitchen. The memo is out.' Michael scooped white rice onto a plate. 'And you're not available for the night shift.'

Checking the bain-marie food warmer, the soup kitchen had only Michael and me on duty at the counter. I had to wear a guise of cheerful friendliness, and not resign myself to Daniel's situation. Memo, my foot! Even Serendipity Sanctuary had politics, mixing work with consanguinity. Daniel's coming out had shattered Uncle Raymond's tolerance ceiling.

'Mama doesn't want to have a burned-toast-coloured granddaughter baking under the hot sun, so no food drive work for me.' I fluffed the rice up from the container.

I looked up and was alarmed by Michael's eyes, which had been observing me.

I cleared my throat. 'I'll talk to Uncle Raymond and Uncle Clement to get me involved in the food drive. I have to be out in the field.' I then informed a volunteer to alert the gourmet side to replenish a few new dishes, urging the crowd to queue up. 'Also, I want to be back on night shift, as I'm perfectly fit for it now.'

Michael was quiet for a moment and then walked closer to me. 'I'll have to be with you working the night shift. Daniel is not here. Mama wants me to take care—'

Everybody was stunned as I dropped the ladle into the stew-gravy pot on purpose. Michael was undeterred, in fact his expression was becoming stricter. I was exhausted being stuck between some bullshit-pseudoscience and Mama's goodwill. Daniel's matchmaking story had gotten the best of me. He'd been ballsy enough to cement his rebellion by running away from home, effectively registering his unwillingness to being treated badly after being slapped by Uncle Raymond—twice. I'd thought about having a chat with my uncle, encouraging him to be kind to his son, but he'd been binge-drinking away his sorrow on the rooftop terrace after work.

'Daniel will be home soon,' I said to stop Michael from probing further.

'Look at the crowded soup kitchen,' is all Michael said in return.

'We shall observe for another week.' I smiled at a man, clasped his hands as he thanked me in rudimentary English after receiving a bowl of dhal. 'For now, respect Uncle Raymond's position as the centre's chief.'

'By the way, Mama had a long chat with me this morning,' Michael said.

'Mama refused to talk to us after the Daniel incident.'

Michael gazed at me.

'Anyway, what has she been telling you?' I asked.

'It was just a simple and heartfelt chat.' Michael's eyes started to get teary. 'She reminds me of my *halmeoni*. I couldn't make it in time to see mine one last time, as I was sitting for my finals in the U.S. And I lost my grandfather when I was ten. He was a tofu maker and unfortunately left to meet the maker without passing on his skill to his sons.'

'I'm sorry to hear that.' This was by far the most emotional straight-from-the-heart talk I'd had with Michael.

'Relatives bring joy to us, though at times they might be meddlesome even if it's usually for a good reason.'

I glanced at Michael. 'My grandfather passed away before I was born. Mama only had one photo of him where he was clad in a police sergeant uniform. Think Mama still keeps his medals. She'd often compliment him and then act all cutesy, repeatedly telling us about their first meeting, and their first cinema-going date and their wedding. But I can't seem to establish any connection with him just by looking at the photo.'

'Michael!'

I was stunned by Uncle Raymond's raspy voice.

'Emily, you're here too. Perfect. Both of you go to the storeroom and bring out two sacks of potatoes, the gourmet side needs it. Hurry up!'

* * *

Michael and I were greeted by particles of mould and dust the moment the storeroom door opened. I blocked the door from closing by placing a thick stopper under the slit. Michael switched on the lights and stayed by the door, coughing non-stop. Uncle Raymond had warned us about the broken knob that was yet to be fixed.

I found the potatoes stacked atop the red onions. While removing the bundle, I heard a loud thud and looked behind to see the door shut as Michael had abandoned his post and moved towards me.

'Didn't I tell you to stay outside?' I asked. 'Look, we're trapped inside.'

'I thought you might need help.' Michael called someone from his phone. However, a few moments later, he hung up. 'No one's picking up.'

I cursed under my breath and bowed my head, walking at a slower pace. To keep a sound mind, I pretended to check on the canned foods in the cramped food aisle. A fleeting chokehold persisted over me. Trapped in a locked room, goosebumps trailed along my neck, down to my spine. I broke out in cold sweat. I switched off the lights that could give rise to excessive heat.

I gathered my strength, kicking at the door once, and then twice.

Michael held me back, dragging me backward as I was about to kick the third time, he cornered me. 'Emily! Stop it!'

'I'm sorry, Michael. I should've waited outside.' Leaning against the wall, my fingernails continued to scratch it. Once I was exhausted, I sank to my knees and tucked my face in between my legs, curling up for protection.

'Listen to me. I am here,' Michael said.

'Such a small thing but I failed to do it.' The intrusive, displeasing thought had invaded. I got up, feeling wonky.

My eyes were swollen with uncontrollable tears, I was afraid to look at Michael's face as I stepped into his embrace. *Warm.* The eerie silence. I pulled away from him and started patting my chest in a four-four cadence beat, and then tapping the platinum necklace, humming to the melody that Edward had composed and that I'd penned the lyrics to at the writer's retreat.

'Try to stay focused, Emily.' Michael gently held my hands. 'Breathe in. Close your eyes.' I did as he said, after each set of four beats. 'You are safe here.' I nodded, despite feeling suffocated. 'I'm here.' He repeated. I felt a little hypnotized by his soothing voice.

Then, a deluge of emotions came over me, pulling me towards the aftermath of an entanglement without closure—Edward's call to Sabrina. A promising visit to clarify his abrupt ghosting. If only I had less to drink that night. If I had stayed awake, waiting for Sabrina to get home, to deliver the *news*. Fiona's underserving to be loved remarks to me just added salt to the wound.

I vented it all out by thrashing—

Then, a pair of hands grabbed mine.

My eyes opened. 'Oh. I'm . . . I'm very sorry,' I apologized, checking on him.

He dismissed my apology. 'I got you.'

I nodded, guilt washing over me.

'Hope they'll get to us soon,' he said looking at his watch.

I tried for levity. 'We aren't growing and harvesting potatoes here.'

Michael chuckled. I pursed my lips as the time slowly passed. And then my gaze met his. 'My father used to lock me in a storeroom,' I muttered.

'I'm sorry to hear that.' He looked at me. 'Is that why your room has disco lights?'

'Well, my crazy, cynical relatives know best.' I chuckled bitterly. 'I was diagnosed with chronic mood disorder after I was discovered in a parking lot by a jogger. The police concluded that I was trying to kill myself.'

'I'm sorry to hear that.'

'Physical abuse is easier to detect because of the nasty scarring or the marks it leaves on the skin,' I continued. 'Emotional abuse is unseen.'

'It is not easy to share this with an acquaintance.'

'Years of being belittled, being made to feel a humiliation that was unforgiving.' I leaned forward. 'Waking up every day is like walking on a rope suspended hundreds of feet in the air.'

Michael's arms bridged the distance between us. A subtle closeness that I could rely on. An emergency. 'Does the promise ring person know about your past?'

'He doesn't,' I said, focusing on my stress-and-anxiety management breathing exercises. 'Who knows, he could've already forgotten about me,' I said bitterly.

Michael didn't reply. A weight then lifted off my chest, his comforting embrace was loquacious and deliberate, bringing us much closer than we had been before.

* * *

Uncle Raymond came to our rescue approximately thirty minutes later.

Twenty-Two

Overlooking Penang Hill, Mama's retreat at the Buddhist monastery had been rather unexpected. I placed her suitcase against the cement accent wall.

Above the open window, the chime danced in circles. My fingers ran along the chalk white paper attached to it, pondering the '安' calligraphy character—Edward's surname in Hanzi—that meant calm and peaceful in both Chinese and Korean.

Daniel leaned against the wall. It'd been two weeks since he'd left home.

'Come here . . .' Mama said to him, taking out something from her canvas bag.

'OMG, you sneaked in a hard-boiled egg.' My cousin grimaced.

Mama glowered. 'Why? Do I need to ask your father's permission?'

'There's no strip-search and interrogation here,' I said.

'Just an egg, not a hand grenade. Oh, pity my Daniel. His cheek looks like a pig's head.' Mama patted him then wrapped the egg with cotton gauze, carefully rubbing it on the swollen parts clockwise. 'Luckily, you didn't end up in the ICU.'

'Old Bean is a big bad daddy.' Daniel sulked, channelling his Peter Pan Syndrome. I checked out the Lucky Bamboo with a red ribbon tied around it.

'One slap is already enough to embarrass you in front of Lily and her parents,' Mama exhaled. 'Then, you risked it for another punch the next day. What an itchy backside you have.' Mama's sugar-coated sarcasm was an attempt to convey to Daniel that he had asked for it.

'I didn't think he could be that merciless to his only son.'

'Serves you right for digging your own grave?' Mama said.

'Ah, pain. Go slow.' Daniel distorted his face in mock-pain, then dragged me to the side and whispered. 'Did you tell Mama' bout my . . .' he meant his sexual orientation.

'Don't manhandle your Biu-jie, it's very rude,' Mama said.

Daniel pouted, grabbing the egg from Mama to rub on his painful cheek.

Mama said, 'Today, you move back home. Do not stay in St Paul's like a church mouse.'

'Mama is talking about your runaway story,' I said through gritted teeth to Daniel.

'Two of you stop talking behind my back,' Mama pointed.

'No,' Daniel answered immediately. 'I refuse to see that old fart's face.'

Mama nonchalantly exclaimed. 'A cold war between my son and me has started because of Smelly-Daniel, one of my precious gold melons. I think our family needs lots of blessings. From now on, I've decided to be a vegetarian, indefinitely.'

'So, this is the reason you want to stay here for a month?' I asked Mama.

Mama avoided my question, which was suspicious because the usual answer would have been a 'yes'.

'Excessive eating of veggies will cause nutrient deficiencies,' Daniel said.

Mama looked up. 'Does a change in my diet need your permission to be carried out? Do you want me to be honest? All of your lives are screwed up, confirmed to be upside-down.'

Unfortunately, none of us could live up to her expectations.

She stood up, gripping the cane. 'I'm the only person that can have a heart-to-heart talk with the Goddess Guanyin, asking her to grant harmony, mercy, and love to our family before I meet her.

There's no perfect timing. It can be any time, since I have one foot in the coffin at this age.'

'We should have a choice, Mama,' I said.

'Yeah, let us choose what is best for us,' Daniel seconded.

'Those wings must've been growing well, look at how very vocal you are.' Mama looked at us.

'Daniel needs to forge ahead to grow up.'

'From getting me a wife to pairing Biu-jie up with Michael, we understand your benevolence.' Daniel was carefully testing the waters.

'Don't you even get me started on Lily's case,' Mama was stomping the cane on the floor, then waving it at me. 'And why are you so blind? Michael is single and available . . .' she stopped for a while then continued, 'and very rich. What do you want then?'

'Money-faced Mama,' Daniel teased.

'How'd you know his family background?' I asked.

'We had a chat over Kopi O,' Mama said.

'Too much kimchi will cause digestive distress,' Daniel added.

Aunt Bridget poked her head in from the window. 'I really don't mind helping Emily make her way into Michael's pants, you know, with my experience.'

Mama released the cord lock of the blinds, shutting them to block my aunt's view. 'Let me focus on Daniel and Lily first.'

'Clarification time,' I barged in. 'Daniel was afraid that his golden grandson status would be revoked due to Michael's existence.'

'How can he be my grandson? He doesn't have any Lau blood.'

'See, I told you so,' I said to Daniel. 'Stop behaving like a scaredy cat.'

'However, he's in the same VVIP list as my grandson-in-law,' Mama retorted.

I rolled my eyes, mentally slapping my forehead.

'I saw Biu-jie's ex-lover. Asian. Much more handsome than Mr Kimchi.'

Daniel screamed the moment I pinched his swollen cheek as revenge.

'Ha.' Mama became inattentive. 'His family name is "An" from Taiwan. Bridget told me about it.' Aunt Bridget walked in, eager to be part of the gossip. 'The one consistent thing I've observed from my eight previous relationships is that women change partners for a charitable cause,' she said sitting beside me. 'We give away our *old toys* to other female desperados.'

'Anyway, I lied about his nationality.' I cleared my throat.

'Like condoms, used once and discarded,' Daniel ignored me, replying to Aunt Bridget's statement.

No one seemed to be attentive. *Great.* 'His name is Ahn Myeongjun, he's a K-pop idol-turned-soloist. His English name is Edward,' I said in one breath.

Everyone was motionless and looked dubious, like three pillars of salt with not a grain of conscience. Meanwhile, at the door, the caretaker announced lunchtime at 1.11 p.m.

'Stop lying,' Mama said, laughing in disbelief.

'You really dated a . . . Korean pop-idol?' Daniel faked a cry.

'Then I've dated James Dean before birth,' Aunt Bridget giggled.

I slid and showed them the photo Edward and me had taken on the bed at the writer's retreat. Daniel, Mama, and Aunt Bridget crowded around and began to whisper to each other.

'Oi—' I clapped. All three of them snapped their head towards me. 'Don't believe me? Fine.'

'Both of you had clothes on. . .' Aunt Bridget wondered.

'We don't take naked photos. By right, there shouldn't be any photos at all but Edward trusted that I won't send it out.'

Daniel read from his phone. 'Former K-pop idol Ahn Myeongjun's second single from his solo album, "Sibjalo" was inspired by a memorable, lovely encounter during his trip to Malaysia.' Daniel looked at me. '*Koreaboo*'s articles are 99.99per cent accurate. He's talking about you, right . . . Biu-jie?'

I gulped, pursing my lips. Dammit, I'd been out-lawyered by Daniel.

'You must've already slept with Edward,' Mama whispered.

I groaned, mortified. 'I didn't.'

'Does he have tattoos similar to yours?' Mama asked.

'I seriously don't know.'

Aunt Bridget winked. 'Hey, foreplay counts too, a man who is willing to go down on his woman is the real fucking deal.' I gestured at her to drop the profanity. Eyes shut, I needed a hideout. 'Like, yes, moisten up the dry firewood,' my aunt continued. 'Only then will it burn fiercely.'

'Since Emily is being brutally honest today, I have a confession too.'

'You have a new boyfriend, Ma?' Aunt Bridget gasped.

'Crazy,' Mama said drolly. 'It's about my dead husband's extramarital affair.'

'What?' Daniel and I exclaimed. 'Ah-Gong had a mistress outside!'

'This is old news to me.' Aunt Bridget left Mama's room.

* * *

It had been a long day at the Buddhist monastery. The eight-course vegetarian meal for lunch and dinner felt like a detox, a spiritual cleanse. Sounds came from the rooftop terrace.

'Hey Emily, do you want to join us for a drink?' Uncle Clement asked.

'For her, only carbonated drinks are allowed,' Uncle Raymond said. 'Let me get her some.' He made his way to the family's kitchen.

'Take a seat. Have some.' Uncle Clement passed me a plate of roasted cashew nuts. 'This is your home. You shouldn't be shy.'

'My cousin told me he's been staying in the church,' I said.

Uncle Clement nodded. 'Oh, you met him today?'

'Yes.' I didn't elaborate further, having survived Mama and Aunt Bridget's interrogation about Edward with mudslinger Daniel cheering them on.

'That's why Michael has been working a lot harder at the kitchens.'

I smiled briefly. 'Well, I took a day off with my uncle's approval.'

'We rarely have foreigners volunteering in the kitchens,' Uncle Clement said. 'But he's the exception. He's like a gem, really.'

'He didn't mind extending his stay due to the shortage of volunteers,' I said.

'Great.'

For once, everything was aligning perfectly—

—or so it seemed.

Uncle Clement added. 'We need sponsors for the food drive charity project.'

Daniel had planned to have Mama's assorted homemade kuih and stage Aunt Bridget's drama script, to manifest his brainchild. Evidently, they'd been underfunded in any case.

I remember Madam Ong taking eight months to two years to fund a single-mother shelter and an orphanage as part of a project I was tasked to work on with Sabrina. We'd have given up if not for Madam Ong's passion and effort. 'I'll take note of that,' I said, wondering what was taking Uncle Raymond so long.

'The church committee has drafted a blueprint ranging from learning courses and training programmes as well as the certificates. I wouldn't have expected you to be so precise.'

I smiled briefly.

'So, have you ever thought of going back to being the legal eagle?'

'You know about my educational background.'

Uncle Clement snapped the melon seed in half and then ate it. 'Raymond told me about it when he proposed to have you join as an intern.'

'You have an elephant's memory,' I said, observing his every move.

'Sorry, it's an occupational syndrome,' he said. 'Something I can never shake off despite having been retired for quite some time.'

'Were you a lawyer too?' I asked as I helped myself to some water.

'Most important is what you want to do in life.' He simply grinned. 'Humans learn from their mistakes. But remember, do not to be fooled twice.'

'What do you think of Michael?' I asked, changing the topic.

'He's very humble despite being from a rich family—'

'I see—' This was the second person alluding to his wealth after Mama.

'His family owns a conglomerate of retail companies in South Korea.'

* * *

I put aside Aunt Bridget's script *Violet Roses Cobalt Blue*.

The one she had almost rolled down the stairs to save—her precious.

Comparable to *Lust, Cautious* and vibing with the dark side of *2046*, the short drama was planned to be the much-anticipated opening act of the fundraising food drive.

I sat there, glancing at Michael reading his lines and marking the script. I was appalled at the idea of acting as his love interest. To complicate things further, I realized my aunt was right—you must act like you're living your script and then once that is done, leave your character on the silver screen.

Aunt Bridget put on her glasses, puffing away from a smokeless pipe, another stolen acting prop from a film location in Vietnam. The script was rolled into a scroll in her grip.

'Now, my dear mentees, turn to page eight, that's the goodbye scene between Rui-er and Lu-yang,' Aunt Bridget said, looking ahead at the pagoda.

'The male protagonist's name sounds so Chinese,' I said.

'He's a Korean spy, fluent in Shanghainese, who has studied political science in Japan and turns the tide by providing aid to the Chinese nationalists.' Aunt Bridget eyed Michael. 'This is inspired by you. So, don't disappoint me.'

'Miss Bridget, you're very creative.' Michael looked bashful.

Aunt Bridget glared. 'Bridget, please.'

Michael looked away and ruffled his hair.

Taking a stroll around Michael, like a cougar, Aunt Bridget examined her prey. 'Now, forget that sexy melting butter in the pot, and the cocaine-like flour . . .'

I braced myself for Infinite Acting Lesson 101, overlooking Penang Hill.

Aunt Bridget waved the thin bamboo cane, looking like a teacher intent to discipline her pupils as her Alexander McQueen heels clacked with every step. 'Emily, the love of your life is leaving, not sure he's ever going to return. He could be killed and then dumped by the street, and you wouldn't even know. It is a warring period. Bloods, guns, grief, and starvation are everywhere. Focus, focus—'

I squeezed my eyes attempting hard to paint this image in my head.

Aunt Bridget snapped her fingers. 'Think of your Edward. It may work.'

'No thanks,' I said sarcastically.

'You can take me as him,' Michael said.

I turned to him to see if he was kidding.

'I mean only for this scene.'

'Michael Kim, you're so professional. I like you,' Aunt Bridget said giggling.

I snickered at Daniel, mimicking the way she talked.

'Mama's got her hands full making her traditional kuih. Of course, I absolutely have to be part of this historic fundraising food drive so I can promote myself as an evergreen actress. I hope to rent a studio to teach drama classes to both adults and children. Acting is an art. It's not only a way to make money, it can also be a hobby or be used for therapeutic purposes.'

I sensed the emotional intensity in Aunt Bridget's words, it was further intensified by the sound of the monks chanting.

'Besides, this is a teary bye-bye scene, are there any happy ones? No one wants to cry enough tears to fill the Mississippi River at the fundraising food drive,' I said to my aunt.

'I remember a scene in *Ghost*, where Demi Moore's tears fell the moment she looked up,' Michael said. 'Natural and perfectly captured, it was pure and nostalgic.'

I nodded, agreeing. 'That was extremely moving.'

Aunt Bridget's hand fanned it off. 'Why pick this among so many?'

Michael blinked. 'It's my favourite. There's an ongoing theatrical stage performance of *Ghost*, and I've watched it so many times in Seoul.'

That's news to me. 'Don't get sidetracked!' Aunt Bridget shrieked, turning red. Daniel, Michael, and I cringed at the loudness. 'So garrulous. Win me over with your climaxing emotional fire.'

'We're just acting part of the script,' I said.

'Unless this is the Oscar-nominated scene,' Michael added.

'Well, I'm crying out for Hollywood,' Aunt Bridget proclaimed.

* * *

I felt Rui-er had taken over me after the rehearsal.

Meticulously created by Aunt Bridget during her admission-vacay in Gleneagles, Rui-er was a learned student, born and raised in 1920s Shanghai. Historically, there could be such a person in reality who lived through a period of insurrection.

Warring period stories were narratives of real events, warnings to never to repeat history. *Supposedly*. But there were some in life that made the same mistake more than once with no intention to repent. Rui-er's characterization was an act of political revolt, resembling Qiu Jin. The slain feminist's brutal death became a pivotal event, a galvanizing voice to motivate the early liberation of Chinese women, such as the freedom to marry and receive education, and the abolishment of the practice of foot-binding. After all, 'Rui' when translated to Mandarin Chinese meant 'razor-sharp'.

This script manifested an overdue farewell to Edward.

Aunt Bridget was right.

It worked magnificently when I invited Edward back into my head—those lips I dreamed of kissing, the scent of the intimate connection I yearned for, to call him mine, his bronze-purplish highlighted strands that felt the raw on my fingertips, that vibrant impish laughter, and his eyes, which always seemed to be getting a load of me.

'Am I disturbing you?' Michael asked.

'Not at all.' I smiled briefly.

'You did a great job acting today.'

'You too,' I looked up. 'Anyway, it's bedtime for me.'

'I'm sorry,' Michael said quickly. 'So, what do you think of the dress?'

My fingers were tracing the lilac lace dress on my bed. I'd almost forgotten about Fiona's engagement party, which was in two weeks. 'Thanks. I didn't know you could get it in such a short time.'

'My family owns a couture house in Kuala Lumpur,' Michael said.

Uncle Clement was right. Mr Kimchi came from a rich family.

'Why'd you want to go knowing you're not welcome? And I wonder why she invited me too.' His brows knitted.

'You don't have to, though. Go, I mean.'

'Well, if you're going then I'm too.' Michael's tone had a note of finality.

I patted my neck, about to reply to him, but realized—

—the promise ring and the platinum chain it was hanging from were missing.

I remembered taking it off and putting it on the desk before going to shower. My breaths were coming heavy and fast. I sat on my bed with my arms around myself. There shouldn't be a fourth blackout. *Please don't let there be a fourth blackout.*

Twenty-Three

I should have been prepped for Fiona's engagement party. But my soul had been floating aimlessly, counting to day fifteen without the promise ring.

Michael walked into my hotel room. 'Why aren't you getting dressed?'

Instead of answering him, I told him to buy me another vanilla latte.

'No more.' Michael said, inspecting my hands, which were shaking slightly. He rubbed his hands over mine to generate warmth and then picked up the AC remote to adjust the temperature. 'You'll get a caffeine overdose.'

I woke up two nights ago, craving that bitter-candy antidepressant.

The alcohol poisoning admission and the urge to get intoxicated were inconsequential in that moment. For now, I could only rely on the lingfu amulet to reduce anxiety; the promise ring together with the platinum chain were yet to be found. If not for my negligence, I would still have it, I would still have *him*.

If only I could upend and search the entirety of Serendipity Sanctuary.

Michael read a text from my phone screen. 'Sabrina is wondering where you are.'

'Please tell her I'm not feeling well enough to—'

'Not this time.' Michael interrupted me. 'I'm going through with this with you.'

I sidestepped Michael and opened the door.

'Going elsewhere, dear cousin?'

Gosh, why would Daniel want to bring Kenneth along?

'Move over, I'm leaving,' I snapped, attempting to push Daniel away.

'Michael, do you mind leaving us alone?' Daniel asked.

I turned to Daniel after Michael left. 'I'm not ready.'

'Remember FEAR: Fight Everything and Rise. You told me that.'

'No. I'm choosing to Fuck-Everything-And-Run.'

'Think about Mama's story—clutching onto that cleaver, rushing all the way down to the next block when she heard from the constable's wife that Ah-Gong was at the mistress's house. Bear in mind, she's only five feet tall.'

'Yeah, Mama got balls.' Anxiety continued to seep in as I sat on the bed. 'Lucky that the blade didn't plunge into Grandpa's head.'

'She might've missed on purpose,' Daniel said, 'Mama only had her spicy, sharp tongue and that valorous heart and soul to save the day.'

I pursed my lips.

My cousin added, 'Biu-jie, you and I are part of Mama's lineage. Bring out that courage. And Fiona isn't T-1000. Her limbs won't nano-morph into stabbing blades.'

I narrowed my eyes at him, my arms still pointedly folded, and chuckled.

'Well, I wouldn't have come over without a trump card under my sleeve.' My cousin took out his phone and then scrolled to a pre-recorded video.

'Oi, listen . . .' Mama's voice was alarming, pointing and poking at the screen. 'Don't embarrass me. You have one-quarter of my bloodline in your veins.'

Then, Daniel pressed the next button.

'This crown is yours when you bring my Jimmy Choo pumps back drenched in blood!' Aunt Bridget was pointing at a Wonder Woman bracer headwear.

Daniel logged off from the phone. 'Sorry, Aunt Bridget took that a little . . . too far.' He looked at me. 'Well, you should know by now that all of us are behind you.'

I just have to bite the bullet, I thought while putting on the dress.

A smile appeared on Daniel's face as he applauded my efforts and then winked at me supportively. Kenneth was behaving wildly, clutching onto the travel make-up box. I pirouetted in a circle, taking a bow. The Sambal-Belacan pair cheered at my sudden transformation, each holding my hand for a dance. Michael was trying hard not to laugh. I giggled when Daniel threw a pillow at Michael for imitating our bad moves. I stole glimpses at Michael from the mirror when Kenneth was curling my hair. Kimchi was buttoning up his sleeve cuffs and probing his defined jawline, revealing the curve of his neck while adjusting the jacquard scarf-tie, and then steadily hand-brushing the undercuts to ensure there was no crimping on both sides.

'I need to fix something on Emily's dress,' Michael said.

'But I haven't got her all dolled up yet.' Kenneth said.

Michael bent down, speaking as he looked at our reflections. 'This looks fine to me.'

'Yeah. I'm disgusted by heavy make-up.'

Michael turned to me, nodding.

'Don't turn Biu-jie into a peacock,' Daniel warned with a smile.

Kenneth, who seemed not to comprehend, was then dragged away by my cousin. Michael shook his head at Kenneth's insensitivity as I looked away.

Michael retrieved a roll of lilac-coloured thread from the metal-box and a medium-length sewing needle from the reusable foam. Carefully, he pulled the strand through the needle's eye, snipped and then knotted the end of the fibre, telling me to remain still.

I gulped, feeling Michael's hands sliding placidly along my shoulder then my back and then my spine, measuring the fabric with delicate but firm pinches. I kept my gaze on the window, looking at the guests in masquerade costumes, who were gathering opposite Hard Rock Café, as his fingers tightened the fabric between my waist and hips and then stitched it well, displaying the curves that I had been craving. Michael then moved to the left side. With a steady, apologetic tone, he rested both of his hands on my rear end, repeating the same process. I let out a silent exhale when I felt him caress my lower back. No one had touched me this way. Except Edward Ahn.

Tenderness hovered as our mutual gazes melded together. His compassion glistened with trust. I gulped and then softly cleared my throat. 'Sewing darts seems to be the dressmaker's imperative task.'

Michael pursed his lips, nodded approvingly.

'So, you brought the sewing kit all the way from Penang?' I asked.

'I borrowed it from the couture house at Mont Kiara,' he said.

'That would've explained why you had to arrive early.'

'This was tailor-made according to the measurements of the Malaysian women. But I know there's some alteration needed when you put it on.'

I gulped as his hand pressed on the flimsy lace netting on my back. 'How long since your family established a fashion boutique here?'

'About a decade or so, our clients are mostly Korean—expats, diplomats, local and foreign entrepreneurs and politicians, businesswomen . . . and their lovers.'

This confirmed Mama and Uncle Clement's not-so-subtle rich, Korean reference.

Michael stood up. 'Every cut of the fabric, from sewing to stitching and even its embroidery has been done by hand.'

'Must be pricey,' I said, jolting in surprise as Michael suddenly pulled the threads together then snipped them. 'Thanks a lot, but you actually don't have to.'

'You're an indisputable beauty,' Michael said, hands on my shoulder as he languidly inspected me. 'Imagine what Rui-er would do if she were in your shoes.'

* * *

The guard in a suit-jacket escorted us to the registration table. A portrait of Fiona and Benedict, her fiancé, was placed along with a billboard at the banquet entrance. A woman at the reception table was inspecting my face, after I signed the hardcover guest book, telling me to help myself to the refreshments.

Michael handed me a glass of some kind of fruit mocktail. 'Do you know her?'

'She tried to break my finger at the door,' I said. 'Now, they can't believe it—seeing a wallflower with a handsome gentleman.' I smirked.

'Don't think you're that substandard,' Michael said to me.

'You both are late!' Sabrina threw her arms around me.

I hugged her back.

'Is it okay if I request to hug a Korean oppa, please?' she requested.

Michael couldn't hide his laughter.

Watching Sabrina melt into his embrace, I wondered how my life with Edward would have been—travelling in a black SUV with tinted windows, escorted by bodyguards, constantly on alert about the paparazzi and fear being attacked by the sasaeng fans.

'Oh,' Sabrina's expression had changed. 'Fiona wants to see Emily.'

My heart sank like it had taken a hit from a sledgehammer.

'The dinner is starting soon, right?' I said, trying to avoid meeting Fiona.

'Do you need me to go with you?' Michael whispered.

'Sabrina is with me. I should be fine.'

'Call me if you need anything,' Michael said.

Sabrina pressed the elevator button.

My eyes closed as the elevator descended to the guest suite. I couldn't pay any attention to Sabrina's chattering. I smiled at my phone when I received a text message from Daniel telling me that he'd be at the bar lounge downstairs, prepared to storm into the banquet if and when I was in need his urgent assistance. Afterwards, I pursed my lips, enduring the burning sensation in my heels, thanks to my aunt's pure black, limited edition diamond stilettos.

The lift dinged. And I wondered what my strength was supposed to be.

We walked a few steps. Sabrina pressed the bell.

Fiona opened the door with a wide grin.

Bottles of champagne, sparkling wine, and hard liquor were scattered across the floor. A glass of wine had been knocked over, like blood dripping from the leather sofa. Sabrina pulled me aside so I wouldn't crash into the dishevelled woman in a blindfold who was wearing a dress with a plunging neckline and drinking from the bottle. A woman with smudged mascara had instructed Fiona to make penalty drinks for me for being late, while she was told to sit through a male striptease before dinner started.

'Why didn't you tell me about . . . this?' I asked Sabrina in disgust.

'I did. In the elevator.' She side-eyed me.

I sighed, berating myself for not paying attention earlier.

'You've missed the fun,' Fiona said, walking up to me.

'Not here for your lifestyle of debauchery,' I said. 'Why do you want to see me?'

'I want to speak to only you,' Fiona said to me, pointedly asking Sabrina to leave.

'Not without me.' Sabrina replied, ready to defend me.

'I'm the host!' Fiona declared. 'The superior!'

I whispered to Sabrina that I would be fine. After much thought, she gripped my hand and squeezed it, letting me go. She instructed Fiona—five minutes and no more—and then left.

Fiona rolled her eyes, then lifted my hands upward to inspect my dress. 'The colour is disappointing,' she hissed at me.

'It's . . . polite,' I said.

'Oh, must be a Korean thing.'

I took a step closer. 'Jealous? You've got yours. Why bother?'

'Not all good things are meant for you. You lied to me. About that K-pop idol!'

My eyes widened. I rubbed my forehead, knowing what she meant. 'Look here, Sabrina and I had to abide to the company's policy. I'm sorry for not telling the truth.'

'Sabrina cleared that up.' Fiona rocked back and forth, leaning against the wall.

'We'll talk when you're sober,' I said after a few moments of silence, not wanting to waste my time.

'I saw Edward Ahn,' Fiona said just as I was turning to leave.

I was immobile, as if I had been hit by a stray bullet, my fingers dug into my palm.

'He arrived at Sabrina's apartment the day you were admitted,' Fiona added.

I loathed the sound of his name on this woman's tongue. There was this excruciating pain like needles pricking my skin, puncturing me for hours. I turned to face her, a machete waiting to strike. 'What proof do you have?'

Fiona cackled so hard she almost choked.

Someone knocked on the door then. I contemplated my escape from this crazy situation.

'The ceremony is starting in ten minutes,' the emcee yelled from outside.

'More to come, stay tuned . . .' Fiona said to me, threateningly.

Part III

Twenty-Four

Michael sat beside me and whispered, 'Go easy on the drinks.'

To be fair, I *had* consumed a variety of alcohol—from hard liquor to red wine—hoping to find some courage at the bottom of every glass. Thanks to my father who had started me with Heineken and Guinness Stout at the age of seven. There were two archetypes of death in the corporate world. The first was that of being overworked—strapped on the chair buried under piles of paperwork. The second was being intoxicated—and as a woman, one aspired to be that unbeatable femme at the pub table.

'You promised Mama and Uncle Raymond that my safety is your priority number one.' I said to Michael, drumming my fingers on the table.

'Pleasure's mine,' Michael whispered back.

I called for the waiter to pour me another glass of champagne.

'So, how was the reunion chat with Fiona?' Michael asked.

I wondered if I should tell the truth. 'Well, catching up on old times.'

Michael studied me closely. 'Oh, I see.'

'Miss-Blaring-Trumpet might be lying.' Sabrina meant Fiona and her love-to-flaunt personality. 'She's like the bride-to-be from hell, going all out on Emily.'

It was utterly impossible that Fiona would've hand-picked Edward Ahn's name from the shrouded sky and then kept it sealed air-tight in her mentally mad box for the past eight months. And the likelihood of Edward escaping from Mr Han's regime was nil. Aside from the missing promise ring, I now also had this piece of clue to analyse. I had to reassemble the pieces before interlocking the jigsaw's tiling to form a complete picture in such a short time. Fiona could be telling the truth, perhaps, but where in the Lord's heck was the proof?

'I've got back-ups.' Michael dabbed at his mouth.

I turned to him, confused.

'That's so sweet,' Sabrina nudged my arm.

After passing a small piece of grilled salmon from my plate to him, Michael fed me a piece of sirloin. Sabrina let out a dreamy sigh, devouring the soup in her bowl. I chuckled as Michael wiped the stain from her lips.

Fiona kept staring at us when Benedict fed her from his plate. There was an abrupt, playful cheer of disgust when her tongue made an appearance while kissing him, the dreadful display of affection continued while Fiona pointedly looked in our direction. Thankfully they were told to behave by both her—I assume—in-laws and other elderly relatives.

The emcee then raised a glass and tapped it with a stainless-steel knife, calling for everyone's attention.

Fiona and Benedict took to the stage. The *loving* couple proceeded with the ceremonial pouring of champagne on a tower of stacked glasses. Fiona then announced that this ceremony had been organized solely for her airline co-workers, her secondary school and college mates. Mid-speech she paused to wipe her tears that her parents had migrated to Singapore and they were too elderly to travel by flight.

The lighting in the banquet hall went off. The spotlights were switched on, one by one, focusing on the couple as a slideshow of pictures were displayed on the projector. It started with photos of Fiona's mother holding her as a newborn baby and went on to childhood birthday parties—from kindergarten to adolescence. Sabrina held my hand when our photos appeared. The photo in the last slide showed Fiona standing between Sabrina and me, taken on the last day of the Christian fellowship camp. From a ponytail, I'd advanced to badass undercut bob.

Once the slideshow was over, they switched on the lights again; they seemed brighter than they had been before.

'There's something you need to know.' I whispered to Sabrina, as the clapping subsided.

Sabrina turned to me. 'What is it?'

I looked at her. 'Fiona knew about Edward and I.'

Stunned. Speechless for one second. 'Wait . . . like . . . he . . . you . . . are you serious?'

'May I invite Emily Chung and Sabrina Ng to the stage,' Fiona said, over the mic.

The crowd cheered and clapped.

My heart skipped a beat. 'Listen to me,' I said, raising my voice. 'That bitch said Edward showed up in front of your apartment that same day I was admitted.'

'No . . . no way,' Sabrina's brows furrowed in thought. 'Hold it, I remembered calling Edward a few days after your admission, but the number wasn't in service anymore.'

I rolled my eyes. 'Is there something you're *still* hiding from me?'

Sabrina looked panicked. 'I thought . . .'

'Is everything all right?' Michael nudged my arm.

I didn't reply; I wasn't looking at him.

Sabrina gripped my hand. 'Should we go over?'

I cleared my throat. 'Let's play this by ear,' I said, taking Sabrina's hand and leading her to the stage.

The emcee passed a glass of champagne to Sabrina, and then to me.

'Don't underestimate her,' Fiona said, taking the glass of champagne and handing me a glass of whiskey instead. 'Queen of hard liquor. Thousands of glasses won't knock her down.'

I placed the whiskey down and took the glass of champagne back from Fiona. As I tugged the glass out of her grip, I noticed her a white envelope in her other hand.

'Growing up, people that I know have complimented how fortunate I am, born into an affluent family and had three servants to handle the house chores. "Ask and you shall receive," my papa said all the time. It was not necessary for me to ace exams to get the latest collection of Barbie, Ken, and their friends.' Taking a big gulp from the glass, Fiona emitted a long sigh.

I patted Sabrina's hand on mine as Fiona ambled towards us looking like a hunter stalking its prey.

'When Ben first proposed to me at the Rockefeller Centre, I said no because it jogged memories of my painful heartbreak. Soon after, the flight I was on almost crashed into the Indian Ocean. After surviving, I decided life was too short and I called him and said yes the moment I touched down in Singapore.'

Benedict wiped his tears with a folded handkerchief.

'I strongly believe there can only be one tigress in a mountain,' Fiona side-eyed me, and then Sabrina. 'Meaning no one can surpass me when it comes to maintaining relationships.'

My mind was at its limit of what it could take of Fiona's chatter, I felt exasperated at the guests' soft derision.

Michael crossed his arms, remaining seated.

'Why? That's because only I deserve the best,' Fiona yelled into the mic.

'Can you see what's written on the white envelope?' I whispered to Sabrina.

'I can't.' Her eyes narrowed in concentration. 'But Fiona seems to be hanging onto it like her life depends on it.'

'I'm not easily defeated. I know my opponent's weaknesses.' Fiona added, peering at me.

Jealousy is your weakness. Your ultimate failure.

Sabrina pointed at Fiona, in shock. 'There's a cockroach on your dress.'

The bitch shouted into the mic.

The guests at the tables in the front immediately covered their ears as the intense loud-pitched squeal echoed around the entire hall. Instantly, I was losing my mind, gripping onto Sabrina's hand, trying to prevent Fiona from coming any closer to us. Sabrina whispered assurances, asking me to stay cool. As I felt my friend grip my hand tighten, a grin appeared on my face, noticing Sabrina keep a proud expression. I'd forgotten that jealousy—and cockroaches—had been Fiona's *weaknesses.*

Finally, the white envelope dropped from Fiona's grip as she jumped around, trying to escape the imaginary bug. Benedict helped her look for it, scanning his fiancée's hair and inspecting the inside of her dress.

Sabrina and I opened the unsealed envelope and found a letter inside.

'It's Edward's letter. To me,' I choked out, on the verge of tearing up.

'Yes, oh my god! I recognize his handwriting,' Sabrina said excitedly.

I scanned the letter, trying to decipher its contents despite the words being scribbled over with vengeful red ink, presumably the jealous bitch's doing. Edward's sign was childlike as usual, with a *tokki* or rabbit icon next to his signature.

'Emily, are you all right?'

'Look, it's Edward's letter.' I showed the paper to Michael.

I suddenly felt something hard hit my head and then drop at my feet.

It was the fucking mic, *served* by Fiona to me.

'Get that letter!' She ordered Benedict and Co.

'Plan B,' I heard Sabrina say. 'Follow me!'

I maintained a tight grip on Edward's letter as I trailed after her. Michael was creating a barricade for us as we ran ahead. Sabrina led us out into a long, narrow pathway that connected to the other side of the concourse area. A maestro pianist was serenading the guests with Richard Clayderman's medleys in the lounge. Fiona threw off her heels, one after another, trying to keep up, while Benedict and Co. were panting like dogs as they tried to evade Michael and catch up to us.

We stopped at the door to the emergency exit.

'Dead end!' Fiona's hair was now gloriously frizzy. 'Where to now, cunts?'

'Let's sort it out in there.' I eyed the emergency exit door, gasping for air.

Michael took off his suit, folding up his shirt. 'Yeah, I'll make sure no one interrupts.'

'Girls' talk. Men stay out.' Sabrina pointed at Benedict and Co.

Fiona's hand intertwined with Benedict's, as she shook like a leaf, her bravado from earlier seemed to have abandoned her. 'Fine. But don't hit me.'

We'll see. I nodded.

Fiona walked in barefoot through the emergency exit with me right behind her. I watched as Sabrina closed the door. Keeping to her cunning ways, Fiona's hand tried grabbing my dress, digging into my pocket.

For Edward's letter.

I grabbed her wrist prompting her to struggle to break away from me. 'It worth a million bucks!'

Sabrina slid in between us and pushed Fiona away. 'Wake up, bitch!'

My mouth dropped in shock at the softie-turned-She-Hulk Sabrina.

Fiona dropped to the ground. 'You knew about them, huh?'

Sabrina didn't reply, rubbing her nose. 'You're not my friend anymore.'

Fiona guffawed. Cold and sinister. 'Expected.'

I shook my head. 'What have I done to make you—'

Fiona's loud exhale cut me off. She fanned herself, as the stuffiness built up along the exit stairway. 'It is years of build-up. Simple as that.' She picked herself up and walked to me. 'From poetry writing to doing well in law, working in prestigious firms, and jumping from front desk to guest relations manager in a short period,' she laughed bitterly. 'Man, I just got promoted this year after working like a donkey for years.'

I took a deep breath to calm myself.

Fiona continued, 'I did the right thing by not telling him about your admission.'

'How could you, Fiona?' I yelled.

Her finger tapped on my cheek. 'You deserve to di—'

I smacked her hand off. 'I deserve to live!'

She cackled. 'K-True-Goss promised to pay me for photo proofs of Edward and you making out in the Saujana Residence back alley. And I managed to get them, thanks to my co-worker who stayed periodically in the aparthotel.' My blood was boiling. Sabrina patted my shoulder in a vain attempt to comfort me. Then, Fiona's expression gradually changed. Angrier. 'But Edward's manager threatened them to take it down prior to publication, else my bank account would have had a five-figure balance right now.'

Tears streamed down my eyes. A betrayal. Such twisted truth.

'That K-pop idol wished you the best when I said you've got a new boyfriend!'

I wanted to slap her so bad I could taste it.

However, I talked myself down. Let's look at the positive side—closure had viciously merged in. Not just through Edward's letter, but from knowing that he'd visited. If only he didn't have to live with the toxic lie that I had moved on from him.

'I've sold Edward's letter to *Dispatch* already,' Fiona said to provoke me.

'Look how foul you are,' I shot back at her, then left with Sabrina.

* * *

'Edward lived up to his promise.' Sabrina said. I swallowed hard, gripping onto her hand. 'I'm so sorry, if only I was at home that day.'

'It's not your fault,' I said, looking out the hotel window. My heart sank. I felt numb.

'Need to go to the ER?' Daniel asked. 'That bitch hit you with the mic.'

'I'm all right,' I assured Daniel with a brief smile, then gave Sabrina a long hug.

Hearing her soft sobs on my shoulder, I patted her back, appreciating her quick wit for remembering Fiona's fear in the nick of time.

After seeing Daniel and Sabrina off at the door, I thanked Michael but didn't elaborate much. 'What a long night, huh?' I reached for the towel.

'Call me if there's anything,' he softly said, then looked at me for a while longer, before closing the adjoining room door.

I exhaled, hearing the door lock, then drew out Edward's letter from my pocket, pressing this newly discovered gem to my chest. My lips trembled, breathed in at 'Dear Emily', hugging my knees and snivelling in sweet rupture.

Dear Emily,

I'm sorry for leaving without a word. It was my fault that I couldn't find the right time to explain things to you. And, once again, my world has fallen into the imperative of publicity, fabrication, and dishonesty from those that I thought I could trust. But I've experienced inner bliss thanks to how unselfish you've been ever since we met. The concrete jungle I'd built to protect myself was torn down by you. Last month, I passed by a cathedral in Seoul. The voices of the choir had me forgetting my worries, the only thing on my mind was our first touch of intimacy—fingers sticky with glutinous dough—and our first overdue kiss(es) when I was teaching you how to play the guitar. I remember how I inspired you to write the most beautiful poetic lines, and the manner in which we behaved so vulnerably under the sheets. From now on, our memory will be celebrated in every song and melody. 너를 영원히 사랑해.

I cried silently at the last line—I love you, always, forever.

* * *

The next day, Daniel and Uncle Clement were surprised by Michael's anxiousness as he rushed into Uncle Raymond's office. I gazed up at Michael, peering at him over my clipboard. 'Is it raining outside? You're drenched in sweat,' I asked, flipping the ballpoint pen.

'I . . . just got off the phone with my mother.' Michael gulped, looking awkwardly perplexed. 'Sorry for interrupting the meeting.'

Uncle Clement passed a sealed white envelope with the St Paul's Church letterhead to Michael. 'This letter has been jointly signed by the committee members of both sides as a show of gratitude for the enormous donation we received from your mother. I thought of giving this to you later, but here you are.'

'The donation is from my mother's personal account. She hoped it would help the fundraising food drive in some way even though it isn't a lot.'

'It is coffee break time, huh?' Uncle Raymond asked.

Uncle Clement got up, adjusting his collar. 'Ah, good reminder, let's go to the pastry kitchen to check out Sean's sweet potato buns switch-up invention.'

'Great, I want to come along too.' I stood up.

'Have you spoken to Michael about the sponsor pitch?' Uncle Clement asked.

'Not yet—' I said.

'Clement and I had decided to have Michael, you and . . . Daniel handle the fundraising food drive project,' Uncle Raymond said.

'But do consult us if you have any problems,' said Uncle Clement.

'Yay, cheesecake and coffee time,' Daniel gathered his clipboard and meeting folder, then whispered to me. 'Have fun being touchy-touchy with your lotus flower.'

I subtly punched my cousin's shoulder on his way out.

As the door closed, Michael reached forward to hold my hand, stopping me from returning to my seat. He seemed to gathering courage to be able to look me in the eye—my gradually narrowing eyes. 'Have you been avoiding me, Emily?'

'What do you mean?' I asked, extracting my hand from his grip and walking to my seat. 'Thought I'd left you a note saying that I'd be taking the earlier flight home. My handwriting is considered readable.'

His eyes looked like they craved more answers.

I couldn't deny he'd helped me to survive that rainforest of bullets.

'Let bygones be bygones,' Michael said.

'The engagement party was not full of unexpected . . . *surprises*, right?'

Michael softly cleared his throat. 'You moved on a lot faster than I thought.'

'I still want that promise ring back,' I said looking into his eyes.

'Anyway, wake me up if you're leaving next time,' Michael said, totally ignoring my demand.

'Why—?'

'I don't like Post-It notes. It makes me feel like I've been discarded.' He pouted.

'Well, the good news is that Uncle Raymond and Uncle Clement have approved of you partaking in my sponsor's pitch.' I clapped my hands together in relief.

'Which company are you targeting?' Michael asked.

'K-Licious-Delish.' I handed him the proposal.

Twenty-Five

'Fiona has blocked me on all her social media,' Sabrina said, her face scrunching in disgust on the screen. We were on video call.

'Honestly, I'm sorry for dragging you into this,' I said.

'She's getting a taste of her own medication,' Sabrina exhaled, then smiled at me. 'Hey, I sent you the magazine cover of *W Korea* that was published a few years ago. Guess who's on the front page.'

The sound of Sabrina munching on snacks was the only sound that could be heard.

I scrolled on my phone, trying to find her message.

When I finally found it, I clicked on the photo she'd sent.

It took a few seconds to download.

The photo opened full screen on my phone.

It was Michael.

'I've been keeping this from you because I needed to confirm with my sister,' Sabrina said, when she realized I'd seen the photo by my stunned expression. 'It wasn't easy for her to dig out her stuff from the basement and I'll have to listen to her complain about this for a while. She was literally screaming over the phone when I sent the photo I took with Michael at the engagement party.'

'Is this magazine available in any major bookstore here?'

'Not really. She bought these back issues from a second hand online shop based in Singapore. She has a thing for Asian male models.'

'But these interviews are in Korean,' I said.

Sabrina reached for a set of the thinly stapled paper. 'My sister is fluent in the language. Bless her for translating the whole interview. Have you heard of *KoreAm*, a defunct English-language magazine for the Asian American community?'

'No,' I said ineptly.

'Michael was featured on one of its covers, too bad that girl misplaced the issue.' Sabrina flipped to the first page and started reading. 'Now, onto the first question for Michael—How long have you been modelling for the runway?' She then imitated Michael's voice. 'At age sixteen after my birthday. I was out with a group of friends. A talent agent scouted me and then gave me her name card . . .'

I was captivated by Michael's powerful influence, palpable even through a camera lens. I couldn't believe that this was the same person as *Kimchi Mike*. The man on my phone screen was exuding masculinity and was extremely photogenic—perfectly representing the beauty of the fashion brand. No one would believe that this model with the intention to pay-it-forward and was volunteering in a constituent island's non-profit food centre.

Straying from Sabrina's thesis-like reading pace, I stumbled upon a photo of Michael slouched on a chesterfield sofa with his hands clasped, staring intensely into the camera lens. Next was a photo where he was standing with his hands in his pockets, and he'd positioned his right leg slightly forward. The overall effect made him look aloof. My fingers zoomed in to get a close-up of his face, mesmerized by the creases of his thick brows, the sharp ridge of his nose, and his plump lips. While I appreciated his chiselled lineament, I couldn't find any evidence of him being emotionally available despite his tender-hearted advances.

'Emily, aren't you supposed to talk to me about something?'

'Oh,' I blinked. 'Your company, by any chance, would it be interested in sponsoring a charity food drive? I know this is very abrupt as well as a pretty long shot.'

Sabrina thought for a while. 'Product sponsoring has always been the task of the retail sales and consumer department. But I'll try to float this idea, just for you.'

'Thank you so much.' I clasped my hands in gratitude.

'You're the daredevil, always known for anticipating the preposterous.'

'We're trying to target the younger ones to volunteer in our centre. In fact, this is my cousin's project. We're just helping him smoothly deliver his baby,' I choked on a laugh, 'anyways that's how he always puts it. Your company is also newly established here.'

'Thank you for thinking of me, my company especially.' Sabrina said.

'By the way, who's the elegant-looking woman photographed with Michael?'

'That's Shin Mikyung, director of Shin and Lambert Couture Limited.'

* * *

Breakfast with Uncle Raymond on the rooftop terrace was a rare occurrence. We were sampling dim sum—a crossover project of the gourmet and the pastry kitchens.

'Lady Di and Sean have been hard at work on this food sampling.' My uncle switched off the small whistling kettle and poured its contents in the cups from the teacup set.

'I really should dig in now.' I took a bite from the *siu-mai*. The succulent chicken meat filling blended superbly with the prawns' umami taste. I nodded approvingly. 'Awesome . . .'

'Guess whose idea that was?' Uncle Raymond passed me the hot Chinese tea.

'Daniel's . . .' I received the tea cup with both hands.

'It was Michael's as well,' my uncle said, narrowing his eyes at me.

'I knew it,' I muttered petulantly under my breath.

'Too shy to pronounce his name?'

'My cousin brother deserves some credit.' I smirked as my uncle took a sip of tea. He probably wanted to know more. 'Daniel and I are very attentive and serious at work, but we do keep in touch over the phone after work hours. And it won't be long before he'll be home.'

My uncle looked at me quietly. 'He's lucky to have a cousin like you.'

'Hey, stop putting food on my plate,' I quickly returned the lotus and custard-filled buns to his plate. 'Breakfast is important, eat more Uncle Raymond.'

'Sometimes I wish you were my daughter,' Uncle Raymond muttered.

I slowed down, glancing at my lap as I felt my stomach tighten. I forced myself to smile at him. How was he to know that this one sentence would resonate through my mind, becoming the backbone of my every wistful thought. The night my father had visited me after the doctor had confirmed the unstable state of my conscious mind. Unlike Uncle Raymond's fond gaze, there was anger in my father's gaze, who had since disowned me the moment Dr Erica recommended either going to rehab to control my alcohol problem or getting psychiatric treatment.

'I'm ashamed that you're my daughter,' my father had said.

'I appreciate that, Uncle Raymond.' I murmured, taking a deep breath. 'Please stop drinking alone on the rooftop terrace. It's not good for your health.'

Uncle Raymond kept quiet, sipping from his tea cup.

'So, when are we introducing this yum-cha culture to the soup kitchen?'

'It is for the food drive at Beach Street,' he said, finally.

'Wow, another soon-to-be-added new location. Kudos to my cousin,' I said.

Uncle Raymond raised his brows. This was Uncle Raymond speak for 'yes' since he'd never admit his son's achievements. But the slight smile within those wrinkled eyes gave him away. He was proud of my cousin, his only son.

'Unfortunately, Mama prohibited me from volunteering at the food drive.'

'You'll get the chance. No hurry.'

I scrunched my face. 'Mama always reminds me of my burnt toast skin.'

'Just apply sunscreen.' Uncle Raymond laughed.

'Sometimes Mama's over-concerned, but I'm lucky that she still cares.'

'I can see Michael and you are like a sub-unit squad.'

'Honestly speaking, I'm not interested in procreating. With him.'

'Now you're sounding like that dirty-mouthed son of mine.'

'Well, I have been wondering about the connection between Uncle Clement and you.' Chewing the shrimp dumpling, I sipped the toasty-fragrant tea.

'What're you going to say this time?' My uncle sounded defensive.

I tried not to laugh at his fear of platonic male intimacy.

'Cheryl's done a great job in bringing up such a polite daughter.'

'A wonderful gorgeous morning breakfast with my beloved uncle means either you're putting knowledge in my pocket or digging for more Dan-Dan info.' I blinked at him innocently.

Uncle Raymond let out a little chuckle at that.

'My probation period ends next month. I've to make a good impression for the reference letter,' I said cheekily, looking at my uncle. On a more serious tone, 'I'm supportive of Daniel's coming out .'

'You knew before any of us?' My uncle was chewing slowly.

'Yeah,' I said, grinning widely, honoured to be the first one in the family he trusted to tell. 'But don't you worry, I'm keeping an eye on him.'

Uncle Raymond shook his head sipping his tea quietly, suggested that he was trying to conform to his son's *brand new* identity.

'What's your opinion about scheduling the fundraising food drive in conjunction with the Mid-Autumn Festival?' I asked, changing the topic. 'Should be no problem.'

'Thanks,' I said, replenishing my uncle's cup with tea. 'By the way, I don't remember meeting Uncle Clement when I was younger and I mentioned him to my mom the other day,' I paused for a second, observing my uncle's reaction. 'She seemed not to know him at all.'

Uncle Raymond wiped his mouth with a cloth serviette, educating me on tea culture for several subsequent hours, without mentioning Uncle Clement at all.

* * *

'Cut!'

Aunt Bridget dropped the loudspeaker, heading to the lawn.

'How many times do I have to repeat myself. Lily, your hand must be like this.' My aunt was guiding the apprehensive girl's hand to rest on my cousin's shoulder, as he stood still as a tree—*frozen*.

Lily was cast to play Ling-Ling in the drama. 'Miss Bridget, I can't. Too much . . . touching.'

Michael and I looked at each other, trying not to laugh.

Aunt Bridget eyed Lily. 'Weren't you the head of the drama club in secondary school for two consecutive years?'

'That's because they combined acting and singing together,' Lily explained. 'I was on the choir side as the mezzo-soprano.'

Aunt Bridget studied Lily very closely. 'Not everyone can sing like Sarah Brightman, act like Helen Mirren, and then twerk like the rebellious queen Madonna. Your school should've employed me as the club's consultant.'

'Miss Bridget is scary today,' Michael whispered to me.

'Have you been asked to submit your curriculum?' I whispered back.

'I will do it soon, but it's only for Miss Bridget's eyes,' Michael said.

'Aren't we all actors and actresses in this life right now?' Daniel started. All of us paid attention to him. 'Whether you're a singer, dancer or an actor . . . we've to feel connected to the role we're given, we have to imbibe emotion in our characters.'

Aunt Bridget pouted as she pondered Daniel's words. She clapped. 'Impressive! Where'd you learn that? Let me guess *Guidebook to Acting for Dummies?*'

'From my godfather, Uncle Clement,' said Daniel. 'The only difference is that there's no second take in life, it's over when the universe yells "cut".'

'Miss Bridget, I want to take a break and polish up my acting skills,' Lily said.

'I don't mind mentoring you, Lily,' Aunt Bridget said, peering at Daniel, Michael and me. 'Unlike those with lukewarm behaviour, thinking this is merely a stage performance.'

'But the last section of the script is so sad for Daniel's character,' Lily said.

'That's the traitor's fate for betraying his own kinsman,' Aunt Bridget said.

'Though I know this is war, I'm kind of disappointed too,' Daniel said.

'Daniel's character Dao-zi initially gaslighted Ling-Ling. He failed to protect her because he did not carry out his duty,' I read from the script intro page. 'In the end he does save Ling-Ling and her family from the ruthless warlords. I'm sold on the part when he seeks Ling-Ling's forgiveness before his last breath.'

'Dao-zi should be given an honourable death,' Michael said. 'He's human too, he was just born in the wrong time and place, but he loved his ailing grandfather and father.'

'One bullet to the back of his head; a merciful death for the WWII Judas,' my aunt scribbled something on the script, 'specially after so many innocent lives perished at the hands of power-hungry people—of course that's shown with special computerized effects.'

Michael shrugged as Daniel and Lily pouted in unison.

'Emily and Mike, you two are next,' my aunt called out. 'We went over the goodbye scene last time. Now, flip to page twenty-eight, the middle paragraph.'

'That's the betrayal scene between Rui-er and Lu-yang!' I said, then turned to my giggling cousin. 'You seem to be so excited.'

'Of course, there's a kissing scene.' Daniel winked at me.

'Yes, this is where Rui-er, inarticulate and angry, discovers Lu-yang's actual identity. It's mandatory to rehearse all the scenes so we can pick the best,' my aunt said. 'You both should be able to do this unlike those two wood-heads.'

'Oh my, there's a love scene on the second last page.' Daniel chuckled and started to read it.

'Be quiet.' Aunt Bridget smacked the back of Daniel's head. 'That's exclusively for Hollywood only. Get into position and ready . . . one, two and three . . . action!'

'Rui-er, listen to me,' Michael recited.

'Don't come any closer, Lu-yang!' I exclaimed, summoning my inner Rui-er.

'This isn't what you're thinking.' Michael was immersed in his character.

'Get out of my room, now.' Rui-er had possessed me.

'What would you choose if your only option is to work for the authority?'

Dropping into a sea of rippling emotion, I said. 'You should've declined. Have you thought of the consequences? Imagine if one of the nationalists finds out who you are.'

'Then, we wouldn't have met.' He immediately took my hand, pressing it to his chest. 'I couldn't have possibly learned the beauty within every scar on your skin, couldn't have known of the tears you refuse to shed just because . . .'

Everyone waited eagerly for Michael to finish.

A brevity of tranquillity settled in Michael's harrowing deep gaze. Every palpitating heartbeat of mine tickled my palm. This felt too real. His arms pulled me in, cradling me gently. My fingers found his lips. I fumbled periodically between the characters of Emily and Rui-er.

'What does love mean? For I do not fear having to face death alone, but I do fear a world without you. In your absence I am but a meaningless being on this earth,' I said as a gust of wind swept in, kissing my skin. 'It must have been hard for you to hide the truth for this long.'

Tears streamed down Michael's face. The luminescent moon highlighted the silhouette of his lashes on his cheek that stood like a dream in astral space. Feeling Michael's hands on my cheek, I sensed that nascent, refreshing candour in that hoarse voice. 'Stay with me.'

'I don't see this part in the script,' I heard Daniel's whispering.

* * *

I typed 'Ahn Myeongjun' in the Spotify search bar.

A list of songs appeared on my phone screen—albums, chart-topping singles, K-drama OST love themes, and Edward's latest photos—available for download—taken in the studio at the lavender farm and the sunflower field.

Furthermore, he had seven million followers on his artist profile.

My heart skipped at every swipe. Edward's intriguing eye contact, revealing his attractive side, and porcelain skin, perfectly altered for promotion. In addition to Korean, Edward had also recorded tracks in Japanese, Mandarin-Chinese, and the latest had been recorded in Spanish. The English album was missing. It hadn't been revealed to the public.

The latest interview Edward did with *Dispatch* mentioned that he would sing in his native language from then on. My heart had reached the final stage of grief—acceptance. I understood his loathing now due to Fiona's deception.

Through the shocking revelation of Edward's impromptu visit, the stars had finally decided to abrogate this love affair. Harsh winter and spicy food aside, I'd always thought I would master the Korean language after memorizing fourteen consonants and ten vowels in its alphabetical system. Some day. A validation of confidence to seal the gap between our social status. Thereafter, our relationship would be accepted by his record label and his management. Now, I knew that not every success is measured by a person's great effort.

'Am I interrupting?'

I brushed away my tears. 'Come in,' I said to Michael.

His gaze was glued to a stack of Edward's letters. 'I want to apologize for . . . what happened at the script reciting just now. It was just acting.'

'You did really well. Even my picky aunt is in love with you.'

He laughed. 'It just feels weird.'

I avoided his gaze, fixing my eyes on the photo garland.

'Thank you very much, Emily.'

'What for?'

'For teaming up with me in the food kitchen in addition to being my acting partner. I admire your dedication to making a great and tenacious effort,' Michael said.

'Thanks,' I said, looking up at him. 'My head hurts looking at your giraffe height.'

He chuckled. 'If you don't mind . . .' he gestured, seeking permission to sit on my bed.

I patted the bed, smoothening the crinkled sheet. He made himself comfortable next to me, as his weight sank in, leaving a space where his right hand stretched out.

'I see Edward's letter found its home,' Michael said.

I narrowed my eyes. The letter was carefully clipped on the garland, surrounded by my birthday photos, Daniel's baby pictures, a Victoria Peak postcard sent to me by Aunt Bridget years ago, and a photo of Mama carrying Daniel and me, seated on the couch with homemade *bedak sejuk* on our necks, to cool us down in the hot climate. I blinked at Michael. 'It's just a letter. Another memory.'

He softly cleared his throat. 'Any plans after your probation period ends next month?'

'How about spending summer in Seoul?' I half-joked looking at him.

'That's awesome,' Michael said.

Twenty-Six

Time for some basic Serendipity Sanctuary refurbishment.

Daniel flipped the bedspread, folding to place it elsewhere, and then adjusting the side of the mattress. We both sneezed as particles of dust dispersed. I switched on the vacuum to clean Daniel's room. Aunt Bridget was at the meeting this morning with the St Paul's godfathers-slash-committee-members, in the presence of Uncle Raymond and Uncle Clement, to get an approval for a non-explicit scene to perform at the fundraising food drive.

'That explains yesterday's speech recital in her room,' I said.

My cousin exhaled. 'Her voice was audible in my dream too.'

I laughed. 'In your opinion, which scene will be chosen?'

'Y'know they're old-fashioned. If they know about the full-on-naked love scene in the script,' Daniel chuckled, 'the godfathers' souls will need to be re-baptized with chlorine. To wash away the pornographic germs.'

I laughed and then frowned at Daniel's incoming message ringtone, which was the iconic Vincent Price *Thriller* monologue.

My cousin read the message, turned off the phone and then slotted it into his pocket. 'Our Devil-Wears-Prada-Aunt has just PM-ed me in all caps with some *very* colourful words.'

'Consider changing that ringtone, it's so eerie.' I pretended to cringe.

Daniel laughed. 'It suits Aunt Bridget. Don't you think so?'

I tried holding in my laughter. 'So, what's mine?'

Daniel unlocked, scrolled, and then pressed onto our chat window, clicking the tone. The song reminded me of Edward waiting for me at the serene bamboo garden in Damyang.

Then, Daniel clicked onto the next tone. 'Guess who's this meant for?'

Eyes filled with joy, I looked at him. '*Autumn in My Heart . . .*'

A tear-jerking K-melodrama that had swept the Asian continent by storm. Its instrumental love theme had been the background music in most shopping malls in the 2000s.

'I remember how Auntie Noon cried in almost every episode. Once she was so engrossed in the show that she mistook the salt for sugar,' Daniel said.

I nudged. 'That sounds sweet to my ears.'

'I knew she cared for me when Old Bean . . . slapped my face. She chased after me and gave me a bottle of medicated ointment that day I left home.' Daniel paused.

Damn—did I just witness my cousin's lips trembling?

'Hearts that are made of flesh beat with dripping blood,' Daniel then added.

'That's deep. So *human.*'

Daniel bit his lips. 'Well, Uncle Clement taught me.'

I was flabbergasted, apart from being creepy, Uncle Clement had impersonated Dr Jekyll with Daniel and Mr Hyde with me. 'We better turn off this sad song,' I said.

'That's Lily's incoming message tone.' Daniel said.

'Are you serious?'

'She's Penang's most-wanted princess of gushing tears,' Daniel teased.

We laughed then turned to the polite knocking at the door.

'Sorry to interrupt, do you mind removing the items that are nearer to the windows in the front rooms? My workers have to start repairing the windowpane before installing the mosquito netting,' said the contractor.

'You can start with my room first,' Daniel said.

'Sure,' the contractor said before turning to me. 'But ma'am, my assistant has to measure the window beside your room.'

'That's Michael's, where is he?' I said to Daniel.

'Old Bean told him to help in the soup kitchen with Lady Di.'

The room had been vacant for years and would have probably remained vacant for many more if not for Michael.

Before, the same contractor had changed my room's windows to aluminium casements, painted the wall, and then installed an armoire. However, the mosquito netting would take half-an-hour to install. I then handed the key to Michael's room to the contractor, which Uncle Raymond had approved. I knew Mama would be hapless, ascertaining that the netting-canopy would trap and inhabit bad spirits. I had to be resolute this time.

At Michael's desk, I put away his leather notebooks. A vast collection from Moleskine and one that looked to be of genuine leather—it felt a little coarse to the touch. Besides Edward, Michael was the other Korean namja who was interested in journalling. Post-it page markers in striking colours with words scribbled in Hangul and English were stuck to the top-right of Aunt Bridget's script.

What a pro.

I arranged and capped all the rollerball pens, setting them aside.

Then, a piece of tri-fold letter was clipped under a book, next to a personalized envelope. The return address was to the Embassy of the Republic of Korea in Malaysia. I contemplated whether to invade another's privacy by reading the contents and decided that a quick glimpse wouldn't hurt. But the name in Hangul in the subject line instantly stopped me.

Kim Hyojin—I silently convulsed at the name.

I remembered Mr Han storming into the employees-only lounge while Sabrina and I had been having lunch, after I had returned from the writer's retreat. If being dumped wasn't enough, the shitty-faced manager then claimed that Edward had blacklisted the capital forever, due to my *cunning, seductive* traits. From the operator and his helpers to the cleaner, everyone stopped their duty. All eyes were on us. Whispers abounded. The name slipped from Mr Han's tongue— 'Edward is dating Kim Hyojin.'

* * *

'I'm so proud of you, my Emily.' Mama pecked my cheek.

I briefly smiled. My mind was drifting elsewhere.

'Your soul has flown out to be with Michael, right?' Mama snapped.

I didn't respond, too dazed from such deliberate confusion being invoked by Mama to put any thoughts into words. I wished to be like Mama, *shelving* in a retreat. 'Michael's identity is *quite* unknown. What'd you think?' Even as I asked this, I was haunted by the name Kim Hyojin.

'He might be working for the Korean Intelligence Agency,' Mama had joked.

I smirked. 'You've clearly been watching too much James Bond.'

'Speaking of that, you should come watch some movies with me.' Mama took her phone out.

'Wait, is that Michael's number?' I asked.

Mama rolled her eyes. 'Yeah, our secret group chat. Two of us only.'

I massaged my temples, distressed at the thought that she was actually being honest.

'Like Smelly-Dan, Bridget, and you have been chatting privately behind my back.'

A mild headache had settled over me now.

On the shore, the microscopic view of beach goers was like looking at an ant colony. Mama hadn't ceased complimenting Michael. I had wondered if this temple would consider accepting a backsliding Catholic to spend a week on a retreat. It would be more like rehab, cleansing and renewing my headspace while also consuming full-course vegetarian meals.

The sound of the great hanging bell bonshō had been my only solace lately, so it seemed like a feasible idea. I hadn't spoken to Michael since yesterday, upon the discovery of Kim Hyojin's name on a letter on his desk. I was attempting to avoid the urge to cross-examine if he'd any relation to Edward, hate myself for still caring, ask myself to not think about it and not care and then go on to think about it and care. Rinse and repeat.

'I plan to go to Seoul after the internship ends,' I said.

'Are you going with Michael?' Mama sounded excited.

I opened my mouth. *Should I tell the truth?* I felt exhausted at the thought of explaining while Mama either glossed-over my words in denial or constantly interjected. I chose to tell the truth. 'Not with him.'

'Take a native to go with you, since you don't speak the language.'

'Michael and I can only be friends,' I said.

Mama changed the topic. 'Where's the ring attached to your platinum chain?'

'How'd you know?' I asked. Everyone was a suspect, including Mama.

'Well, you've been wearing it all the time but not recently.' Mama shrugged.

'Someone stole my precious gift.' I narrowed my eyes, my tone was cold. 'I'd forgive that person if he or she returned it to me tonight.' With that, I walked away.

'Emily—' Mama called out. 'You've found that grit in you after destroying the engagement party. Please don't smash the bottle on the culprit.'

I turned, cloyed by Mama's justification. 'Well, unless you.'

Mama gulped. 'It could be a sign from the Guanyin Goddess. The cruel truth is, my dear child, the K-pop lover of yours is not coming back.' She stroked my hands tenderly. 'You're lucky not to be married to him or pregnant with his love child. So, you can always begin a brand-new relationship whenever you're ready.'

Tapping Mama's palm, I mentally relocated her back to Position #1 of aiding and abetting. 'So, what went through your head when that mistress was sleeping beside Ah-Gong?'

'Why asking that?' Mama shied away.

'That, my dear Mama, is exactly how I feel now. That sting of betrayal from the one who deprived us from receiving the genuine love we deserve,' I said, acrimoniously. 'Ah-Gong slept with two women and fathered three children with you. But that K-pop lover . . . Edward is my only love-memory.'

Mama's quietness was replaced by the tintinnabulation of a wind chime.

'Edward left that promise ring with me,' I affirmed. 'Yes, I'm moving on from this but what if . . . what if Edward returns one day to claim the ring back? My parents raised me to be a "woman of her word". And I want to show him that.'

'But promise me not to smash that person's head with the bottle.'

'Why——?'

Mama's lips pursed, avoiding my question. 'Sometimes, a good man is hard to find.'

'I promise.' I mouthed, patted Mama's hand.

Alleged suspect confirmed. Time to bait him out.

'Did you know I wanted to chop that mistress up?' Mama asked suddenly.

I couldn't believe her words.

Mama's lips trembled. 'That was my first reaction when I found out about her.'

'I'm so sorry, Mama.' I hugged her tightly.

'I forced myself up from bedrest. Bridget was only two-weeks old.' Mama wiped tears from her eyes. 'Then I found out the mistress was three months pregnant.'

Twenty-Seven

'Are you sure you're going to do this?' Daniel asked, kneeling on the prayer cushion.

'Little Niece, maybe you should think twice?' Uncle Sean asked, because my family did not believe in asking anything once.

Receiving the oracle lot, I thanked the temple caretaker with courtesy. 'I'm all ready to get back what I truly deserve.'

'Today is the most blessed day, I come before you with these two young ones asking for your assistance,' Uncle Sean glanced at us, then at the Gautama Buddha golden statue. 'Even though Little Niece Emily is not a Buddhist, may the oracle stick point her in the right direction in life and grant her peace, so she won't burn the egg tarts and overcook the custard batter like she did yesterday.'

Daniel chuckled with a snort, hearing Uncle Sean's prayer.

Never would I have thought to allow my future to be predicted by Chinese fortune sticks.

I only had one chance—shake the lot and wait for one random stick to fall onto the ground, unlike the multiple chances granted by the moon blocks. The soul reclaiming sound of the oracle lots vibrated with the flute music, bestowing the purest intention and positivity.

The smell of burning incense had been transmitted into the dream I had last night—the same lotus-flower attached to a translucent gemstone. I fell into the lake while trying to grab it. My back landed on the floor when I woke up. In Mama's room just now, I spotted the wind chime with the missing 'An' character—a possible conspiring sign, petitioning me to accept Michael.

What if Michael chose to return to Seoul? And took the promise ring along? Also, the mysterious unisexual name Kim Hyojin had been pecking at my head, though it hadn't been broached in Edward's last letter. Koreans generally refer to both men and women as beautiful, as Sabrina had mentioned. Seoul had a population of 25 million. The chances of us celebrating Christmas and New Year with Taylor Swift, singing an all-star duet together, were about the same as that of Michael Kim and Edward Ahn being connected. But why did Edward bring a letter over if his purpose was to see me?

Another undiscovered truth. *Forever.* My talk-therapy sessions with Dr Erica had ended. I had to search for an alternative method to attain catharsis in lieu of relying on medications.

Finally, a stick fell from the oracle lot.

Taking it with me, I returned the lot bucket to the priest.

At the interpretation corner, Uncle Sean listened to the interpreter and frowned while Daniel waited in the queue. I waved when Daniel looked behind. His face was boiling red due to the roasting weather. Two elderly persons thanked him as he left his seat to queue beside me. 'What took you so long in Mama's room?' asked Daniel.

'It was about Michael,' I turned, scrutinizing him. 'I have a suspicion that there's something about him.' I leaned closer and whispered, 'He could've taken the promise ring.'

Daniel chortled. 'Hang on, what's his motive behind doing that?'

'Remember how his eyes were glued to the promise ring when Aunt Bridget first put it on? He was already showing *that* flip side,' I said.

Arms folded, Daniel thought for a while and shook his head. 'Michael is a *chaebol*. His family owns a business conglomerate.

Why would he want to steal a customary promise ring when he can own thousands of Tiffany & Co. flagship stores around the globe?'

Goddamn it. I felt like I was being neurotic, magnifying even the tiniest thing. I partly agreed with Daniel. There was no way the moneyed Kimchi stole the promise ring belonging to a newfangled forbidden lover. Likewise, his portrayal of Lu-yang stemmed from method acting, or was he—ah, *jeopardizing* the project by going off-script?

'Any plan to celebrate the end of your internship?' asked Daniel.

I ignored his question. 'By the way, have you heard of Rocking Fire Entertainment? They're South Korea's prominent record label.'

Daniel pointed at me. 'This is about Edward, *riiight*—'

He got me. Before I could reply, Uncle Sean stood up and shot us a brief grin.

'You two, who wants to go first?' The interpreter at the table asked.

'Ex K-pop girlfriend.' Daniel pushed me towards the table.

I gestured a slap at him when the folks in queue turned to me.

The interpreter bowed and then received the oracle stick from me. I looked on as he retrieved a piece of pink paper from a numbered compartment.

It felt like I was being lectured in Greek as the interpreter read from the quatrain in Chinese with the grandiloquent prose, believed to be the answer from the gods that matched with each number on the oracle stick. 'What do you want to ask?' The man asked me.

'Destiny in life and . . . will I able to find the missing *thing*?' I meant the promise ring.

He pondered. 'The querent here says an individual is waiting for someone to return. But the absence has evolved into a dormant inferno. This can be the landmark decision in an event you're pursuing or closure for something unanswered. Additionally, it can be a lesson that will stir you, becoming an unforgettable experience in your lifetime.'

'That's pretty far-reaching,' I said.

The interpreter smiled. 'The flame will either be slow and gentle or it can also horrifyingly eat you up, depending on how you perceive it.'

'Hence, I should toe the line?'

'Our life is defined based on the choices we make. People often fail due to being asleep at the wheel. Go with your values, beliefs, and your desired intention.'

* * *

At the table, Uncle Sean mixed the plate of water spinach and boiled pre-soaked brown squid with thick, dark sweet sauce, took a bite and then said, 'The temple's interpreter hinted that the love of my life is at my workplace.'

Daniel and I raised our beer glasses and proposed a 'drink to victory' toast.

'Can't be Lady Di, we're like sworn siblings,' Uncle Sean murmured.

'Should we start preparing for a wedding like now?' Daniel said to me.

'The Lau-d & Praud has decided to leave me alone and be heed Uncle Sean's happiness,' I said. 'Let's celebrate with a plate of grilled chicken wings.'

Uncle Sean smacked the table. Daniel and I were stunned. The food vendor next to us looked on and several customers would've thought Thor and his Mjölnir had materialized.

'Please not her.' Uncle Sean pointed the plastic spoon at us.

Daniel and I started to grin and then nodded.

'Do not show me the face. No, it can never ever be her.'

We re-enacted the pottery-wheel romantic scene from *Ghost* with our plastic bowls and plates, then counted to three. 'Aunt Bridget!'

'No way, Ray-Ray will kill me.' Uncle Sean shook his head.

'It must've been difficult to bury those feelings, huh?' I said.

'We have this brotherhood policy and . . .'

'Just fuck the whatever-da-hood policy.' Daniel stole a piece of squid from Uncle Sean's plate. 'Stop being a pussy. You never know what turn life's gonna take.'

'Yeah.' Uncle Sean smirked arrogantly. 'As if I will die tonight.'

'Shut up!' Daniel and I yelled at such inauspiciousness.

'Little Niece, when is your first date with that Kimchi?' Uncle Sean asked.

'Don't change the topic.' I waved the fork at him, a warning sign.

'Don't cry like a cow if you miss the boat,' Uncle Sean said.

'You're becoming exactly like my aunt,' I said. 'She says that all the time.'

'The two of you have been defying me.' Uncle Sean expressed annoyance.

We returned our gazes to our plates.

Then, a familiar sedan passed in front of the tables and parked in the designated box at the corner end of the junction. I looked at Daniel malignantly when I recognized the driver and the passenger. I glared at Daniel as he was furrowed his brow at me.

'You invited that old fart behind my back.' Daniel accused me.

I spotted Michael with my uncle. 'Did I ask you to invite Kimchi over?'

'Told you I am not ready to go home,' Daniel added.

'Not that promise ring-burglar.' I said after him, gritting my teeth.

'Shut up! I called them over.'

In shock, Daniel and I blinked.

Uncle Sean pointed at Daniel. 'You, time to go home Don't be like Clement, only talking about the Bible and Jesus.' Then, he gazed at me and sighed. 'Lately, Michael's been complaining of your rigid coldness towards him.'

That Kimchi's audacity to get the Monk involved too.

'We're going to settle everything here!' Uncle Sean said confidently.

'Anybody want another plate of *lobak* meat rolls?' I said to escape.

Daniel raised his hand. 'I'm going with you.'

I avoided Michael as he looked on while my cousin moved past his father.

Uncle Sean ordered two bottles of large beer and poured full glasses for Michael and Uncle Raymond. Michael raised his glass with a polite bow, then he turned away and drank.

The seller placed the chicken wings on the hot grate, glazed them with honey, and then grilled them till they were a juicy golden brown. The chicken was cooked directly above the hot coal. I wondered what would happen if I were to stir the heat between Michael and the unknown, and what would happen if it was proven that it was not him. It could be another stupid mistake, an evidently ludicrous plan. I patted the lingfu in my jeans pocket for strength.

A man suddenly fell on me.

Daniel and I helped him up.

'Going somewhere, pretty . . .' The man smelled malodorous— inflamed eyes and jittery limbs kept blocking us from moving on.

Uncle Sean and Uncle Raymond had been keeping an eye on the situation.

Michael stood up, but they told him not to cause a scene.

'What's the matter?' a voice yelled.

A crowd of people that looked suspiciously like a gang parted way for the man to walk through.

Clad in an unbuttoned leather jacket, his torso was covered in with tattoos, and he was laughing at us. 'Lovers with a wide age gap . . .'

'Dai-lou, this prick pushed me,' the halitosis-afflicted man said, pointing at Daniel.

'Wait, listen. He fell on my Biu-jie. We helped him up. That's all.'

'Yes, what my cousin said is true,' I said, gulping.

The gang leader's hand tapped the table, his gaze alternating between Daniel and me. He then whispered to one of his gang members. Daniel covered his mouth when a crate of beer was kicked in our direction. 'Finish these if you didn't lie,' he said to halitosis-afflicted man.

'Don't play. There are twenty-four of them.'

The gang leader leaned in. 'Think my pet crocodile is hungry by now.'

Daniel swallowed hard. A chill ran down my spine, hearing that.

'Two of you are the witnesses,' the gang leader said to Daniel and me.

Refusing to be a reptile's meal, the halitosis-afflicted man uncorked the first bottle, gulping its contents down. However, his bloodshot eyes hadn't left mine and Daniel's, drinking up to five bottles in a couple of minutes. He wasted a quarter of each starting from the sixth, spilling from his mouth and down his chest. He dropped by the leader's feet to the time he was on the fifteenth bottle.

'Don't make me lose face or else I'm not your Dai-lou,' the gang leader said.

The halitosis-afflicted man said, gasping, 'Four for me. Four for those two. My apology to them.'

Daniel and I turned to each other, mouthing 'shit'.

The gang leader nodded after some consideration.

One of the members passed the bottles to us. Daniel and I were staring at the extra-large bottles as two of each were placed in front of us.

I'd drank way more on the event of my past overdose, and I'd had quite a lot during Fiona's engagement party too. *Nothing would kill me.* I picked up the bottle after Daniel, made a toast and prepared to drink' em up—

'Hold it.'

We turned to Uncle Raymond and Uncle Sean, who were walking to the table.

My uncle swiftly took his son's bottle while Uncle Sean took mine. Both drank till the bottles were empty. Not a drop was wasted. They drank. One after the other. Without pause. The rest of the members tried to interfere, but the leader held them back. Michael slipped in between, providing a layer of protection to Daniel and me. Both then let out a sound of satisfaction after they'd finished. The leader stood up, clapping with a draconian expression.

'Both of them are with us,' said Uncle Raymond.

'Now, we're taking them,' Uncle Sean added.

The gang leader smacked the table. 'How dare you!'

Daniel covered his ears as I hid behind his shoulder.

The gang outnumbered us by then, circling the table as their leader sat on the stool with his right leg folded upward, pouring a beer into a chilled glass, sipping it and then spitting it out after a hostile gargle.

Michael walked in between Daniel and me. 'You two must leave with me.'

'Not without Old Bean,' Daniel whispered back.

'Yeah, we do not leave anyone behind,' I said.

'It's Uncle Raymond's order,' Michael added.

'Like the old rules, forgive the young ones.' Uncle Raymond smiled at the leader.

'I only respect the OG Three-Star Leopard.' The leader puffed a cigarette at my uncle.

Uncle Sean pointed. 'Don't be too much—'

My uncle stopped his bestie, then said to the leader. 'One last time, let them go or not?'

I gulped in fear as Michael gripped Daniel and my wrists.

The leader threw the cigarette bud on the ground.

The rampage was on.

Uncle Raymond and Uncle Sean lifted the wooden table as the gang members darted over, retracting backward as a barrier to protect the three of us.

There was a roar of the nemesis and rattling footsteps coming from behind.

Daniel pulled me to run faster.

'We should wait for Michael,' I yelled, watching Michael grab the table to shield himself, dodging punches and then kicking the assailants on the concrete.

'He's Korean, must've done military duty,' Daniel said.

We quickly got in the campervan and locked the door.

Heck, I couldn't let Michael tackle that legion alone. We'd won the rainforest of bullets fight. Whether he was that Edward's Kim Hyojin or the one that stole the promise ring—I owed something to him. How could I be so cruel? To sit back and watch Uncle Sean battling these crooks? Stuck in-between Fuck-Everything-And-Run and Fuck-Everything-And-Rise, I was gripping the lingfu, chanting the prayer for strength and courage.

'I just called Uncle Clement,' Daniel said.

'I'm going back there.' I confessed loudly.

'Are you nuts?' Daniel pulled me back.

'Stay safe here, the Lau male heir.' I hugged him.

I kissed the lingfu and ran. Daniel's screaming disappeared slowly.

Once in the zone, I grabbed and threw two chairs at the battlefront with one landing on the attacker. Michael was agile in combat and made do with mixed self-defence practices. I felt someone push me. It was Uncle Raymond, saving me from being attacked by a young hooligan. I turned, blocking her with my left arm so I could defend Michael and my uncle by taking the blow. She lurched forward and fell as I grabbed and then twisted her arm. Michael screamed at the sight of the leader holding a shiv that was now dripping blood.

Uncle Raymond had been maimed.

I ran to grab the leader's foot. Unwilling to let it go even as he dragged me to the ground.

Blood escaped from my left arm as it was cut by pieces of shattered glass.

The leader dragged me past a knocked-out Uncle Raymond. I sank my teeth into the leader's ankle, to stop him. He bawled, cursing at my hardcore fangs on his nauseating flesh.

Then, I heard my uncle's faint voice.

Be well my niece. Daniel . . . my son.

That was the last I heard from my uncle.

I bit onto the lingfu, counting four-beat cadences, as the leader continued to drag my body over broken glass. But I refused to let go. I won't let this fucker get away with hurting my family.

If I must go down, I will do it with dignity.

Twenty-Eight

My body crawled to reach for the jewel in the lotus flower.

Floating in the lake, the bijou became ruby-red, luminous below the dampened zephyr. Edward was walking barefoot along the shore and against the moving current. An instant chill seeped into my bones as I pounced into the water. Defenceless, ungoverned, and wayward across the rapids of eroding rocks, Edward had disappeared, and so had the lotus flower.

The loud beeping of lifesaving machinery clashed with the sound of scalpels and scissors. I felt no pain, just an indescribable chill seeping in my bones, like my skin was being cut open. A suction tube was attached to my mouth, strapped over my nose bridge. I couldn't even twitch my pinkie as a needle-like instrument penetrated my skin.

Noises and speech garbled in multiple frequencies.

Then, two latex-smelling fingers pushed open my eyelids.

'Her left arm is severely inflamed,' a voice said hastily.

'We'll try our very best, otherwise amputation is needed.'

Once again, I fell unconscious after being sedated.

* * *

A flash appeared. Rumours of my promiscuity were spreading in my workplace.

Despite the current guest being a food blogger, I could still feel Edward's presence, the scent of his acidic ocean cologne, and the sound of a guitar strumming whenever I walked into the suite even after the clean-up was done by the housekeeper. That'd changed when Mr Krishna handed me a temporary suspension notice.

Seemingly Mr Han had reported my 'obnoxious, indecent, and obsessive behaviour' towards Edward, causing him to return to Seoul. Madam Ong had insisted that I should stay instead of resigning while Sabrina had been my only pillar of support. Either way, I'd grown out of all shitty, ill-fated, dramatic storylines. What angered me the most was Mom recommending a one-week spiritual prayer retreat, saying it was in my best interest.

At times I wondered if Mom *really* ever knew what I wanted.

* * *

'Clear . . .' A jolt of electricity shocked me.

My heart started to beat again.

'This is the third time, doctor.'

'We almost lost her yesterday.'

'Like the other one as well, her uncle I mean.'

Then, there was another loud 'clear' before the defibrillator shocked me again.

My soul had commanded all heartaches into a colossal vault of vapour. My face was moistened by my tears as I waited for my last breath.

'Have you called her family?'

'Yes, her mother,' a woman's voice echoed.

'Ready! Last one. Clear!'

* * *

'Daniel said you almost collapsed a few days ago.'

That—Mom's voice.

'Just low platelets after donating blood to Raymond.'

Uncle Clement.

'Sean will be discharged in two days,' Uncle Clement said.

'Thank you for saving Emily and my brother.' Mom's voice was cold.

'Don't mention it.'

'I mean during Emily's so-called suicide. My brother explained everything to me.'

'I know for sure it was an accident or else Emily wouldn't have left the tiny-slit open in the window. Also, there was no suicide note.'

'The allegation was due to the alcohol bottles and the excessive inhaling of CO_2. I know my daughter won't be that dumb to die for a pop star.' Mom was confident.

'The burden of proof lies with Emily and, of course, with the best lawyer.'

There was a long silence.

'Emily is blessed and lucky to be alive, not once but twice. You volunteering in the church for years must've paid off.'

'It provides me inner peace,' Mom said. 'I did it not only for my Ma, Bridget, Raymond, and my daughter, but also for the years of emotional detachment I suffered at the hands of my father ever since childhood because he had a mistress outside.'

There was another interval of silence.

'If you don't mind, I need some quality time with my daughter.' There was the sound of mom sniffling and the rustle of her swiftly pulling facial tissue. 'I'll come back later,' Uncle Clement murmured.

'I appreciate all that you've done for my family. Get what I mean?'

'This is not the time to bring up old scores and grievances, Cheryl. I'm part of the Laus, and Emily is my niece too.'

'You're not obliged to shoulder what your mother has done, Clement.'

* * *

I felt a hand fervently stroking my hair, stopping only to hold my right hand in the softest grip. This person had delicate lips. I know because they pressed their mouth to my hand. I heard a quiet sniffle and warm tears drenched my right arm. The hand rested on my face, inhabiting regret and sadness. I gulped as my forehead was kissed. The touch was . . . *familiar.* My left arm—cumbersome, immobile, bandaged (perhaps), in-between numbness and soreness. The lips were pressing on the back of my right hand again. I wished I could open my eyes. Could it be *him?* Impossible. Could it be . . . Michael? Footsteps hastily retreated and just as quickly came back. A quick kiss on my lips, followed by a quick whisper—*saranghae.*

* * *

'Be well, my niece!'

Uncle Raymond's voice came alive in my head.

I could hear the non-stop beeping of the heart monitor and the soft thud of footsteps rushing in and out amid the cacophony of mumbling voices. The smell of . . . sickness . . . of sterility greeted me. My body was trying to move. Cold moisture trailed from my neck down my spine. I couldn't decipher the difference between sweat and other bodily fluids. A woman screamed as a bottle fell and broke apart with a piercing sound.

My right hand gripped onto the IV drip.

Eyes opened, then closed.

'She's awake!' a woman shouted.

'Get the doctor.'

'Aunt Cheryl! Biu-jie is up!' Daniel's voice was lightning struck.

* * *

It'd been two weeks since the near-death experience. Uncle Sean had been discharged the day before and had already returned to the pastry kitchen. I'd been transferred into the single-bed room. Orizuru or paper cranes folded in polychromatic shapes had been stringed then hung from the ceiling, like chandeliers that brought hope.

'Christmas comes early,' I was stroking the origami. 'It must be Daniel. But don't think he could do it alone, there are way too many of them.'

Michael nodded. 'Kenneth and Lily helped. A Japanese legend has it that if you fold one thousand paper cranes, your wish will come true.'

'Unfortunately, I can't do it for Uncle Raymond,' I said, looking at my left bandaged arm. I felt kind of useless. Suddenly, I thought of that kiss. 'Michael, I—'

'Yes, Emily?'

My fingers briefly caressed Michael's left cheek; the wound had a bandage over it. 'Does it still hurt? I saw there were some bruises on your arms.'

He shrugged it off. 'Just minor injuries. No worry.'

Eyes narrowed, I studied his expression.

Mom knocked on the door. 'Is everything all right here?'

'How long do I have to be admitted?' I asked as a jolt of stabbing pain radiated through my body, with an on-off shocking effect on my arms, I looked elsewhere. 'Can I visit Uncle Raymond?'

'Later dear, the skin reconstruction surgeon will be here soon,' said Mom.

'How bad is my arm?' I asked, too scared to see for myself.

'Don't worry, Emily.' Mom pulled me into her embrace. 'You'll be fine. Let me get you something to eat.' She let me go, hanging her tote bag over her shoulder, preparing to leave. 'Michael, you stay here and keep Emily company.'

I needed to speak with Mom about Uncle Clement, his background along with the story behind my pseudo-suicide. Wasn't it Uncle Raymond's assistance that had saved me?

Then why was Uncle Clement involved? Damn, these unsolved puzzles wouldn't let me off the hook.

I grabbed the pillow and threw it at Michael. He turned away from the wall of paper crane decorations.

'Bring my pillow here.' I stretched forward, sulking.

Michael gently leaned my shoulder towards the bed after slipping the pillow underneath. I leaned on the light comfortable contour. My gaze never left his as he sat on the chair, softly lifting my right foot to his lap, massaging my knee, and then repeating the process with the other one. I winced. He apologized. Karma had seemingly reverted the rigid coldness back to me.

'Let's go for a walk later.' I tried breaking the ice between us.

'I've to return to work at the pastry side. Uncle Sean is on a half-day today.'

'How's he doing?' I cocked my head at him.

'Just aching muscles. Surprising, huh?' Michael retracted from me, and then sat up straight so he could punch the air. 'You remember this? At the pastry kitchen . . .'

I thought harder. 'Wait, isn't that the towel strike? The one where Daniel . . .'

'Yeah, it took him years to learn those Taichi techniques,' Michael imitated Uncle Sean's uppercut and left hook. 'Only those at the Grandmaster level could defeat the crooks.'

I laughed at his attempt at humour, but eventually my smile subsided.

Michael searched my expression. 'Uncle Raymond will be fine too. The blade missed by an inch.' With this, I exhaled in relief. Then, Michael took something out from his pocket. 'I found this.' He placed it in my hand. 'I thought I'd save it before it disappeared.'

I beamed and took the lingfu from him. My lips trembled, as I examined the contorted surface. 'Thank you for everything,' I murmured.

'Emily, I . . .' Suddenly, Michael held my hands.

Then, I felt his thumb brush along my cheek before pulling me forward. I froze in shock. The beating of our hearts was only two fabrics apart. I looked up into his eyes. This wasn't Aunt Bridget's script rehearsal, and Rui-er was hibernating in my creative mind, lost in my recent misfortune. My lips pursed, then moved away. However—

Michael placed his lips on mine, pressing in.

My eyes widened, arms by my side, rendered motionless.

Other than perceiving his tenderness, all I could feel was a racing heart—an intensifying dread. I pulled away as Michael blinked softly.

'Have you been crying beside me almost every night?' I murmured.

'Think the surgeon is here . . .' Michael said, then slinked out.

Is that what guilt looks like on him?

* * *

Daniel threw his arms around me, pulling Uncle Clement in— who didn't mind joining in on the hug-fest. Thank goodness my cousin had survived the ordeal with only a few cuts on his face.

'You two, stop crying like babies.' Uncle Clement wiped our tears.

I rubbed my nose, briefly smiled at this *unconfirmed* elder of mine.

'Blessed be that Raymond has surpassed the critical period,' he said.

'What'd the surgeon say about your arm?' Daniel asked.

'Skin reconstruction surgery followed by physiotherapy sessions.' I said.

'Any chances you'll be able to re-ink the black rose tattoo?' Daniel asked.

'Unlike regular skin, tattooed skin needs a period of time to recover,' I said. 'The doctor said I was lucky that the injury didn't damage the nerves. My worry is getting back to the kitchen after this.'

* * *

'You should go to bed now,' Michael said to me. 'Mama's coming over tomorrow.'

'Don't think she's coping well with all this,' I murmured.

'Your mom and Uncle Sean told her everything.' Michael looked at me, biting his lips. 'Mama was very calm at first but started crying while standing outside Uncle Raymond's ward. The ICU wouldn't allow an elderly visitor to enter.'

'All mothers' hearts hurt more than the wounds of their children,' I said.

'Well, not all the time,' Michael expressed strictly.

Feeling that something was amiss, I turned my gaze to his. 'Daniel said you've been burning the midnight oil after work to fold Orizuru for me and Uncle Raymond.'

Michael smiled reluctantly as I massaged his fingertips.

Just what's going on in your mind, Michael Kim?

* * *

Later, Daniel came over with Penang *laksa*, stir-fried Chinese rice cakes takeout, and Korean spicy cup noodles. To wish me luck for my consultation with the surgeon tomorrow.

On our way to visit Uncle Raymond, we spotted Michael walking into the adjacent elevator in haste. Daniel raised his hand, to greet him, I held my cousin back with mixed feelings. The red signalling of numbers continued to descend and stopped at the lobby area.

I quickly pulled Daniel by his shirt into the other elevator.

'Is there anything I need to know?'' Daniel glanced at me, almost tripping.

'Sorry for getting you involved,' I said.

'Your expression definitely could slice metal,' my cousin muttered.

My leg fidgeted, tapping away the anxiety. Right arm folded over my belly. 'It rubs me the wrong way suddenly. By the way, Michael kissed me on my lips.'

'He's proven his feelings. Yes!' Daniel's voice echoed.

I stepped out. We turned left at the lobby area.

'Wait, is he a two timer?' Daniel covered his mouth.

I ignored him and spotted Michael, taking a sharp right turn. The directory plate above pointed towards the basement. I followed. Daniel started to slow down, periodically hiding behind pillars then tiptoeing when Michael meandered further towards the end. Then, a figure appeared, who Michael might've been covering up for, presumably a man a head shorter than him.

Michael looked over his shoulder. Had he spotted us? He then pushed the figure into the black luxury MPV. The vehicle had driven off by the time Daniel and I arrived at the scene.

'It's you.' Michael shot me a *fake* smile. 'Not sleeping yet?'

Daniel was gasping for air.

'What's the hurry?' I asked Michael, panting.

The sound of a screeching vehicle approached nearer, then stopped before me. I lifted a hand over my eyes as the piercing headlights momentarily blinded me. A figure stepped out. 'Let me talk to her, Hyojin-ssi.'

My heart raced. *That voice.*

'I'll handle it. Reporters could be outside.' Michael's tone was disapproving.

'I'm prepared to face the consequences, whatever they may be.'

Tears clouded my vision as Edward Ahn moved closer.

'Myeongjun-ssi,' Michael called out. 'I would advise against this. Unless you want to destroy your career.'

My eyes stared at those long-forgotten arms that I wished to be held in. Like Daniel's expression, the situation was in the shambles. 'Yeah, listen to Kim Hyojin.' I could barely get the words out.

Edward was dumbfounded.

Michael looked shocked at my literary *ambush*.

Daniel cleared his throat. 'Visiting hours have ended. My cousin needs rest.'

'I'm dropping by tomorrow,' Edward said to me, then left in the MPV.

I entered the elevator with Daniel, ignoring Michael.

Twenty-Nine

In the consultation room, I held my breath as the doctor removed the dressing gauze, careful not to disturb the scarred skin on my left arm. The doctor instructed me to squeeze a soft ball. I peeped at the patient's checklist while the doctor ticked away at the square boxes.

Only six-and-a-half upon ten stars on my agility level.

Make it seven—*how stingy!*

'How's my daughter's arm?' Mom asked.

'The skin reconstruction must be done as soon as possible,' the doctor explained. 'Next week if possible, since the operation theatre is available.'

I couldn't stop appreciating these *brand-new friends* on my left arm.

Crinkled plum blossoms cruising along the serpentine river, dunes and craters mapped out on my skin. The pain I felt when my clothes rubbed against my damaged skin was similar to needles jabbing my skin. It was like a getting a tattoo from a sadist. The doctor had labelled me as 'very fortunate and very close to losing a forearm'. The surgery was to remove the remaining glass fragments lodged in my skin.

'What're the chances of full recovery?' Mom asked. 'Any possible side-effects and what should she keep an eye out for after the surgery?'

The conversation between my mom and the doctor had begun to take the shape of a topiarist in my head, clipping ill-favoured shrubs to form ornamental fresh wounds from the surgery risks involved to the estimated rate of recovery and the mandatory after-care.

Last night, I'd swallowed a mixed cocktail of emotion.

I had questions. I had *so* many questions.

What were Michael's true feeling when he kissed me?

Would Edward accept my black rose tattoos and injured left arm?

How did Michael slide his way into St Paul's Church?

Did Michael ever tell Edward the truth that I haven't moved on?

'Is next Wednesday all right, Emily?' Mom asked.

I was confused.

'I'm talking about your skin reconstruction surgery,' mom continued.

'Should be fine,' I said to Mom. Then, I thanked the nurse for bandaging my left arm. The lock screen alerted me of an incoming call. 'Yes, Daniel.'

'Come back to your room now, right now.'

* * *

I yelled at the two strangers in my room as they manoeuvred to the side, removing the paper cranes from the ceiling, supervised by Michael.

'Tell your men to stop right now!'

Michael instructed his men to stop. 'Let's talk, Emily.'

I told Daniel to leave. He did so after sufficiently glaring at Michael.

'I'm taking you to the first-class ward,' Michael said. 'Myeongjun-ssi is paying for everything including your surgery.'

'Oh great,' I said, sarcastically. 'Call him here. I need to have a word with him.'

'He'll be coming over at eight,' Michael said.

'Yeah, I saw him last night for the first time in a while.' I clenched my teeth.

'He's been . . . here with you for the past few days,' Michael said.

I pursed my trembling lips, feeling bad about doubting Edward's love, sincere in its care even at the risk of being exposed.

'It's been five years since I've been working as Myeongjun-ssi's fashion stylist. His solo career is currently managed by my mother, Director Shin.' Michael continued, 'You have the right to be angry, as there have been heaps of misunderstandings . . .'

'Then how do you fit in, Kim Hyojin?' I sneered. 'For putting up the best volunteering showmanship in Serendipity Sanctuary, acting over-friendly with my family, and then getting me that expensive dress to the engagement party.' I took a step forward.

Michael stared at me. 'How'd you know my full name? From Uncle Clement?'

'Edward's manager Mr Han.'

'Former manager you mean.' Michael crossed his arms.

I gazed deeply into his eyes. 'Did you steal my promise ring?'

'Yes, I did.' Michael's expression turned uncompromising.

'Goddamnit!' I turned away.

Michael exhaled. 'I've returned it to Myeongjun-ssi.'

I pivoted over to face the wall so Michael couldn't see what his words had done to me.

'He suffered from insomnia after returning from Kuala Lumpur. That person had stopped loving him and had moved on with someone new. And that ring was his promise to her.'

My heart went out to Edward. To have lived with this lie for months—working on his studio album and trying hard, day and night, to forget heartless Emily. I wondered how Michael had found me. My whole family. All the way in Penang. In the secluded Serendipity Sanctuary.

Chills ran down my spine, one after another, like a climber, conquering peak after peak.

'Then why bother to stay?' I choked out, at this fresh betrayal.

Michael's lips pursed.

I took a deep breath. 'Volunteers are replaceable.' *Be positive.* 'But it's all right if you want to leave after the fundraising food drive. We've to finish from what we started, right ?'

'Emily, I . . . I'm sorry.'

I swallowed hard, then brushed away my tears.

He titled his head, avoiding me, then cleared his throat. After a while, he turned to face me. 'About the kiss.' His eyes were slightly swollen. 'It was . . . my first time.' My heart skipped a beat. If Edward hadn't returned. I might've taken his hands, like he'd held mine in the storeroom. And his attentiveness before we kissed. 'Please . . . stop.' I warned.

'And I truly meant it.'

There was a thunderous sound, of flesh hitting cement, echoing with vibrations. A bouquet of flowers was discarded outside the door and a shadowy presence was storming off.

* * *

'You should've stopped me from talking further.'

Daniel apologized. 'Well, I was shocked when Edward stood there with . . . flowers . . .'

We hurriedly rushed to the upper mezzanine.

I gasped. The storm that had been brewing was reaching its end.

Daniel pulled me back as I opened the door into the corridor.

'Emily is mine!' Edward was holding Michael by his collar.

Michael was wiping blood off his bleeding lips.

Edward yelled something distasteful in Korean when his attempt at kneeing Michael in the groin failed as the latter was quick to dodge. Two ferals alike—fists clenched and bloodshot eyes. Undeterred, Edward bent low, using his body weight to throw Michael against the wall. He held him there with a shoulder pressed in Michael's belly, putting all his body weight on Michael's kidneys. Michael screamed in pain. The veins on Edward's forehead looked like they were about to burst as he put his full weight on Michael. Attempting to escape, Michael's elbow started to knead hard into Edward's upper neck, making the other man yowl.

I rushed in to pull Edward off. 'Stop it, both of you.'

Daniel grabbed Michael. 'Can't you both sit down and—'

'Still denying your feelings, huh?' Edward pointed a threatening finger at Michael.

'Then I would've run away with Emily.' Michael said, trying to get his breath back.

Edward tried to move forward, but I grabbed him, holding him back.

Michael continued. 'You wouldn't have known about Emily's overdose and subsequent hospitalization if I'd left earlier. And did I mention you left Seoul an hour before the fan meeting?' he said the last part staring at me.

'Yeah, my passport was compounded by Director Shin and she forced me to rewrite all the songs in Korean. Didn't I pay my dues?' Edward's eyes swelled with emotion. 'The English album was my love for Emily, and for my international fans.' Edward held my hand, looked into my eyes. 'Leaving Emily at the writer's retreat was a mistake, if only Mr Han hadn't lied about my parents' car accident.'

My grip tightened around Edward's, furious at Mr Han's deceitful, dirty tricks.

'Your solo career would be over if Director Shin hadn't stepped in!' Michael looked like he wanted another go at Edward.

Daniel interrupted both men with a sharp exhale. 'Biu-jie, your arm . . . your arm is bleeding.'

'What'd you know about love, Kim Hyojin?' Edward quickly picked me up and left.

* * *

After the consultation, Edward wheeled me into my room.

The paper cranes had been redecorated as before alongside the plush teddies, get-well-soon cards, and, balloons, all arranged on the top of the cabinet. Sabrina's get-well-soon gift was carnations with miniature teddies attached to the bouquet.

'Thank you very much for your help,' Mom said.

'I'm sorry for causing Emily pain,' Edward replied in a small voice.

I looked at Mom smiling at him, adjusting the pillows behind me.

'Oh, please don't.' Mom waved his apology away. 'I'm glad you were there for her.'

'If you don't mind, can I stay for a bit?' Edward turned to my mom.

Mom gave me a quick hug and left.

'What're you doing?' Edward asked as I flipped the blanket over.

'I need some water.'

'I'll get it for you.' Edward filled the paper cup from the thermos flask, added some cold water from the other jug and handed the cup to me.

I carefully took a sip. 'If I hadn't stopped the fight, Michael would've thrown you off.' Edward remembered that I preferred to drink warm water when facing the aparthotel's teeth-chattering air-con. An ache had crept in as my thumb brushed Edward's face, skimming over his inflamed cheek.

'His tiger-mom would have annihilated him for killing their agency's most bankable virtuoso soloist.' Edward chuckled, narrowing those beautiful eyes. 'He's been hiding under his mother's skirt for far too long, that's the price to pay as a chaebol.'

Meanwhile Edward had to choose between a successful career or a life with the woman he loved. 'What a snob.' I rolled my eyes. 'I'll get you a band-aid.'

Edward was quick to cradle me in his arms. 'We really need to talk.'

'I need rest.' I extracted myself from his embrace and pulled the thermal blanket over my head. While forcing my eyes to shut. *I don't want this to end. I don't want him to say it.*

Edward sneaked in with that softest grin. His smile had found its way beneath my skin. A heartrending love that had traversed between the polemic and the abyss, was now gravitating towards an unexplainable pace. We'd returned to each other at long last. My fingers were trailing across his chest, Edward was kissing my lips. I stirred at his gentleness. With my eyes closed, it felt like that kiss—the similar sharing of breath during my coma. Edward's sudden return had created a detour (again) in my life. I slowly pulled away as tension mounted.

'I've been waiting and praying for you every night,' he whispered, resting his head on my cheek. 'I wanted to be the first thing you saw when you woke up.'

My eyes locked with his. I wiped the tear making its way down his cheek.

'I spoke to your mother about your follow-up treatment in Seoul.'

Shocked, I exhaled a sharp breath. 'I bet she dissented.'

'Of course.'

'Yeah, I won't be going anywhere either.' I said, adamantly.

'But South Korea ranks first on a per capita basis in cosmetic surgery. There's a hospital located out of Seoul with English interpreters. You don't have to worry about the expenses—'

'Edward . . .' I murmured, fervently.

'What—?'

I took his hands and pressed my lips to them. Breathing in. Slow and steady. Feeling his skin on mine. In no rush. Repeating his confession in my head. I felt his kiss on my forehead. I didn't stir. I wanted to remember this moment. This moment that belonged to Edward Ahn and Emily Chung.

'Is something bothering you?' Edward whispered.

He got me. 'Am I losing to your career?' I looked down. 'And then my arm . . .'

He cupped my face. 'Please remember, you're never a burden. You're the most joyful addition to my life.'

I raised my hand and intertwined my fingers with his. I felt how thin his hands had got. Edward has lost a lot of weight.

'If you're worried about your surgery tomorrow, don't be. You're very important and I wouldn't survive losing you. I'm certain my desperation by itself would be enough to persuade the universe to let you make it through.' Edward was tearing up. 'We've been fooled by two scumbags. I don't ever want a repeat of the pain we were put through, the grief we lived with.'

'Hypertrophic scars aren't for the faint-hearted.' I cupped his face, smiling at him.

'I'm asking for one more chance to prove my love.' Edward's sincerity pierced my heart.

* * *

Mom helped me wear the surgical gown the next morning. Then, Mama put a new lingfu amulet over my neck. She'd requested the temple for it so I wouldn't accompany the Chinese bull-head and horse-face reapers—who could plan to snatch my soul at the operation table—to purgatory. Daniel, Aunt Bridget, and Mama already knew that I once dated a former K-pop-idol, and Mom took this breaking news fairly nonchalantly.

Later, I received a brief good luck text message from Michael.

I took a deep breath as the team of nurses wheeled me into the elevator.

At the patient waiting lounge, my family members could only look in from the outside sliding window panel. Mom passed a facial tissue to Mama. I wiped my tears with my sleeve. It made me feel a little better to see Aunt Bridget and Mom gripping onto Mama's hands. Her wish had come true—her two princesses were by her side, now if only Uncle Raymond, Mama's prince, could wake up from his coma.

I received a well-written text message from Uncle Clement with photos of Uncle Sean's new pastries, a bribe to make it through. My reward would be trying their delicious invention.

The doctor explained the surgery procedure to me before I signed the consent form. As an experienced plastic surgeon, he was confident that the surgery would be a success.

Edward walked in after the doctor's permission. He took out the promise ring with the necklace from his pocket and dangled it in front of me. 'Hyojin-ssi already returned it to me. Now, I want you to wear it.' He tried to put it over my head but realized the lingfu amulet was on my neck. He smiled and unhooked the clasp of the necklace to retrieve the ring. 'Have you tried wearing it before?'

'No, but Sabrina told me she was part of this.' I rolled my eyes.

'There's no secret between you both,' Edward chuckled, putting it on my finger. I tried not to burst into tears, feeling his lips on my knuckle. 'It's beautiful . . .'

'I panicked when it disappeared because this is the only reminder I had of you, of our memories and the time we spent together.'

'The ring is now back with its rightful owner.' He took my hand. His fingers trembled. 'Please don't leave me.' A whispered plea.

* * *

The incandescent LED light shone directly on me in the operation theatre.

The doctor and his assistants were in their surgical gowns. Sounds of surgical tools clattering filled the theatre as everyone gathered around the table, stirring my anxiety.

The doctor turned off the classical music playing in the background and plugged in a USB flash drive into the stereo, tweaking the volume to an admissible level.

'That gentleman gave it to me. He said you'd like it.'

The doctor meant Edward. I mouthed, 'thank you' and closed my eyes.

It was the demo of a song in English— 'Sibjalo' or 'Crossroad'.

The lyrics went, 'From strangers to lovers we meet halfway, never star-crossed; no upholding the finale'. The piano scales in the background lured me in. The bowed strings arranged with the padded drums, syncing with the pulsation.

A memory floated up—the writer's retreat. Edward had taken a polaroid photo of me then drawn a sunflower on the paper, scribbling the chords above the lyrics written in English and in Korean. Edward's kisses had liquefied my lips.

Thirty

'Remember, don't add water in the coconut milk,' Mama instructed.

The pastry kitchen was closed for the Laus' family affair. Daniel was blending a handful of pandan leaves to make a concentrated juice. The pastry kitchen smelled earthy, of petrichor after a light tropical rain, magnified by the whiff of the pandan leaves, unrefined and mysterious.

I popped an antibiotic and then swallowed it with a glass of water. This was one of the post-surgery treatments to combat the possibility of inflammation and bacterial infection. The other treatments were the application of an antibiotic ointment and aloe vera gel to my skin.

Blessed be that the dermis had begun to heal as the days progressed.

'Do not pour the pandan juice all at once. You must do it slowly and by feel,' Mama said combining the batter by hand. '*Kuih talam* is a soft and bouncy steamed sweet cake. The green pandan at the bottom layer is topped with flavourful milky coconut.'

Everyone was attentive in Grandma Betty's kuih-making masterclass.

'It was my husband's favourite—an apt preference because it represented his two-faced character of having a legal wife and a mistress.' Mama added.

No one stirred at the grim humour.

Mama then poured the green coloured batter onto the tray, evened it out and then tapped on the folded towel to release the air bubbles. 'Steam for twenty minutes on medium heat, leave it to cool for ten to fifteen minutes before pouring the coconut batter, steamed for sixteen minutes, and then serve well after an hour of refrigeration.'

Mom jotted down the recipe step-by-step in her spiral notebook.

'That Sean Monk said he wants some for his old ma?' Aunt Bridget asked.

'Sure, how's she doing?' Mama asked.

'Just the usual old-people rheumatism, I guess.' Aunt Bridget replied.

'I will visit her after things get better.' Mama exhaled.

'Time to start the campervan engine,' Daniel hollered and then left.

'My dead husband's genes are confirmed to have skipped a generation and manifested in Emily.' She was alluding to the love triangle between Michael, Edward, and me. 'But this unfaithful husband impregnated and committed to two women.'

'Your granddaughter is a one-man woman,' I said.

'I would choose wisely if I were to meet two similar men,' Mom said.

'Edward knew the importance of my internship as well as my arm's route to recovery,' I said. 'One step at a time, y'all.'

'We'll see . . .' Mom turned to Mama; both nodded with a smirk.

* * *

Glaring at the black and white photo, I bowed before Ah-Gong's columbarium.

My cousin was arranging two plates of kuih talam on the communal table of offerings. I'd heard of my grandfather's integrity and efficiency in his assigned police duties. No one among the Laus had ever spoken ill of him.

Uncle Clement walked solemnly into the hall.

Daniel and I greeted him with a nod and then took a few steps back to stand beside Mom. Mama clasped her hands, mumbling prayers as Uncle Clement placed a bouquet of white chrysanthemums on the table, gazing at the black and white plaque next to Ah-Gong; a woman with shoulder-length permed hair and a pleasant smile, resembling Uncle Clement's. I would've assumed she was Uncle Clement's late mother, Ah-Gong's mistress.

'I dreamed of Old Bean last night,' Daniel muttered, outside the prayer hall. 'Tubes were all around him, hanging onto life support. Besides pulling my ear, he was slapping my back for disobeying his will to accept Lily as my wife. She appeared to be quite pretty wearing that two-piece quan kwa dress and a traditional headgear.'

'Very filial.' I restrained myself from giggling. My thoughts flew to Uncle Raymond's critical condition.

'Yeah, but I got up sweating like crazy.'

'They probably wanted to solemnize the marriage by way of *choong-hei* to banish the family's bad luck, replacing it with an auspicious occasion,' I said.

Daniel nudged my elbow. 'Who knows, perhaps your and Edward's wedding will be arranged to hasten Old Bean's recovery, to counteract the bad omen.'

I plucked a yellow flower off the bonsai plant and threw it at Daniel.

'Seriously now,' Daniel's hand blocked my attack. 'Kenneth has been hurrying me to bring him to meet the family.'

'Does he know it is not a good time?'

Daniel exhaled. 'He's been making that bitter gourd "meh" face. Being in a relationship isn't easy, so complicated if one behaves tactlessly.'

'Yeah, family is most important right now,' I patted Daniel's back.

'My Biu-jie is always a step ahead in thoughts,' Daniel pursed his lips. 'Did you know I dreamed about mamie two nights ago for the first time after so bloody long?' I put my arms around him as he snuggled against my shoulder. 'I woke up crying.'

I patted his head, understanding Daniel's tension, as the probability of losing his father was a bleak 60/40. Blood was thicker than water—now, I believed this.

'I've been manifesting in abundance for this kuih talam magic to work. The sweet cakes are to appease Ah-Gong's spirit, to protect Old Bean from unseen ghosts dawdling in the hospital hunting for weaker spirits so they may reincarnate as mentioned by the temple's fortune teller.' Daniel said.

'No spirit has visited me throughout my stay,' I said.

'Wandering spirits love abandoned and quiet spaces. Your room has had visitors in and out, their noises and the energy would've caused irritation—from Aunt Cheryl, Aunt Bridget, and myself . . . Michael and then . . .' he winked. 'Edward.'

I rolled my eyes, blushing a bit.

Suddenly, I thought of Michael. Ever since his fight with Edward, I hadn't seen that Kimchi anywhere in the kitchens. I hadn't had the heart to send him a text. Perhaps, it was time for us to stay apart—for a while.

'It's been like bats flying out from hell's cave for these past few days,' my cousin shook his head. 'Mama woke up from a nightmare one night, convinced that a ghost had come to claim Old Bean in the ICU and was begging that thing to take her instead. Poor Mama was shivering, she was so spooked she lost her appetite and then had a fever for the next three days.'

'Mama has to go through such turbulence at this age,' I muttered.

'All of us are destined to be born and die as a cursed Laus.' Daniel said grimly.

'Aunt Bridget should start writing a family saga reality show,' I joked.

'Please don't get her started.'

I laughed.

Daniel continued. 'Aunt Bridget stepped into the family kitchen to make freshwater fish and chicken soup for Uncle Sean. I somehow became their delivery man, delivering the food to him twice a day until he was discharged from the ward.'

'Sounds like a blessing in disguise?'

Daniel looked bemused.

'Uncle Sean and Aunt Bridget have reconciled,' I said. 'Mom has returned to Penang. And you're not in a bull fight when talking about Uncle Raymond.'

'I've been forced to grow up after this incident, exhausted by this year-long hatred.' Daniel said. 'Oh, allow me to clarify further; now that you have two lotus flowers. Plural.'

I owed Michael a heart-to-heart talk.

'For now, I'll be replacing you in the kitchens until your next consultation has ended. You're a ghoulish workaholic, just like Edward. He said in one of the interviews that he was able to finish composing, lyrics writing, and then arranging a song within one day.'

'Professionally and privately, I love him for who he is. Honestly, the romance between us has . . . everything is different now. We need to work things out.'

'Don't tell me . . .' Daniel leaned forward. 'Are you in love with that Kimchi?'

'No—' I yelled, pointing. 'Wait, did you tell anyone about that kiss?'

'Oh, please.' Daniel shrieked. 'My jewels are precious,' he said grabbing his crotch.

I rolled my eyes.

'Michael was very kind to inform Edward about your hospitalization unlike that hellish bitch Fiona,' Daniel reminded me. 'That Kimchi had the choice not to, y'know.'

I felt indebted. The Laus had also owed Michael his kindred spirit after the rumble ordeal. 'But twist of fate, Uncle Clement's really one of the Laus.'

'I'd been hoping he's part of us,' Daniel said.

'Expected.'

'It started when Old Bean needed a blood transfusion. His AB positive type is fucking rare in Penang. I thought he was going to die in my arms. Uncle Clement did it without me having to ask him. He put his life at stake for his half-brother.'

'I owe Uncle Clement for utilizing his past connections to save me from my alcohol poisoning. He trusted this incompetent half-niece that he hadn't met. Uncle Raymond had to lie to Mom in order not to cause further misunderstanding.'

Daniel patted my back. 'By the way, did Aunt Cheryl tell you all this?'

'I heard the conversation between Mom and Uncle Clement in my coma,' I said. 'It was quite a horrifying situation, I could hear crying and could feel Mom and Mama touching my skin. Mom's been shouldering this family trauma ever since she was young. And I've also been hearing you crying beside my bed.' I briefly smiled.

Daniel covered his mouth. 'That's so embarrassing.'

'You were snorting and blubbering all over me,' I joked.

'Every family has skeletons in their ancestral cupboard; bitter wounds that are unable to heal overnight.' Daniel said. 'Forgiveness takes a lot of effort. It is impossible when all the heart has borne is resentment and hatred.'

'I finally understand Uncle Raymond's painstaking effort.'

'The meet and greet was a good example for Mama and Old Bean competing over their stubbornness. Old Bean surrendered to Mama when she insisted on meeting Uncle Clement to fix the roster. Mama has a way to keep her son in line.'

'I've learned the hard way to embrace cunningness and kind-heartedness together.' I brushed my hand on the pruned bonsai in the terracotta pots.

'We need more gossip to drive off all the negative vibes,' Daniel winked at me.

'Come join us in the communal hall for some kuih and tea.' Uncle Clement said to us.

Daniel and I looked at each other. The short circuit of closeness between the Laus and this half-uncle had fused fast.

'It's your Mama's instruction. I'm just a messenger.'

'Yay! Time to eat!' Daniel walked ahead of me.

'Thank you Uncle Clement for everything.' I stopped in front of him. His silence proved my arrogance. That I was indomitable. I exhaled and then conceded his smile, at the one I'd prejudice against from the start. If Uncle Raymond had given me a home to rebuild my life, Uncle Clement had given me the courage to spread my wings and fly.

'Remember my advice at the rooftop terrace,' Uncle Clement held my shoulder. 'Dispel the sadness as it comes. Don't let a haunting past take control.'

'You're slowly becoming my therapist.'

'Time will bear witness. Be patient, my niece.' Uncle Clement raised an eyebrow. 'By the way, Michael is moving back to St Paul's Church. With another person on board.'

Thirty-One

Michael had been waiting on the porch.

Mama gave him a hug after getting down from the campervan, thanking him for his company during lonely nights when she wept for Uncle Raymond's condition. Mom shook his hand gratefully for taking care of me while Aunt Bridget ordered him to keep in touch.

'Sorry for my hurtful words,' I said to Michael, feeling empty.

'So long as the misunderstandings are settled.' He grinned softly, slinging the backpack over his back. 'The room can't fit two adult men, one of us has to leave.'

Edward and my gaze met; he was watching from the upstairs window.

Mama had warned me that I wouldn't be able to look at Michael without any sweet reminiscence. She was right. Aunt Bridget had suggested picking the best one based on their dominant qualities and similar interests while Mom held my hand, praying to the Chaplet of The Divine Mercy. Ah-Gong's lothario trait had cast an inglorious curse on me.

'Where're the clothes you previously bought from Uniqlo?' I asked Michael.

'They're mostly for Myeongjun-ssi, I didn't have time to send them previously. I guess there's no need to . . .' Michael shrugged. 'The only clothes for me were the t-shirts.'

I looked at the paper bag in his grip. My heart had attempted to open up to Michael after the gang fight; caught somewhere between platonic feelings and a sprinkle of affection. But his impromptu kiss had taken me by surprise. I hadn't liked it. 'So, I'll be seeing you around still?'

He nodded. 'You know the fundraising food drive . . .' But then, he didn't complete his sentence or mention the drama script recital—which is where I thought this was going. 'Better not keep Uncle Clement waiting,' he said glancing up.

Edward was nowhere to be seen by then.

'See you later.' I hugged him.

'Yeah, take care.'

I closed the door after he left.

* * *

Leaving the bathroom tap running was kind of therapeutic.

I turned it off and almost screamed when I saw Edward leaning against the door. I wondered how long he'd been there staring at me through the reflection in the mirror.

Water dripped down my face, then onto my shirt. Edward quickly passed me a towel.

Once I was done, I placed the towel back, a peculiar grief striking me suddenly like honeyed poison. *The adjustment without Michael.* I felt Edward's fingers trailing over my skin, his breaths laboured as he looked at me with those inscrutable eyes, enthralled by this yearning.

Starting with quick butterfly pecks, we kissed behind the door, as Edward lifted me, his open mouth reaching for my neck. An unhurried pace. He kissed along my jawline and then my collar bone. I breathed heavily as his tongue slipped in, tasting mine.

Once we were in the room, the trepidation in our hearts disappeared as we kissed harder. He pulled away, panting as he rested one hand on my cheek. With our foreheads softly pressing together, we breathed in our heated passion.

Four large Uniqlo paper bags were arranged underneath the desk. There used to be five. That Kimchi had been shopping for clothes. It was after the meeting with Uncle Clement at St Paul's Church. I remembered Michael being extra careful with the denim jeans, the flannel long-sleeved shirt, and the hooded jackets. I thought it was just him being fussy. Looking at the bags under the table, I finally knew the reason for his careful handling of the apparel. Michael had been shopping for Edward.

'A pop star stocking up on non-designer clothes,' I teased Edward. Michael had purchased an assortment of coloured tees, including the one he'd dared me to put on him that night.

'Designer clothes are for airport fashion and radio station interviews.' He unbuckled the empty suitcase. 'Basically, anywhere where there are fans.'

'This is why everybody wants to be a celebrity,' I said. 'Complimentary facial treatments and free skincare samples aside, it's the fame and the huge fortune.'

'An idol is a trendsetter, packaged by the company in a pretty outer covering. Other than being talented, they also need to be hard workers and passionate, and have leadership qualities.' Edward finished arranging the denim jeans atop the flannel long-sleeved shirt. 'I remember at the peak of my idol career, one or two of the least popular members would receive only a tie or a pair of socks, but I can't reveal who the unlucky ones are.' He put the luggage away, then dragged the other one. 'And I swear it was definitely not me.'

'I've never been a fan of K-pop, despite their cool choreographies.' I locked the suitcase. Madam Ong had assigned Edward's airport pick-up to me because she thought I wouldn't be charmed by him. But the universe had its own plans.

'It's a blessing to wear Karl Lagerfeld's designs, to visit the finest leatherwork factory in Milan, to fine dine with other famous local designers, and attend fashion week.' Edward wheeled the two suitcases to the side of the desk. 'Idols return to their authentic selves after the spotlights fade. And being a soloist, it feels like I'm starting anew, alone on the stage once again.'

The room was infused with the pleasant fragrance of a scented candle, reminding me of our first intimate moment at the aparthotel suite; the memory gradually eliminating Michael's presence. 'I heard Uncle Clement had a video conference with Director Shin before heading to my grandpa's columbarium for prayers. I know he took full responsibility for Michael's safety .'

'Your half-uncle was impressively calm and collected even as he was dealing with South Korea's most perilous manager. But I don't blame Director Shin, it's her duty to ensure I'm in good hands. Hyojin-ssi's trip to Penang was on my account, I wanted him to check out a business venture here.'

'Yeah, to steal the promise ring, huh—?' I leaned closer.

'Including that lace lilac dress.'

'What a sweet retort,' I said, rolling my eyes.

Edward looked at me with seriousness. 'The moment of truth. I pushed you to become a killer.' I chuckled at his dramatics. 'Michael was really mugged though,' he added.

'Wait, you're not kidding?' I felt bad for him. *Poor Kimchi.*

'The irresponsible taxi driver dropped him at the junction and he had to walk a long road. Michael's the type to separate cash and documents. A very meticulous man.' Edward's tone was approving.

Though I had apologized to Michael before, I still felt like kicking myself.

'You seem to have quite a big family.' Edward's voice interrupted.

I smiled. 'I'm so grateful to have them.'

'Ever thought of adding one more?' Edward whispered. 'I'm staying here for one week to make up for the time we didn't spend at the writer's retreat.'

'Director Shin seems to be an affable person?' I smiled.

'She thinks our relationship can develop further after considering your half-uncle's background and his former position in the Narcotics CID. And I know about the toxic relationship between you and your father.' Edward rested his hands on my cheeks, stroking gently. My arms were over his shoulder. Edward continued. 'Hyojin-ssi briefly spoke about it. You had to undergo such hardships and I'm sorry for not being there.'

'Your manager must have known about my past and upbringing,' I murmured as Edward planted a kiss on my hands, pulling me to sit on his lap.

'I owe it to Director Shin's PA and his team. I mentioned your retired actress aunt and they were able to excavate the rest. Their efficiency and insightful teamwork frighten me at times. Famous celebs aren't supposed to have a relationship without their artist management's approval. We can't risk our career by placing it in the hands of a stranger. The PR side will handle the media agencies and the paparazzi when they find out about our relationship.'

* * *

The dinner had been good, aside from Uncle Raymond's absence. Edward was sitting on Michael's usual seat. Daniel and I had made kimchi from scratch, which Edward had generously complimented. Later, Sabrina called to confirm she received my sponsor proposal via email and chatted briefly with Edward.

I had stopped applying the antibiotic ointment twice a day on my left arm due to skin dryness and only applied it once after showering. Three weeks post-surgery, the scars were slowly healing.

'Choco pie was so hard to come by during those days,' Edward took an indulgent bite, putting the draft and guitar away. 'We were allowed to eat it maybe once a week. It's expensive and calorific and we had to be thin and fit. No refined sugary carbs.'

I sipped on the semi-sweetened prune juice; an attempt to reduce my caffeine intake. The oral antibiotic had caused indigestion. 'You survived the trainee days' ordeal.'

'I remember sneaking out one night to the nearby mall, waiting for a girl at the alley, the same alley where the other ParadiZo members would meet their girlfriends.'

'Young hearts run free with the exes.' I giggled. The band consisted of seven 'boyz' including Edward, like seven sins cast from paradise to steal many hearts.

'Someone's jealous.'

'Why should I be?' I turned to Edward. 'So, what happened then?'

'Adolescence is about recklessness and making silly mistakes. I called her when the group finally debuted,' Edward chuckled. 'She broke up with me because she'd started dating her best friend. I was suspended from a month of training for dating without consent.'

'The universe has given you more that you've lost,' I said. 'Your group has gained fans from around the world, and you have toured many countries, done interviews for local as well as with the international magazines, you've done TV shows and travel documentaries.'

'Some of us have even acted in TV series and movies.' Edward nodded. 'You're right. The emptiness has been replaced by screaming fans and loud cheering at concerts, at airports, outside radio stations and at the award ceremony shows.'

'And you've also written a love song dedicated to your ex-lover.'

He was staring at me. 'I thought you didn't listen to K-pop?'

I covered my face with a blanket.

He pinned me to the bed. 'Say it—'

'I've been listening to your songs ever since last month, only yours.'

Deborah Wong 307

His gaze fixed on my lips, he didn't even look up when he said 'nice canopy'.

I playfully covered my face with mosquito netting.

'Can't wait to be my *sinbu*?' Edward teased. 'Hello, my bride.'

I pulled his collar, looking at my reflection in his soft, brown pupils. My heart skipped a beat when I felt his lips on my forehead. 'Can't wait to have me?' I asked.

'It's dinnertime, *yeobo*,' he pretended to call, grabbing the netting. 'The wife shouts and turns off the stove. The husband sets the table and makes sure the kids are seated properly. Her face blooms into a smile when she sees her husband and the kids savouring the rice with the seaweed soup and the banchan she's prepared.'

'After dinner, the kids have strawberries or apple pie, then run and scream with joy while the husband joins in the fun,' I added. 'They bathe the kids in the tub, later teaching them to draw or reading them bedtime stories, kissing the kids and wishing them good night, tucking them in bed. They unwind in front of the TV, watching their favourite movie, chatting away.'

'I'm confident that the day will arrive, Em.' His thumb brushed my cheek. 'From abiding to the vows of "I do" to our kids taking their first baby steps . . .'

A tear made its way down my face. Edward rubbed it away.

My heart swelled the more we kissed.

* * *

The day for the sponsor pitch presentation had arrived.

Meeting the K-Licious-Delish management team for the first time, I recognized each of them, thanks to the organization chart Sabrina had emailed me the night before. They were welcoming, helping with my nerves. The pressure to be perfect had barely receded with Edward's encouraging words and kisses before leaving the house.

The decision would be finalized after lunch time.

I took over the wide projector screen when Daniel finished his part.

I fought the urge to throw up while delivering my speech.

I glanced at Michael and then Uncle Clement, determined to do my best.

I craved for this uncertainty to be over, afraid that the management wouldn't agree to the sponsorship. Sabrina and Daniel silently cheered me on.

I stammered during the project evaluation pitch.

Uncle Clement furrowed his brows, prepared to come to my rescue. I removed the promise ring on my finger and the lingfu amulet from my jeans pocket, placing them side by side, I'd prolonged my dependency on these sources of protection. Michael gazed in my direction then tapped the 4/4 beat cadence on the conference table.

I hit it on the fifth, then finished, in addition to summarizing the closing paragraph like a professional statement. Thunderous applause followed. Sabrina and Daniel gave me a standing ovation. Years of succumbing to belittlement had made me underestimate my capability. Besides Edward, I owed this victorious moment to Michael.

* * *

A hotpot party was held to celebrate the successful agreement. The management team had said yes.

'We'll be spending Christmas with Taylor Swift this year.' Sabrina eyed me, arranging the tofu and slices of meat, placing them beside the chopped scallions and fermented kimchi that encircled the electric pot that was currently cooking *budae jigae* or army stew.

'Better than winning the jackpot,' I said, sarcastically.

Edward and Daniel looked in my direction, chewing and drinking soju straight from the bottle.

'That's our sisterhood of secret codes.' I winked at them.

Edward and I took turns to fill up each other's plates with food. Michael was munching on a green chilli pepper, pretending not to notice our interaction. He'd been volunteering at the soup kitchen nowadays and could therefore *successfully* avoid me. Edward's face had become rosy while feeding me the spicy rice cake which he'd eaten half of was a public display of affection.

'My father used to say, throw in the soju and *nakji bokkeum*,' Edward burped. 'You'll never regret eating spicy stir-fried octopus. I miss drinking *makgeolli* under the moon and discussing poetry with him. I'm planning for a meet-the-parents session for my poet-girlfriend and them very soon.' He eyed me affectionately then kissed my cheek.

Everyone clapped and cheered.

Except Michael who uttered a hoot.

'Oh, thanks for your greasiness.' I stuck my tongue out at Edward.

'Thanks, Michael, we owe you this success.' Daniel raised his glass and proposed a toast.

Michael smiled briefly, raised the soju bottle and finished it in one gulp.

'Of course, to my Biu-jie,' Daniel added.

I sipped from the cup. 'You're still the leader in this project, though.'

From the victorious pitching event to the warmest gathering, there wouldn't be any iced-water-bucket treatment after midnight. My thoughts had been with Uncle Raymond. At this time, Uncle Clement could be praying over Uncle Raymond in the ICU.

'Emily is always the smartest and the prettiest,' Edward grabbed my hand and kissed it. Everyone continued to rant and rave while Michael stared into space, eating from his bowl.

I narrowed my eyes and excused myself.

In my bedroom, I removed the non-stick gauze then the compressor, slowly flexing my arm. Aside from the PDA and the celebrated occasion, I felt a weird tug in my windpipe; unable to breathe properly with Michael's feelings, suspended in the air.

Suddenly, Edward ambled in and grabbed the aloe vera gel from the vanity table. 'This is the job of your namja.' He had a bad no-knocking habit.

'He's to be as strong as a king, as emotional as a human,' I said gazing at him.

'And, more beautiful than a flower.' Edward squeezed quite an amount onto his palm. I fell when he pulled me softly. He rolled me over carefully. 'Someone is becoming greedy.'

'I'm picky about his rightful scent, crisp and refreshing like the deepest, bluest ocean, something my olfactory senses would adore.' I looked at him.

Edward capped the tube and set it aside, cutting the dressing cloth to wrap it around the wound. The universe had listened to Mama and Mom's fervent prayers. The granulation tissue over the cut appeared unevenly bumpy red. I had an urge to scratch it. On the contrary, the healed wound on my left arm would lose its glossy black ink. Some lines would break after the scabbing, and it would be harder to absorb new ink when it would be redone, as it would smudge due to the scar tissue. My only consolation was this fragility was a gentle reminder to be resilient despite difficult setbacks.

'Why'd you bring a letter to Sabrina's place—?' I sat up.

'In case you refused to see me,' Edward looked at his handwritten letter that I'd clipped on the garland. 'That Fiona could've tried eating it, look at the condition.'

I caressed his cheek. 'Would you have come for me if I didn't get admitted this time?'

'Yeah, I broke my own rule.' He chuckled.

'Remember when you said a man's tears are shed for his parents and for his country.'

Edward's lips pursed. 'I'm indeed grateful that Hyojin-ssi stayed on. Otherwise, I wouldn't have known about your . . .' He was at a loss for words. 'Sorry for being a *babo*.'

I shook my head, cupping his cheek. 'Well, I don't mind being the most foolish version of me with you.'

Edward laughed. We kissed.

Daniel was right. Michael had a choice to keep me away from Edward.

'So,' Edward inquired, 'may I ask why you were sharing a room with Hyojin-ssi in the hotel? I heard it back at the hospital.'

'Kenneth dropped by and I got kicked out by my cousin.'

'Playing dress-up the whole night?' His fingers pinched my chin. 'Am I still the first man you've undressed?'

'And the first whose name I wanted to moan.' My forehead was pressed against his.

Edward pulled away, then removed his shirt—two cursive handwritten lines of poetry were tattooed on the left side of his rib cage. 'I did it six months ago.' He said.

I traced my fingers over this emotional inking—*for each love it holds so dearly, for each breath it becomes you*. I had written these lines not long after we had first met. At the airport, from the moment Edward had removed his sunglasses, I was lost in his gentle masculine gaze. Then there was the comfort of physical presence, which then changed to intimacy when he attended my open mic night, right before I had the guts to surrender. 'Did you have to get approval from your manager for the tattoo?'

'Luckily, Director Shin is open-minded about this.' He then whispered. 'She even personally recommended the tattooist.'

I laughed as he struck a muscular pose.

'So immaculate, picture perfect. Your black rose tattoos and my poetic ink complementing each other,' Edward smiled widely, admiring my arms.

'I'm not sure about redoing it.'

'You've passed the torch to me. For now.' Edward whispered.

I murmured a thank you and then pulled him in. With each kiss, I enjoyed teasing his skin more, appreciating the needling pain he had to tolerate. Our tongues had found a way to entice and ignite passion. Forget breathing, I wanted to be lost.

'I know Hyojin-ssi likes you.'

I stopped, gazing at him.

'But you're mine, forever and ever,' he declared with pride.

'Biu-jie—' Daniel barged in, suddenly. 'Oh . . . sorry,' he mumbled, covering his face.

Edward smacked Daniel's back playfully, then put on his shirt.

'The hospital called. It's about Old Bean,' Daniel said.

Thirty-Two

Mama and Mom were reciting their prayers outside the ICU ward. The corridor filled with vibrations of positive zen mantra ritual healing and the Prayer for the Sick, the flow to circulate healing in the spiritual pathways. I prayed to the Almighty One, manifesting good health for my uncle.

The nurse walked out with the doctor, who approached us, removing his stethoscope once he was standing in front of us.

'Mr Lau is confirmed to be in a stable condition—' the doctor started.

That was all Daniel and I had waited to hear as we rushed in, throwing ourselves into Uncle Raymond's embrace, crying with relief. Too dramatic—we didn't give a *damn*.

'Be careful with the wound,' Mom said to us, holding my uncle's hand.

These weren't crocodile tears, but an emotional release of withholding fears.

The ICU housed a mix of Japanese and Chinese traditions, decorated with paper baubles and bunches of paper talismans with handwritten calligraphy on the wall, like the House of Jiangshi—stiff, hopping corpses wrapped in Chinese grave clothes. Mama believed the magical power of these sealing spells would eradicate the Chinese grim reapers from snatching my uncle's soul, or turning him into a jumping-zombie that would absorb the *qi* from humans.

313

Aunt Bridget and Uncle Sean took turns to clutch onto Uncle Raymond's feet, imitating our sobbing—it was somewhat overdone.

My uncle winced, ticklish. 'Hey, don't kill me again.'

Aunt Bridget was wiping tears from her eyes. Mama smiled, mumbling the Amitabha chant. A mother's kiss on her son's forehead—the emperor's baby had returned from slumber.

Michael was standing beside Kenneth outside the ward.

Uncle Raymond held onto Daniel and me, turning to Mom. 'Cheryl, you don't know just how hard I fought with the hell demon only to come back and find these two mosquitoes crying.'

Daniel and I laughed wetly, holding him tighter.

'Son, I dreamed that your father wants to take you away,' Mama said.

Uncle Raymond thought then spoke slowly. 'I dreamed of a man in a police uniform, smoking a cigarette and wiping his pistol under a shady tree. He warned me not to cross into the thick fog because they are waiting, he didn't say anything else just kept repeating the same over and over again, "They are waiting." I just turned and continued running.'

'Yay, the kuih talam's miracle is working,' I said.

'Yay, I don't have to marry Lily,' Daniel shouted.

Uncle Raymond grabbed his son by his hair. 'I know you've been crying like a cow. If I were able to get up and smack your head, I would, just to shut your mouth.'

'You can whack me but never on my handsome face,' Daniel said.

I rolled my eyes, looked at Uncle Clement. 'Well, it is the siblings' moment . . .'

Mom didn't respond as I made quick eye-contact with Daniel.

'Yes, we should be hungry by now,' said my cousin.

'It should be a husband-and-wife moment,' Mom pulled Auntie Noon, taking over my seat next to my uncle. 'I'm hungry, too, may I join you both?'

'It's okay Aunt Cheryl. Uncle Sean is joining us.'

'But I'm not hungry.' Uncle Sean was perplexed.

Daniel and I pulled Uncle Sean out of the ICU ward, despite his protests.

Michael and Kenneth waved at Uncle Raymond, grinning when he awkwardly waved back.

I made eye-contact with Daniel, who then took Kenneth into the ICU. Michael and I chatted about the fundraising food drive's progress. Kenneth smiled as he walked out with Daniel. Both gestured an 'okay' sign to me. I was glad that my cousin was taking small steps like I'd advised him.

Then, I broke it to my uncle that I'd reconciled with Edward and looked forward to him meeting Edward when he was discharged from the hospital. My uncle looked animated, tearing up with joy.

* * *

'Sorry, am I interrupting?' I heard a voice.

Edward pecked my cheek, bowed to greet Mom and then left.

'Why not spend more time with Uncle Raymond?' I asked Mom.

'It's after midnight. Your uncle needs rest.' Mom popped a macadamia nut into her mouth, sitting next to me, concentrating on the constellated sky from the veranda.

'Are we analysing astrology?' I asked, gazing at the lush garden.

'The demons that haunt our generation should be laid to rest,' Mom said when I stood up, 'instead of passing it on to the younger ones.'

'A daughter should be allowed to share her mother's burdens,' I said. 'Uncle Clement has been holding onto every stake of that exhaustive fortress for the past few weeks. I can't be a selfish-*biatch* when it comes to the Laus.'

Mom shook her head at my sugar-coated swearing. 'Clement's been talking to you . . .'

I softly cut in. 'I believe that God works in His own miraculous way.'

'My daughter has started to worship God. My prayer came true.'

'The Sunday catechism teachings are just mere guidelines. My ritual is to pray every morning,' I said. 'Wearing Mama's lingfu is a sign of respect. I've come to realize that life is like bouldering; some give up before reaching fifteen feet while some persevere.'

Mom's lips trembled as she reached for facial tissues from the round box. 'Thought I was going to lose you when your heart stopped beating, all I could do was pray.'

'Uncle Sean's big chest indirectly saved Uncle Raymond and my life,' I said. Mom looked extremely surprised. 'Michael, the eyewitness, said so. I wouldn't be sitting here talking to you. I would be dead if not for Uncle Sean.'

Mom's lips trembled as she took a deep breath in. 'Yeah, that's his Iron-Chest nickname.'

'Whoa, so deserving, huh? Grandmaster . . .'

Mom shook her head ruefully. 'Gor and Sean were . . . in the gang. Once upon a time.'

Stunned, I glanced at her. 'No way, you're being dramatic.'

'The family has seen its fair share of inglorious pasts,' Mom looked straight at me.

I held my breath for what I knew was going to come next.

'Boys who dropped out of school in the seventies would either work as hard labour or loiter at Acheen Street, waiting to be scouted by gang leaders. Unfortunately, Gor and Sean were hand-picked by Pothead-Kwan of Three Stars Leopard. Ma wasn't happy and Pa threatened to remove Gor's name from the Laus' genealogy register.' Mom wiped her eyes.

'Pothead, huh? Drug trafficking?' I asked hesitantly.

Mom nodded. 'But he never tried it for himself, at least that's what I was told.'

'Like a vegan slaughtering livestock.' I chuckled. 'Did . . . Ah-Gong use other ways to stop Uncle Raymond from . . . plunging further besides threatening to erase his name?'

Mom narrowed her eyes, contemplating. 'It came to the point where Pa got the news that the narcotics department was to conduct a raid at Pothead-Kwan's factory, where Gor and Sean were. He came home and told Ma he intended to save . . . Sean only.'

I let out a startled breath. 'He would rather see his blood hang by the noose.'

'That's Pa.' Mom said nonchalantly. 'Very strict towards his sons.'

My throat felt tight. Ah-Gong's tough-love routine had been inherited by Uncle Raymond and was then passed on to Daniel. What a harsh way to *punish* a disobedient son. 'One gone and another to love, huh?'

Mom kept quiet, she must've been battling too many bad memories. I put my hand over hers, and she gradually patted mine. 'That was the first time I stood up for Gor against Pa. I told him that Gor was my only brother. I remembered begging him while Ma was crying like on the brink of losing her child.'

A woman could grow iron wings for her loved ones.

Mom let out a sigh. 'Yeah, then Pa met up with Pothead-Kwan that night. God knows what deal they negotiated. To cut a long story short, Gor and Sean were told to be home the next day.'

I shook my head in disbelief. 'A gang leader and a police enforcer colluding together?'

'The police are like licensed gangsters, the legal line walkers.'

I blinked. 'But Uncle Clement was the ultimate surprise.'

'We meant to keep it from you and Daniel,' Mom said.

I nodded slowly. 'I see.'

'I remember meeting Clement when he was just a young boy, always with that big big smile on his face. He would share his medals with me during long jump and shot-put events on the sports day. But I would pull away each time Pa tried to bring us closer. And Bridget is the neutral kind who's always most interested in herself. Generally, no woman wants to share their husband with another. Ma suffered a lot being married to an unfaithful man.'

'Surprised that Mama remains buttoned-up about Uncle Clement?' I asked.

'They met for the first time at Pa's funeral. I called Clement,' Mom said. 'After all, he's still part of the Laus. Just the other day, Ma got pissed-off when she learned that Gor has been in contact with Clement, but she mellowed down and accepted it eventually. Especially since Gor has just woken up from coma.'

'And Uncle Clement is a stakeholder in Serendipity Sanctuary.'

Mom looked surprised that I knew.

'I had an honest chat with Uncle Clement outside the ICU just now.'

'Anyway, I heard Ma took you to the temple for jiaobei months ago.'

'To search for peace, yeah.'

'You know that's conflict of divine interest.'

'Honestly speaking, I find strength in these two,' I confessed, showing Mom the lingfu attached to Edward's promise ring on the platinum necklace. 'I'd lost faith in my life, but these have been protecting me after what had happened and after years of emotional neglect . . .'

Mom cupped my face. 'I've failed you as a mother. I'm sorry.'

I shook my head, my eyes watery as I told her no, smiling the best I could at her. 'I forgive your unhealed wounds within.'

Mom pulled me in a tight hug.

Perhaps, the Lau daughters are roses destined to grow in the concrete.

* * *

I closed Mama's room door after kissing Mom on her cheek. She'd been sharing the bed with Mama ever since she got here. When asked how she could handle Mama's snoring, Mom shared that she made liberal use of her ear-plugs.

Edward was already asleep when I sneaked into his room.

I tried not to laugh when I noticed that he had taken over the middle of the bed, arms spread like he was making snow-angels. His suitcase had been packed and was kept next to the desk. The velvety blossom scented candle had burned halfway. I gently snuggled up beside him, adjusting till I got comfortable, kissing his cheek. My sweetheart. My lotus-flower.

His eyes opened. 'You've awakened the sleeping tiger.'

'Hey, not asleep yet,' I giggled.

Rubbing his eyes, Edward stretched. 'Your Mama brewed me a type of coffee known as Kopi O. It smells robust, love it. I'm now in-between sleep.'

I laughed at Mama's pseudo-creativity to utilize a speed-freak addictive potion to interrogate another potential grandson-in-law by *sedating* him with the bold and highly caffeinated black coffee. Michael had tasted a cuppa, it was now Edward's turn.

'Poor you, so what have Mama and you been talking about?'

'About Hyojin-ssi,' Edward was staring at me. I froze. Motormouth-Mama seemingly back in action after the storm cleared up. He picked up on it. 'It was just a chat.'

'Look,' I started, 'whatever Mama has told you—'

Edward shushed me. 'Hold it, Em. Like I said, it was just chatting.'

I exhaled, arms covering my face, pouting because I was a little embarassed.

He pinched my nose. 'Feeling hungry? Let's chat and eat ramen together. This is how couples do it back in Korea late at night.' He wiggled his eyebrows suggestively.

'You're leaving at six and it's already 2 a.m.'

'I can't hear you,' Edward conveniently ignored my concern, pinning me to the bed.

I traced Edward's beautiful lips and his chiselled jawline.

Mom and Mama were asleep and no one else was home.

Best part—I'd latched the door.

Edward bit my neck, licking the spot he'd just bitten to soothe the sting. He teased me with soft, butterfly touches on the skin near the hem of my shirt, slipping his fingers underneath after what seemed like a torturously long time to me. I swallowed Edward's feverish kiss, intoxicated by the pleasurable rush. I wanted. *God, I wanted.* But I knew that it wasn't the right time.

We were not there yet.

Slowly, I broke off the kiss, snuggling up in his arms, trying not to feel too sad about him leaving. I wanted to cherish these few hours with him. Be strong at the painful idea of sleeping alone tomorrow night onwards.

Thirty-Three

The crowd had begun to grow. Children were carrying the handmade lanterns of Chinese zodiacs that we'd given them. We also gave each adult attending the fundraising carnival a balloon at the K-Licious-Delish welcome booth. At the seafront, paper lanterns had been displayed along the railing along the row of lamp posts straight up to the pier. The Mid-Autumn Festival, also known as Mooncake Festival among the locals, had arrived with the fundraising food drive. Pop-up stalls of imported, Korean snacks had been set up for sampling. Party bags were being lined up beside stacks of product catalogues, packet snacks, and discount vouchers for each attendee.

Daniel had stopped Uncle Sean and Aunt Bridget from bickering while setting up the stage. I pretended to cough, instead of laughing, when I walked past them.

At the stall, Lily was stacking up the mooncakes in boxes. These sweetly baked pastries were Uncle Sean's apprehended recipe from a Hong Kong-inspired bakery in Singapore where he had worked as a trainee baker. This massive quantity of lotus and red bean paste had taken Daniel, Michael, Lily, and me two days to whip up into satiny sheen in the Canto-style carbon steel wok, *rowing* the dragon boat as we raced—coxswain Kimchi had led his team to the finishing line.

'This wouldn't have manifested if not for your connection,' said Lily.

'A fluke though,' I said. 'I would hate to see Daniel's effort go to waste.'

Lily smiled graciously.

'Anyway, thank you for volunteering.'

'I just want to be closer to Daniel.' Her long ponytail danced along her tiny frame. *How straightforward, take the key and slot it in.* Instead of being in love, she would rather fall into the endless loop of unrequited love. Lily smiled. 'No time has gone to waste. I'm content just sharing a workspace with him.'

'What do your parents think about this?' I asked, curiously.

'No point in telling them. They won't understand. Sometimes, a kind of attraction is so unique yet bizarre. Every love story is different. Some are at first sight or with second glances. Some take time. In the end, it is all worthwhile.'

Building a castle in the sky could be bliss. 'Have you been in love before?'

'I dated a former colleague while working in Johor a year ago. We taught in the same Chinese vernacular school. He broke up with me immediately when I asked to be transferred back here to take care of my ailing father.'

'That must be hard.' I said to Lily then smiled as a child ran up to me, giggling when I fed her a piece of lotus paste filled mooncake. Her mother then dropped a small sum into the donation box.

'People want an easy relationship, that's understandable. I heard his wife was three months pregnant before they got married.' Lily accepted the cut, red bean paste mooncake I passed her. 'Guess they didn't want the child to be born out of wedlock.'

I remembered Daniel had attracted both boys and girls in school, but would be interested in non-chauvinist men, for he'd always been different.

'I'm grateful for this friendship with Daniel.' Lily winked at me after bidding another child goodbye. 'Any good news heading our way soon about you and Edward?'

'Nah, he'll be arriving at eight later,' I said, pretending to misunderstand her question.

Lily didn't press for more. 'That's why you're not joining them at the Rasa Sayang Resort later?'

'Grateful for every moment that I can spend with Edward.' I smiled.

'Ladies and gentlemen, my name is Sabrina, from the K-Licious-Delish PR department, wishing you the warmest welcome to the fundraising food drive jointly organized by St Paul's Church and Serendipity Sanctuary, Penang's prominent non-profit food centre.' Sabrina cleared her throat, adjusting the wireless mic. 'Hope you're enjoying this glorious morning at Karpal Singh Drive. Please stay tuned for our drama sketch, performed by the most beautiful and affectionate on-stage couple!'

'Get ready, Little Niece,' Uncle Sean said, squeezing in between Lily and me. 'The volunteers can't wait for your drama performance with that Kimchi.'

'Give a standing ovation to this scriptwriter,' Aunt Bridget pointed at herself, winking at me. 'But, of course, both their acting has improved to a great extent.'

'I look forward to the romantic scene only,' said Uncle Sean.

My aunt rolled her eyes, her fake lashes fluttering. 'It's true what they say about a man's brain existing in their pants, concentrating on the physical action only.'

'The Church's godfathers choose "The Farewell" among others,' Daniel said, before turning to Lily. 'So, that's a wrap. I think I nailed that dying-in-your-arms scene with real tears. Save on the eye drops, right?' His fingers were tapping together, looking anxious.

'I had fun reciting the dialogue with you. That's good enough.' Lily blushed.

I nudged Daniel's arm. He made a distorted 'what' expression at me. Uncle Sean and Aunt Bridget stepped aside, sharing a brief glance at Lily's subtle obsession. Mixed-signal tea bags

324 Me in Your Melody

were brewing slowly. Daniel hadn't directly rejected her yet. I'd reprimanded him for not being transparent about the situation and taking advantage of her feelings.

'That's supposedly the opening scene of the script,' Aunt Bridget said, breaking the awkward silence. 'I've been devoted to the Goddess Guanyin lately, relying on full-fledged vegetarian meals and meditating three times a day hoping to hit the Hollywood spotlight. There could be casting assistants walking by today.'

'Yeah, in fact there are quite a few of them,' Uncle Sean said—liar.

'Where?' Aunt Bridget lifted her sunglasses. 'Tell me where . . .'

'Look, a smart-looking officer patrolling in plain-clothes,' Uncle Sean said. 'Oh sorry, that's Clement, your retired half-brother police officer, not a casting agent.'

'I want my name at the Avenue of Stars in Hong Kong.'

'When pigs climb trees maybe.' Uncle Sean laughed.

Daniel and I counted to three. 'Go, go Aunt Bridget. Go, go Hollywood!'

'Oi, stop giving her false hopes,' Uncle Sean said.

'Have you considered the role of a nun before?' Mom asked as she walked up to us.

My aunt shook her head. 'Good choice, sis. Make it a sexy, stripping one.'

Uncle Sean suddenly pushed past Aunt Bridget, knocking shoulders with her.

We couldn't stop laughing when Aunt Bridget ran to catch up with Uncle Sean.

'Did I say something wrong?' Mom whispered to me, perplexed.

'For triggering the Monk's jealousy.' I waved her concern away, still laughing.

* * *

I was strolling along the promenade. A man was handing a larger-than-life teddy to a girl in pigtails at the game stall. Both must've been father-and-daughter from the manner they were communicating. A woman fed them bites of what looked like a choco-vanilla sundae while the man picked up his daughter, sharing the cone with his two precious diamonds.

Such a family portrait made me envy their father–daughter relationship.

I kept my father's contact number, so I could pick up if he ever called. I had learned of the best, most healthy way to communicate with him to get a handle on him and the situation. Edward's theory was that a man's arms were constructed to protect and provide for his family's health and wellness and create an autonomous space for his kids.

Mama was tugging at Michael's sleeve when I arrived at her kuih stall.

'Your girlfriend is here,' Mama said. I stopped myself from commenting further. 'What? Both of you should immerse yourselves in your roles for today's drama acting.'

Michael smiled. 'Thank you, Mama.'

'Ask your *eomeoni* whether I can take you as my sworn-in grandson.'

'There's no such arrangement in Korean culture.' Michael sounded apologetic.

Mama narrowed her eyes at the sweets—kuih talam, kuih bingka, and kuih lapis. The latter was made by Michael and me. This could've all been a part of Mama's plan.

'What's the time now? You've almost finished selling them?' I asked Mama.

'The kuih lapis sells like hot cakes.' Mama's gaze hadn't left mine, keen on changing the topic. 'Anyway, I'm craving a bowl of *tom yam* flat rice noodles.'

'I'll get some for you from Auntie Noon's stall,' I said.

'You stay here,' Mama ordered, pulling me over till I was standing beside Michael.

'Uncle Raymond's stall was so crowded earlier on,' Michael said.

I turned to Michael, who kept his eyes glued to Mama until she reached Auntie Noon's stall. Uncle Raymond waved at us while Auntie Noon did the same with a ladle. 'Any food cooked authentically is fervently supported by the locals and the tourists,' I said.

'A woman came and bought almost half the trays from each of Mama's kuih.'

I glanced at Michael, then cut two pieces of each type and placed them in a plastic bag.

We thanked the person as he put some money into the donation box.

I turned to Michael. 'Traditional homemade tastes are hard to come by. Cottage industries are facing challenges due to the mass-production in factories, who are probably eliminating the smaller companies by using artificial edible colourings, which makes the process faster and cuts costs significantly.'

'Ever thought about being a businesswoman?' Michael asked earnestly.

I smirked. 'You gotta be kidding me.'

'You never know.'

'Currently, I'm pleased to have my life going in the right direction,' I said.

Michael looked at me, as if thousands of riddles were squabbling to be solved inside his head.

Auntie Noon was feeding Uncle Raymond and Mama her tom yam noodle soup—her mother's recipe. She'd proposed this to be the optional dish for the soup kitchen next month. They were joined by Uncle Clement and Mom. Mama fed them, starting by feeding Mom the sweet coconut rice dumplings. Further away, Aunt Bridget was biting a red rose between her teeth, flamenco dancing with Uncle Sean, pushing him back, closer to where the ocean washed up against the pier. There was a roar of applause as Uncle Sean managed to keep his footing and not slide back into the water. Instead, he grabbed onto my aunt's waist. His poor back must have been cursing him.

'Oh, the ring is back around your neck,' Michael said suddenly.

'Because Rui-er shouldn't be wearing it on her finger.'

'Uncle Clement has agreed to change the dialogue in the script. This'll for sure boost your aunt's chances of being in the limelight.'

I felt a little strange. 'Shall we go through it once more?'

'There must be strong correlation between the performers, a so-called real-life chemistry to fool the audiences. I'm sure you're brilliant enough to take the lead.'

* * *

The front row seats were occupied by the church's godfathers and Uncle Clement. Aunt Bridget was seated on the foldable black chair with her name at the back, a filming prop she had ordered two months prior. She sat there stroking her embroidered silk qipao's collar, with a handheld sakura paper fan, sunglasses on the ridge of her nose and her red Chanel stilettos making a statement.

'The moment you've been waiting for,' Sabrina announced on the stage. 'A short sketch written by the famous retired Hong Kong-based screen siren, starring the Serendipity Sanctuary volunteers and St Paul's Church representative . . .'

'This is it,' I said, at the waiting corner.

'Do or die, all or nothing,' Michael said.

'Please welcome Michael Kim and Emily Chung for *The Farewell*.'

The music cued to the heighten the epic, cinematic melodrama. Michael exhaled, following my steps as we walked forward, holding hands. The projector screen showed a background of rain splashing against a Renaissance-era window. The sound of applause died down. Our dialogues were delivered through our lapel microphones. The sad and dramatic background music inspired the rapid intensity of this 'farewell'. Rui-er became part of me, I immersed myself in her character by adding my own impressions to the emotional roller-coaster she was living in the script. There was a living spirit in every role you played.

Michael's gaze caught mine. 'Will you come with me?'

This wasn't part of the script.

Either I would nail it or fuck it up.

I took a step forward, running my fingers along Michael's lips, then across his chest. 'We'll meet as the moon resurfaces from depths of the Han River.'

Michael's hand slowly let me go. The crowd applauded as he shot me a grin. I blinked. Tears fell from his eyes, and he quickly left the stage. The background music continued as whistles, compliments, and flowers were tossed on the stage. There I was, facing the crowd, accepting the denouement of Rui-er and Lu-yang, a little mislaid.

* * *

Fangirling-Sabrina gave her Korean oppa Michael an embrace outside the departure hall. Then, I stood back and smiled when Michael spread his arms, inviting us in. Instead, Lily took the chance to hug Daniel. We cheered at her bravery. Daniel didn't reciprocate and kept his hands up. Kenneth wasn't at the fundraising event, for he'd returned to his hometown.

'I'm going to miss this grandson of mine.' Mama hugged Michael.

'I'm going to miss you and your kuih.' Michael hugged Mama in return.

'Finally, you can celebrate Chuseok with your eomeoni,' I said.

He glanced at me softly, pursing his lips.

'Will you be my tour guide when I visit Seoul?' Sabrina interrupted.

'Of course, but inform me earlier, I'm a busy man.' Michael winked.

'I should be free this Christmas,' Sabrina said laughing at his little self-deprecating joke.

'Meanwhile, the soap flakes are replaceable with snowflakes,' said Daniel.

The intercom announced the opening of the Korean Air departure gate.

After hugging my family, Michael gave me a hug. It felt decent and sociable.

Michael whispered to me. 'We'll meet again, soon.'

I smiled, with no further thought.

Thirty-Four

Mama showed me the lotus paste filling she got from Uncle Sean. 'Made so much for the mooncake, but forgot to keep some for your sweet, sweet date.'

'Thank you for reminding me, Mama,' I said, blushing.

'My daughter is now a certified pastry princess,' said Mom, 'from mooncake to kuih lapis, and now she's going to make the snow skin version.'

'Isn't that the easiest? No baking. Just mould it up.'

'Someone blushes whenever the "E" comes up,' Auntie Noon teased.

'Think the kitchen is getting hotter.' I tried to cover up, covering the bowl of lotus paste with a transparent cling wrap.

'Oh,' Auntie Noon and Mama nodded in unison. 'Hotter eh . . .'

'Why is there an additional batch of lotus paste filling?' asked Mom.

'I'm assisting the pastry side next week to make deep-fried Shanghainese pastry with Sean,' said Mama. 'Lotus paste represents sweet union, like you and Edward.'

I hugged her for blessing our love.

'Raymond is recovering fast and Cheryl, you've decided to stay longer, and Clement too.' Mama's lips trembled. 'I chose to disillusion myself to see the world through the very flawed eyes of mortals. No more resentment will be buried in the grave with me.'

'Don't say that,' we said in unison.

'Now, if only . . . this kitchen were filled with children's laughter.'

'I don't mind being your forever five-year-old, Mama.' I quickly cut in.

'Let's see how it goes tonight with Edward.'

'Mama, don't think dirty.'

'I told her to behave, Ma.' Mom gave me a stern look.

Mama rolled her eyes, playfully. 'Oh, too bad, can't help it.'

'I've made some lemongrass juice to bring to the Rasa Sayang Resort later,' said Mom. 'Let's brainstorm some recipes during our pre-bedtime talk.'

'That's great.' Auntie Noon did a happy-shoulder-dance.

'Cooking and baking is an ongoing creative exercise,' Mama explained. 'Take this grain of salt as an example, how much is needed to balance the taste? Just a pinch? Would it be enough? Let's judge by its taste. Why is there always "a pinch of salt" in every recipe? The taste is based on the individual.'

'That's seriously deep.' I shook my head, amazed.

'I need extra notebooks to jot down Ma's philosophy of life,' Mom said.

'Salt is like love.' Mama said to me. 'Take a pinch, feel the excitement.'

* * *

Edward picked me up from the ground after Aunt Bridget had shown Minrin-ssi, his PA, to his room upstairs. A little dizzy from the swinging, I begged Edward to put me down. I felt warm in his embrace. We pecked each other on the cheek, and then on the lips— once, twice. I stopped after hearing footsteps coming closer to us.

Minrin-ssi apologized, spoke to Edward in Korean then left in a black Audi sedan.

'Is everything all right?' Uncle Raymond asked, smiling.

'They're picking me up at six in the morning.' Edward said. 'Nothing more important than spending time with Emily.' He held my hand.

Daniel whistled. 'I only want good news from Biu-Jie.'

'Edward is older, is that how you talk to him?' Uncle Raymond reprimanded Daniel.

Daniel hung his arm over his father's shoulders. 'Biu-Jie hereby has chosen her *mate*. All she needs is blessings from us. So, welcome to the Lau-d & Praud, Edward Ahn.'

Edward laughed, fists-bumped my cousin, and bowed with his hands clasped before Uncle Raymond. 'Thank you for arranging this for us, sincerely from my heart.'

'Don't mention it,' Uncle Raymond said.

'Better make a move. Clement's waiting at the hotel lobby.' My aunt winked.

'Don't burn the kitchen.' Mom gave me a hug, patting my back.

I hugged her in return, then, said to my cousin. 'Drive safely.'

'Enjoy your trip.' Edward said, waving to everyone.

'Now, go burn the bed.' Mama's voice echoed as Daniel drove off.

Edward and I couldn't stop laughing even after I locked the door.

* * *

A racy kimono had been placed nicely on my bed courtesy Aunt Bridget. There was a post-it note.

Let the moonlit night waltz into the voluptuous reflections.

I headed to the kitchen after a shower, putting on the silk nightwear.

Having the house to ourselves was the rarest privacy. Edward had decorated the cabinet tabletop with some candles. 'Ever since the onde-onde making, I'd feel your presence whenever I was in a kitchen, including the company's pantry section.'

He finally able to pronounce it. 'Hiring me as your personal chef?' I asked.

'That's my dream realized.'

My lips pursed, suppressing my smile at the thought of cooking up a storm for Edward. For our children too.

'Seemingly durable.' Edward lifted Mama's wooden mooncake mould, peering inside at the traditional flower pattern. 'Has it been passed to you already?'

I briefly coughed. 'I would have my mom and my aunt to fight for it, but I've been warned to handle you with care,' I said, inhaling the scented lotion on Edward's neck.

His laughter echoed in the empty house. 'So, what are you making?'

I smiled, pouring the pre-fried glutinous rice flour and all-purpose flour into a separate bowl, measuring the coarse sugar. 'We're making a snow skin mooncake. It's less oily and can be served instantly. These are the main ingredients to make its crust.'

Edward scooped to taste the lotus paste with a spoon. 'Hmm, *mashisoyo*, really a lot less sweeter than I'd expected. I'd eaten a similar filling at the dim sum restaurant in Hong Kong.'

I poured the fresh milk into the flour batter for the crust. I tried to concentrate on my tasks as Edward's finger drew heart shapes on my left arm and his warm breath tickled my ear as he hummed a random tune. Then, I pinched portions from the paste with a crystal-like sheen and rolled them into clumps then roughly measured them on the digital scale.

'Chestnut-Emily is now the baker,' Edward whispered. 'I am obsessed.'

I chortled at my nickname, feeling his hands on my waist. 'That's scarily encouraging.'

'What's your pick between baked skin and snow skin mooncakes?'

'When I was a child, I would separate the paste from the baked skin crust and then eat the latter,' I laughed. 'My father used to get so goddamn pissed.'

Edward kissed my hair.

Feeling safe, I continued. 'Most traditional bakeries here sell baked skin dough in piglet, fish, and coin shapes all year round. The pastries come with a small plastic basket, like animals for sale in the ancient Chinese marketplace. Kids love them. But refrain from eating too much. It has lye water that could upset your stomach.'

Edward blinked, softly. 'Adorable. Childhood is always the best.'

'The innocence.' I turned to him. He looked back at me. Could it be that he lost his during his trainee days? 'The good and genuine love and memories.'

'I've got a better idea.' Edward pinched a portion from lotus paste then rolled it into a ball.

'Don't you want to bring some for your parents?' I asked.

'I took the whole week off and had meals with my *bumonim*.' Edward said. 'My parents have made plans with their friends to go on a trip to Jeju-do. They told me to take good care of you.'

My heart bloomed like sakura petals. 'I plan to visit Jeju-do.'

'Let's go there for our honeymoon.' Edward's chin rested on my shoulder. His fingers intertwined with mine.

I gazed at him. 'Don't forget you've promised to take me to NYC.'

'From JFK Airport we'll go to Jeju-do.' Edward caught my gaze, I felt his arms tighten around me. In his embrace I'd found security and the sense of being home, yet there was fear within, not the Fuck-Everything-And-Run or Fight-Everything-And-Rise abbreviations—but the fear of the inevitable, painful separation.

'Did you know I've been whispering your name every night, hoping the moon and stars will keep you company while you stay up late working?' I confessed.

'That's . . . so kind of you.' His voice was emotional.

'And the Mid-Autumn Festival represents reunion, like the round mooncakes. The pastry's surface is engraved with idioms of prosperity and harmony.' I took his hands in mine. 'I hope to make *songpyeon* and mooncakes with you, connecting the two cultures in your parent's kitchen.'

'I love you, Em.' He kissed my forehead then checked on my left arm. 'I've been offering morning prayers to the universe, to protect you and to heal the scarring.'

'They're fading like a sand-painting,' I said bitterly.

'You're always the most beautiful to me,' he whispered.

With butterflies in my stomach, I rolled the last of the lotus paste, arranging it on the tray.

Edward pulled out a red, woven string from his pocket, to bind around our wrists. 'With this, you won't go elsewhere. According to Korean tradition, the red string must be tied around the pinky fingers.'

'Talk about dependency.' I teased.

'With this, you won't leave me anymore.'

I laughed.

'Hey, I haven't been this close to anyone except my future wife.'

'Not even the girl you met in the alleyway when you debuted?'

The kitchen was full with the sound of our laughter.

'Anyway, we're heading to Seoul tomorrow,' Edward said, gasping for breath.

'You're pulling my leg again.' I murmured.

His finger tapped on my lips. 'Kissing you all the way to the flight . . .'

I giggled so loud that it echoed around the whole house. He burst out laughing again. I felt my heart melt. Edward could be himself. With no pretence. Utterly imperfectly perfect.

'But first, how to get rid of the fans?' I asked.

'Remember our airport marathon? We made such a great team.'

'Burning calories, huh?'

'Still not as intense as this one . . .' Edward scrolled through his phone.

I stared at the moving screen in awe. It was my acting from the fundraising food drive. 'Must be Daniel, huh.' Edward nodded. 'Damn, you really bribed my whole family.'

Edward leaned in to share the screen with me. He then paused at the part where I turned to look at Michael. 'Hyojin-ssi and you made a great pair. On-screen only.'

I smiled at his over protectiveness. 'What do you think of my acting?'

'Passionate and exquisite.' His hand was on my cheek. 'My baby is so talented.' His voice was husky.

I gently kissed his fingers.

'Is there anything I don't know about you?' His raspy voice excited me.

'I'm afraid you need more time . . .'

His eyes were half-lidded.

I watched as his hands ran along the silky fabric of the kimono. 'Let's make this our lifetime,' Edward nuzzled my neck, his familiar crisp, herbal scent drove me crazy. I let out a moan. 'I don't mind the next lifetime too,' he whispered against my skin.

We kissed for a long, long time.

I stopped and scooped some lotus paste from the bowl. Edward's breathing accelerated as he watched me spread the delectable lotus paste on the corner of my lips. 'I only want us. Now,' I whispered.

Edward pulled me in and kissed me hard. My heart skipped a beat as he licked the paste from my lips. I leaned into his kiss, sucking on his tongue, chasing the taste of him. We parted just to breathe. I leaned my back against the tabletop, panting as I caressed the nape of his neck.

Edward swept the robe from my shoulder.

We kissed, I loved the sound of his coarse moans as I sucked on his lower lip, wanting all of him. Shivers tingled down my spine as he carried me to my room.

* * *

I woke up on my bed with Edward's lips on my forehead. My fingers were drumming against his tattooed hip bone—a new melody and the colossal feeling of bliss.

'Last night was like a dream,' I murmured, my eyes still closed.

He bit my shoulder. 'Hmm, you taste heavenly.'

I winced then poked at his waist.

Edward grabbed my hand a little too quickly. 'Hey, don't do that . . .'

'Ahh, so that's your weak point.' I clicked my tongue.

Edward covered my face with the mosquito canopy. Giggling with a snort, I watched my reflection in his deep eyes. The kiss was long enough to moisten my lips even separated as we were by the thin lace. I felt so daring for sharing that innermost, fragile, personal part of me with a man that deserved every inch of my being. Raw & Praud. With my chosen lotus-flower.

'We should've met earlier . . .' His voice shattered.

'When our souls have completed a certain amount of inner work,' I said, fingers trailing up his chest, 'the alchemy of destiny will gravitate towards us.'

Edward looked like I was the only thing that mattered. 'I'm with the right woman.'

'And very experienced in bringing her out.' I tilted my head.

Edward rolled over, kissing my lips. 'You're mine, for the rest of our lives.'

Thirty-Five

Daniel and I were racing ahead and then our shoulders collided in the narrow doorway. I squeezed through and pushed Daniel's face away, rushing to the Parisian baby crib with a mini canopy. My cousin narrowed his stare as I was quick to grab Coco, patting her back and humming a lullaby.

'Shouldn't you be mingling with the guests instead?' My cousin was still a sore loser.

'Aunt Bridget is handling it well by wearing her flamboyant Cantonese Opera ceremonial costume.' We heard our aunt test the mic in the hall. 'Ask her to sing a happy song, not that tragic "Butterfly Lovers" in Cantonese opera.'

'It is bloody loud.' Daniel rolled his eyes, tickling Coco's rosy cheeks.

'Why not ask Lily to sing "My Heart Will Go On."' I smirked.

'Oi, don't!' Daniel warned.

'*Ghost* has been blacklisted and now *Titanic*.' I teased, laughing.

'Stop that Romeo of yours from spoiling Coco with such great gifts.' Daniel said. 'Both your parental clocks are ticking, and I want to be Coco's favourite.'

Uncle Raymond joined us in the nursery. 'I've arranged for you to attend the next matchmaking dinner, Daniel. That'll be next week.'

I chortled at my uncle's wit as Coco stirred in my arms.

'Biu-jie should get married first.' Daniel complained. 'Especially Uncle Sean. He can't wait for you to serve him a cup of oolong at your wedding tea ceremony. Both of you have already sworn-in as uncle and niece, remember?'

I stuffed the baby rattle into Daniel's mouth, shutting him up.

'Now that Lily is a professional make-up artist, consider hiring her.' My uncle laughed at us. 'Last month, she just received a diploma in baking.'

'Kenneth can quit his job at Urban Decay,' Daniel annoyingly put the rattle aside. 'Don't mind if Lily and he were to set up the make-up empire, I'd be the MD of the business-enterprise.'

'Business savvy but in such a reckless rush,' I said to Uncle Raymond.

'That's what I'm expecting at the very least,' Uncle Raymond said. 'Good to see he's learning how to manage Coco, especially at night, as an older brother.'

This father-and-son had fought against all odds and had finally accepted each other.

'Someone's on video conference.' Uncle Raymond reminded me.

Alerted, I quickly handed Coco over. 'I'll be right back.'

'Hurry up, don't let my cousin-in-law wait.' Daniel pushed me out.

It'd been fifteen months and three weeks without Edward.

I had been happily kicking the basket of denial. A grieving stage with hope, I'd spent an extended amount of time hustling in the three kitchens, including at the food drive. Every so often, I would still feel Michael's presence, living rent-free in my head at the dining hall, in the pastry kitchen, and the guest room. At times, I would smile like a fool, reminiscing about his dry humour.

A month later, I had been experiencing drowsiness, fatigue, food craving, and breast changes, all of it making sense when I missed my period. I could be baking love dough in my womb.

I craved for Edward to be by my side.

Mama had planned her glamorous attire for my wedding in Penang and then in Seoul already. Daniel had been brainstorming baby names with Aunt Bridget. Coco's name had come from Chanel and Louis Vuitton, if the latter were a boy. Mom wasn't too thrilled knowing about my misbehaving night with Edward but was happier to know that I had hormonal irregularities and was not pregnant, as confirmed by the gynae. The doctor had also said it could be early menopause. Menopause as a thirty-five-year-old unmarried woman.

A few weeks later, Auntie Noon had announced her pregnancy. Everyone had forgotten about my so-called midlife crisis.

'My honey looks so exhausted.' Edward appeared on the LED monitor.

I walked into the room that had once been inhabited by two beautiful men. 'Auntie Noon needs plenty of rest. Daniel and I had pulled another all-nighter with Coco yesterday,' I said, pulling the chair over.

'I spoke to Uncle Raymond just now and congratulated him.'

'Everyone has been saying how fortunate he is to have a baby girl at this age.'

'Baby Coco is blessed with so much love from her family,' Edward said. 'So, have you introduced this uncle to her yet?'

I leaned closer to the screen. 'I did, by listening to your songs every night.'

'I'm sure you had fun changing diapers.' Edward said, eating oatmeal with mixed berries from a bowl. Minrin-ssi entered the camera frame and waved at me.

I greeted her in my rudimentary Korean, then said to Edward. 'Not really an expert, it's a learning process. Daniel and I have survived the first month of Coco's crying nights. She's really a handful but we've figured out that whenever her lips start smacking and she starts trying to eat her hand, it could be feeding time.

At times, I'd have to swaddle and softly shush her. One night, Uncle Raymond found me falling asleep while holding Coco—' I stopped. 'Why are you giggling?'

Edward pursed his lips. 'No. Please continue.'

I felt a little hot. 'Well, that's about it.'

'So well-prepared, can't wait to do this with you,' Edward teased.

I pursed my lips. 'Definitely looking forward to it.'

That day, Edward had been ready to leave for the airport, and told me to put the ring on his finger. I couldn't stop crying, but they were happy tears. Two rings, one committed heart.

I showed him my finger. 'See this. I'm wearing the ring today.'

Edward pursed his lips, placing his hand on the screen. *'Bogoshipo . . .'*

I gazed at the ceiling, willing my tears to not fall.

Honestly, dating a pop star isn't for the faint-hearted. It was harder to breathe when my hand was virtually pressing in, as if to prevent a physical contact. With exhaustive schedules, Edward *belonged* to his fans. 'I'm happy for your sold-out Asia tour,' I said as I smiled.

I had to be strong for us.

Hand on the screen, he exhaled. 'I plan to drop by the day after the Macau tour.'

A deep breath in. My heart blossomed. 'Miss your future cousin-in-law?'

He leaned in. 'Yeah, like I miss you.'

'I miss you too. Good luck for tonight,' I said.

'Thank you,' he exhaled.

'Eat my share of Portuguese tarts and stroll the streets of Macau.'

'We'll meet right after this one.' Edward was so confident.

'Promise?' I waved my pinkie finger.

'*Yag-sog-hae.*' He did the same.

'Emily, there's a human-bouquet surprise downstairs for you. Go pick it up,' said Aunt Bridget then waved at Edward. 'Anyeonghaseyo, do you miss me?'

'When are you coming to Korea?'

'I only want to visit Grand Walkerhill Seoul.' My aunt elbowed me.

'You've a sharp eye for a wedding reception garden, Aunt Bridget.'

'You get me, my dear soon-to-be nephew-in-law.'

Edward chuckled, then to me. 'Go check out the human-bouquet, quick.'

* * *

I spotted a familiar figure at the banister from the corner of my eye.

Descending the stairs, I saw Mom talking to Mama's legion of relatives from Chew Jetty. A child bumped into Michael's leg. He asked her if she was hurt as he bent to pick her up. The child's parents arrived soon, thanked him and then took her away.

'It's like the whole of Penang has come to greet Little Coco,' Michael said.

'Mama's hosting approximately seventy family members, living in shelters made from wood and zinc.' I smiled. 'What you see is just a little portion.'

Michael shook. 'What would happen if you were to get married one day?'

I tilted my head, whispered. 'Just don't invite them.'

He laughed with his mouth full, holding a plate of sweet cakes. 'I finally got to taste Mama's kuih. This is my third helping of kuih talam and kuih lapis.'

I kept quiet, despite the urge to continue our banter; careful not to be overly friendly. 'Did you happen to RSVP to anyone in my family?'

Michael placed the plate aside, asking me to follow him to a less merry atmosphere.

The noises from inside faded as I slid out the door. The gardeners greeted me at the veranda then left to work on the other landscaping portion. Michael's gaze never left mine. He took in my puff-sleeved floral, square-neck sundress. I pretended to clear my throat when his gaze lingered for too long. His actions contradicted his sophisticated look that was completed by gold framed glasses. He retrieved a thin stack of admission passes from a navy-blue leather pouch.

'Myeongjun-ssi wants you to have these,' Michael said.

I inspected the priority seating concert tickets.

They had my name—

—for Yokohama, Osaka, Nagoya, Sapporo . . . and other major cities in Japan. I opened the last envelope; a reserved priority seat with a premium VIP hospitality package and an exclusive, private backstage pass at Tokyo Dome to meet Edward after the concert.

'All expenses paid from business class flights to staying in five-star hotels,' Michael continued. 'As duly signed and stamped by Director Shin, our priority is to secure your privacy and the safety of your journey throughout.'

There was a letter addressed to my full name by Shin Mikyung.

I became aware of Edward's assertiveness.

'You came just for these?' I asked Michael.

'That was part of it.' He gazed at me, unperturbed.

'I need some time to think.'

'The Japan Tour starts next month,' Michael said, strictly. 'You have a week from now to decide. Hopefully, you won't let Myeongjun-ssi down.'

'I need to plan my work schedule beforehand.' I said earnestly.

'I almost forgot. Congratulations on your promotion, Assistant Senior Pastry Chef of Serendipity Sanctuary.' Michael bowed and smiled.

'Thanks. The news really travelled fast. I was just notified yesterday.' I nodded at him. 'Anyway, let me talk to Edward about this arrangement.'

'I'm taking over Myeongjun-ssi's personal matters from tomorrow onwards,' Michael said. 'Aside from vocal practising, team and management meeting for the concert arrangements, and other related matters, now is his best opportunity to rise to popularity.'

I didn't take my eyes off Michael's.

Michael then grasped my arms. 'Director Shin doesn't want any distraction. You're a brilliant woman. I'm sure you don't want to see him fail.'

I flung Michael's arms away.

'Remember when I said we will meet soon?' Michael handed me a business card. 'I know it's been a year or so but my feelings haven't changed.'

'I have never taken this off ever since he left.' I showed him the promise ring.

'It is unusual for a non-celebrity to have two famous male figures smitten with her; must be your beauty, endearing even to the gods.' Brushing his undercut, he leaned in. 'Myeongjun-ssi wished for your recovery on every single one of the thousand paper cranes he folded, like every melody that has ever been broken.' I sensed his green-eyed tone.

I gripped onto Michael's new name card—Senior Artist Manager. 'Congratulations,' I said as he nodded. 'We both have unlocked our achievements. More busy days to come.'

'Yeah, I love challenges, as you know.'

'I'd settled in with Rui-er's character. Lu-yang should be smart, too.'

Michael grinned. 'Your wit never ceases being attractive.'

'Well, thank you.' I bowed and left as he looked on.

* * *

The living hall was decked with a garden-like party.

The table had been graced with hard-boiled eggs in red edible colour, pickled ginger, and a variety of Mama's homemade kuih, including *ang ku kuih*. These red-hued, tortoise shaped glutinous cakes wrapped around a sweet mung bean central filling were custom-made with two peaches on the surface, signifying the gender of the child. Daniel and I had baked some cupcakes too.

Coco's name and her age had been ballooned in gold colour against the pink curtain wall. Uncle Raymond held Auntie Noon, cuddling and then tickling Coco's cheek in her arms. A calming sense precipitated over me as I observed my one-month-old cousin sister giggle in a lace floral dress and a custom-made cotton bow headband that tamed her fluffy hair. The photographer was instructing us to get in the line. Mom and Aunt Bridget were leaning cheek-to-cheek against Mama, having their picture clicked.

For once, Mom had banished that so-called Sister Act outfit and had her hair tied in a messy bun adorned with a rubescent rose, identical to the one in Aunt Bridget's hair. Daniel stood near his father, tickling Coco's cheek as she yawned and scrunched her tiny nose.

'Is everything all right?' Uncle Clement walked up to me.

'Who dares to bully my Little Niece?' Uncle Sean cracked his knuckles.

'I'm all right. But today is Coco's full-moon celebration,' I said. 'The house only welcomes elated and heaven-sent vibes. Other than that, bugger off.'

Michael stood not far from the seasoned photographer.

'Shall we invite Michael for the next shot?' Uncle Clement asked.

Every pair of Laus' eyes was on me.

I shrugged. 'Bring him in.' My hands went to the promise ring.

Michael ambled over as he was invited by Uncle Clement, who switched places with Daniel and stood in between Michael and me, dropping his arms onto our shoulders.

'Do you remember what I said when we first met?' Uncle Clement asked.

'I'm like a son to you.' Michael repeated.

'Ready—one, two . . . ' The photographer gestured.

'And you always will be,' Uncle Clement said.

Click.

Acknowledgments

Me In Your Melody wouldn't have seen the light of day without the refulgent spellworking of these Godsent folks. Many thanks to those who made this dream of mine come true.

Nora Nazerene Abu Bakar, my publisher, for recognizing this manuscript out of the 'topaz-gem' piles, saving this child from her darkest moment. Amberdawn Manaois and Swadha Singh, my MasterChef editors, for reinvigorating this book-baby with your sharp-eyed and insightful viewpoints and critiques. It's been an honour and pleasure working with Garima Bhatt, Chaitanya Srivastava and Almira Ebio Manduriao—the Penguin SEA marketing, publicity, and sales forces. Grateful for your swift response and your continuing patience when I *spammed* your inboxes with questions and suggestions. And cover designer Divya Gaur for the best illustration to accentuate Emily Chung's character.

My wonderful family—Mom Sharon and Mama Elaine for your unconditional love and pragmatic advice. God willing our stories will be written in many books to come. Sherri Ee-Ee, Uncle CK, Nicole and Andrea, for your love and support. And for the real Uncle Raymond. Your niece has found a method to immortalize you. In pages. Church members and family friends— Uncle Terry, Uncle Richard, Auntie Furzanne, Auntie Angie, and Auntie Rosalind, much obliged for your help and assistance in recent years.

My beta-readers—Megan Stadnik, a zillion thanks for pulling through my half-baked draft when I was at the verge of surrendering as well as for your review prior to the book release. Kate Doughty, for suggesting the engagement party. Trish Caragan, my sweet K-pop yeodongsaeng for your book review, your comments with fan-girling notions on each and every paragraph. Thank you for rooting for this ever since day one. Christine Wang, my Twisties and Hawaiian pizza Twinsies, for our epic ongoing messages, publishing rants, K-Dracula and Sashimi-K, Krueger-Antonio and the slinging sundae cone jokes!

Amanda Woody, Lily Mehallick, Stefany Valentine, Amy Leow and Jean-Maré Gagliardi—for contributing your thoughts and opinions on the query letter and the first three chapters of the book. Shoutout to my gorgeous HoneyBies™ — Tanvi Singh (Pocky and Pepero Twinsies), Ryoko Hirosue, Natalie Jacobsen, Jaime Hunter, Ai Jiang, Sarah Dorko, Emma Yuan, Jude Lee Baet, Karlein Kwong, Millica, Bria Fournier, Boon Carmen, Alex Morán, Samantha Chong, Tien Lee, Mel Reynard, Ashley Detweiler, and Stacey L. Pierson.

I believe education makes a person and the right one lays the foundation—Cikgu Hj Mohd Yusof, Puan Saadiah, Mrs Molly Wu, and Madam Bong my powerhouse language teachers; Mrs Joyce Xavier and Miss Anne Moses, for making the Literature in English the best moments in my upper secondary and in A-levels. Madam Wang Hwee Beng, and Madam Chong Ik Poh, for transforming a nice girl into the toughest cookie through your disciplinary action. Mr Tan Eng Lin, Madam Meera Badmanaban, and Madam Sharon Amen, for the tips in building reasonable and prudent arguments and not being lawyered in return.

Graham Lawrence, Glenn Lyvers, Kris Williamson, Sukhbir Cheema, Rob Carroll, Katy Lennon, Yilin Wang, Katrina Vera Wang, Emma J. Gibbons, Holly Lyn Walrath, AJ Odasso, and

Debbie Berk—my amazing editors for publishing my poetry and prose on online journals, in paperback magazines, and in anthologies.

Tina Isaac, Sharon Bakar, and Tsiung-Han See, for providing me a reading space to showcase my work ever since 2014.

Amy Walton, Marissa MacDonald, and Debra Fleming, for still keeping in touch after decades of friendship through pen-palling. Chan Xiao Huey, Michelle Chen, Ellen Whyte, Foo Siew June, and others who know me, thank you for your unending support. YJ Han, Takako Takizuka, Lara Gabriele, and Mark McDonald, my writing buddies at the Summer Intensive Creative Writing at the University of British Columbia, thank you for the memories.

Arley Sorg, for your encouraging congratulatory note and your personalized feedback on my short story. Amy Bishop-Wycisk, for championing Emily and Daniel's kinship from the start. Nic Caws, for your interest in the Malaysian sweet treats. Vicki Lame, for hyping this manuscript during the #APIpit Twitter pitching event. Stephanie Maricevic and Nancy Lee, the most admirable creative writing instructors I've ever had, who helped me make my decision to become a storyteller.

To other author-friends and readers on the Twitter #WritingCommunity, for hitting the 'like' button and leaving messages on my posts, adding cheers whenever rejections bit.

Jean Kwok, Yangsze Choo, and P. P. Wong—your books and words of wisdom have been my motivation and inspiration to continue writing.

Lastly, to Donghae and Eunhyuk (of Super Junior), and J-Dub for writing the splendid title track 'One More Chance', finally sealing the deal to this story idea I had back in 2016.